James Harrison Wilson, Charles Anderson Dana

The Life of Ulysses S. Grant, General of the Armies of the United States

States

Vol. 2

James Harrison Wilson, Charles Anderson Dana

The Life of Ulysses S. Grant, General of the Armies of the United States
Vol. 2

ISBN/EAN: 9783337416638

Printed in Europe, USA, Canada, Australia, Japan

Cover: Foto ©Raphael Reischuk / pixelio.de

More available books at **www.hansebooks.com**

OF

Ulysses S. Grant,

𝔊eneral of the 𝔄rmies of the 𝔘nited 𝔖tates.

By CHARLES A. DANA,

LATE ASSISTANT SECRETARY OF WAR;

AND

J. H. WILSON,

BREVET MAJOR-GENERAL U. S. A.

PUBLISHED BY

Gurdon Bill & Company, Springfield, Mass.

H. C. Johnson, Cincinnati, Ohio.

Charles Bill, Chicago, Ill.

1868.

SPRINGFIELD, MASS.:

SAMUEL BOWLES AND COMPANY,

ELECTROTYPERS, PRINTERS AND BINDERS.

Preface.

WHEN so many biographies of General Grant are announced as about to be published or actually ready for delivery to purchasers, several of them by writers of acknowledged capacity and distinction, the authors of the present work feel that if they do not owe to the public an apology for their undertaking, it is at least their duty to tender a frank statement of the reasons which have induced them to engage in such an enterprise. First among these is the fact that they have been urged to do so by their excellent publishers; but this alone would not have been sufficient, had it not been their fortune, at various critical epochs of the War for the Union, to be thrown into the midst of decisive events, and to see with their own eyes, and often quite intimately, a great deal that is important in history. In many of these transactions, General Grant bore a controlling part, so that to know the facts was to know the man. It is hoped that the desire to record this knowledge in a manner somewhat permanent, and to preserve the impressions gathered in the campaigns of Northern Mississippi, and of Vicksburg, the rescue of Chattanooga, the battles and marches of 1864 in

Virginia, and the crowning events which culminated at
Appomattox Court House in April, 1865, may of itself,
be thought a satisfactory motive for the production of this
volume; but to this is to be added the wish to do justice
as far as possible to a man, who, highly as he is admired
by his fellow-citizens, is not yet sufficiently esteemed for
heroic steadiness and courage, his transparent simplicity
and honesty, and his profound and disinterested wisdom.

Another consideration which has seemed to be of some
weight is the fact, that most of the biographies, completed
or projected, are either of a special nature, exclusively
devoted to some particular portion or aspect of General
Grant's career; or else they are framed upon a plan of
extensive elaboration and exceeding fulness of detail. It
has accordingly seemed desirable that there should be a
book of convenient compass, covering the entire ground,
and putting within the reach of the people in a single
handy volume, all the information which they naturally
desire respecting this great soldier, sincere patriot, and
naturally astute statesman.

With these remarks the subject is committed to the
candid judgment of the public.

New York, *April*, 1868.

Table of Contents.

CHAPTER V.

GRANT IN CIVIL LIFE.

CHAPTER VI.

FIRST DAYS OF THE WAR.

CHAPTER VII.

FORT HENRY.

CHAPTER VIII.
FORT DONELSON.

CHAPTER IX.
THE BATTLE OF SHILOH.

CHAPTER X.
IUKA AND CORINTH.

CHAPTER XI.
PREPARATIONS FOR THE VICKSBURG CAMPAIGN.

CHAPTER XII.

THE REBEL STRONGHOLD ON THE MISSISSIPPI.

CHAPTER XIII.

PORT GIBSON AND GRAND GULF.

CHAPTER XIV.

VICKSBURG REACHED.

CHAPTER XV.

THE SIEGE AND CAPTURE.

CHAPTER XVI.

THE ARMY OF THE CUMBERLAND.

CHAPTER XVII.

KNOXVILLE.

CHAPTER XVIII.

PLANS FOR THE NEXT CAMPAIGN.

CHAPTER XIX.

GRANT IN THE CHIEF COMMAND.

CHAPTER XX.

THE SITUATION.

CHAPTER XXI.

THE WILDERNESS.

CHAPTER XXII.

SPOTTSYLVANIA.

CHAPTER XXIII.

BUTLER AND HUNTER.

CHAPTER XXIV.

ON THE NORTH ANNA.

CHAPTER XXV.

PETERSBURG.

CHAPTER XXVI.

EARLY'S INVASION.

CHAPTER XXVII.

SHERIDAN AND EARLY.

CHAPTER XXVIII.

SHERMAN.

CHAPTER XXIX.

THE ATLANTA CAMPAIGN.

CHAPTER XXX.

MINOR MOVEMENTS.

CHAPTER XXXI.

IN FRONT OF PETERSBURG.

CHAPTER XXXII.

THE MARCH TO THE SEA.

CHAPTER XXXIII.

THOMAS IN TENNESSEE.

Life of Ulysses S. Grant.

CHAPTER I.

GRANT'S BIRTH—LINEAGE—PARENTAGE—BIOGRAPHY OF HIS FATHER
—ULYSSES DECLINES TO RECEIVE ANY OF HIS FATHER'S PROPERTY—
NOTE—ORIGIN OF THE GRANTS—CHARACTERISTICS OF THE CLAN.

ULYSSES S. GRANT, was born on the 27th day of April,
A. D., 1822, at the village of Point Pleasant, situated in Cler-
mont County, Ohio, on the north bank of the Ohio River,
twenty-five miles above the city of Cincinnati. He is descended from the Grants of Scotland, and possesses many of
the characteristics of that sturdy race.

His father, Jesse Root Grant, was born in Westmoreland
County, Pennsylvania, on the 23d day of January, 1794, and
is the son of Noah Grant, Jr., who was born in Connecticut,
and served as a Lieutenant of militia at the battle of Lexington, subsequently sharing all the dangers of the Revolutionary
war. The father of Noah Grant, Jr., was Captain Noah
Grant, of Windsor, (now known as Tolland,) Connecticut,
a sturdy, robust and courageous man.

He and his brother, Solomon Grant, seem to have been
highly honored and respected by their neighbors. Noah
Grant commanded a company of colonial militia, called into
service during the French and Indian war, while Solomon
served under him in a subordinate capacity. Both were killed
in the battle at White Plains, fought in 1776. Nothing further is known of the ancestors of the family in this country,
except that two of them, brothers, came to America early in

2

the eighteenth century, and one is said to have settled in Canada, and the other in Connecticut.

Jesse R. Grant, whose father had removed to the North-West April. 1799, lost his mother when he was eleven years old, and at the age of sixteen was sent by his father to Mays-ville, Ky., where he was regularly apprenticed to his half-brother, for the purpose of learning the tanners' trade. He served his time faithfully, became a skillful workman, and soon after arriving at his majority went to Ravenna, Portage County, O., where he began the tanning business for himself. At the time his father went to that part of the North-Western Territory, known as Ohio, there were but a few weak and widely scattered settlements in all that region now containing a highly civilized population of over three millions. The adventurous pioneers, who had gone to the frontier for the purpose of subjugating the wilderness and making homes for their children, found themselves beset by many troubles, and continually menaced by sickness and danger. The Indians were discontented, and, under the influence of British emissaries, kept the country in continual disorder. Not till after the peace of 1814, did it become possible for the frontier settlers to establish schools, or to devote themselves closely to agriculture and the useful arts, which necessarily preceded the higher refinement and civilization of the present day. The constant struggle which circumstances forced upon the family of Noah Grant precluded all idea of giving the children a liberal education. Jesse went to school only about five months, but his father being a man of culture, gave such attention to his instruction during childhood, as their check-ered and unsettled life would permit. Notwithstanding early disadvantages, and a life of great industry and activity, Jesse R. Grant has succeeded in acquiring a vast amount of inform-ation upon almost every subject, and is in many respects a remarkable man. Blessed with a strong constitution, a robust and stalwart body, a shrewd, penetrating and comprehensive judgment, and being honest, frugal, industrious and persever-ing, he soon became prosperous, and gradually extended his business, establishing branches in various cities and towns throughout the West. It is not within the scope of this work to enter into the details of his long and successful career. Let it suffice to say that he is a man of strict integrity, a ready and effective speaker, and a pleasing writer. Having amassed an ample fortune, he gave up business at the age of sixty, leaving his sons Orville and Simpson (the latter since dead) to continue it. With a rare degree of liberality he subsequently determined to divide his property equally among his children, reserving only enough to support himself and wife the rest of their days. Ulysses, with a liberality still more remarkable, declined to receive any part of his father's fortune, forgetful of his own industry in boyhood, modestly asserting that he had done nothing towards its accumulation.

Jesse R. Grant was married at Point Pleasant, O., in June, 1821, to Hannah Simpson, the second daughter of John Simpson, a well-to-do farmer and land owner, formerly of Montgomery County, Pennsylvania. As the name indicates, she is also of Scotch origin, though at what time the family came to America is not known. Mrs. Grant is described by those who know her as a woman of great steadiness, firmness, and strength of character; an exemplary and consistent member of the Methodist church from her girlhood; a faithful and devoted wife, a careful, painstaking and affectionate mother, and at all times and in all troubles the chief stay and comfort of her family.

Mr. and Mrs. Grant, are now living at Covington, Ky., full of years and honor, widely respected and beloved for their unaffected simplicity and true worth of character.

It is not strange that the offspring of such parents, should be virtuous, honest, and truthful. But if there is anything good in blood or race, aided by judicious training and honorable example, such a family should contain within itself a model of all that is excellent in woman or admirable in man.

Note.—"Playfair's British Family Antiquity," vol. viii., states that the origin of the Grants is somewhat doubtful, and whether they were originally Scotch or came from Denmark or France, cannot now be positively stated. It is probable, however, that they were Norman, and arrived about 1666 with William the Conqueror. It is certain that the clan had become great and powerful in the early days of the Scotch monarchy. Gregory Grant was "Sheriff Principal" of Inverness, between 1214 and 1249. John Grant commanded the right wing of the Scotch army at Halidoun Hill, 1833, and was defeated. About 1400, the clan became divided into clan Chiaran and clan Allan. They held great possessions in the Strathspey country, and in the Jacobite troubles adhered to the Protestant and Whig cause.

The Strathspey country, the original home of the Grants, lies in the northeastern part of Scotland, along the course of the picturesque River Spey, in the shires of Inverness, Moray and Banff, and is remarkable for its beautiful scenery and noble forests of fir.

In "Collectanea Topographica et Geneologica,' vol. vii., it is stated that Lieutenant General Francis Grant was buried in Hampshire, England, December 2, 1781, and that his monument bears as a crest a burning mount with the motto: "Steadfast." In "Fairbairn's Crests of the Families of Great Britain and Ireland" twenty-one different crests of the Grant family are given. One of them represents a burning hill with four peaks, each surmounted by a flame, with the motto: "Stand sure: Stand fast: Craig Ellachie!" Another Grant had as a crest an oak sprouting and sun shining, with the motto: "Wise and harmless."

Robson's "British Herald" gives twenty-four crests of different Grants. Grant of Jamaica has a burning mount—motto: "Stabit;" Grant of Grant, a burning mount supported by two savages—motto: Stand sure;" Grant of Currimony, a demi-savage—motto: "I'll stand sure;" and Grant of Lieth, a rock—motto: "Immobile."

One of the most distinguished regiments of the British army in India during the Sepoy rebellion, was a Highland regiment composed almost entirely of Grants, bearing upon their colors the motto: "Stand fast Craig Ellachie!"

The reader cannot help being struck by the remarkable description of Grant's most noticeable peculiarities contained in the foregoing mottoes of his sturdy clansmen.

CHAPTER II.

IT IS curiously related by Jesse R. Grant, that soon after
the birth of his first son, a discussion occurred in the family
in regard to the name which should be given him. His
mother and one of his aunts proposed Albert, in honor of
Albert Gallatin, at that time a prominent statesman. Some
one else proposed Theodore, and his grandfather Simpson
suggested Hiram. His step-grandmother, represented as
being a great student of history, and an ardent admirer of
Ulysses, as described by Homer, proposed that name. After
due deliberation he was christened Hiram Ulysses.

The boyhood of Ulysses, as he was commonly called,
passed in a comparatively new country, did not differ materially from that of other boys surrounded by similar circumstances. From a series of interesting biographical papers
by his father, written for Mr. Robert Bonner of New York, we
learn that he began to manifest an independent, self-reliant and
venturous disposition at a very early age, and from the time
he was first permitted to go out alone, he lost no opportunity
of riding and breaking horses, driving teams, and helping his
father in whatever work his strength and size would enable
him to do. At the age of seven and a half years, during his
father's absence, he harnessed a three-year-old colt to a sled,

and hauled brush with him for an entire day. He became
accustomed to harness horses when he was yet so small that
he could not put the bridle or collar on without climbing into
the manger, nor throw the harness over their backs without
standing upon a half-bushel measure. Before he was ten
years old he had got to be a skillful driver and used to do
full work in hauling wood, carrying leather to Cincinnati and
bringing passengers back to Georgetown, where the family
then lived. He became a good rider at six years of age, having begun like most farmer boys by riding the horses to water.
Continuous practice makes perfect in horsemanship as in other
things, and long before Ulysses had reached his twelfth year
he could ride horses at full speed, standing upon their backs
and balancing himself by the bridle reins. It is told of him,
that he succeeded in riding the trained trick pony of a circus
company, in spite of the pony's and ringmaster's efforts to
dismount him, aided by a monkey which fastened itself upon
the head and shoulders of the young rider. His quiet and
gentle disposition, together with a remarkable degree of firmness, rendered him particularly successful in controlling horses,
and in breaking them to the saddle and harness. This he
always did for his father, but his fame soon spread beyond the
family circle and caused his talent to be called into requisition
by the neighbors who had troublesome horses to break. At
that time pacing horses were in great demand for the saddle,
and to teach a horse this gait required no slight skill and patience. Ulysses was quite an adept in this as in other things
relating to horses, but from some idea of pride he would not
exercise his skill for money, although not unwilling to do
real work, or go on errands of business. One of his father's
friends had a fine young horse which he wished to use as a
riding horse, but he could not teach him to pace. Knowing
Ulysses' unwillingness to set about such a task as this for
hire, he engaged him to carry a letter to a neighboring town,
and as the lad was riding away called out to him, "please
teach that colt to pace." Ulysses returned the horse at night
a perfect pacer, but having ascertained that the letter was

simply a sham, he could never afterward be induced to teach a horse to pace.

Sometime after this incident occurred, his father took a contract to build a jail for the county in which he lived, and Ulysses agreed to haul the logs of which it was to be constructed, on condition that his father would buy a certain large horse, as a mate to one he already owned. The bargain was made and the horse bought; but the lad being very small, although then twelve years old, his father had no idea that he could hold out over a week at such heavy work. A man was hired to assist him; but after a short time he told his employer that there was no use in his following the boy around any longer, as he was amply capable of driving and taking care of the team without anybody's help. After that, the boy was permitted to do his part of the work as agreed upon, and did it honestly and faithfully. One day, after hauling a load of logs, Ulysses unhitched his team, and said to his father that there was no use of his going back for another load, as the men were not hewing, and he could keep up with them the next day; besides that, there was no one to help him load. "Nobody there to help load?" said his father; "Why, how did you load this morning?" "Oh, Dave and I loaded," replied the sturdy little fellow. Dave was the name of the big horse that he had induced his father to buy, and Ulysses and Dave had actually loaded the wagon with logs, any one of which would have been a heavy lift for twenty men. This difficult task was accomplished in the following way:—A tree had been felled, one end of which rested upon a stump, and the other upon the ground. Ulysses hitched his horse to the logs, and pulled them, one after the other, across the fallen tree, till their ends were raised off the ground sufficiently high to permit the wagon to be backed under them. As soon as this was done, he chocked his wagon, and made the horse draw the logs upon it, one at a time. This seems to have removed all doubt from his father's mind in regard to his capacity, and certainly showed a great deal of ingenuity and self-reliance. It is needless to say that Ulysses finished his part of the contract, which his father had undertaken, although it continued for over seven months. During the latter part of this time he went to Louisville on important law business, which he transacted satisfactorily, although he was yet so young and small that the steamboat captains would not allow him to take passage without a passport from his father.

At about the age of twelve, he displayed, in a remarkable manner, that calmness and presence of mind which has so eminently characterized his career as a soldier and general. Having been sent with a light wagon and pair of horses to the village of Augusta, in Kentucky, twelve miles from Georgetown, he permitted himself to be persuaded to remain all night, in order to take back two young women who could not be ready to start before morning. The Ohio River had swollen rapidly in the meantime, and the back-water in White Oak Creek, across which his route lay, had risen so much that when he reached it in returning, he was surprised to find, after the first few steps, that his horses and wagon were swimming. The young women, finding themselves in water up to their waists, became badly frightened, and began at once to cry for help. In the midst of this exciting scene, Ulysses, who was on the front seat, coolly guiding his horses towards the opposite bank, turned to the women, and with an air of perfect assurance, said: " Keep quiet; I'll take you through safe!"

Although exceedingly modest and quiet, he was fond of all the games and sports of boyhood. His resolute spirit and cool temper made him a leader among his companions; but his disposition inclined him to seek the society of persons older than himself, and this quality he is supposed to have inherited from his mother, of whom it is said, " she had as much the deportment of a woman at seven as most girls had at twenty." Those who have had the good fortune to know him in manhood, will readily perceive that he must have been an exceedingly good-natured, amiable, patient, cheerful, modest light-hearted boy; full of courage, good sense and self-reliance, without a particle of that disagreeable self-assertion, or aggressiveness of temper which would lead him into difficulty with others. He could read by the time he was seven years old, and was fond of going to school, learning easily and rapidly whatever was taught, but showing particular aptitude in mathematics.

He had always a peaceable, and even disposition, without any inclination to quarrel, and yet he would never permit himself to be imposed upon, neither would he stand by and see a little boy abused by a larger one. His sense of justice and fair play would always cause him to join the weaker side, and fight it through on that line at every hazard. His father bears testimony, in boyhood, to what many who served under and with him during the rebellion, can assert with perfect truthfulness; he never used a profane or obscene word, no matter how great his anger or provocation. "Confound it" is the hardest phrase he ever gave utterance to, but this is an ample vehicle for his wrath, as those can attest who have witnessed its blighting effect upon those who have called it forth.

Although a very industrious boy, he was never fond of working in his father's tannery; the beam-room was particularly distasteful to him, and as he preferred to drive the team and do the out-door business, he generally managed to keep out of it. By the time he had reached his fifteenth year, he had fully made up his mind, and gave his father warning that he would not be a tanner, but would work at the trade till he should become of age, though not a day longer. He expressed a desire to have a liberal education, and to become a farmer, or trader to the States at the South. Fortunately for the country, his father did not fancy the plan of allowing his son to be a farmer or trader, but sagaciously suggested the idea of sending him to West Point. Fortunately, too, no great difficulty was encountered in securing a cadet's warrant, through the kind offices of Senator Morris, and the Hon. Thomas L. Hamer. The last official act of the latter as member of Congress was to make the nomination of Ulysses S. Grant to the Secretary of War as a suitable person to receive the appointment of cadet at the United States Military Academy.

It seems that when his father solicited his appointment as cadet, he designated him as Ulysses, and that the member of Congress who made the nomination, knowing that his mother's maiden name was Simpson, and perhaps that she had a son also named Simpson, sent in the name as Ulysses S. Grant instead of Hiram Ulysses Grant. As a matter of course, the cadet warrant was made out in the exact name of the person nominated, and although the young candidate might have written his true name on the register when he presented himself for admission, it would have probably resulted in his suspension, till the warrant of appointment could be corrected. Foreseeing this trouble and wishing to avoid it, he entered the academy as Ulysses S. Grant, and trusted to getting his name set right at some future day. This, however, he did not succeed in accomplishing, but in order that there should be nothing lost on that score, his class-mates and comrades, looking about for a suitable nickname, gave him the familiar appellation of Sam, which was often expanded into Uncle Sam. Since arriving at the age of manhood, he has not regarded the S. in his name as having any signification whatever.

CHAPTER III.

On the 1st day of July, 1839, Ulysses S. Grant,* then about seventeen years of age and slightly above five feet in hight, was regularly enrolled amongst the cadets at the Military Academy. Although his previous education had not been conducted with any special reference to the requirements of West Point, he had no difficulty in passing a searching preliminary examination in reading, writing, spelling and the ground rules of arithmetic. The battalion of cadets having removed from barracks to the usual summer encampment, young Grant soon found himself in common with his class-mates, rapidly inducted into all the mysteries of cadet life. Under the skillful hand of a third class-man, who had already been thoroughly, " set up as a soldier," he was rapidly taught the military position, squad drill, and manual of arms. Guard duty, field artillery, and academic exercises followed in their turn. Having satisfactorily passed the semi-annual January

---

* There were two Grants in this class, " Grant E." and " Grant U. S." The latter, as was stated at the close of the last chapter, was called " Uncle Sam," and thus distinguished from his class-mate.

examination, which is usually fatal to the hopes of dull and
incorrigible candidates, he subscribed to the oath of allegiance
to the United States, and bound himself to serve the nation
honestly and faithfully against all its enemies and opposers
whatsoever.   Grant did not take a high position in his class,
except in mathematics and the kindred studies,—engineering
and military science.   He preferred to be at a safe distance
from both head and foot, equally removed from plodding
wearisome study, and the danger of being sent away from
the academy.   He excelled in all military exercises, and as
might have been supposed, surpassed nearly all of his class-
mates in horsemanship, and the cavalry drill.   He had the
good luck to escape much of the playful hazing usually inflicted upon the new cadets of that day, though he doubtless
received enough of it to give him a relish when he got to be
a third classman for running it judiciously upon those who
came after him.   He was then as now, cheerful, amiable,
good-natured, and tender-hearted to a degree rarely attained
by men, and hence did not approve of nor enter into the rude
and boisterous pranks, so commonly in vogue among cadets ;
but in his own quiet way he doubtless got all the pleasure
that the circumstances by which he was surrounded would
permit.

At the end of his second year, he was granted the usual
furlough of two months, and, after a visit to his home, returned to his studies, with renewed vigor and determination,
heightened by the approaching prospect of honorable gradua-
tion, at the end of his term.

While at West Point he made the usual unauthorized expeditions to Benny Havens', but was never induced to taste
liquor of any sort, nor to learn to smoke, nor to use tobacco
in any other way.   His fun was all innocent, and his amuse-
ment only such as might have been expected to please an
even-tempered, well-behaved, and high-minded young man.
While, on the one hand, he was not enthusiastic in anything,
on the other, he was always attentive to his studies, and
prompt and faithful in the performance of his duties.   He

was never at enmity with his companions, and had no prejudices against his instructors. He submitted readily to discipline, and was never guilty of a wanton violation of regulations.

During Grant's term of service at the Military Academy, Captain C. F. Smith, a gallant and highly accomplished officer, and subsequently an able and distinguished General, was Commandant of cadets. The Superintendent of the academy and post of West Point was Major (now General) Richard Delafield, to whom, after Colonel Thayer of the same corps, the academy is more indebted, than any other man for the deservedly high reputation it has attained throughout the world.

Mahan, Bartlett, Bailey, Church and Weir, were Professors in the various sciences, and discharged their duties with remarkable ability and fidelity. It is not too much to say that the academy at that day was under perfect discipline, and admirable administration. The course of instruction, comprehending algebra, plain, spherical, descriptive, and analytical geometry, differential and integral calculus, natural and experimental philosophy, mechanics, chemistry, mineralogy, geology, French language and literature, rhetoric, logic, constitutional, international and military law, ordnance and gunnery, architectural, industrial and topographical drawing, civil and military engineering, besides the practical duties of infantry, artillery, cavalry and engineer troops, was thoroughly and rigorously taught. In view of the fact that Grant had such men as Sherman, Thomas, Meade, Humphreys and William F. Smith, for his cotemporaries, and Franklin, Ingalls, Reynolds, Augur, Ripley, Gardner, and others afterwards distinguished in both the national and confederate armies, as class-mates, and that out of a class of over one hundred, only thirty-nine succeeded in graduating, it may be fairly assumed that his scholarship was of no mean order. It has come to be too much the fashion to deny the graduates of West Point the credit of being well educated, because they do not as a class excel in oratory, the intricacies of statute law, nor understand the mazes of commercial and financial affairs. It is difficult to see how any man can go through with the course of studies indicated above, without having his mind so disciplined as to render him capable of performing creditably the duties of any position in either civil or military life. Grant graduated twenty-first in his class, but could have easily taken a higher standing had he thought it worth the extra trouble it would have cost him. It is a well known fact, that it is not always, nor often, the head-man at West Point, nor the first honor man in the colleges at home or abroad, who carries off the first honors, or reaches the highest station in the ordinary pursuits of life. Occasionally a head-man, endowed with superior powers of comprehension, aided by common sense, and the favoring circumstances of life, has reached like Lee and Johnston, the high places of power and command; but more frequently fortune has chosen for her favorite the Grant, Sherman, Thomas or Sheridan, of his class, who left the petty rivalries of school-boy days to petty minds, and from among the ways before him:

> —" Chose considerately
> With a clear foresight not a blindfold courage,
> And having chosen, with steadfast mind
> Pursued his purposes."

CHAPTER IV.

ON the 1st of July, 1843, Grant was appointed Brevet
Second Lieutenant in the United States Army, and temporarily assigned to duty with the Fourth Regiment of Infantry.
Early in November after the three months' leave of absence
usually granted to the graduating class of cadets, which he
spent among his friends and relatives in Ohio, he reported
for duty with his regiment then stationed at Jefferson Barracks near St. Louis. This was the principal military station
in the West, and contained by far the largest garrison of infantry then to be found at any post in the country. Constant
drill and rigid discipline under experienced and excellent offi-

cers brought the regiment to an admirable state of efficiency, and at the same time inspired the young officers attached to it with a high degree of *esprit de corps*.

Early in the summer of 1844 Grant accompanied his regiment to Camp Salubrity at Natchitoches, La., whither it had been ordered for the purpose of being in readiness to carry out the policy of the Government in regard to Texas. Grant's duties as a subaltern here were not dissimilar from those at Jefferson Barracks, though the life and surroundings were not nearly so agreeable. It was during the year passed at this encampment that he smoked his first cigar, and laid the foundation of a practice which has since become so eminently characteristic of him.

In the summer of 1845 the Fourth Infantry joined the army of observation then assembling at Corpus Christi under Taylor, for the purpose of watching the Mexican army menacing that frontier, and while Grant was one of those officers not quite able to perceive the justice of the Texas claim to the country lying beyond the Nueces, he accompanied his regiment and performed his duties with unswerving fidelity.

On the 30th of September, 1845, he was promoted to the full rank of Second Lieutenant to fill a vacancy in the Seventh Infantry, but having become attached to his comrades of the Fourth, he made application to the War Department for permission to remain with them. This request was granted, and he had the good fortune to participate shortly afterwards in the battles of Palo Alto and Resaca de la Palma, on the 8th and 9th of May, 1846. He also took part in the operations of the army under Taylor, previous to and during the bloody battle of Monterey, September 23d, behaving with noticeable coolness and gallantry whenever an opportunity presented itself.

As these battles were fought, against greatly superior numbers, by a small army, unused to warfare (except with the Indians,) every man and officer was called upon to do his utmost, to maintain the honor of the flag. Defeat would have led to capture and imprisonment. Victory was an absolute necessity, of which every man had become convinced by the fate of those who had fallen into the hands of the Mexicans, and hence a spirit of individual prowess characterized the whole army. The different regiments and arms of the service vied with each other in deeds which transformed them into veterans, while officers of every grade gained in a few weeks more professional experience than a lifetime of frontier service would have given them.

Soon after the capture of Monterey, Grant's regiment was withdrawn from the army under Taylor, and was sent to join Scott, then assembling a large force at the Island of Lobos, for an attack upon Vera Cruz, preparatory to his great campaign in the interior of Mexico. Grant was, therefore, at the siege and capture of Vera Cruz, March 29, 1847. Having displayed great perseverance and activity, both there and elsewhere, he was about this time appointed Regimental Quartermaster, and held the office, discharging all its duties with patience, regularity and efficiency, till the army was withdrawn from Mexico. According to the usages of the military service this appointment always excuses the officer holding it from duty with the troops; and as the Quartermaster is required to take charge of trains, depots and equipage, it is his business to remain with them while on the march; it also entitles him to the privilege of doing so during actual battle, if he prefers it. Grant's brother officers bear witness to the fact, and tell it to his praise, that he never availed himself of this privilege as many others had done, but made it a point to rejoin his regiment at the approach of every battle, and to stay with it till the fighting had ceased.

Acting in accordance with this chivalrous principle, he took a gallant part in the two days' battle of Cerro Gordo, on the 17th and 18th of April. After active operations were resumed, he took part in the capture of San Antonio and the battle of Churubusco, August 20th. At the splendid affair of El Molino del Rey, his bravery was so conspicuous that it won for him shortly afterwards the brevet rank of First Lieutenant, for "distinguished and meritorious services;" but

3

having received in the meantime his promotion to the full grade, to fill one of the vacancies caused by the casualties of that battle, he declined the compliment. At the storming of Chapultepec, Grant volunteered with a detachment of his company, and assisted in the assault which carried the enemy's entrenchments. During the action he took command of a mountain howitzer and served it with such effect as to materially hasten the retreat of the Mexican forces. His conduct upon this occasion attracted the special notice and commendation of his regimental, brigade and division commanders,* and following so closely upon his spirited behavior at El Molino del Rey secured for him the brevet of Captain.

After the assault and capture of the city of Mexico, in which his bravery was again conspicuous, Grant for awhile became absorbed in the duties of Regimental Quartermaster. His station being in the city, he made the acquaintance of many of the officers of our army; and after the declaration of peace organized several excursions into the neighboring country for the purpose of gathering information. He lost no opportunity to become acquainted with the Mexican people and their institutions, and is now one of their firmest friends. He was at this time only twenty-five years old, had served two years in camp and garrison under the best officers of the army, had accompanied Taylor in his brilliant campaign from Corpus Christi to Monterey, and finally, in the double capacity of staff and company officer, had shared in the labor and honor of Scott's memorable conquest. He took part in every battle of the war except Buena Vista, and by zeal, energy and courage, distinguished himself above most of his companions holding the same rank.

The careful observer of character will not fail to see in the foregoing narrative ample evidence of Grant's peculiar quali-
• ties, as they were more fully developed by the events of the great struggle in which he became the central figure. His zeal, enterprise and courage, were conspicuous. His endurance, regularity, and promptitude in the performance of duty,

* Reports of Major Francis Lee, Colonel Garland and General Worth.

gained for him the notice of his superiors, while his modesty and amiability made him a general favorite, both among his companions, and the Mexicans with whom he came in contact. After the treaty of peace with Mexico, Grant accompanied his regiment to New York city.

In 1848 he was married to Julia T. Dent, eldest daughter of Mr. Frederick Dent, a successful and widely known merchant of St. Louis, and after a short leave of absence returned with his wife to Sackett's Harbor, where his regiment was then stationed. He remained at Sackett's Harbor till 1849, and in September of that year he was again appointed Regimental Quartermaster, which office he held till 1853.

In the fall of 1849 his regiment moved to Fort Brady near Detroit, where it rested two years and then returned to Sackett's Harbor. In 1852 it was sent to Fort Columbus in the harbor of New York, preparatory to sailing for the Pacific coast, where a rush of emigration was then setting in toward the newly discovered gold-fields, and troops were needed to protect the growing settlements from the depredations of Indians. The regiment proceeded by way of Panama, but the Panama railroad had not then been built, and the transit of the Isthmus was attended with great difficulty, and much exposure to the hurtful influences of the tropical climate. During the passage, and after they had reached the Pacific side, many of the officers and men fell sick and died of fever and cholera, but Grant's rugged constitution defied the malaria, and enabled him to be of great assistance to his less fortunate companions. The cholera became so general that the regiment could not continue its voyage but was compelled to encamp on one of the islands in the bay of Panama, where it remained for several weeks. After it reached Oregon, decimated in numbers, one battalion, including Grant's company, was ordered to take post at Columbia Barracks, near the Dalles of the Columbia River, where it remained for some time, making occasional expeditions against the hostile Indians, in all of which Grant took an active part, adding to his varied experience, and gaining useful information in regard to the Indian character and the resources of the neighboring country.   In August, 1853, while on duty at Fort Vancouver he was promoted to the full rank of Captain, and shortly afterwards he was assigned to the command of Fort Humboldt, on the northern coast of California.   He remained at the latter place about a year, but seeing no chance of further promotion, and having nothing to compensate him for separation from his family, but the doubtful pleasures and uninteresting occupations of a nomadic life upon the frontier, he resigned his commission on the 31st of July, 1854, and rejoined his wife and children at St. Louis, from whom he had been separated for over two years.

CHAPTER V.

WITH no fortune of his own and with few acquaintances, and fewer friends in civil life, Grant was thrown at once upon his own resources. Without hesitation he settled upon a small farm near St. Louis, which had been presented to Mrs. Grant by her father. He threw aside completely the habits of army life and went to work bravely with his own hands to better his fortune. His first labor was to assist in hewing the logs, and building a house upon his farm. As soon as it was finished he occupied it with his family, so that he might be entirely independent of the world, as well as close to the fields he intended to cultivate. It has been said that he did not make a successful farmer, but that is a mistake, which may have arisen from the fact that his farm was small, and only partially ready for cultivation. Grant worked hard himself and displayed excellent judgment in all that he did. To be sure his profits were not large, at any time, but they were his only dependence for the support of his family.

He took great interest in his stock, and being really fond of his new occupation, he devoted himself to it with a will. During the winter season he employed men to clear land, and chop wood, and hauled it to St. Louis for sale, driving one team in person, while his little son drove another, thus saving the expense of two extra hands. He ploughed and planted in the spring, and when the summer had ripened his crops he was the foremost hand in the harvest-field.

Several years before the war began, one of his friends, happening to be at St. Louis, heard that Grant was living near by, and drove out for the purpose of seeing him. Calling at the house, he inquired for Captain Grant. The servant who answered his summons at the door informed him that the Captain would probably be found in the meadow, harvesting. The officer walked down to the field, as the servant suggested, but not discovering the Captain, sat down in the shade of a tree for the purpose of waiting for the approach of four men whom he saw mowing at a distance. After a short time the mowers came abreast of him, and going out to meet them he was surprised to find that the leading mower, covered with perspiration, and in his shirt-sleeves, was the friend for whom he was seeking. It has been said that "the ways by which men get money lead downward," and this may be true when applied to the tricks of special trades, or to the devices and uncertain calling of the gambler in stocks; but if every man could be induced to get money by such an honest exhibition of industry, the world and our country would certainly be the better for it.

Grant was economical as well as industrious, and if he could not make money rapidly for himself, he could tell others how to save it. While living at his father-in-law's, he observed that all the rooms in the house were warmed by wood fires, in ample old-fashioned fire-places, and that it kept one man continually busy to cut fuel for them. Near by was a colliery, the owners of which were paying fifty cents apiece for stout saplings with which to shore up the roof of their mine. Grant suggested that he could cut and haul poles enough in one day to buy coal for an entire month, and in two more to pay for a grate or stove in every room. This was a new idea, and a few days thereafter was put into successful application.

After four years of farming, Grant resolved to try something else. He leased his farm, and removed to St. Louis, where he established and conducted for a short time a real estate office.   Shortly afterwards a situation was offered him in the custom-house, which he accepted and held till the death of the Collector brought a new man into office, who had his own friends to reward.   Being again out of business, he applied for the position of city engineer, and although thoroughly qualified by his military education and practical experience to perform the duties of the office, his influence was not sufficient to secure it.

Early in 1860 he accepted a proposition from his father to remove to Galena, and join his brothers in the leather business.   Devoting himself with industry and good sense to his new occupation, he soon became familiar with all its branches, and achieved a fair degree of success.   But not being at all demonstrative in his manners, nor inclined to take an active part in the affairs of the town, he made but few acquaintances, and those mostly among the people with whom he had business.   A few of the best citizens had broken through his natural reserve, and discovered the sterling qualities of the man, though it is but fair to say that no one then suspected that the modest, quiet, and obscure leather-dealer would ever become the most distinguished man of his time.

When the rebellion was precipitated upon the country by the attack upon Fort Sumter, Grant had just attained his thirty-ninth year, and having been blessed with a strong and elastic constitution, an equable temper, a stout and well-set figure, capable of great endurance, he had passed through the varied experiences of his life with continually increasing powers.   He had not reached full mental development with manhood, but had increased steadily in mental and moral stature by the trials through which he had gone, rather than by the years that had passed over his head.   He had never been a great student, not even a great reader; but having a remarkably retentive memory, coupled with a thorough appreciation of all that is practical and useful, he was fully able to grapple with whatever question might be presented for his consideration.   He had neither whims nor hobbies, neither

pet theories nor visionary schemes; but was entirely free
from prejudice of every sort, and, better than all, he had
reached that perfection of common sense, which, combined
with truthfulness and steadfast courage, is superior to genius.
Plain and simple in his address, "with manners unspotted by
the world," direct in his purposes, slow to anger, sparing of
words in public, free from guile and shams of every sort, and
faithful in all things, he was regarded as a true friend, a good
citizen, and an honest man! Adversity or prosperity,—
whichever came,—would find him ever cheerful and ready
for the duties of life, no matter whether they should lead him
in the ways of peace or through the dangers and trials of
war.

CHAPTER VI.

GRANT, while living at St. Louis and Galena, took no part in political matters, farther then to keep himself well informed as an intelligent citizen should, of what was taking place throughout the country. Having been educated as a military man, and been denied the opportunity of voting during his service in the army, he had no bond of sympathy with purely partisan movements, and no taste for public meetings of any sort. From an army acquaintance with the character and real merits of Fremont or his real lack of merit, he was induced to cast his vote for Buchanan; but before the weakness of the latter had actually enabled the secessionists to plunge the country into civil war, Grant had become convinced that his first and only vote had been a grevious mistake. He had never been a democrat but rather favored the moderate opin-ions of such men as Everett, Crittenden and Bell. He hoped that peaceful counsels would prevail, and that civil war would be averted, but when all the measures looking to conciliation had failed, he was not the man to occupy a neutral or doubtful position. Having been educated at the national expense, and repeatedly taken the oath to uphold and defend the Constitution of the United States against all its enemies and opposers whatsoever, his duty was too plain to admit of a moment's hesitation. Like Sherman and many other former officers of the army, he was inspired by an ardent and patriotic loyalty and therefore determined to support his Government and uphold its flag at every hazard.

Beauregard opened fire upon Fort Sumter on the 11th of April, 1861. Four days afterward the President issued his call for seventy-five thousand three months' men; four days later a company was enrolled at Galena, and Grant being the only man in the town who knew anything whatever of military matters, the duty of drilling this company was naturally assigned to him; still four days later, he went with it to Springfield, and reported to the Governor for service.

From Springfield he addressed a letter to the Adjutant-General of the army, offering his services to the Government for whatever duty it might be thought his past experience would fit him, but to this letter he received no reply. About this time he visited his father at Covington, Ky., and while there he took occasion to go twice to Cincinnati, where General McClellan, then commanding the Ohio militia, had established his head-quarters, hoping that his past acquaintance with that General might secure for him an offer of employment. But in this, too, he was disappointed.

While at Springfield waiting for an opportunity, his knowledge of military organization and the details of service enabled him to become exceedingly useful in the organization of troops. Volunteers were pouring in from all parts of the State, calling for arms, clothing, camp and garrison equipage and instruction; and although the Governor and his staff of military civilians did all in their power to meet these urgent demands, the confusion and disorder accompanying their labors were almost inextricable. The want of an experienced army officer was severely felt, so the Governor was compelled by force of circumstances rather than choice to call upon Captain Grant,—although on account of his obscurity he had received him at first with decided coldness. The ordnance department required Grant's first attention, the adjutant-general's next, and in their turn all the others. He had all the forms at his finger's ends,—knew how every paper should be drawn and where it should be sent. His information was in constant request, and when not engaged in one of the offices he was called upon to assist in drilling troops. So thoroughly and yet so quietly did he perform the duties assigned him, that before a month had expired the Governor had sagaciously discovered his sterling characteristics, and lost no further time in finding a place for him.

Accordingly when the Twenty-first Regiment of Illinois Volunteers arrived at Springfield, in a bad state of organization, under an inefficient Colonel of their own choice, the Governor declined to commission him, but put the regiment under the charge of Captain Grant, and a few days thereafter, while Grant was absent at Covington, sent him the commission of Colonel. Nobody was more surprised at this piece of good fortune than Grant himself, for with characteristic modesty he had scarcely hoped for a higher grade than that of Captain, and having received but little encouragement even in this aspiration, he had almost made up his mind to return to Galena. Accepting, however, the trust so fortunately confided to his care, he assumed command on the 16th of June, and soon had the satisfaction of seeing his regiment noted for its excellent discipline and proficiency in drill. In his report to the Adjutant General of Illinois, he says: "Being ordered to rendezvous the regiment at Quincy, Ill., I thought, for the purpose of discipline and speedy efficiency for the field, it would be well to march the regiment across the country, instead of transporting by rail. Accordingly, on the 3d of July, 1861, the march was commenced from Camp Yates, Springfield, Ill., and continued until about three miles beyond the Illinois River, when dispatches were received, changing the destination of the regiment to Ironton, Mo., and directing me to return to the river and take a steamer, which had been sent there for the purpose of transporting the regiment to St. Louis. The steamer failing to reach the point of embarkation, several days were here lost. In the meantime a portion of the Sixteenth Illinois Infantry, under Colonel Smith, were reported surrounded by the enemy at a point on the Hannibal and St. Joseph Railroad, west of Palmyra, and the Twenty-first was ordered to their relief. Under these circumstances, expedition was necessary; accordingly, the march was abandoned, and the railroad was called into requisition. Before the Twenty-first reached its new destination, the Sixteenth had extricated itself. The Twenty-first was then kept on duty on the line of the Hannibal and St. Joseph Railroad for about two weeks, without, however, meeting an enemy or an incident worth relating. We did make one march, however, during that time, from Salt River, Mo., to Florida, Mo., and returned, in search of Tom Harris, who was reported in that neighborhood with a handful of rebels. It was impossible, however, to get nearer than a day's march of him. From Salt River the regiment went to Mexico, Mo., where it remained for two weeks; thence to Ironton, Mo., passing through St. Louis on the 7th of August, when I was assigned to duty as a Brigadier General, and turned over the command of the regiment to that gallant and Christian officer, Colonel Alexander, who afterwards yielded up his life, whilst nobly leading it in the battle of Chickamauga."

Early in August he was assigned to duty as a Brigadier General. His name having been suggested by the Hon. E. B. Washburne, and unanimously recommended by the Congressional delegation from Illinois, the President appointed him to that rank to date from May 17, 1861, one month anterior to his appointment of Colonel by Governor Yates. He was immediately assigned to the command of the military district of Missouri, including the south-eastern part of the State, from which it took its name, Southern Illinois, and all of the territory in Western Kentucky and Tennessee, then or afterwards under the control of the national forces. Simultaneously with this assignment he was ordered by telegraph to proceed to St. Louis and report in person at the head-quarters of the department. In order that no time should be lost, a special train was sent from St. Louis for him—but when the General presented himself the same day at head-quarters as directed, they were so surrounded by sentinels, and hedged about with aids-de-camp in waiting, that he was delayed over twenty-four hours, before he could reach the presence of General Fremont. Having received his instructions, on the 1st of September, he went at once to Cairo, where he established his head-quarters, and assumed the command to which he had been assigned.

At this time the rebels under Polk held Columbus, a strong point commanding the river twenty miles below Cairo, and in connection with Bragg, at Bowling Green, were making vigorous efforts to provoke Kentucky into an abandonment of her assumed neutrality. They had also a force operating in South-eastern Missouri, under Thompson; they controlled the Mississippi River throughout its length, below the mouth of the Ohio; held the Tennessee and the Cumberland, and seemed to be looking to the control of the Ohio, by the seizure of Paducah and other strong points on the western border of Kentucky. Perceiving the true condition of affairs almost at a glance, and properly appreciating the strategic importance of Paducah, situated at the confluence of the Tennessee and Ohio Rivers, Grant determined at once to forestall the movement which Polk had already begun toward that point; and on the 5th of September he notified his intentions to Fremont and the Legislature of Kentucky. On the night of the same day, having received no countermanding order from Fremont, and having made an arrangement with Commodore Foote for a convoy of two gun-boats, he set out with two regiments of infantry and one battery of field artillery, embarked upon steam transports. An accident to one of the transports caused a slight detention to his flotilla. Nevertheless, it

arrived at Paducah by half-past eight o'clock the next day.
A small force of rebels, under General Tilghman, had reached
there before the national troops, but fled upon their approach,
leaving Grant to take quiet possession of the town, and the
rebel stores already gathered there.   Having disembarked
the troops and occupied the telegraph office, railroad depot,
and marine hospital, he issued a proclamation, saying that he
had nothing to do with opinions, and would deal only with
armed rebellion, its aiders and abettors.   The same day he
returned to Cairo, where he found permission from Fremont
to take Paducah, if he thought himself strong enough.   But,
in the meantime, Fremont, had sent him, by telegraph, a
severe reprimand for corresponding with the Kentucky State
authorities in regard to his contemplated movement, and informed him that General C. F. Smith had been assigned to
the command of Paducah, with orders to report directly to
Fremont's head-quarters.   As a matter of course, Grant's
promptitude was an exasperating blow to the disunionists in
Kentucky, and was severely denounced by the rebel authorities as a flagrant violation of the neutrality declared by a
sovereign State.   Its effect was to give the national forces
firm control of the Ohio River, as well as of the Lower Tennessee and Cumberland.   At the same time it served to
unmask the real intention of the rebel leaders, while it
strengthened the hands of the Union men in the Legislature
sufficiently to enable them to carry resolutions favoring the
Union cause, thus putting an end forever to the rebel fiction
of Kentucky neutrality.   During the next ten weeks, Grant
was prohibited from engaging in important operations, and
by the order of Fremont was kept in a strictly defensive
attitude.

A few weeks after the capture of Paducah, Smithland, at
the mouth of the Cumberland River, was taken possession of
by C. F. Smith, acting under special instructions from Fremont.   Grant, in the meantime, was engaged in strengthening the defenses of Cairo, and in building those at Bird's Point
and Fort Holt.

Cairo had come to be recognized by the Government as a point of great importance. Being situated at the extreme southern end of Illinois, thrust in between Kentucky on the one hand and Missouri on the other, with ample railway communication with the north, and covered from attack by the Mississippi and the Ohio Rivers, it was early selected as a base of operations against the rebels in the lower Mississippi valley.

New troops were now pouring in from all parts of the North-west; and while they were filled with ardor, and inspired by an exalted spirit of patriotism, they were, men and officers, entirely ignorant of warfare. Here and there was an occasional soldier who had served in the Mexican war, but that was a memory of the past. Officers and men alike required instruction. The task of organizing and giving this instruction naturally fell to Grant, the commanding general of the district. At that time he had not a single trained soldier or officer of the regular army under his command, and hence he was compelled to direct everything in person. He was actually obliged to teach the regimental and company officers how to make requisitions for rations and equipage. McClellan and Buell had so completely monopolized the officers of the regular army, that Grant was also forced to select his staff entirely from officers of the volunteer service. They had first to be taught their duties before they could be of any assistance; so that for much of the time Grant had to act as adjutant-general, quartermaster, commissary, ordnance officer, and aid-de-camp. He was busy from morning till night, and frequently from night till morning, in writing orders, endorsing papers, and doing the multifarious work incident to such a command.

Fortunately, in this emergency, he displayed that profound knowledge of character for which he has since become so justly distinguished. Lieutenant John A. Rawlins, (now Brigadier-General and Chief-of-staff,) a young lawyer of talent, with whom he had become acquainted at Galena, was chosen for the position of Adjutant-General, and entered upon the discharge of his duties with great eagerness; bringing to his assistance habits of regularity and order in the transaction of business, a remarkably retentive memory and a powerful understanding. Under the instructions of his chief, he was not long in acquiring a thorough knowledge of administrative details.

During this period of two months Grant's forces were increased to 20,000 men, from whom he organized the nucleus of that army with which he afterwards repossessed the entire valley of the Mississippi, and which throughout a career extending to the end of the war, never met the rebels but to conquer them. Whilst engaged in this work he more than once advised the capture of Columbus, a strong point on the left bank of the Mississippi, twenty miles below Cairo, which the rebels were fortifying, and where they were gathering a large and well appointed force. This position being naturally one of the strongest on the river, enabled the rebels to completely bar the navigation of the stream, and to menace either Paducah or Cairo. By holding Belmont also, a point on the west bank of the river, directly under the guns of Columbus, they could cross troops at all times for the purpose of making incursions into Missouri and menacing Cape Girardeau, and under favorable circumstances, even St. Louis itself. As early as the 10th of September, Grant wrote that if he were permitted to use his discretion, and could have slight reinforcements, he could take Columbus, but he received no reply to his letter.

On the 21st of October a spirited fight took place at Fredericktown, in South-eastern Missouri, between the rebels under Jeff. Thompson and a detachment of Grant's command, sent out from Cape Girardeau, under Colonel Plummer, assisted by Hawkins' Missouri cavalry and Colonel Carlin's regiment of Illinois volunteers, moving from Pilot Knob. The movement of the Union detachments having been well timed, Thompson was considerably outnumbered by the united force, and, although strongly posted, he was overpowered after two hours' severe fighting, and compelled to fly, leaving sixty killed upon the field.

On the 1st of November, Grant was directed by Fremont to make demonstrations toward Norfolk, Charleston, and Blandville, but was cautioned against bringing on an actual engagement. The next day Fremont informed him that a force of three thousand rebels had taken position on the St. Francis River, about fifty miles south-west of Cairo, and ordered him to detach a force to assist a column, already moving from Ironton, in driving them away. In compliance with these instructions, Grant sent one regiment from Cape Girardeau, and Colonel (now Governor) Oglesby, with a small brigade of mixed troops from Commerce, in the direction of Indian Ford, on the St. Francis. But the next day Grant was informed that Polk, at Columbus, had begun to send reinforcements to Price, who was at that time confronting the national forces in South-west Missouri. Fremont therefore ordered a demonstration towards Columbus, and Grant immediately sent the regiment of W. H. L. Wallace to reinforce Oglesby, and directed Oglesby to turn his column towards New Madrid,—a point on the Mississippi below Columbus,—with instructions to communicate with him at Belmont. General C. F. Smith was requested to send out a force from Paducah, for the purpose of menacing Columbus from the rear, while two smaller detachments moved out from Bird's Point and Fort Holt, with the intention of giving the demonstration the appearance of a general movement.

Having made these dispositions, on the evening of the 6th of November, Grant embarked the rest of his available force, consisting of five regiments of infantry, one section of artillery, and two squadrons of cavalry,—in all about thirty-one hundred men,—and, under the convoy of two gun-boats, began the demonstration towards Columbus. But having heard during the night that the rebels had been crossing troops from Columbus to Belmont, and fearing for Oglesby's safety, he at once decided to convert his demonstration into an actual movement against the rebel camps at Belmont. This purpose was favored by the semblance of a landing which he had made the night before on the Kentucky side, ten or twelve

4

miles below Cairo.   At early dawn of the 7th the transports
steamed down the river, and landing at Hunter's Point just
outside the range of the heavy guns at Columbus, the troops
were rapidly disembarked, and moved by the flank to within
two miles of Belmont.   Here they were halted long enough
to form in order of battle, and then marched forward to the
attack.

The rebel camp had been established in an open field on
the bank of the river, its front covered by a wooded slough
running through several small lagoons, and further strengthened by a line of abattis.   The enemy under Colonel Tappan
having been warned by the lookout from Columbus, were on
the alert, and lost no time in disposing themselves to resist
Grant's approach.   General Pillow, with four regiments of
his division, hurriedly crossed the river and took command
of the rebels.

The national forces moved forward to the attack as soon as
circumstances would permit, covered by a heavy line of skirmishers meeting with determined opposition at every step.
By nine o'clock they were all engaged, except one battalion
left to guard the transports and landing.   The rebels fought
with determination, disputing every foot of the way, and holding to every tree till the last minute; but after four hours'
hard fighting, with varying fortunes, Grant's raw volunteers
swept everything before them,—pushed the rebels beyond the
lagoon, burst upon their camp, captured their artillery and
equipage, and took many prisoners.   During the action the
men had behaved like veterans, but in the moment of victory they forgot what little they had learned of military
order.   The four hours' hard work through which they had
gone, had necessarily disorganized them considerably, and
instead of forming again and pressing the rebels, who in the
meantime had taken cover under the river bank, they began
to plunder the rebel encampment and count the fruits of their
victory.   Many of the field officers carried away by enthusiasm, and not realizing the dangers of their situation, wasted
their time and breath in making speeches.   But the rebels

though beaten were not disheartened. General Polk, overlooking the entire scene from the heights of Columbus, had become thoroughly alarmed for the safety of Pillow, and hurried reinforcements to him as fast as possible. Three regiments under Colonel Marks reached him first, soon followed by General Cheatham's brigade, thus increasing the rebel force to eleven or twelve regiments,* over twice as many as Grant had with him. Pillow lost no time in reorganizing his command, or in getting it into a suitable position from which to assail Grant in flank and rear. In the meantime, the latter having observed the rebel transports crowded with troops crossing from Columbus, and discovered the movements of Pillow, saw that he had nothing left him but to withdraw his forces promptly to the transports. He directed the camps to be burned, and after much hard work, with the aid of the rebel guns at Columbus, he succeeded in recalling his men to their colors. The march in retreat was begun without further delay, but had hardly commenced when the combined rebel force was discovered between them and the transports. One of Grant's officers hurried to him with the information, and in an excited manner, exclaimed: "We are surrounded, and will have to surrender!" "I guess not," said Grant with composure. "If we are surrounded we must cut our way out as we cut our way in."

When the troops discovered that their chief was determined to fight his way out, all hesitation was at an end. The attack was made with vigor, and resulted as had been expected,—in a second defeat of the enemy. The transports were reached in due time, and the command embarked under cover of the gun-boats without further loss or confusion.

The loss of the national forces in killed, wounded and missing, was 485 men, while that of the rebels reached 632.† This was the first battle of any magnitude in that theater of operations, and is justly claimed by Grant as a substantial and important victory. Officers and men had behaved with great gallantry. Colonels Logan, Lauman, Dougherty, and

* "Southern History of the War," pp. 206–8.   † Ibidem, p. 209.

Fouke, and General McClernand led their men with conspicuous bravery throughout the action, while Grant himself
exhibited his usual coolness and determination.   In the heat
of the action his horse was killed under him.   After the
larger part of his command had reached the transports, he
went out again, accompanied by an aid-de-camp for the purpose of withdrawing the battalion that had been left to cover
the landing, and such small parties as had not yet got in, but
had gone only a few rods when he found himself in front of
the entire rebel line not sixty paces distant.   Being dressed
in a soldiers blouse, the rebels took no particular notice of
him.   He saw that all his stragglers had been picked up or
cut off, and therefore turned to ride towards the boat, but as
the rebels continued to advance rapidly in the same direction,
he was compelled to put his horse to his best speed, and succeeded in reaching the boat just as she was pushing off.   The
rebels, now under Polk in person, reached the shore a few
minutes afterwards, and opened a severe musketry fire on
the transports, but as they fired low, little or no damage was
done.   The gun-boats replied with canister and grape and
drove them back in confusion.

The rebel historians claim this as a great victory, but nothing is more certain than that Grant accomplished his purpose,
captured and burnt the rebel camps, took their artillery and
compelled Pillow's command of five regiments to seek safety
under cover of the river bank.   After the rebel force had
been doubled by two additional brigades, and had succeeded
in surrounding Grant, the latter again broke the rebel lines
and forced his way to the transports, inflicting almost twice as
much loss upon the enemy as he had received.   Oglesby's
movement was entirely protected, and the rebels in all that
region were thrown upon the defensive, lest their strong
places should be wrested from them.   The national troops
engaged in the battle of Belmont had no doubt whatever
that they had gained a substantial victory, and the memory
of their deeds gave them a confidence and steadiness in action
which transformed them at once into veterans.   Neither offi-

cers nor men who participated in that battle were ever known to falter in the hour of danger, but wherever hard work was required or hard blows were to be given, a regiment with "Belmont" upon its flags was sure to be found. And yet the country at large did not realize these facts, but regarded Grant with distrust and looked upon the battle as at best a glorious misfortune.

CHAPTER VII.

THE rebels now set about strengthening their position in
West Tennessee and Kentucky, and accordingly Albert Sid-
ney Johnston, who had been sent West by the Davis government, with discretionary powers, determined to establish a
strong defensive line extending from the Mississippi to Central
Kentucky. He concentrated at Bowling Green, on the extreme right of this line, covering Nashville and Central Tennessee, a large and well appointed army. Columbus was
rapidly strengthened by all the heavy guns which could be
obtained, while the garrison was swelled by a large force,
designed to cover Memphis and hold the Mississippi. The
centre of the line was occupied by two strongly entrenched
camps, Fort Henry situated upon the east bank of the Tennessee River, and Fort Donelson on the west bank of the
Cumberland. These positions had been selected and fortified
with considerable care by experienced engineers, and were
well placed, for the purpose of barring the navigation of the
two rivers penetrating into the interior of Tennessee. Every
exertion was made to render them entirely secure. Magazines
were constructed, guns of heavy calibre were mounted upon
the water fronts, and troops were gathered from all parts of
the South with great dispatch. The rebel leaders seem to

have become thoroughly alarmed, even at this early day * by the activity which the Union forces were displaying, and did all they could to give an exaggerated idea of their own numbers and resources.

Owing to the failure of Fremont's administration of civil affairs in Missouri, he was relieved on the 9th of November and was succeeded the same day by General Halleck, with enlarged authority both civil and military.

The new command was designated as the department of the Missouri, and included Arkansas and Western Kentucky in addition to the territory which had heretofore been within the limits of Fremont's department. About the same time all that part of Kentucky and Tennessee lying east of the Cumberland River, was erected into an independent command to be called the Department of the Ohio. General Buell was designated to relieve General Sherman, who had succeeded General Anderson a short time before

General Halleck, continued Grant in the command which he had held under Fremont, but changed its designation to the District of Cairo—and extended its jurisdiction to include Paducah. During the two months which followed Halleck's accession to command in the West, no important operations were conducted from Grant's district, but the time was passed in instructing the troops, and in perfecting their organization.

Early in January, 1862, Halleck ordered Grant to make demonstrations from Paducah and Bird's Point towards Columbus for the purpose of preventing the re-enforcement of Buckner then collecting a large force at Bowling Green. In compliance with these instructions six thousand men under McClernand, were sent out from the neighborhood of Cairo, while a somewhat larger force under C. F. Smith moved at the same time from Paducah. These troops were marching and countermarching through the swamps of Kentucky, something over a week, and although they were not engaged in fighting they suffered greatly from exposure, and hardships. A few days after they started the order to send them was

* "Southern History of the War," p. 210.

countermanded. In the meantime, as early as the 6th of
January, Grant had conceived the idea of taking Forts
Donelson and Henry, and had applied to General Halleck for
authority to visit him at St. Louis in order that he might
obtain permission for the movement. Buell had asked Mc-
Clellan then General-in-Chief, that a demonstration might be
made in the direction of Nashville, from Cairo, but neither
Halleck nor McClellan seemed to realize the full importance
of the suggestion. The latter in fact, declared the capture
of Bowling Green and Nashville to be a matter of secondary
importance at that time. But on the 22d of January General Smith, who had just returned from a reconnoissance of
Fort Henry, reported that the place could be easily taken by
the iron clads and a strong co-operating land force, if the attack should be made within a short time. Grant sent this
information at once to Halleck, and on the next day set out
to visit him. Halleck however would not sanction the undertaking, but sent him back to his command with an intimation that it would be time enough to make suggestions when
they were asked. Fortunately, however, Grant was not convinced by Halleck's ideas of strategy, but on the 28th of
January, he telegraphed for permission " to take and hold
Fort Henry," following it the next day by a letter stating his
reasons more fully than he had yet done, for believing that
the place could be taken and that considerations of sound
policy would warrant the attempt. These repeated applications, supported as they were by Commodore Foote, commanding the naval forces in the vicinity of Cairo, at last
prevailed, and Halleck issued the necessary orders for the
movement. Detailed instructions were sent on the 30th of
January, and reached Cairo on the 1st of February. On the
2d, Grant, accompanied by seventeen thousand men on transports, and seven iron-clads under the command of Commodore
Foote, set out upon this expedition and two days thereafter
the troops were disembarked a few miles below Fort Henry,
for the purpose of marching upon its rear while the gun-boats
should attack it in front.

The rebels had erected batteries on both sides of the river and had garrisoned them by about 2500 men under General Tilghman. The main work was however on the eastern side and consisted of an enclosed bastioned line mounting seventeen heavy guns, with a strong line of outworks, covering the approach by the Dover road. Fort Heiman, on the opposite side of the river overlooked Fort Henry, but not having been finished the rebels abandoned it at the first intimation of danger. The Tennessee River at that time being very high, Fort Henry situated on the bottom land, was entirely surrounded by water. Grant desired to make his movement entirely certain and to capture both forts with their garrisons. He therefore delayed the advance till the next day, employing the interval in bringing up additional troops, and in making his final dispositions for the attack. Not knowing that Fort Heiman had been evacuated he ordered C. F. Smith with two brigades to invest and take it at daylight, while McClernand was ordered with the remainder of the forces to move to the rear of Fort Henry and to take position on the roads to Fort Donelson and Dover. The iron-clads steamed up at the same time and by noon opened at short range upon the water batteries. The rebel artillerists under the direct command of Tilghman in person, served their guns with accuracy and effect but after an hour and a half every gun was silenced. They could not hold out against the heavier metal of their assailants though they inflicted severe injury upon them. The Essex, was struck by a shot, which penetrated her boiler, causing a terrible explosion from the effects of which forty-eight soldiers and sailors were killed and wounded. The fort surrendered, with General Tilghman and staff, and about ninety men, but the main force, having been posted in the outworks on the high ground fled by the road to Fort Donelson as soon as they saw their flag hauled down. McClernand did not succeed in reaching the place assigned him till some time after the retreat had begun, his delay having been unavoidably caused by the high water, bad roads, and difficult character of the country, and the victory was therefore not so complete as it might have been.   Grant announced his success to Halleck, in a brief and modest telegram, closing with the information, that he should take and destroy Fort Donelson on the 8th and then return to Fort Henry.

NOTE.—The conception of the movement against Forts Henry and Donelson is doubtless due to Grant, for, although others, as Sherman and Buell, may have seen the necessity of this movement as soon as or even before Grant, there is no evidence that either of them ever suggested it to him, or to any one else who did suggest it to him.   Badeau's "Military History" gives a full and clear exposition of all the correspondence in regard to this matter, and shows clearly that it was Grant's persistence alone which succeeded in geting authority for the movement.

CHAPTER VIII.

In anticipation of further operations on the part of Grant's
column, General Pillow assumed command at Fort Donelson
on the 9th of February, and began at once to make preparations for the coming struggle. The remnant of Tilghman's
force had already arrived, and on the 13th, the garrison was
further strengthened by a considerable force from Russellville
under the command of Floyd. Johnston, who was then at
Bowling Green in supreme command, called a council of his
Generals, and after fully considering the condition of affairs,
decided to fight the battle for Nashville and Middle Tennessee
at Fort Donelson. He therefore detached all the troops that
could be spared from the army confronting Buell, and did
everything in his power to provide the army at Donelson
with ammunition and the means of defense.*

But Grant was equally prompt to perceive the advantage
of activity, and made all haste to gather the means of assailing that important point, although he had been cautioned by
Halleck to "strengthen Fort Henry and hold it at all hazards."
Re-enforcements were hurried forward with admirable rapidity

---

* See "Southern History of the War."

by the Department Commander at St. Louis, but with them came shovels and picks in abundance, and the urgent advice to have them used by the slaves of the country, who might be impressed for that purpose. Grant with the instinct of a true soldier, had no notion of wasting his time in such work. He had no sympathy with the excessive caution and timidity, which even at that day had begun to control the policy of the future General-in-Chief.

The rapid rise of the Tennessee River made it impossible to collect the forces in the neighborhood of Fort Henry, and get them ready for the advance. The gun-boats had not yet returned from their expedition up the Tennessee, so that notwithstanding Grant's impatience, he was forced to wait as patiently as he might, although he knew that every moment's delay was making his task more difficult.

On the 11th, a part of McClernand's command moved out several miles, and on the 12th, the whole force, consisting of McClernand's and Smith's divisions, about fifteen thousand strong, including eight batteries of artillery, marched by the telegraph and Dover roads towards the rebel stronghold. The wagons, tents, and all "encumbrances" were left at Fort Henry under the protection of Lewis Wallace's brigade. Such re-enforcements as had already arrived, were ordered to remain on their transports and to accompany the gun-boats by the way of the Cumberland River to the neighborhood of Fort Donelson.

The rebels made no effort to delay the advance of Grant's army, although the broken and heavily wooded country between the two rivers would have rendered it an easy matter for a small force to give the national troops great annoyance.

By this time the rebels had succeeded in making Fort Donelson the strongest place in that theatre of operations. It was situated on the west bank of the Cumberland, on a rugged and heavily timbered range of hills, overlooking the river in one direction, and commanding the country in the other. The lines had been laid out by skillful engineers and were so arranged on the water front as to completely sweep all the ap' proaches on that side. At the foot of the hills on the same side were two powerful and well constructed sunken batteries mounting ten thirty-two-pounders, one ten-inch columbiad, and one heavy rifled gun. On the land side the main and inner line of breastworks was continuous, and followed the hills and ridges with re-entrants, curtains and salients, so as to enclose over a hundred acres of ground, and to give a front of over two miles, covered throughout by heavy slashing and abattis. Both flanks of this line rested upon creeks, the banks of which were overflowed by the back water from the river. Still outside of this line, encircling the fort and the town of Dover, was a line of detached rifle trenches, surmounted by log breastworks. The rebel force consisted of twenty-six regiments of infantry, two independent battalions, and Forrest's cavalry,[*] numbering in all about twenty-three thousand muskets, and sixty-five guns, of which, seventeen were heavy, and the rest field pieces.

On the 10th Pillow held command of the rebel forces, but he was superseded by Floyd, (secretary of war under Buchanan) on the 13th. The other prominent rebel commanders were Buckner, and Bushrod Johnson, the former having command of the fort and inner line, while the latter assisted Pillow in the command of the rebel left.

Shortly after noon of the 12th the advance guard of McClernand's and C. F. Smith's columns drove in the rebel pickets and came within sight of the stronghold, in front of which they gradually took up their position, Smith on the left and McClernand on the right. Slight skirmishing ensued at intervals along the lines, but nothing like an engagement took place that evening. The rebels seemed undecided, while Grant did not care to strike till he could have the powerful assistance of the turtle-back iron-clads. The next day was spent in reconnoitering the ground, extending and adjusting the lines, and perfecting the investment. Sharp skirmishing, and some desultory fighting took place, but the rebels still refrained from attacking. The non-arrival of the gun-boats

---

[*] "Southern History of the War."

and of the expected re-enforcements, was a sufficient reason
why Grant should not seek to hasten the action. By the
second night, he had made the investment as complete as it
could be made by the force then at hand. His line was about
three miles in extent, the left resting on Hickman's Creek
and communicating with the Cumberland while the centre
occupied an open field, and the right extended well out
through the wooded country towards Dover. Batteries of
field guns occupied favorable positions along the line, but no
entrenchments had been thrown up, notwithstanding General
Halleck's foresight in sending forward axes, shovels and picks.
Neither Grant nor his army had yet thought it necessary to
resort to such weapons during the progress of an active campaign. Everything was in readiness for an assault or a siege,
as circumstances might require, as soon as Foote and the
transports should make their appearance. At this time, it
will be remembered, that Grant's forces consisted of only two
divisions of infantry, one regiment of cavalry and six field
batteries, about 14,000 men, or nearly ten thousand less than
the rebel force in their front.[*]

Foote reached the neighborhood of Fort Donelson during
the night of the 13th, bringing with him the long-expected
re-enforcements. These were disembarked at once, formed
into a new division under General Lewis Wallace and assigned to a place between Smith and McClernand, near the
center, while McArthur's brigade of Smith's division was
moved to the extreme right of the line. These dispositions
were perfected by noon of the 14th, and at three P. M., the
flotilla, under Foote steamed up the Cumberland and opened
fire at close range upon the rebel works. The rebel batteries
replied at once and with great spirit, and having an elevation
of thirty or forty feet above the water, they were enabled to
deliver their shot with telling effect. The iron-clads continued

_____
[*] "Campaigns of General Forrest," p. 95, states: "As it was, Grant, landing with a petty force of fifteen thousand in the very centre of a force of nearly
forty-five thousand, having the interior lines for concentration and communication, by railway at that, was able to take two heavy fortifications in detail,
and place *hors de combat nearly fifteen thousand* of his enemy.

their approach to within four hundred yards, and would doubt-less have succeeded in driving the rebels from their guns had not two of the best boats been disabled.   The action continued an hour and a half with great desperation, but at the end of that time all the gun-boats were so severely crippled that they were obliged to haul off.   They had lost fifty-four men, killed and wounded, including among the latter, Commodore Foote and several other officers.

McClernand had made a gallant but unauthorized attack on the right of the line, in which Colonels Wallace, Haynie, and Morrison, and the troops under their command behaved with great intrepidity; sharp skirmishing had been going on all day in front of the other divisions, it having been Grant's intention to order a general attack in case the navy should succeed in silencing the rebel batteries.   This not having been done the army continued immovable.   The losses up to this time were insignificant, not exceeding three hundred and fifty killed and wounded.

The rebels deluded themselves with the belief that they had gained important advantages, and were greatly elated by their partial success, from the fact that the batteries had beaten off the gun-boats.*

The entrenchments on the land side seemed to be so strong and so well manned as to forbid the hope of a successful as-sault by new troops.   Grant had begun to contemplate a resort to the slow and tedious process of a regular siege, but the idea that he had lost the day, or would not ultimately reduce the place, never entered his mind.   In the words of Colonel Oglesby: "he had gone there to take that fort, and intended to stay till he did it."   Re-enforcements had begun to pour in rapidly, and although the men were entirely un-trained, they were of the right material to encounter danger and hardships.   Up to the 13th, the weather was fine and warm, but during that night a storm of sleet, hail, and snow set in, and before morning the mercury stood at twenty de-grees below the freezing point.   The tents had been left be-

"Southern History of the War."

hind, the troops were without rations or fires, and many had even thrown away their blankets during the march from Fort Henry, yet there was no faltering. Every man stood to his post, and every officer did his duty cheerfully and willingly.

The rebels seeing the Union lines strengthening day by day, seemed from the first to have had no hope of maintaining their position. They were kept constantly on the alert lest the attack should fall upon them unexpectedly, while the cold and wet pinched them as unrelentingly as it did the hardy northerners. The situation was far from being an agreeable one, and in the vivid imagination of Floyd and Pillow, it appeared worse than it really was.* On the night of the 14th, Floyd called a council of his Generals, in which it was represented that it was absolutely impossible to hold out for any length of time with their inadequate numbers and indefensible position. On this statement of the case, after much discussion, it was decided that " but one course remained by which a rational hope of saving the garrison could be entertained, and that was to drive back the molesting force on the Dover side, and pass their troops into the open country in the direction of Nashville." † But as a matter of course, this determination was not discovered till the rebels had nearly succeeded in their attempt to carry it into effect.

At two o'clock A. M., Grant was sent for by Commodore Foote, and before dawn of the 15th, he had gone on board the flag-ship, where he received the information that the fleet would be compelled to return to Cairo for repairs. In the meantime the rebels had made arrangements to carry out their desperate policy, and as soon as it was light they sallied from the left of their line in heavy masses. The attack fell at first upon McArthur's brigade of Smith's division, but soon extended along the brigades of Oglesby and W. H. L. Wallace, of McClernand's division, and ultimately to Cruft's brigade

* " Campaigns of Forrest," p. 70, states that a council was held early on the morning of the 14th, at which it was decided to make a sortie and escape to the open country, but it was abandoned for some reasons not made public.

† " Southern History of the War," p. 247.

of L. Wallace's division. The national troops fought with great courage, stubbornly holding their own as long as it was possible, against the superior weight and impulsion of the enemy's columns. Even when they yielded their ground, it was only because their ammunition was exhausted. General McClernand, and Colonels McArthur, Oglesby, Cruft, Logan, Lawler, W. H. L. Wallace, and Ransom, together with the field and line officers of every grade, behaved with the most conspicuous gallantry. Taylor's, Dresser's and McAllister's batteries were well posted and swept the advancing rebels with a storm of canister and grape. Everything that valor and endurance could do to stem the tide of defeat was done, and yet with varying fortunes and occasional success, the Union troops were slowly pressed back. The ammunition of nearly all the troops engaged had been exhausted, and the crisis of the battle seemed to have arrived, when taking advantage of a halt in the fight, Thayer's brigade of Lewis Wallace's division, moved into the post of danger, while the hard pressed regiments of the right refilled their cartridge boxes. So great had been the rebel success, that Pillow paused in the heat of his advance and sent to Johnston at Nashville, the following message: "On the honor of a soldier, the day is ours." But he had claimed the victory before it was won, for, although the tide of battle in the morning had set strongly in his favor, he was destined before night-fall to have it rolled back upon him with resistless force.

At nine o'clock, Grant having finished his interview with Foote, set out to return to his head-quarters, but received no intimation of what was taking place, till he met an aid who had been sent to inform him of the rebel sortie. On his way to the field of battle, he encountered C. F. Smith, who had not yet been engaged, and at once ordered him to hold himself in readiness to assault the rebel right with his entire division. Pushing on rapidly, he soon came in sight of his broken and disordered troops. The condition of affairs was nearly as bad as it could be. Logan, Lawler, and Ransom, were wounded, and a large number of the best officers

5

and men were killed. Whilst riding over the field in the midst of the confusion and uncertainty which prevailed, Grant discovered that the knapsacks of the rebel dead were packed, and that their haversacks were filled with rations. Knowing that no soldier would have made such preparations for an ordinary sortie nor even for a general battle, he saw at once that the rebels had been fighting for a road to the open country. Fully appreciating the situation, he said to those about him: "Whichever party makes the first attack will win the day, and the rebels will have to be very quick if they beat me!" He sent his staff at once to reassure the troops by telling them of his fortunate discovery, and with the promptitude of genius, gave the word for an advance along the entire line. Having done this, he put spurs to his horse and galloped to the place where he had left Smith, and ordered his division to assault the enemy's works. Immediately afterwards he requested Foote, in writing, to steam up with his fleet and make a show of renewing the attack.

At about four o'clock, everything was in readiness. On the center and right, Wallace's division, Cruft's and M. L. Smith's brigades in advance, supported, as occasion required, by McClernand and McArthur, moved against the enemy, and after a gallant struggle, recaptured the lost guns of the morning and pressed him back into his works.

In obedience to the orders of his chief, C. F. Smith had lost no time in forming Lauman's brigade, composed of the Second, Seventh, and Fourteenth Iowa, with the Twenty-fifth and Fifty-second Indiana, into a column of attack. Having ordered Cook's brigade to make a demonstration on his left, he rode along the lines of the forlorn hope, and in a few soldierly words taught them what must be done. It was late in the afternoon when the sharp rattle of musketry, mingled with the sullen roar of artillery from the center and right, told the gallant veteran that the time for his advance had come. Throwing himself between the two lines, he gave the word "forward." His men sprang to the attack with a zeal and rapidity rarely surpassed, and although the ground over which they had to move was broken, covered with a dense growth of small trees, and swept by the sharp and unrelenting musketry of the rebels, they pushed forward, through brush and abattis, scaled the heights and burst upon the rebel line with a force that nothing human could resist. Artillery and re-enforcements hurried forward, securing the advantage which had been gained, and pressing the enemy still farther back, while McClernand, Wallace, and McArthur, pushed their advance with renewed vigor.

When night closed, the desperate struggle was no longer doubtful. It found the Union army flushed with victory, and filled with hope for the morrow. It had regained all the ground lost during the day; re-established and strengthened its lines, and what was better, had secured a firm lodgment within the enemy's stronghold. Grant's generalship, after his timely appearance upon the field, aided by the valor of Smith and the steady courage of his undisciplined volunteers, won the day, even after it had been lost.

During the night which followed, Floyd again called his officers together, but this time for the purpose of finding some one brave enough to relieve him from the duty of surrendering. Conscious of the many injuries he had inflicted on the country, whilst secretary of war, he feared that, once a prisoner, summary justice would be executed upon him. He therefore made over the command to Pillow, who with pusillanimous haste, " passed " it to Buckner the third in rank.* This being done, these men took possession of two small steamboats, and with a small brigade of troops, stole away from their comrades. Colonel Forest with his regiment of cavalry, went out by the river road. Buckner did not hesitate in the only course left him, but called at once for a bugler, and wrote a note to Grant asking for an armistice and the appointment of commissioners to arrange the terms of capitulation. Grant having issued orders the night before for an early attack, declined the armistice, and replied at once : " *No terms other than an unconditional and immediate surrender, can be accepted. I propose*

* Rebel Official Reports.

to move immediately upon your works!'" These words were as startling to the rebels as the attack which they portended would have been, and were answered by the " unconditional and immediate surrender," of Fort Donelson and all its garrison, consisting of 14,623 men, with 17 heavy guns, 48 field pieces, over 20,000 stands of small arms, and about 3,000 horses, besides large quantities of military stores of all kinds.

The news of this splendid victory spread like lightning. The name of Grant was hailed with joy, while the deeds of his gallant army were read with eager delight by every loyal citizen and true soldier, throughout the land. The President hastened to express his gratitude to Grant by sending him the commission of Major-General. Everybody rejoiced at this act of justice, except General Halleck, who did all in his power to give exclusive credit for the victory to C. F. Smith, and to secure for that officer the reward which Grant had so honestly won. On the other hand, Grant never for a moment withheld the praise which was due to his subordinates, but with the least possible delay, recommended all who earned it, for promotion, and yet there were some among them who did not scruple to charge him with incompetency, or to circulate caluminous reports against his private character.*

* For a full explanation of Halleck's action towards Grant, see Badeau's " Military History of Ulysses S. Grant."

CHAPTER IX.

THE damage inflicted upon the rebel cause by the fall of
Fort Donelson was not limited by the prisoners and spoils
captured at that place. Southern Kentucky and a large
portion of Middle Tennessee, were cleared completely of all
insurgent force, and including the strongly fortified camps at
Columbus and Bowling Green, as well as the important city
of Nashville with large quantities of military stores that could
not be removed, passed at once under the control of the Union
armies. The entire North was electrified with hope and inspired by renewed vigor, while the South was correspondingly
depressed.

General Johnston, the rebel commander, realizing when it
was too late to avert it, that the Confederacy, through his
policy of dispersion, had received a vital blow, set himself
to work vigorously to concentrate and reorganize his broken

and widely scattered forces. After much trouble and some delay he succeeded in collecting at Murfreesboro, an army which, according to the rebel historian, Pollard, numbered seventeen thousand men, though in all probability it was considerably larger; his object now being to coöperate with Beauregard, and ultimately to join with him in the defence of the lower Mississippi valley and the railroad system of the South-west. This required the establishment and maintenance of a new defensive line, of which Island No. 10 and Murfreesboro at first, and Corinth and Chattanooga afterwards became the principal points.

General Halleck, soon after the great victory on the Cumberland, set movements on foot under the direction of General Pope, which resulted in compelling the evacuation of Island No. 10. This event occurred on the 8th of April, and in connection with the operations which we are about to describe, gave the control of the Mississippi River to the Union forces, as far down as Memphis.

In obedience to an assignment from Halleck, Grant assumed command of the new military district of West Tennessee, with limits undefined, on the 17th of February, and was succeeded in command of the District of Cairo by General W. T. Sherman, who had been stationed at Paducah during the operations against Fort Donelson. This officer had exerted himself to the utmost in forwarding re-enforcements and supplies, and lost no opportunity to encourage and support our army in the field, and although he was Grant's superior in rank, he expressed a willingness to join and serve under him, without raising the question of precedence. Grant heartily appreciated this zealous and patriotic conduct, as well as the kindness and confidence with which Sherman had offered his services. It speaks well for both that henceforth these men were firm and devoted friends.

Immediately after the fall of Fort Donelson, Halleck telegraphed to Grant to be cautious in his movements—to risk nothing by sending out detachments, and that it would be better to retreat than to risk a general battle. But Grant, with the true instincts of a General, sent C. F. Smith, on the 21st of February, to take Clarksville, and on the 27th, went in person to Nashville for the purpose of conferring with Buell, whose advance had reached that place. He was anxious to know in what direction he should have to strike next, and therefore did all he could to keep himself informed of the enemy's movements. During this time he wrote and telegraphed daily to Halleck and his Chief-of-staff, in regard to the condition and whereabouts of his command, and neglected nothing which should have engaged the attention of a careful and painstaking General. And yet his dissatisfied and envious superior, charged him with neglect of duty and disobedience of orders, and shortly afterwards reported him to Washington as irresolute and insubordinate.

On the 4th of March, Halleck, having already ordered the army from Fort Donelson to Fort Henry, with the view of operations up the Tennessee River, inflicted the further indignity upon Grant of compelling him to place Major-General C. F. Smith in command of the expedition and to remain himself in command of Fort Henry. Smarting under the unjust rebukes which were continually coming from Halleck's head-quarters, and feeling keenly the crowning act of injustice which had been inflicted upon him, Grant made a truthful and soldierly statement of his conduct up to that time, closing with the request "to be relieved from further duty in the Department." Instead of granting this request Halleck reiterated his unwarranted rebukes, to which Grant replied by requesting to be relieved from further duty till he could place himself right in the estimation of those higher in authority. The decided and spirited tone of this letter seems to have brought Halleck to his senses at last, for about the middle of March he answered Grant that he could not be relieved from duty, but as soon as it could be assembled in the field, he must resume command of his new army and lead it on to new victories.

In accordance with this authority, Grant took command of his troops, and began at once to make preparations for putting

them in the field. But the first order he received from Halleck was: "Don't bring on a general engagement; if the
enemy appear in force, our troops must fall back—General
Smith must hold his position without exposing himself."

In the meantime General Smith had pushed forward to the
neighborhood of Eastport for the purpose of making a movement against the Memphis and Charleston Railroad, somewhere between Decatur and Corinth, but under the influence
of Halleck's timid and vacillating policy this movement was
paralyzed, almost at the outset, and was finally abandoned
without resulting in serious injury to the enemy. The rebels,
having sent a small force from Corinth, which seemed to
threaten Smith's rear, he fell back from Eastport and disembarked his forces at Savannah, and at Crump's and Pittsburg
Landings.

By this time the rebel policy of concentration had begun
to develop itself, and in order to counteract it, Buell was ordered from Nashville to Savannah by the way of Columbia
and Waynesboro, and every effort was made to re-enforce the
army on the Tennessee, and to prepare it for a desperate
struggle. Volunteers from all parts of the North-west were
rapidly sent forward. They were composed of good and true
men but none of them had seen service, and many of them
were not even provided with arms and camp equipage. As
a matter of course, no forward movement except with the
older troops could be made till these deficiencies had been
in a measure supplied. The new regiments were assigned to
brigades and divisions as fast as they arrived, new encamp-
ments were formed, and whatever could be done, was done to
get the army into shape.

On the 17th of March, Grant assumed direct command
of the troops, with his head-quarters at Savannah, a small
town on the east side of the Tennessee River, from which
communication could be kept up with Buell, now known to
be moving in that direction. He found McClernand's and
Smith's divisions, the oldest and best part of the army, encamped at that place; Wallace lay at Crump's Landing, still

farther up the river, but on the opposite side; while Hurlbut
and Sherman with their new levies were some miles further
on at Pittsburg Landing. Seeing at a glance, that in the
event of an attack, his army would be at the mercy of the
enemy, Grant determined to concentrate without delay at
Pittsburg Landing.

Accordingly, McClernand and Smith were sent thither as
fast as the steamboats could carry them. Wallace was regarded as being within supporting distance, and was therefore left in his old camp, with orders to keep a lookout for the
enemy in the direction of Purdy.

The point at which the troops were concentrated, is on the
west bank of the river, twenty miles north-east from Corinth,
and was first selected by General Smith. It was well chosen,
for although it lay upon the side of the river next to the
enemy, it gave our troops the power of moving out for battle
at any time as a unit, and being partially covered in front by
Owl Creek, flanked on one side by Lick Creek and on the
other by Snake Creek, both of which are difficult to pass at
all times, and specially so during high water, it was susceptible of an easy defense. Had Savannah, or any point on the
east bank of the river been selected, the army would certainly
have been safe so long as it remained stationary, but as soon
as it should become necessary to advance, the lack of steamboats or pontoons to cross the entire army at once, and the
danger of crossing by detachment, would have more than
counter-balanced the danger incurred by concentrating at
Pittsburg Landing. Grant had also determined to remove
his head-quarters to Pittsburg Landing, as soon as the troops
could all be collected there, but owing to a deficiency of
steamboats, it required a longer time to do this than had been
expected. On the 4th of April, however, just as everything
was in readiness for the abandonment of Savannah, Grant received a telegram asking him to meet General Buell at that
place the next day. Desiring to confer with Buell, the order
for the movement was suspended, but Buell did not reach
Savannah as expected, and Grant was compelled to wait till

the 6th.   Buell began his movement on the 15th of March, and although the distance to be overcome was only one hundred and twenty miles, it took his army twenty-three days to reach the Tennessee River.

It is not within the limits of this work to give the details of the correspondence between Grant, Halleck, and Buell, concerning the events of the three weeks which preceded the battle of Shiloh.   But after careful study of those documents in connection with the fact that there was no considerable force of armed rebels at that time, in all Middle Tennessee, it is hard to imagine how the warmest partisan of Buell can claim that he moved with proper celerity.   The simple truth is that he was culpably and tardy in all his movements, then as well as frequently afterwards.   To him alone belongs the blame, if there is any due, for whatever advantage the rebels gained by having the preponderance of force in the first day of the battle at Shiloh.

Grant has been severely and unjustly criticised for the condition in which his army was caught by that battle.   He has been charged directly or indirectly with the responsibility for the absence of pontoons, the insufficiency of river transportation, the delay of Buell, both in the march and in crossing the river, the alleged disadvantages of the field on which he fought, the rawness of the troops, and the three weeks of inactivity after he arrived at Savannah.*   But when it is remembered that Halleck with his head-quarters at St. Louis, five hundred miles away, held general command and directed the movements of all the loyal forces in Kentucky, Tennessee, and Missouri, forwarded the re-enforcements, controlled the supplies of every kind, including pontoons and river transportation, assigned commanders, and dictated the minutest details of the policy which they were to pursue, it may be justly stated that he was mainly responsible for the deficiencies which embarrassed the movements of the army.   He it was who forbade all movements against the enemy after the fall of Donelson, " till re-enforcements were received," who super-

* See " Swinton's Twelve Decisive Battles of the War"—Article, Shiloh.

ceded Grant, and kept him in disgrace at Fort Henry, till the advance of the army, had been arrested, and who, even after the restoration of Grant to his command again, forbade him to move against the enemy till Buell should arrive.

Following sharply upon the commencement of Smith's operations in the direction of Eastport, the concentration of rebel troops at Corinth began. Beauregard, who had been sent to the South-west, with unlimited authority, exerted himself to the utmost to consummate this movement. Having determined, wisely for the rebels, to inaugurate a new policy that should be aggressive instead of defensive, he ordered Polk to withdraw from Columbus, and sent a part of his force to Island No. 10, which had been fortified for their reception. But the larger part consisting of two strong divisions, were hurried rapidly to Corinth. Bragg's fine corps, said to be "the best troops in the Confederacy," were brought up from Mobile and Pensacola, while Johnston's army consisting of Hardee's corps and Breckenridge's division, were brought by rail from Murfreesboro and Chattanooga. In addition to this, the Governors of Alabama, Louisiana, Mississippi, Georgia and Tennessee, were called upon for volunteers, and in speedy response sent forward their people towards Corinth by regiments, companies, squads and singly. Johnston being the senior officer assumed the general command, though Beauregard was the controlling spirit. Scouts and spies kept them informed of everything going on in the national camp, and advised them promptly of Buell's progress. When Buell's bridge over Duck River was finished, and news reached them of his advance towards Savannah, they determined to fall at once upon Grant. On the 3rd of April, this movement began, but on account of bad roads and difficult marching, it was not till night of the next day, that the main interval had been passed. The expectation of the rebels was to attack at dawn of the 5th, but before that time a furious rain-storm set in and suspended all further operations for twenty-four hours. The rebel cavalry and small detachments had made their appearance along the Union outposts, as early as the 2d of

April, so that skirmishes were of almost hourly occurrence, till the battle itself finally burst upon the army.*

The general features of the field upon which the battle of Shiloh was fought, may be briefly described as follows: It is a rugged plateau, ninety or a hundred feet above the river, seamed and broken by ravines, and covered throughout its extent, by dense forests, and underbrush, except at wide intervals, where small fields have been cleared for cultivation. Falling off gradually towards the interior, it is limited on the north and south by Lick and Snake Creeks, which empty into the Tennessee about four miles apart, and both which are impassible during high water. Between two and three miles from the river, the heads and affluents of these streams interlace and seam the plateau into ugly and difficult ridges. Pittsburg Landing, with its two or three log cabins, had been at one time an important shipping point, but since the days of railroads its glory had departed. The roads, however, which connect it with Purdy, Corinth, Hamburg and Crump's Landing, rendered it easily accessible from the surrounding country.

The morning of Sunday, April 6th, which broke clear and bright, found Grant anxious and uneasy still detained at Savannah for the purpose of conferring with Buell. The continuous skirmishing of the few days just passed, together with the information gathered from scouts and rebel prisoners had put him on his guard. The army was encamped in the following order: Hurlbut and Wallace held an interior position, stretching from the Tennessee River across the lower bridge on Snake Creek, while Sherman, McClernand and Prentiss occupied an irregular line, something over a mile farther out, of which the key point was near Shiloh Church on the main road to Corinth.

---

* "Campaigns of General Forrest," p. 111: "But General Beauregard earnestly advised the idea of attacking the enemy should be abandoned, and that the whole force should return to Corinth, inasmuch as it was now scarcely possible they would be able to take the Federals unawares, after such delay, and the noisy demonstrations which had been made meanwhile."

Same, p. 113: During Saturday, "there was a good deal of unimportant but lively skirmishing."

The right of this line was held by McDowell's brigade of Sherman's division, occupying a position on the Purdy road near the crossing of Owl Creek; the left resting on the Tennessee, was held by Stuart's brigade of the same division, well posted on the Hamburg road just north of Lick Creek; while the center was held by the two remaining brigades of Sherman's division, posted near Shiloh Church, nearly three miles out on the Corinth road, assisted by Prentiss, whose division still farther to the left, covered a net-work of paths connecting the main roads to Corinth and Hamburg. McClernand lay from a quarter to a half mile behind Sherman with his right somewhat refused; Lewis Wallace was at Crump's Landing. Thus it will be seen that Grant's army was formed in two lines, something over a mile apart, with the advanced line strongly re-enforced on the right. His entire force on the field was thirty-three thousand men, or thirty-eight thousand with Wallace's division. It has been stated that Grant's army was surprised in its camp, but this statement like many others, has not stood the test of investigation. Neither Halleck, Grant nor Buell, expected the rebel army to sally from its works to offer battle, but when it did so, its coming was no secret. Both Sherman and Prentiss were on the alert at an early hour; their outposts, more than a mile and a half in advance, had discovered the enemy on the 5th, and had been strongly re-enforced. At early dawn both divisions were under arms and ready for the conflict about to burst upon them.

The rebel army advanced to the attack along all the roads leading from Corinth, with its three corps formed in line, one behind another, Hardee leading, followed by Bragg, and then by Polk and the reserve under Breckenridge.* The outposts of Prentiss and Sherman, received the first onset of the

* "Forrest and his Campaigns" gives the rebel force as follows:

1.	Polk's corps,	2 Divisions,	4 Brigades,	10,000 men, effective.			
2.	Bragg's "	2 "	6 "	15,000 "	"		
3.	Hardee's "	2 "	6 "	13,500 "	"		
	Cavalry,			4,500			
	Total,			43,000 men and 50 guns.			

enemy, but stubbornly disputing every step of the ground, falling back slowly from tree to tree, and making every log and ridge a breastwork, they stayed the enemy's advance, for an hour and a half. By half-past seven o'clock the battle had begun to rage heavily along the entire Union center. Hardee, with his two wide stretching divisions had pressed close in upon Prentiss, overlapping him on both flanks and extending well across Sherman's front, but by this time his lines had been broken and filled with intervals, into which Bragg lost no time in pushing his well disciplined regiments and brigades. The force now converging their fire upon Prentiss' front, consisted of nearly three full divisions, and several batteries, while the rest of the rebel forces, under Hindman, Cleburne and Wood, were pressing forward heavily against Sherman. Fortunately they were met by men who were as brave and steady as themselves, though far newer in the service of battle. By eight o'clock the struggle was raging furiously at every point. Sherman and Prentiss were indefatigable in their efforts to hold their hard pressed and overmatched battalions to the deadly work; their batteries were well posted and well served, and their infantry delivered a fire as deadly as that they received. But Polk's divisions soon swelled the ranks of the enemy. Johnston and Beauregard seemed determined to sweep everything before them by the very force of numbers, and in a fury of determination pressed forward, regiment, brigade and division, with unrelenting vigor. Gradually the flanks of Prentiss' division were pressed back, and then the center, by the overwhelming force which fell upon them. Sherman's left, composed of raw recruits, was also compelled to give ground shortly afterwards, but that gallant General still held his right and center at Shiloh Church, with the tenacity of a bull-dog. By this time his left, strengthened by four regiments from Hurlbut's division, and three regiments and several batteries, (the veterans of Donelson,) from McClernand's division, had filled the gap between Sherman and Prentiss, and with a gallantry rarely equalled they stayed the rebel advance.

Grant had taken an early breakfast, at his head-quarters near Savannah, and was about starting to meet Buell, when he heard the opening guns of the enemy. With his usual promptitude he dispatched an order to Nelson, commanding Buell's leading division, to push forward to Pittsburg as rapidly as possible. He also wrote to Buell, telling him that the action had begun—and then set out for Pittsburg Landing, where he arrived at eight o'clock, having stopped on his way at Crump's, and ordered Wallace to hold himself in readiness either to march to the battle-field or to defend his camp.

Grant hastened at once to the front, encouraging men and officers, pushing forward supplies of ammunition, ordering stragglers to rejoin their colors, sending re-enforcements to various parts of the line, and fearlessly exposing himself on every part of the field. His efforts were unceasing but his hard pressed army was gradually driven back. At 10 o'clock he had reached the extreme advance, and was helping Sherman to hold his staggering forces to their work. By this time Hurlbut, W. H. L. Wallace (with Smith's veteran division), and McClernand, had moved up to strengthen the center, lying between and across the two roads to Corinth. Every brigade was now engaged; Stuart held the left, then came Hurlbut, then the remnant of Prentiss' division, next Wallace; next McClernand, and finally Sherman. In this order, our troops, although assailed by nearly double their numbers, fought the battle through. First one part and then another of the line receiving the full force of the rebel attack, the army was gradually driven towards the Landing. Hurlbut's line was repeatedly broken but not disheartened; he re-formed it and held on, yielding only when overpowered. Prentiss, by dint of extra stubbornness, or being more fortunate—perhaps more unfortunate—maintained his position till he had been surrounded and captured with nearly three thousand of his men. Wallace was killed, and his division pressed back simultaneously with Hurlbut, carrying back McClernand's left; and finally even Sherman was compelled to yield, yet the day was not lost irrevocably. If Buell or Wallace would only

come, victory might be snatched from the jaws of defeat.
Many men had fled from the field early in the fight, and
sought safety at the Landing—but the heroes of Fredericks-
town, Belmont, and Donelson, showed themselves to be veterans in every sense, their splendid valor remaining unshaken,
though their ranks had been terribly thinned.

Early in the day, Grant dispatched orders for Lewis Wallace to march to the battle; and as the fight grew in fierce-
ness, couriers and staff officers were sent to hurry his laggard
footsteps.   But through some untoward fatality, night closed
upon the struggle before Wallace had overcome the few short
miles which separated him from fame and the stricken field.
Nelson and Wood, commanding divisions of Buell's army,
now known to have reached the river, were also urged to
lose no time, in crossing to Grant's assistance.

It was the middle of the afternoon when Buell, in person,
arrived upon the field, in advance of his troops.   Almost his
first question was: "What preparations have you made for
retreating, General?"   Grant, to whom the question was addressed, replied with the courage of a paladin: "*I have not
despaired of whipping them yet!*" *

Nelson's troops began to arrive upon the field at a little
before five o'clock, and were ordered into position on the left
of the line, but not till the action had nearly ceased.   They
lost only three men before darkness put an end to the battle.

Johnston had been killed early in the afternoon, but Beauregard took his place and continued to press his jaded troops to
the attack.   By four o'clock the Union forces had been driven
nearly two miles backward, into the angle between Lick Creek
and the river.   The left flank resting upon the ridge just below the landing, was strongly posted and covered by a battery
of some forty guns of all calibres which Colonel Webster of
Grant's staff, had posted and manned with volunteer artillery

---

* Buell is said to have renewed this conversation several days afterwards,
and by way of reproach said to Grant: "You hadn't steamboats enough to
carry away 10,000 men."   "Well," replied Grant, "there wouldn't have been
more than that many left by the time I should have got ready to go."

men. The right rested on the creek a mile and a half away, covering the road by which Wallace was expected to arrive. Two gun-boats had taken their stations opposite the mouth of a deep ravine, behind which our troops were posted.   In this position the national army received and repelled again and again the final attacks of the enemy; but again and again did Beauregard, Bragg, Hardee, Polk and Breckenridge lead their soldiers to the assault.   They did all that human nature could do.   Webster's artillery, poured out its ready canister, the gun-boats swept the rebel flanks, while the broken but still undaunted regiments of the Union delivered their withering fire.   Before night closed upon the scene, Beauregard saw that to struggle longer could have no other result than to swell the list of his killed and wounded.

With his usual sagacity, Grant rode towards the right and told Sherman the story of Donelson—how the armies had fought till both were nearly exhausted, and how he had seen that the next blow struck would win the battle.   It was too late and his troops were too much jaded to take the initiative then, but he ordered Sherman to attack at dawn in the morning.*   •

During the night, Nelson, together with most of McCook's and Crittenden's divisions of Buell's army, nearly twenty thousand men in all, arrived upon the field, and took position along the left of the line of battle.   Lewis Wallace, after marching and countermarching all day, within five miles of the field, also made his appearance at nightfall after Grant had superintended the re-adjustment of his line, assigned the new divisions to their stations, and visited the different Commanders giving each his orders to advance at early dawn.   Both hosts slept upon their arms.   The wounded remained uncared for except by Providence ; the dead leaves of the forest in

---

* From "The Campaigns of Gen. Forrest," it appears that Beauregard was entirely ignorant of Buell's arrival upon the field, and even when informed by Forrest of this fact, refused to believe it. It seems that he had received intelligence that Buell was moving with his whole force upon Florence, and therefore could not understand the possibility of a junction between Buell and Grant. P. 135–6.

6

which they lay, took fire, but shortly afterwards a rain storm broke upon the field and extinguished the flames. At intervals of ten or fifteen minutes, throughout the night, the gunboats threw their ponderous shells into the enemy's camp.

Early on the morning of April 7th, the national troops with renewed confidence and vigor, began the battle afresh. The divisions of McCook, Crittenden and Nelson formed the left; Hurlbut's, Sherman's and McClernand's divisions, between which Wallace's division and the remnant of Prentiss' had been distributed, held the center; and Lewis Wallace's division the extreme right. In this order they moved out to the fight. The rebels had not heard of Buell's arrival, and yet they had not ventured to attack. The confident advance of the Union army, and the steady rattle of musketry soon convinced them that the tide of victory had turned for good and all. They resisted stubbornly, disputed every ravine, and wooded knoll, and seemed determined for honor's sake, if not for victory, to hold what they had won; but the splendid battle tactics of Buell, the gallantry of his magnificent army, the steady courage of Lewis Wallace's division, and as much as all other things combined, the keen anxiety of Hurlbut's, McClernand's, and Sherman's gallant men to wipe out the misfortunes of yesterday, carried the Union flags triumphantly forward. Beauregard made desperate efforts to advance his right, strongly formed and supported by his batteries, and although he checked for awhile the advance of McCook, Crittenden and Nelson's new and well drilled regiments, he was soon compelled to give way in order to save his line of retreat. Sherman, McClernand and Lewis Wallace had pressed forward with such ardor as to crowd back the rebel left beyond all hope of recovery. This relieved the pressure from Buell's front, and enabled him to renew the onset successfully. The rebels fought well, but at no time did they check any considerable part of the Union line. Grant, being Buell's senior, was in command of the entire army, and spared no effort to make his victory complete. He exposed himself fully whenever occasion required it; and at one time he took command in person of a wavering regiment and led it forward to the assault of the enemy's line. Shiloh Church was regained, the lost guns were recaptured, and others were wrested from the enemy. After this, the resistance grew weaker and weaker at every step. By the middle of the afternoon the rebels were in full retreat and fighting only for safety. They retired sullenly but covered by Breckenridge's division which had seen less fighting than the rest of the army, their retreat did not become a rout. Rain had again set in, the roads were bad, and all parts of the army were much fatigued by marching and fighting. Nothing more could be done. Grant was compelled reluctantly to rest upon his victory, but sent two brigades of Wood's division with a part of Sherman's to watch the enemy and press his retreat.

The rebels in this battle had intended to destroy Grant's army before Buell could reach it; they had fought with great desperation, without much effort at grand tactics or combination, resting their entire hopes upon superior weight and impulse to drive Grant into the river. It has been claimed that had Johnston not been killed, or had Beauregard renewed the action after five o'clock, his plan must have been successful. Others have asserted that Grant's army would have been destroyed but for Buell's timely arrival. But Grant, Sherman, McPherson, Hurlbut, McClernand with every officer of spirit under their command have asserted over and over again, that the rebels could not force their last position, though they tried it with all the valor of desperation.* They had done their best, and even admit in their official reports that their progress was stayed in the full tide of victory not by night, for still one hour of daylight remained when their last assault was made, but by the determined resistance of Grant's army, aided by the fire of the gun-boats. A careful study of all the

* This view of the case is confirmed by "Forrest's Campaigns." That vigorous fighter denies the efficiency of the fire from the gun-boats, and shows that the desperate fighting of the Union forces, aided by the difficult ground in their front, was the cause of Beauregard's failure to carry Grant's last position.

official reports, both rebel and national, leaves scarcely room to doubt that had Lewis Wallace arrived upon the field by four o'clock, Grant would have gained a complete victory before nightfall. Buell's arrival was opportune, and when brought into action his troops behaved admirably, rendering that secure which fortune might otherwise have left in doubt; but it will be remembered to the credit of Grant as long as fortitude and steadfast courage are looked upon as virtues, that he had not despaired of beating the rebels when the tide of defeat seemed to have set heaviest against him.*

The Union losses, including those of Buell's army, taken from official returns, amounted to about 1,750 killed, 7,400 wounded, and 3,200 missing, in all 12,350, while the rebels report their losses at 1,728 killed, 8,012 wounded, 959 missing, total, 10,699. Omitting the missing on both sides, the rebels lost nearly six hundred more men than Grant. This simple fact of itself ought to put to rest forever the story that Grant was surprised. It is not too much to say that no army fallen upon by surprise ever fought such a battle as that of Shiloh.

---

* Shortly after the battle of Shiloh, General Grant telegraphed to Halleck : "To Sherman, more than to any other man is due the salvation of the army." Halleck immediately sent a message to Washington ignoring Grant entirely, but using his very words in commending Sherman. These words from Grant were a graceful and well merited compliment to a gallant subordinate ; but their use by Halleck was an indirect and treacherous blow at Grant's reputation.

CHAPTER X.

IT has been seen how two armies, whose combined force could not be far from seventy-five thousand men, united upon the field of Shiloh ; and how on the second day, they swept Beauregard's shattered battalions in confusion and dismay from the field. Everything was now in our favor. The rebel leaders had carried out their policy of concentration with skill, and had hurled their united forces into battle with frantic vigor, but all to no purpose. The Union host had but to press their advantage to carry their victorious colors to the remotest corners of the South-west. Grant saw this, and had he been left in untrammeled command, would have given the rebels no place of rest.

His advance under Sherman had pressed to within sight of Corinth, while the main body of the jaded army was reform- ing its disordered ranks, burying the dead and gaining a par- tial respite from the fatigues of battle and the march. At this time, the 9th of April, Major-General Halleck appeared upon the scene, and immediately assumed command. The army thenceforth made no movement towards Corinth, except for the purpose of entrenching. The musket and carbine were discarded, while the shovel and axe were in constant requisition. Grant was again practically removed from all control of troops, but this time under the pretext of making him "second in command." The army was reorganized, and called the army of the Mississippi. It was divided into a right, left, center and reserve, Buell's force being made the nucleus of organization. Thomas commanded the right, composed mostly of Grant's troops; Pope commanded the center, made up principally of the troops which he had brought from Island No. 10; Buell commanded the left, while McClernand commanded the reserve. Re-enforcements and materials of all kinds were hurried forward from the North, with boundless liberality, for the country had been taught to believe through Halleck's spiritless policy and the persistent misrepresentations which had been circulated far and wide against Grant and his troops, that Shiloh had been a disastrous defeat instead of a splendid victory. Six precious weeks were squandered, in what Halleck, with ridiculous pedantry, called the "Siege of Corinth." During all this time the rebels made no show of advancing, but remained quietly in their entrenchments, studying how they might abandon them without appearing to have done so. The national troops, now increased to one hundred and thirty thousand in number, were converted into ditchers instead of being used as soldiers. Every foot of ground, between Shiloh meeting-house and the rebel works, was laboriously shoveled behind the army, in order that it might get within sight of fortifications which it found empty, or guarded only by Quaker guns. Fortunately for his reputation, Grant, as before stated, was permitted to take no part in this business. When orders were given in his presence, it was either done in a whisper, or the person receiving them was led aside so that Grant should not hear what was said. Upon one occasion he ventured to advise an attack, but Halleck scouted his advice, and intimated too plainly to be misunderstood, that when his opinions were thought to be sufficiently important they would be duly asked for.

During this entire campaign, or "siege," Grant's position was a false one, in which, injustice was continually inflicted upon him. He was looked upon by everybody as being in disgrace—and therefore asked for a leave of absence in order that he might escape from unmerited obloquy. It is said that for a time he thought seriously of resigning, and did ask for a leave of absence that he might give Halleck a chance to get rid of him. Sherman counseled him to remain, and fortunately for the country his counsel prevailed.

This volume is not concerned with what Halleck might have done, after, or during the siege of Corinth, but did not do, for that would swell its bulk beyond all proportion. The policy of dispersion, or "pepper-box strategy," as it has been derisively but not inaptly called, which he inaugurated after the evacuation of Corinth—sending Buell towards Chattanooga, and burying Grant's army in the towns, villages, crossroads and elaborately entrenched camps of Northern Mississippi and West Tennessee, demands the severest condemnation, for it lost to our cause the advantage of its past successes, delayed and endangered those that remained yet to be gained, and inflicted upon the country a long series of disgraceful delays and indecisive combats. Neither can we do more than make a passing allusion to the campaign of General Mitchell into Northern Alabama, ending with the occupation of Huntsville and Decatur, about the time of the Corinth campaign.

Shortly after Buell had been detached, Halleck went to Washington, for the purpose of entering upon the duties of General-in-Chief, to which position he had been called by the President, but before starting, he shot a Parthian arrow at Grant—by offering the command of the army to Colonel Robert Allen, chief supervising quartermaster in the West, an educated soldier and an able man. It was only when Allen positively declined, that the command was restored to Grant, but with still restricted authority. He was ordered to garrison a large number of points and to send re-enforcements to Buell, in doing which he was thrown upon the defensive. But while Halleck was thus scattering the national forces, the rebels had been taught a lesson, which made them concentrate all their available means, east of the Mississippi. Price and Van Dorn were ordered to remove their troops from the trans-Mississippi department, and to form a junction with Beauregard's army at Tupelo. Bragg had already crossed into Alabama and Tennessee, in pursuit of Buell, whom he ultimately compelled to fall back to the Ohio River, fighting him finally at Perryville—and then retreating to Murfreesboro.

On the 10th of September, Price having reached Northern Mississippi with his army of about twelve thousand men, started towards Iuka, where he arrived on the 19th, having driven in small detachments of the national troops from Jacinto and Chewalla. He made a feint of following Bragg in his northern march, in the hope that Grant would pursue him, and thus leave Corinth an easy prey to Van Dorn. But Grant, whose head-quarters were at Jackson, Tennessee, was too sagacious to fall into such a trap. Knowing from his scouts that Van Dorn could not reach Corinth for four or five days yet, he determined to crush Price by sending out a heavy force under Ord and Rosecrans, who had succeeded Pope.* He therefore threw Ord towards Iuka, on the north side of the railroad, re-enforcing him by Ross' brigade from Bolivar, bringing his force up to about five thousand men, and directed Rosecrans, with Hamilton's and Stanley's divisions, and Mizner's cavalry, about nine thousand men in all, the bulk of the force from Corinth, to move towards Iuka by the way of Jacinto and Fulton—hoping thus to cut off the rebel retreat and to concentrate a force sufficient to overwhelm Price. This combined movement commenced at an early hour on the 18th of September, and although the distances to be overcome did not exceed in either case thirty miles, the rebels discovered it before it was fairly executed. For some reason not satisfactorily explained, Rosecrans failed to occupy the Fulton road. In addition to this, it was exceedingly difficult to communicate between the different columns or between them and Grant's head-quarters, on account of the heavily wooded

---

* Most of Pope's troops had been already sent back to Missouri.

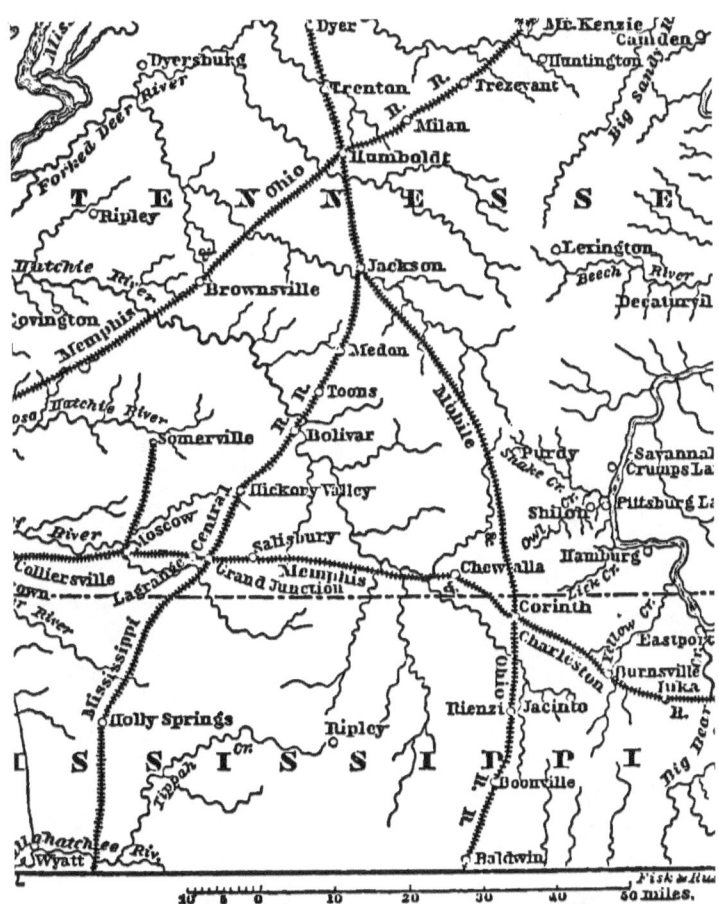

BELMONT, DONELSON, SHILOH, CORINTH.

country and intricate roads.   Hence the junction of Ord and Rosecrans did not take place till after the latter had had a desperate and only partially successful engagement with Price. This took place on the 19th, in front of Iuka.   Rosecrans' troops fought well, but owing to the exceedingly difficult nature of the ground, he was not able to bring his whole command into action.   The rebels were finally defeated after a sanguinary battle, and under cover of night retreated rapidly southward by the Fulton road.   Their loss is stated by Pollard the rebel historian " at about eight hundred killed and wounded," not counting over a thousand prisoners left in the hands of the victors.   Hamilton and Stanley went in pursuit of the retreating rebels, but did not again come up with them.

On the 22d, Grant ordered the pursuit to be discontinued, and directed Rosecrans to return to Corinth, where he arrived on the 26th.   Ord was sent to Bolivar, and Hurlbut in the direction of Pocahontas.   Price, by a wide circuit, joined Van Dorn at Ripley.   The united force then moved in the direction of Pocahontas.

On the 2d of October, Van Dorn and Price, with three divisions advanced thence towards Corinth by the way of Chewalla.

Shortly after Halleck left for Washington, Grant, seeing that the old works were too extensive to be held by any reasonable force, directed the construction of an inner and much shorter line of entrenchments at Corinth, and by the time the rebels made their appearance in front of these works they were sufficiently near completion to be used for defensive purposes.   Rosecrans had withdrawn his outposts upon the first appearance of the enemy and formed his line over a mile in front of the fortifications.   Stanley held the left with a brigade and a battery, advanced still farther to the left.   Davies occupied the center, and Hamilton the right, with Mizner's cavalry, posted where occasion required it.   The rebels advancing on the Chewalla road, soon drove in Stanley's advanced brigade, which, being supported by another, made head for a time.   But the rebels, continually developing their front, soon hotly engaged Davies' division also, and finally the entire line. Pushing their attack with great vigor, they finally compelled Rosecrans to fall back with the loss of two guns, and to occupy the fortifications. He was not again attacked that night. The comparative ease with which this advantage was gained led Van Dorn to believe that he had achieved a great victory, and in emulation of Pillow's example, he sent to Richmond a hasty and exultant dispatch, announcing the capture of Corinth. But like Pillow again, his exultation was destined to end in bitter disappointment.

At an early hour on the morning of the 4th, the action was renewed by the rebels, who opened upon the Union lines with their batteries, and at half-past nine o'clock, Price assaulted the Union center with desperate determination. A storm of canister and grape was poured upon the rebel columns, but with only partial effect. Cheered on by their gallant but mistaken officers, they renewed the attack, now become general, and soon succeeded in breaking Davies' division and in forcing the head of their column into the town. But Rosecrans concentrated a heavy fire of artillery upon them, and pushing forward the Tenth Ohio, and Fifth Minnesota regiments, followed closely by Sullivan's brigade, succeeded in driving the rebels beyond the works and in re-establishing Davies' line. In the meanwhile Van Dorn had formed the right of his army into column of attack, and under cover of a heavy skirmish line, was leading it in person to the assault of the Union left. But Rosecrans was ready on that side also. Stanley's division and the heavy guns of Battery Robinet, manned by the veterans of the First Regular Infantry, made answer to the rebel musketry, and with round shot, shell, grape and canister, played dire havoc among the advancing troops. But still they held their forward course till within fifty yards of our works. Here they received a deadly rifle fire, and after struggling bravely for a minute to face it, they were compelled to fall back. Again the rebel leaders led their men forward, to the very ditches and parapets of the defenses, but again were they bloodily repulsed; this time, however, to be followed by the gallant soldiers of Ohio and Missouri, who, seeing the enemy falter, poured over the works and drove them routed and broken, back to the woods from which they had advanced. The battle had spent its fury, the rebels were no longer able to make head, and lost no time in withdrawing their disorganized battalions to a place of safety. They left dead, upon the field, 1,420 officers and men, and more than 5,000 wounded, besides losing 2,248 prisoners, 41 colors and 2 guns. The next day Rosecrans, re-enforced by McPherson's brigade, began the pursuit, but he had lost eighteen hours and could not regain the advantage which had thus escaped. The following extract from Grant's order of congratulation tells the rest of the story :

" 'The enemy chose his own time and place of attack, and knowing the troops of the West as he does, and with great facilities of knowing their numbers, never would have made the attempt, except with a superior force numerically. But for the undaunted bravery of officers and soldiers, who have yet to learn defeat, the efforts of the enemy must have proven successful.

"Whilst one division of the army, under Major-General Rosecrans, was resisting and repelling the onslaught of the rebel hosts at Corinth, another from Bolivar, under Major-General Hurlbut, was marching upon the enemy's rear, driving in their pickets and cavalry, and attracting the attention of a large force of infantry and artillery. On the following day, under Major-General Ord, these forces advanced with unsurpassed gallantry, driving the enemy back across the Hatchie, over ground where it is almost incredible that a superior force should be driven by an inferior, capturing two of the batteries, (eight guns,) many hundred small arms, and several hundred prisoners.

" To those two divisions of the army all praise is due, and will be awarded by a grateful country.

" Between them there should be, and I trust are, the warmest bonds of brotherhood. Each was risking life in the same cause, and, on this occasion, risking it also to save and assist the other. No troops could do more than these separate armies. Each did all possible for it to do in the places assigned it.

" As in all great battles, so in this, it becomes our fate to mourn the loss of many brave and faithful officers and soldiers, who have given up their lives as a sacrifice for a great principle. The nation mourns for them."

In this campaign of fifteen days, although weakened by detachments sent to Buell and hampered by imperative instructions from Halleck to hold the points which had been garrisoned under his orders, Grant had fought and won two battles, against superior forces of the enemy, and had shown his capacity, if permitted to concentrate his forces and leave conquered territory to take care of itself, to assume the offensive with an ample force to sweep every vestige of rebel power from Mississippi. This is the only period in his military career when he was compelled to receive attack rather than give it, and nothing could have been more galling to his feelings. His combinations were made with great promptitude, his orders were issued with clearness and precision, and although at times they were not so well executed as they should have been, they resulted in gaining substantial and valuable successes for the national cause. The resolution, readiness and perfect comprehension of topographical details, including the strategic relation of important points, exhibited by Grant in this campaign, show him to have been, even at that day, a General of the highest order, and yet Rosecrans received the reward for the victories gained, by being sent to relieve Buell of the command of the largest and best appointed army then in the West.

A full and detailed history of the operations in West Tennessee and Northern Mississippi, from August to October, would of itself make a volume of exciting interest.

CHAPTER XI.

ON the 25th of October, 1862, in compliance with orders
from Washington, General Grant assumed command of the
Department of the Tennessee, which he immediately divided
into four districts, allotting one division of troops to each.
Sherman was assigned to the District of Memphis and the
first division; Hurlbut to the District of Jackson and the
second division; C. S. Hamilton to the District of Corinth
and the third division; and Davies to the District of Columbus
with the fourth division.

The rebels having been defeated and again thrown upon
the defensive at nearly every point in the West, Grant now
determined to take the offensive as soon as the necessary

authority could be obtained. He made every effort in his power to prepare his command for an active campaign. Organizations were perfected, the troops were re-clothed, transportation was diminished, and baggage of every sort was reduced to a minimum.

The entire country, and specially the North-west, had by this time come to regard the opening of the Mississippi River, as a military necessity, not only for the purpose of providing a commercial highway to the sea, but as the means of severing the Confederacy and affording the national armies a base of operations against the vital points of the rebel territory. Grant had long since recognized this necessity, and as soon as his army had been relieved of its immediate troubles, he set about devising the means of carrying forward the work so effectively begun. But while he was working in the field, with the legitimate means which the Government had placed in his hands—a movement had been put on foot in Washington, by one of his ambitious lieutenants, having the same object in view. General McClernand had grown tired of serving in a subordinate capacity, or as he expressed it in his own figurative language—"furnishing brains for Grant." He therefore obtained a leave of absence and went to Washington, where he laid before the President a plan for capturing Vicksburg, and operating eastward in Mississippi. Having formally proposed this movement, he proceeded upon parliamentary precedent and requested the command of, an expedition for the purpose of carrying his plan into effect. The President and Secretary of War, seem to have approved the plan and listened to the request for an independent command with decided favor, but General Halleck opposed it, upon the ground that it would necessarily assume proportions of such magnitude as to pass beyond the limits of a secondary operation, and urged that it should properly be given to Grant, within whose department it would fall. Both sides were stubborn; but as Halleck at that time was believed by the country to possess great military capacity, his opinion prevailed so far, at least, as to induce the President not to interfere with Grant's army. But he ordered McClernand to Illinois for the purpose of raising a new army, with the promise that when it should be ready to take the field, it should be charged with the duty of opening the Mississippi River, and be commanded by McClernand in person.

In the meantime, Grant had collected the available part of his command, now designated as the Thirteenth Army Corps, at LaGrange and Grand Junction, important points on the Memphis and Charleston Railroad, near the northern border of Mississippi, and had ordered Sherman, then commanding at Memphis, to march with his movable force towards Wyatt, on the Tallahatchie, for the purpose of menacing the enemy's left and forming a junction with the main body of the army under McPherson and C. S. Hamilton. Expeditions composed of cavalry and infantry, had already scouted the country in the direction of Ripley, Lamar, and Holly Springs, driving back Van Dorn, and giving Grant a thorough understanding of the enemy's position and force. The rebel government at Richmond appears to have had its confidence much shaken in the leaders of the rebel cause in the South-west. Bragg had been driven from Kentucky with heavy loss; Beauregard had thrown up his command in disgust, and retired to the interior to restore his shattered health; while Lovell, Price, and Van Dorn had been defeated at Iuka and Corinth. In order to repair these damages as far as possible and to raise the hopes of the rebels, Davis assigned Pemberton, a northern renegade, to the chief command of the department of Mississippi.

Grant did not delay his movements an hour longer than necessary, but pushed forward with great celerity and vigor, reaching Holly Springs on the 29th of November, and the Tallahatchie—where he formed a junction with Sherman—on the 1st of December. During this advance from LaGrange, Hovey and Washburn, under Grant's instructions, crossed the Mississippi at Helena and moved out towards Grenada for the purpose of menacing the rebel communications and rear. Under the influence of these combined movements, Pemberton abandoned his strongly entrenched camp on the south side of the Tallahatchie near Abbeville, and fell back rapidly, closely pressed by the cavalry under Colonel Dickey. Sharp skirmishes occurred at Water Valley and Springdale, and a combat of some magnitude took place at Coffeeville between the rebel rear guard, consisting of a part of Lovell's corps, and Dickey's mounted force, and although the latter was worsted, it was only after a well-contested struggle of several hours, during which Colonels Dickey, Hatch and McCullough (the latter of whom was killed), handled their commands with skill and bravery. The rebel force composed of infantry, cavalry and artillery, were in great preponderance; and as the national infantry, owing to bad roads, had not been able to keep up with the advance, Dickey was compelled to fall back. He was sent immediately, however, towards Okolona and Tupelo, for the purpose of breaking the Ohio and Mobile Railroad.

But the overland movement towards Jackson, had already been paralyzed by the winter rains which had set in some days before. The roads in Northern Mississippi naturally bad, had become almost impassable for an army accompanied by wagons and artillery. This thickly wooded region, cut up by streams with broad alluvial bottoms, presents even under the most favorable circumstances, an extremely difficult theatre for military operations. Grant was not slow in reaching the conviction that further operations in that direction were out of the question. He had also received information that the President and Secretary of War, were about to precipitate the movement of McClernand's expedition against Vicksburg—in spite of Halleck's opposition—and having received permission from the General-in-Chief, on the 8th of December, he issued the following orders to Sherman:

"You will proceed with as little delay as possible to Memphis, Tenn., taking with you one division of your present command. On your arrival at Memphis, you will assume command of all the troops there and that portion of General Curtis' force at present east of the Mississippi River, and organize them into brigades and divisions in your own way. As soon as possible, move with them down the river, to the vicinity of

Vicksburg, and with the co-operation of the gun-boat fleet, under command of Flag-officer Porter, proceed to the reduction of that place, in such manner as circumstances and your own judgment may dictate.

"The amount of rations, forage, land transportation, etc., necessary to take will be left entirely with yourself. The Quartermaster at St. Louis, will be instructed to send you transportation for thirty thousand men. Should you still find yourself deficient, your quartermaster will be authorized to make up the deficiency from such transports as may come into the port of Memphis.

"On arriving at Memphis, put yourself in communication with Admiral Porter, and arrange with him for his co-operation.

"Inform me at the earliest practicable day of the time when you will embark, and such plans as may then be matured. I will hold the forces here in readiness to co-operate with you in such manner as the movements of the enemy may make necessary.

"Leave the District of Memphis in the command of an efficient officer, and with a garrison of four regiments of infantry, the siege-guns, and whatever cavalry may be there."

While this movement was in progress, and the force under Grant at rest on account of the heavy rains, the rebel cavalry under Van Dorn, assumed the offensive, and marching rapidly beyond the left flank of Grant's army, struck the railroad at Holly Springs, captured the place and destroyed a large quantity of stores. This movement was successful, through an unfortunate array of disadvantageous circumstances. Grant's cavalry as already mentioned, had been detached to break up another railroad, and although they crossed Van Dorn's line of march, just as he was passing out of Pontotoc, they were too much fatigued and weakened by long marches, to make rapid pursuit. A brigade of infantry which was sent by Grant to re-enforce the garrison at Holly Springs, failed to reach it in time, owing to the precipitate haste with which Colonel Murphy, the ranking officer, surrendered his command, amounting to nearly two thousand men. This officer had ample warning of Van Dorn's approach, and with the force at hand, could have easily defended the place, had he shown the least enterprise or soldierly spirit. Having acted in a similar manner at Iuka, he was disgracefully dismissed for his conduct by Grant, a few days thereafter. The rest

7

of Van Dorn's campaign was a failure, for he was held at bay by all of the little garrisons which he undertook in succession to capture, and was finally compelled to make a wide circuit and return towards Grenada.

This interruption of communication with his base of supplies, gave Grant an opportunity to withdraw from his advanced position in North Mississippi, under the appearance of compulsion. He had already seen that the Mississippi River would afford a line of operations which could not be cut by raiders, and which led directly to the principal objective point in the theater of operations; and that he ought, therefore, to lose no time in transferring his entire army by that route to the immediate vicinity of Vicksburg. It was vain to hope that the rebels would allow that place to fall by a *coup de main*, and unless it should so fall, its natural and artificial strength would necessarily require a large force and much time to overcome it. These considerations, and as has already been stated, the extreme difficulty of continuing the movement towards Jackson, together with the natural anxiety to direct in person the main body of his army, influenced him to remove his head-quarters to Memphis, and soon after to the neighborhood of Vicksburg. The army was slowly withdrawn to the north side of the Tallahatchie, where it was encamped and thoroughly taught the lesson of making war support war. The interruption of railway communication with the rear, deprived the army of its usual supplies, but Grant had given up the idea of treating the rebels in such a manner, as not to exasperate them. He therefore issued orders putting the army on "half rations" and requiring it to live off the country. The country being neither populous nor highly cultivated and having already been marched over by two armies and various detachments, was regarded as unable to furnish support to so large a force for any length of time. But under the thorough system adopted by McPherson, Hamilton, Logan, Denver, McArthur and others, aided by the enterprising men of their commands, an abundance of corn, bacon, poultry, pork and beef was obtained. All parts of the upper Tallahatchie and Cold Water vallies were ransacked and foraged; the mills were set to work and kept running night and day by detachments from various brigades and divisions; and although they were neither numerous nor large enough to keep the army provided with a full supply of meal, the men were not long in filling up the deficiency. In the lack of bread, they made hominy. This was done by burning hickory wood to ashes, leaching them and then soaking the uncracked corn in the lye till its skin could be easily removed. After this it was only necessary to boil the hominy till tender, thus making a healthy, nutritious and agreeable article of food. On Christmas day, McPherson's pioneer corps sent him as a specimen of "half rations," an admirable dinner for himself and staff, made up of roast turkeys, chickens, meat pies, well baked wheaten bread, corn bread, cakes, hominy, and stewed fruits.

The irregularities consequent upon the system of foraging, were not conducive to a high state of discipline, but as the necessities of the case were somewhat pressing, breaches of regulation could not be severely punished. Logan, with his usual ingenuity, forbade his men to burn fence rails, but allowed them to use as much dry, twelve foot split wood as they could find corded up outside the fields. He also forbade them to forage, except under direction of officers, but they could not entirely resist the temptation. Logan was vigilant and active, however, and caused his Provost Marshal to arrest all men caught bringing in hogs or cattle on individual account, and pen them up together till discipline had been vindicated. As a matter of course the accumulated supplies thus obtained were divided by the proper staff officers, equally among the troops. These instances serve to indicate the general rule followed in the different divisions, and to show how Grant was accustomed to leave subordinate details to subordinate commanders, subject only to general orders and regulations of the army. The Commanding General of an army, may undertake to regulate the details of duty in the field of battle, and in camp, for every subdivision of his force, or he may announce general principles and rules, and leave the details

of tactics and administration to his Lieutenants. The former
course necessarily converts him into a martinet, annoys and
harasses himself and staff as well as the Generals below him,
and seldom accomplishes any important result; while the latter
leaves him free to attend to the more serious business of
his office, and confines the corps, division, brigade and regimental commanders, more particularly to the duties which
concern them. Grant had at this time but two regular officers on his staff, and only three others within his whole command, and he would therefore have been compelled to adopt
the latter policy, had he not had the sagacity to see it was
better of itself.

On the 22d of December, 1862, Grant issued from his
head-quarters, at Holly Springs, the following order:

" By direction of the President, the troops in this Department, including those from the Department of the Missouri, operating on the
Mississippi River, are hereby divided into four army-corps as follows:

" 1. The troops composing the Ninth Division, Brigadier-General G.
W. Morgan commanding; the Tenth Division, Brigadier-General A. J.
Smith commanding; and all other troops operating on the Mississippi
River below Memphis, not included in the Fifteenth Army-Corps, will
constitute the Thirteenth Army Corps, under the command of Major-
General John A. McClernand.

" 2. The Fifth Division, Brigadier-General Morgan L. Smith commanding; the division from Helena, Arkansas, commanded by Brigadier-
General F. Steele; and the force in the ' District of Memphis,' will
constitute the Fifteenth Army-Corps, and be commanded by Major-
General W. T. Sherman.

" 3. The Sixth Division, Brigadier-General J. McArthur commanding;
the Seventh Division, Brigadier-General I. F. Quimby commanding; the
Eighth Division, Brigadier-General L. F. Ross commanding; the Second
Brigade of cavalry, Colonel A. L. Lee commanding; and the troops in
the District of Columbus, commanded by Brigadier-General Davies, and
those in the district of Jackson, commanded by Brigadier-General Sullivan, will constitute the Sixteenth Army-Corps, and be commanded by
Major-General S. A. Hurlbut.

" 4. The First Division, Brigadier-General J. W. Denver commanding;
the Third Division, Brigadier-General John A. Logan commanding; the
Fourth Division, Brigadier-General J. G. Lauman commanding; the
First Brigade of cavalry, Colonel B. H. Grierson commanding; and

the forces in the District of Corinth, commanded by Brigadier-General G. M. Dodge, will constitute the Seventeenth Army-Corps, and be commanded by Major-General J. B. McPherson.

"District commanders will send consolidated returns of their forces to these head-quarters, as well as to army-corps head-quarters, and will, for the present, receive orders from Department head-quarters."

Soon after the issuing of the foregoing order, Grant went in person to Memphis, where he established his head-quarters, and exerted himself to the utmost to prepare for the work before him. Having great confidence in Sherman's courage and generalship, he left him untrammeled in the first descent upon Vicksburg, giving only general instructions, and leaving him to carry them out as circumstances should demand. Sherman landed at first, near Young's Point, sent an expedition to destroy the Vicksburg and Shrevesport Railroad, so as to cut off the rebel supplies from that quarter; made a demonstration upon Haines' Bluff, on the Yazoo about twelve miles above its mouth; and finally on the 29th of December, landed at Chickasaw Bayou, a few miles lower down, and moved thence across the almost impassable swamps against the rebel lines along the slopes of the Walnut hills. But the natural and artificial defences, together with the strong rebel force behind them, were too much for Sherman to overcome. In the nature of things his movement could not be made a surprise, and he therefore found himself compelled to relinquish the expedition without further effort, or to make a bold and vigorous attack. He chose the latter course and failed, but from no fault of his own nor of his men. The troops after a most gallant fight, in which they suffered severe loss, were withdrawn to the river and re-embarked on the 1st of January.

General McClernand, who, in accordance with the promise of the Government, had been hurried forward to take the command, under the advice of Sherman moved at once against the Post of Arkansas on the White River, which place, he, in connection with the naval squadron under Admiral Porter, captured on the 11th of January. The fruits of this victory were 6,000 prisoners, 17 guns, 12 colors, 6,000 stands of small arms, and a large amount of military stores.

During this time Grant was still at Memphis,* but when McClernand joined the expedition and its first failure became known, Grant obtained authority from Halleck to strengthen it with all his available forces, and to assume command in person. His first movement was to visit the forces near the mouth of White River, on the 17th of January. After conferring with Admiral Porter, and Generals McClernand and Sherman, he ordered the expedition to rendezvous in the neighborhood of Vicksburg and then returned to Memphis. Soon after his arrival at that place he received a letter from McClernand, protesting in an insolent and insubordinate manner, against being superseded in command, on the score that he had been assigned by order of the President and could not be removed except by him. This was not McClernand's first offense, for he had long been in the habit of grumbling, protesting, and acting with marked disrespect to his superiors. Grant was therefore urged by his staff to test the question of authority at once by relieving McClernand from all command, and sending him to the rear; but with a degree of magnanimity rarely equalled, he sank all personal feeling, and answered: "No! I cannot afford to quarrel with a man whom I have to command." Acting on this principle he treated McClernand with the greatest consideration, giving him in nearly all cases the post of honor and more than his share of the troops, knowing that nothing else would satisfy his inordinate ambition, and feeling that McPherson and Sherman would regard themselves as amply rewarded by the simple privilege

---

* While here Grant was approached by an acquaintance from St. Louis, with a proposition to permit the sale of salt, along the Mississippi River, within the rebel lines, upon condition that he should receive half the profits—which would have been enormous. It is hardly necessary to state this offer was scorned, and the person making it treated with such contempt as to overwhelm him with shame. The news of this attempt and its signal failure doubtless spread among the cormorants who were fattening upon the misfortunes of the country ; for nothing like its repetition was ever known to have occurred.

of obeying orders with alacrity and zeal, no matter what they might be, nor what sacrifices they might exact.

Without delay, Grant sent the engineer officers of his staff to join the army and gather information; ordered McPherson with his corps, already withdrawn from the Tallahatchie to Memphis, to proceed to Milliken's Bend as fast as transportation could be obtained; assigned Hurlbut with the Sixteenth corps to the command of West Tennessee, and to the task of keeping the river open as far down as Helena; and then proceeded in person to Young's Point, where he arrived on the 28th of January. While perfecting these arrangements, being thoroughly impressed with the magnitude and difficulty of the operations in which he was about to embark, he advised the Government to unite the various military departments in the West, into one command, in order that all its resources might be directed to the accomplishment of the one great object. And for fear that this advice might be looked upon as an effort to extend his own power, he declined in advance the supreme control. This suggestion, based as it was, upon strategic considerations of the highest character, is enough to show that Grant had already attained the stature of an able General and a far-sighted, judicious statesman. It was not acted upon, however, until Rosecrans' defeat at Chickamauga rendered a consolidation absolutely necessary. It will be seen in the meantime how Grant showed his worthiness to have the supreme command, in spite of his exceeding modesty.

;

CHAPTER XII.

IN order that the reader may understand a part of the difficulties which the army of the Tennessee (not "the army of
the Mississippi," as McClernand persisted in calling it,) had
to encounter, he should bear in mind that Vicksburg is situated on a bluff some two hundred and fifty feet above low
water mark, and is covered in front and flank by the almost
illimitable bottom lands of the Mississippi. These lands are
intersected in all directions by impassable swamps and tortuous, fever-breeding bayous, filled with quagmires and quick-
sands, treacherous bottoms, and steep banks, almost impassable by troops in summer, and entirely so, except by boats,
during the rainy season. They are covered by a dense forest
and incumbered by a luxuriant growth of cane and vines.
No roads have been constructed through them, and none can
be except at an excessive cost. The swamps, forests, jungles,
bayous and rivers of this remarkable region, are the most
perfect defense that could be devised for important points situated on the highlands which lie beyond them. To the army
operating along the main river, they proved to be a perfect
barrier, for although they were frequently penetrated, it was
always with such great labor and loss of time, that the rebels,
moving by rail or along the better roads of the highlands,
were enabled to meet our forces in superior strength, or to
block their way by impassable fortifications.

As fast as the troops reached Milliken's Bend and Young's Point, they were disembarked, and the transports were sent to bring forward others. In the meantime, Grant undertook to devise a plan which should give him either the immediate possession of Vicksburg itself, or a footing on the neighboring highlands with an accessible base from which he could operate against the city and its communications. To secure the first of these ends, there was no course possible but to land a picked force by surprise from steamers and flat-boats at the levee of the city, and to carry its works by a vigorous attack. But this was clearly too hazardous an undertaking with troops unused to such desperate adventures. It was therefore apparent that some other scheme must be adopted. The various plans which suggested themselves may be classified under three general heads:

First.—To enlarge the canal, commenced the year before by Butler, across the peninsula in front of Vicksburg, and to send through it a strong force by flat-boats and steamers if practicable, to land at or below Warrenton, whence the highlands might be reached and the defences of Vicksburg carried. It was also hoped that this plan would result in turning the river through the canal and thus in a measure depriving Vicksburg of its importance.

Second.—The probability of capturing the rebel works at Haines' Bluff by a combined land and naval attack was thoughtfully discussed, as was also the possibility of turning this place by operations along the bayous leading from the Mississippi to the Yazoo above it.

Third.—In the event of all other plans failing, General Grant carefully considered the feasibility of running the batteries with the fleet, and taking his entire army to some point on the Mississippi below Vicksburg, by whatever means should be found most practicable. By this plan it was hoped to secure a footing at Grand Gulf or Rodney and thence to move at once into the interior of Mississippi, or to form a junction with Banks—then occupying the Red River country—and with the combined armies to maneuver so as to draw out and destroy the rebel army under Pemberton.

The first of these plans proved impracticable on account of the faulty location of the canal* and the impossibility of giving it a sufficient width and depth to admit the passage of boats. The rapid rise of the Mississippi and the consequent pressure of the water broke the levees of the peninsula and canal, and instead of cutting a navigable channel as had been hoped, inundated the country for miles around. But even had this canal been finished as intended, it is not probable that it could have been used by the steamboats, as the rebels had established batteries of heavy guns, within a mile and a quarter of its outlet, enfilading it throughout. They had rendered it untenable for the dredge boats before the levees broke.

Grant had probably but little faith in it from the first, for the very day he arrived in front of Vicksburg, he sent Lieutenant-Colonel Wilson of his staff, to Helena, for the purpose of opening and exploring Yazoo Pass—a tortuous bayou leaving the Mississippi a few miles below Helena and with the Cold Water and Tallahatchie, after nearly two hundred and fifty miles of twisting and turning, connecting with the Yazoo River. A few days afterwards McPherson was ordered to open a way through Lake Providence to Bayou Baxter, and Bayou Macon, and thence through the Washita into the Red River.

Yazoo Pass, in the earlier days of the Mississippi settlements, had been used by trading boats as the means of reaching the country along the Tallahatchie and Yazoo, but in later years it was obstructed by a levee across its entrance, near the bank of the Mississippi. The supply of water having been

---

* General Halleck in his annual report of operations, states that this canal failed because of its faulty location, there being an eddy at the lower end, but this is only partially correct. The water failed to run through it and across the peninsula because the middle of the peninsula, in accordance with the general law in such cases, was lower than either side; as a consequence the water ran in at both ends, and after the guard bank was broken, spread out over the swamps and lowest land first.

cut off, its bed was encroached upon by a rank growth of cotton-wood and willow, so that when it came to be considered as a possible line by which the Yazoo could be reached, its mouth had become almost obliterated. But when the levee was cut, the flood of water which poured through the crevasse in a few hours, uprooted the young trees, swept away the fallen timber, and left an open channel wide enough for steamboats to descend. The rebels, however, anticipating the intentions of Grant, before the gun-boats and troops could be got ready, filled the lower part of the pass, felling into and across it, the forest trees growing upon its banks, and overlapping their limbs above it. These were, however, removed by the troops, under the direction of General Washburne and Colonel Wilson, after infinite labor, and ceaseless exposure for nearly two weeks. The expedition consisting of two rams, two powerful iron-clads, six tin-clad steamers, and one division of troops under General Ross, embarked on about twenty small steamboats, left the river on the 24th of February, and by the 1st of March they had mostly succeeded in pushing their way through the wilderness to the Coldwater. Thenceforward it was supposed to be plain sailing, but the naval force was commanded by an officer of extreme caution and timidity, who managed upon one pretext or another to delay the expedition so that it did not reach its final station, near the mouth of the Tallahatchie, till the 11th of March. Pemberton, in the meantime, had sent a strong force from Vicksburg under Loring, and while the expedition which promised so much was moving with such deliberation, this force took position near Greenwood, and threw up a line of works some five hundred yards long, extending from a bend in the Tallahatchie, to a corresponding bend in the Yazoo, and covering the mouth of the Yallobusha. They also sank an ocean steamer, and constructed a heavy raft in the Tallahatchie under the guns of their fort. When the iron-clads made their appearance, they were greeted by a well directed fire from two heavy rifled guns, and although they replied in due time with their nine and eleven inch Dahlgrens, aided by the fire of a battery erected by the troops on the narrow spit of land not overflowed, they did not succeed in dislodging or silencing the enemy. Nearly the entire face of the country being under water, and the rebel fort being covered on all sides by the river, and impassable sloughs, it was out of the question for the infantry to attempt either a turning movement or an assault. After spending a week in futile efforts to devise means of getting into the Yazoo, the expedition was abandoned, though Grant had entertained such hope of its success that he ordered McPherson to withdraw his detachments from the bayous leading southward from Lake Providence, and to join the Yazoo Pass expedition with his entire corps. It was also hoped that an expedition sent from the mouth of the Yazoo through Steele's Bayou, Rolling Fork, and Alligator Bayou, might reach the Yazoo, above Haines' Bluff, thus taking the position at Fort Pemberton in reverse. Admiral Porter undertook to carry out this part of the plan, and succeeded in penetrating over two hundred miles into the net-work of bayous, but the rebels, gathering in his front and rear, and felling trees into the streams, soon obstructed the navigation so much that it was equally impossible for the gun-boats to advance or retire. The officers and men were driven below by the annoying fire of sharp-shooters lying behind the trees within a few yards of the boats, and had it not been for the timely arrival of General Sherman, with a succoring force, it is not improbable that the Admiral would have lost his vessels and been taken prisoner with all his officers and men.

Thus it will be seen that Grant was foiled at every step, and in every plan. The interminable forests, tortuous bayous, and impassable swamps of the Yazoo country, were too much to be overcome by human effort. These side expeditions were therefore abandoned and the troops rapidly concentrated again in front of Vicksburg.

Though no substantial advantage had been gained, and the high land seemed farther off than ever, these preliminary operations were not entirely without benefit to the national

cause.   The army was kept busy and therefore healthy, while
the rebels were greatly annoyed and harassed.   Holding not
only Vicksburg, but nearly all of Western Mississippi, they
were compelled to move constantly from one place to another,
scattering their strength and keeping on the alert at all points.
But the greatest advantage was that the Union commander
became convinced by his failures that there was but one way
left for him to accomplish the object in view, and, "at that
very stage when an intellect of less determined fibre would
have been resigning itself to a seemingly implacable fortune,
Grant, overleaping fate and failure, rose to the height of that
audacious conception on which at length he vaulted into
Vicksburg." *

* Swinton's "Twelve Decisive Battles of the War," p. 283.

CHAPTER XIII.

M'CLERNAND AND M'PHERSON MARCH TO NEW CARTHAGE—ADMIRAL
PORTER WITH THE IRON-CLADS AND TRANSPORTS RUNS BY THE BAT-
TERIES—DESCRIPTION OF THE SCENE—SUPPLIES ARRIVING—NAVAL
FIGHT AT GRAND GULF—THE GUN-BOATS AND TRANSPORTS RUN BAT-
TERIES AT GRAND GULF—TROOPS CROSS THE RIVER AT BRUINS-
BURG—M'CLERNAND ENCOUNTERS THE ENEMY—BATTLE OF PORT
GIBSON—THE REBELS DEFEATED—EVACUATION OF GRAND GULF—
GRANT PUSHES FORWARD—BASE OF SUPPLIES AT GRAND GULF—
HALT FOR SUPPLIES AND RE-ENFORCEMENTS.

As before stated, Grant never felt entire confidence in any
of the plans for taking Vicksburg by operations north of it,
and therefore, while he gave all of them the best trial circumstances would allow, he held firmly to the idea of transferring
his army to the southward. When the canal across the peninsula failed, his fertile genius discovered another route promising better results. By examining the map of the country
adjacent to Vicksburg it will be seen that there is a system of
bayous, leading by a tortuous course of thirty miles from the
neighborhood of Milliken's Bend—the rendezvous of Grant's
army—to New Carthage, some twenty miles below Vicksburg.
Engineers were sent to examine this route, and soon reported that it could be prepared for steamboat navigation, by
cutting a canal from Duckport to Walnut Bayou and then
clearing the bayous of the trees which had grown up in their
beds. Grant gave the necessary orders for beginning the
work; but without waiting for its completion he began the
movement by ordering McClernand's corps to march along the
levees bordering the bayous, to New Carthage. The country
being inundated nearly everywhere, except along the banks

of the bayous, causeways had to be thrown up, in one instance over a mile in length, before the troops could pass. Madison Parish, through which the line of march lay, has been brought under a high state of cultivation, but the roads, owing to the freshet, were at that time as bad as they could possibly be, so that the march was made with great difficulty. When the advance reached Smith's plantation, New Carthage, two miles beyond, was an island which could only be reached by ferrying. Boats were built and others collected from the neighboring plantations, by which means one division succeeded in reaching the village, but the rest of the corps was sent twelve miles farther, striking the river at Perkins' plantation. McPherson's corps followed soon after.

By this time, owing to a subsidence of the flood in the river, and the difficulty of cutting off the trees below the surface of the water in the bayous, it was necessary to abandon this route also as a means of keeping the army supplied; and should the river continue to fall, which it was likely to do at that time of the year, it would be utterly out of the question to send transports through the bayous, even after the trees were removed. Grant therefore determined to overcome all difficulties on the score of supplies and transportation by sending the transports and iron-clads, under the fire of the Vicksburg batteries, to join the army below that place.

Accordingly, on the night of Thursday, April 16th, Admiral Porter, with six iron-clads, one tug, one steam ram, and three river steamboats, the latter manned mostly by volunteers from the army, ran past the batteries of Vicksburg under a terrific and almost incessant fire.

It was a clear, starlight night, but the rebels set fire to houses near the river bank; and one of the transports also took fire from the effects of a bursting shell, so that the whole scene was soon under a glare of light, almost as bright as day. The fleet, instead of going by under a full head of steam, drifted with the current, the gun-boats answering shot with shot. The passage required nearly two hours, during which the rebels were enabled to work their heavy and well posted guns with telling effect. The reverberation of artillery, the howling of rifle shot, and the constant bursting of shells made the scene one of the most terrific ever witnessed in warfare. Grant accompanied the fleet with his own steamer to within range of the rebel guns, and from that point anxiously watched the entire movement. By twelve o'clock he had the satisfaction of knowing that it had proved entirely successful. The gun-boats were uninjured; one transport was abandoned and burned, and another had her steam-chest pierced, but with all, it was now certain, that by using the gun-boats, tugs, and transports, the entire army could be ferried across the river at any point, in a few hours. This end being secured beyond a doubt, Grant felt that his campaign could not fail. Supplies for immediate use were forwarded by barges and flat-boats which also ran the batteries under the cover of darkness; and as the flood gradually subsided, and the country emerged from the water, roads were constructed on the west side of the river, leading from Milliken's Bend and Young's Point, to Bowers' * Landing, just above Warrenton. Under the efficient direction of Colonels Bingham and Macfeeley, Chief Quartermaster and Commissary, every want of the army, until it finally cut loose from all connection with the river, was promptly supplied. The greatest danger had already been overcome, when the army and transports passed below Vicksburg. To Grant, and Grant alone, is due all the credit of carrying this movement into effect, for although circumstances may have in a manner driven him to adopt the plan of which this was the first and most important step, he perceived from the day of his arrival at the point opposite Vicksburg, all the great strategic advantages to be obtained by operating against that place from the southward, and therefore bent all his energies to placing his army in such position as would enable him to gain those advantages. The persistency with which he tried to find some other route than the one finally adopted, shows his

* Located by, and called after T. S. Bowers, A. A. G., an efficient and valued officer of Grant's staff.

anxiety to avoid unnecessary risk; but when all other routes had failed, there was nothing left to a man of his temper but to go forward in the one that remained. He was counseled to wait for the dry season, and in the meantime to send a part of his army to help Rosecrans overwhelm Bragg. Sherman advised him to return at once to Northern Mississippi, and renew the overland campaign; McPherson and Steele rather favored the same plan. So long as the question was open for discussion, Grant was almost entirely alone in the opinion which he held. He was not insensible to the fact that his plan was a hazardous one, or that in the event of any serious misadventure, his army would be in great peril; but he also knew that he could not afford to turn back, even to gain a victory elsewhere. The country had begun to clamor for his removal, and it was rumored that the Government had determined to replace him by McClernand. Under such circumstances success was an absolute necessity, and as at Shiloh, he had "not yet despaired" of winning it. It must not be understood from the foregoing, that Grant at any time called a council of war, or solicited through any other means the advice of his subordinates. No General was ever more easily accessible than he, and no one ever listened with more attention to the voluntary suggestions of those in whom he had confidence; and yet it is not too much to say that neither McPherson nor Sherman, (not even McClernand,*) "furnished him with brains," then or thereafter, either for the conception or the execution of his plans. It is but fair, however, to add that when he announced his determination, and issued the final orders for the march, every officer from the highest to the lowest gave him unqualified support.

The movement of the troops to firm footing on the banks

---

* Should the future historian ever get hold of the records kept by General McClernand, he should not waste too much time in trying to reconcile them with this remark, but should bear in mind it has been said of that sagacious Commander, that after the receipt of orders to execute a good movement, he not unfrequently wrote to his Commanding General advising the same movement, antedating his letter and carefully forgetting to mention the instructions already received.

8

of the Mississippi, below Vicksburg, was one of the most
difficult ever accomplished by an army. Canals were dug,
bayous were cleared out, roads were thrown up and cordu-
royed, boats were built, wagons and artillery were with incredible labor drawn through the swamps, before the army
could be assembled within striking distance of the enemy.
During this march, over three thousand feet of bridging, including four bridges of over six hundred feet in length, were
built, and that without the use of a single military bridge
train. Cotton-gins and flat-boats afforded all the materials
required by the hardy and self-reliant soldiers of the Union.
Nothing could have been more admirable than the spirit with
which the army overcame difficulties. It shared to the fullest
extent the qualities which mark their indomitable Commander,
as the most peculiar General yet known to history. If no
other General would have undertaken such a campaign, it is
not too much to say that no other army, except one composed of Americans, could have carried it successfully to its
completion.

By the 29th of April, just one month from the commencement of the movement from Milliken's Bend, Grant had assembled McClernand's and McPherson's corps, a force of about
thirty thousand men, at New Carthage and Perkins' Landing,
five more transports* had run past the Vicksburg batteries,
and were added to the fleet below, and all were in readiness to
assist in ferrying the army to the Mississippi side, which had
been carefully reconnoitered from Warrenton to the mouth of
the Big Black, without finding a landing place connected with
the high land by a passable road. There was nothing left
for it but to select some point at which the river washed the
foot of the bluffs. The first point of this kind, was Grand
Gulf, just below the mouth of the Big Black, and as the rebels
had fortified and garrisoned the place, a landing could not be
made till their batteries should be silenced. In order to mis-
lead the enemy in reference to his real designs, Grant ordered
Sherman to make a demonstration with two divisions and the

* Nine river steamers ran past the batteries, only two of which were lost.

gun-boats still above Vicksburg, on the rebel position at Haines' Bluff, and after attracting all the attention that he could, without making an actual attack, to withdraw and follow rapidly upon the footsteps of the main force.   Sherman carried out his instructions so efficiently as to deceive Pemberton completely.

On the 30th of April, Porter made a determined attack with his iron-clads, upon the rebel batteries at Grand Gulf, passing and repassing the town, pouring out first one broadside and then another; holding his armored vessels, including his own flag-ship, for six hours to the desperate work, but all to no purpose.   The rebel guns were too far above water to be dismounted, and too well manned to be easily silenced. They returned shot for shot, with great regularity, occasionally pausing for awhile but renewing the fire whenever favorable range could be got upon their antagonists.

Grant was again an anxious spectator.   He had embarked a part of McClernand's corps, and held them ready to make a landing and scale the heights when the rebel batteries should be silenced; but Porter's gallant fight had shown that the navy was incompetent to do the work assigned it, though it was as fit for action after the six hours' work as before, only one iron-clad having been seriously damaged and thirty or forty men killed and wounded.   It was plain that some other point must be selected.   Accordingly as soon as it was dark, the transports, under cover of the fleet ran past the batteries, as at Vicksburg, under a heavy fire, while the troops marched across, after dark, to Hard Times Landing, two miles below Grand Gulf.   Early the next morning they were re-embarked on board the transports and, accompanied by the gun-boats, started down the river again.   It was generally supposed that a landing could not be effected short of Rodney, but Grant was fortunate enough to learn from a negro that the highland could be reached by landing at Bruinsburg, about ten miles below Grand Gulf.   The troops had been already supplied with rations, and stripped of all impediments, and when the advance reached Bruinsburg, which was found unoccupied, no time was lost in pushing out a party as far as the hills, by the road along the south bank of Bayou Pierre. This party was soon strengthened; and by the middle of the afternoon enough of McClernand's corps had obtained a firm footing on dry land to render the lodgment entirely safe. Transports and gun-boats vied with each other in ferrying the army from Hard Times to the landing place, while Grant busied himself in pushing them to the front. So anxious was he to get his army united on the Mississippi side, that he issued orders forbidding even the Generals to take their horses till every man who could carry a musket was across. The infantry crossed first, and then the artillery, but wagons of all kinds were left behind; Grant even left his own horses and personal baggage and required his staff to do the same. In order to go to the front he was compelled to borrow a horse from a small detachment of cavalry which he had allowed to cross for the purpose of acting as scouts and couriers. The ferrying was continued throughout the night and by daylight on the 1st of May, all of McClernand's and a part of McPherson's corps had crossed. McClernand, who had pushed out his leading division five or six miles during the afternoon and night, renewed his advance at early dawn, and by sunrise had begun to feel the enemy. The sound of artillery soon afterward bore to Grant's ears the assurance that Pemberton had not been inactive. Ordering McPherson to hurry the remainder of his troops to the front as fast as they arrived, he mounted his borrowed horse and, accompanied by two staff officers, rode rapidly to the field of battle, about eight miles from the river, and assumed direct control of the troops. McClernand had found the enemy composed of infantry and cavalry, posted upon a succession of heavily wooded ridges covering the two roads leading into Port Gibson, and although not in very great force, able to make a successful and stubborn resistance, owing to the natural strength of the position. The divisions of Hovey, Carr and A. J. Smith, were thrown against the enemy along the right hand road while Osterhaus' division pressed him back on the left. The rebel General Bowen felt that he must hold Grant back with all his might, and defeat him if he wished to save Grand Gulf, and bar the road to Vicksburg long enough to make its defense sure. He therefore disputed every foot of the field, with stubborn and determined bravery. But Grant pushed forward his troops with the greatest celerity, driving the enemy steadily but slowly all the while, till the arrival of Logan with McPherson's leading division enabled him to re-enforce both Osterhaus and the troops under Hovey, Carr and Smith, and by a vigorous attack all along the line and on both flanks, to drive the rebels broken and defeated from their last position, with the loss of 150 killed, 840 wounded, and 600 prisoners, besides 3 guns and 4 flags. Night put an end to the pursuit, but the rebels continued their retreat through Port Gibson, and beyond the Bayou Pierre. They burned the bridges across the forks of the bayou, and fell back the next day to the north side of the Big Black River, having blown up the magazines, spiked the guns and abandoned Grand Gulf, during the night of May 1st.

Grant pushed forward, and repaired the bridges, and while the army continued the pursuit to Hankinson's Ferry, he rode to Grand Gulf reaching there at nightfall on the 2d. Admiral Porter had already taken possession. Grant directed the proper staff departments to transfer the base of supplies at once to Grand Gulf, sent orders to Sherman to cross the river there, and wrote despatches to Banks informing him of his success, and telling him that he should not turn towards the south, nor detach any part of his troops for operations in that direction. At midnight he mounted and rode rapidly back to the army, which he joined on the morning of the 3d, at sunrise. The night before he had slept upon the ground, without a tent, in the midst of his soldiers, with his saddle for a pillow and without even an overcoat for covering. Now, throwing himself upon a hard wooden bench he took two hours' sound sleep, this time without even the luxury of a saddle.

The rebel writers have tried to palliate the soreness of their defeat at Port Gibson, by saying that they were outnumbered

two to one, but they forget that it was Grant's good generalship which enabled him, by the concentration of superior
forces on the field of action, to make his first step sure.   No
General ever displayed greater activity or clearness of judgment than Grant did during the preliminary movements of
this campaign ; but the rebels having fallen back towards
Vicksburg, he now suspended his advance for the purpose of
waiting for Sherman to join him.   The delay was improved by
bringing forward supplies, making reconnoisances and gathering information for future use.

CHAPTER XIV.

AFTER Beauregard's retirement, the Richmond authorities put the control of all their military operations in the South-west, into the hands of Joseph E. Johnston, who made his head-quarters with Bragg—receiving daily reports from all parts of his extensive command. Pemberton gave him the impression that Grant would relinquish the campaign against Vicksburg, but, as has been seen, he sadly misconceived the temper of his adversary.

During the progress of the battle near Port Gibson, Johnston ordered re-enforcements from Tennessee, South Carolina and Georgia, and directed Pemberton to gather all his forces and "drive Grant into the river;" but that officer was not only incapable of doing this, but of understanding the principles of warfare upon which the order was based. Instead of abandoning Vicksburg at once and concentrating his entire force in the direction of Jackson—a railroad center—he collected his troops within the fortifications which had already shown their inutility, and waited for the blow which was menacing him.

In pursuance of Grant's instructions, Hurlbut sent out from West Tennessee, in the latter part of April, a detachment of cavalry under Colonel Grierson, with instructions to ride through Mississippi for the purpose of destroying rebel property, breaking the railroads, and scattering rebel conscripts, and finally joining either Grant, or Banks, as circumstances should determine. This raid proved to be eminently successful, demonstrating clearly to the country that the Confederacy was but a shell—empty within and only strong on the outside—a piece of information upon which Grant was by no means slow to act.

Sherman, with the Fifteenth corps, joined the army on the 8th of May; wagons and supplies had been brought forward in the meanwhile, and definite information obtained, touching the enemy's movements. Grant's force was now not far from forty-five thousand men, and everything in excellent condition, when the word for the advance was given. His plan was to sweep around to the eastward of the Big Black, with Sherman's and McClernand's corps, marching by the roads towards Edwards' Depot and Bolton, on the Vicksburg and Jackson Railroad, while McPherson was to be thrown well out towards the interior—if necessary as far as Jackson—by the way of Raymond. Rations of sugar, coffee and salt, together with " three days of hard bread to last five " were issued to the troops; everything else was to be gathered from the country. In pursuance of these instructions, the different corps pushed rapidly forward, encountering but little or no resistance. On the 12th of May, McPherson's leading division, under command of the gallant and irrepressible Logan, encountered the enemy in strong force under Gregg and Walker, recently arrived from Port Gibson and Georgia, posted on the north side of Fondreau's Creek, near Raymond, and after a brilliant combat of several hours, in which a part of Crocker's division became finally engaged, drove them from the field, with the loss of 120 killed, and 750 wounded and prisoners. Our losses were 69 killed, (from Colonel Richards' Twentieth Illinois infantry, and Major Kaga's Twentieth Ohio,) 341 wounded, and 32 missing. The rebel force was about 6,000 strong, and fought well. McPherson and Logan behaved with great gallantry, and displayed excellent generalship in this affair, while Stevenson, Dennis, Lieutenant-Colonel Sturgis of the Eighth Illinois, and all the officers and men showed the highest soldierly qualities.

This battle, in which a second detachment of the enemy had been routed, gave Grant great confidence in the following steps of the campaign. Instead of pushing McClernand and Sherman, who had both crossed Fourteen Mile Creek and got within seven miles of Edwards' Depot, directly upon the latter place, he determined to make sure of Jackson first and to scatter the force now known to be assembling there under Johnston in person. To this end McPherson was pushed towards that place by the Clinton road; Sherman was ordered to move rapidly by the way of Raymond and Mississippi Springs, to the same place; while McClernand was directed to withdraw by his right flank from his menacing position in front of Edwards' Depot, and to march to Raymond whence he could support either McPherson or Sherman. These movements were made with precision and celerity, and on the 14th, Grant entered Jackson in triumph, after a sharp fight of several hours between McPherson's leading division under Crocker, and a force of rebels under Johnston. The latter, finding that the city could not be held, had posted guns in front of Sherman and thrown this force out upon the Clinton road for the purpose of resisting McPherson's advance long enough to permit the evacuation of the city by the Canton road. Large quantities of military stores, including six or eight guns and an abundant supply of sugar, fell into our hands. Grant was one of the first persons to perceive the ruse which his wily antagonist had adopted, and at once galloped into the town closely followed by the troops. Charging Sherman with the demolition of the bridge across the Pearl River, and the destruction of all the rebel military property not needed by the army—not forgetting the railroads north, south, east and west, Grant apprised McClernand that evening of his success, and directed him to move Carr, Osterhaus and Hovey, the next morning towards Bolton Station, and A. J. Smith towards Edwards' Depot. General F. P. Blair commanding a division of Sherman's troops, not yet arrived, and Ransom with a brigade of McPherson's corps, were also directed to move upon the same point. Soon after arriving at Jackson, Grant learned that Johnston had sent the night before, three different couriers with positive orders for Pemberton, requiring him to march out and fall upon the rear of the national army. Without giving McPherson an hour's rest, Grant directed him to countermarch his corps and push with all possible haste towards Bolton, for the purpose of uniting with McClernand's corps, and anticipating the rebel attack. Sherman was left to finish the work which he had so thoroughly begun, and then to follow the main body of the army by the Clinton road. Grant in person left Jackson on the morning of the 15th, and encamped that night at Clinton. Before daylight on the 16th, he was informed by two citizens just from Vicksburg that they had passed Pemberton's entire army, estimated at twenty-five or thirty thousand men, the evening before, at Baker's Creek, and still marching towards Bolton. Their information was so explicit and circumstantial that Grant despatched a staff officer at once to McPherson and McClernand with orders to prepare for a general battle, but not to bring on the action till all the troops were thoroughly in hand. A short time afterwards he rode rapidly to the front himself, arriving on the field about ten o'clock. He found Hovey's division with artillery, posted and drawn out in line of battle at Champion's plantation, on the Edwards' Depot road, two miles east of Baker's Creek; McPherson's corps was in readiness to support Hovey; McClernand, with Carr and Osterhaus, occupied a position on the same line, on the middle road from Raymond to Edwards' Depot, but about a mile and a half to the left of Hovey; while Blair and A. J. Smith were still farther to the left, converging on the same point. Sherman at the same time was well on the way from Jackson. Grant threw forward Logan's division to the right of Hovey, and gave the latter orders to advance. The skirmishing had already become pretty hot and by twelve o'clock the troops of both armies were in full battle array. A prelude of sharp skirmishing with an occasional shot from the cannon of either side introduced the terrible shock of arms which followed. The rebels held the advantage in position, their lines being formed along the heavily wooded ridges lying in the bend of Baker's Creek. Their center on the main road held Champion's Hill, the key point of the field. Upon this point Hovey impelled his enthusiastic men with terrible vigor and by two o'clock had carried it in the handsomest manner, capturing four guns and several hundred prisoners. The enemy did all in his power to withstand the onset, but were steadily pressed back. Logan advanced almost simultaneously with Hovey, pushing through an open field, along the northern slopes of Champion's Hill, and also driving back the enemy in his front. In the meantime the enemy had rallied in Hovey's front and being strongly re-enforced threw themselves upon him with great determination, in their turn pressing him back and threatening to wrest from him the heights which he had gained at such a fearful cost. At this critical juncture McPherson, who had fortunately brought forward Crocker's division and posted it behind the interval between Hovey and Logan, under Grant's direction, ordered it at once to the support of Hovey whose hard pressed regiments were now greatly fatigued and some of them entirely out of ammunition. Boomer's brigade, on the left, was marched rapidly by the flank to the top of the hill, and reached there just in time to catch the full force of the rebel onset. For fifteen minutes the rattle of musketry was incessant. At the same time several batteries had been collected near Grant's head-quarters, and converging their fire upon the woods from which the rebels were emerging, Boomer was enabled to drive them back with great loss. McPherson and Logan were meanwhile swinging the right of the line well forward, steadily driving the rebels, and finally overlapping their left and striking them in the flank and rear, capturing two batteries and nearly a thousand prisoners. This movement in connection with Boomer's splendid assault, resulted in driving the enemy from the field, broken and routed. By four o'clock they were fleeing in confusion rapidly towards Vicksburg. McClernand, although frequently ordered, did not succeed in getting either Carr or Osterhaus heavily engaged. Smith and Blair were too far to the left to produce any decided effect, although their artillery and skirmishers were engaged with Loring's division for a short time. Ransom marched across the country towards the heaviest firing and joined McPherson after the action had ceased.

The victory could scarcely have been more complete, and as has been seen, it was gained almost entirely by three divisions, Hovey's, Logan's and Crocker's, not exceeding fifteen thousand men in all, while the rebels could not have been fewer than twenty-five thousand. The rebel historians excuse this defeat also on the ground that they were vastly outnumbered; and it is true that Grant had in the short space of twenty-four hours, transformed the rear of his army into the full front of it, concentrating some thirty-five thousand men in all within supporting distance of each other, but it is also true that he won the battle with less than one-half of this force. His combinations were admirable; nothing in warfare was ever more praiseworthy, and had McClernand forced the fighting in his immediate front, as did Hovey, Boomer and Logan, under Grant's immediate supervision, it is difficult to see how any part of the rebel forces could have escaped. As it was they lost about 500 killed, including General Tilghman, 2,200 wounded, and 2,000 prisoners, besides 18 guns and a large number of small arms. Grant's loss (mostly in Hovey's division and Boomer's brigade,) was 426 killed, 1,842 wounded, and 189 missing, total, 2,457.

The pursuit was continued to Edward's Depot that night, the leading troops capturing at that place an ammunition train of ten or twelve railroad cars. At dawn of the 17th, the pursuit was renewed in the direction of Vicksburg; and by seven o'clock McClernand's advance, under Osterhaus and Carr,

came up with the rebel rear guard posted in strong entrenchments nearly a mile in extent, covering the railroad and military bridges across the Big Black. These divisions were
developed without delay under a strong fire from the rebel
artillery, during which Osterhaus was wounded. Carr held
the right, his right brigade commanded by General Lawler,
resting upon the Big Black. After some desultory artillery
firing and skirmishing, Lawler found a weak place on the
extreme left of the rebel works, and lost no time in leading
his brigade, composed of Iowa and Wisconsin men, to the
assault. Advancing across an open field several hundred
yards in width, they received a deadly fire, but without faltering they rushed gallantly through the ditch and over the
rebel breastworks, sweeping away all opposition, and capturing eighteen guns and nearly two thousand prisoners. In
this gallant affair, Colonel Kinsman of the Twenty-third
Iowa was killed, and Colonel (now Governor) Merrill of the
Twenty-first was wounded,—both, while cheering forward
their men in the most conspicuous manner.

This put an end to the campaign in the open field. Pemberton immediately abandoned his camp on the Big Black, and
retreated in disorder to Vicksburg. Johnston had gone in
the direction of Canton, but did not attempt a diversion in
Pemberton's favor, though he might have fallen upon Sherman's flank and harrassed him considerably.

During the night four floating bridges were built across the
Big Black by the troops under the direction of the engineer
officers. McClernand built one out of the ruins of the railroad bridge, near the railroad crossing; McPherson built two
further up the river, one of timber obtained by pulling down
cotton-gin houses, the other of cotton bales rafted together;
while Sherman made his of the india rubber pontoons.
After night-fall, Grant rode up the river to see Sherman,
whom he found at Bridgeport, engaged in crossing his command. The two commanders crossed the bridge, and seated
themselves on a fallen tree, in the light of a pile of burning
fence rails, and had a friendly conference, while the eager and

swift marching men of the Fifteenth corps filed by them and disappeared in the darkness. Grant recounted the results of the campaign and detailed his plans for the next day, after which he returned through the forest to his own head-quarters.

On the next day, the 18th of May, the army marched by the various roads to the rear of Vicksburg, and after slight skirmishing drove the rebel pickets inside of their works. Communication by signal was opened at once with the gun-boats and transports lying above Vicksburg, and measures were taken to establish communications with the Yazoo River. The rebels had already evacuated Haines' Bluff, and the navy took possession of the place, and proceeded to burn the gun-carriages, camps, and stores, and to blow up the magazines. This, however, was done in mistaken zeal, and inflicted an actual damage upon us rather than upon the enemy.

We may now pause to consider what had been accom-plished. Within these eighteen days, Grant had won five bat-tles, taken 40 field-guns, many colors and small arms, and nearly 5,000 prisoners; killed and wounded 5,200 of the enemy; separated their armies, in the aggregate, nearly 60,000, strong; captured one fortified capital city; compelled the abandonment of the strong positions of Grand Gulf and Haines' Bluff, with their armament of 20 heavy guns; de-stroyed the railroads and bridges; and made the investment of Vicksburg complete. In doing this McPherson's and McCler-nand's corps, had marched an average of 156 miles, while Sherman's had marched 175 miles. During this time the united strength of these three corps did not exceed 45,000 men. The limits of this work will not permit us to dwell upon the brilliancy of this campaign nor to descant upon the surpassing boldness and vigor of the generalship displayed by Grant, in conducting it. There is nothing in history since Hannibal invaded Italy to compare with it.

CHAPTER XV.

THE rebels though badly beaten were at last concentrated within the fortifications of Vicksburg, and availing themselves of its great advantages they were enabled to make a protracted and desperate defence. In order that the reader may have a definite understanding of the rebel position and the difficulties that yet remained for the Union army to overcome, let him imagine a plateau two hundred and fifty feet above the surface of the Mississippi, originally level, or sloping off gently towards the Big Black, but now cut and seamed in all directions by ravines from eighty to a hundred feet deep, with steep sides made more difficult by a heavy growth of fallen timber, which the rebels had cut down for the purpose of encumbering the ground and giving them fair range upon troops

trying to advance over it.   These ravines leading into three
creeks emptying into the Mississippi, one just above Vicksburg, another within its limits, and the third entirely below
it, were divided by high and difficult ridges, along which had
been thrown up a series of open and closed redoubts, armed
with artillery and connected by single and double lines of well
constructed rifle trench for infantry.   The entire line, including three miles of river front, was nearly eight miles in extent, for the defence of which the rebel General had something over twenty thousand effective men.

Grant's army was posted in the following order: Sherman's corps, composed of Steele's, Blair's and Tuttle's
divisions, held the right, extending from the ridge road around
to the river; McPherson, with Logan's, Crocker's and Quimby's divisions, held the center on both sides of the Jackson
road; while McClernand, with Carr's, A. J. Smith's, Osterhaus' and Hovey's divisions, held the left extending well
around to the south side of the city.*   The ground had been
reconnoitered in front of the different divisions, and although
seen to be exceedingly difficult it was not regarded as impassable.   Grant had been informed by his cavalry that Johnston
was gathering a strong force on the east side of the Big
Black with which to fall upon his rear, and knowing that
Pemberton's army must yet be in considerable disorder, if not
actually too much demoralized to make a determined resistance, he decided upon an assault of the enemy's line.

Accordingly he issued orders for all the field batteries to
open fire upon the rebel works at half-past one, and that at
precisely two o'clock, the entire army should move to the
attack.   These orders were promptly obeyed; the batteries
poured forth an incessant fire for over a half-hour at close
range, dismounting and silencing nearly all the rebel guns;
and promptly at the time appointed, the infantry sprang cheerfully forward, confident of sweeping over the rebel works as
they had done at the Big Black bridge.   Steele, Blair, Logan

---

* Lauman's, Herron's and McArthur's divisions were afterwards added to the
investing force.

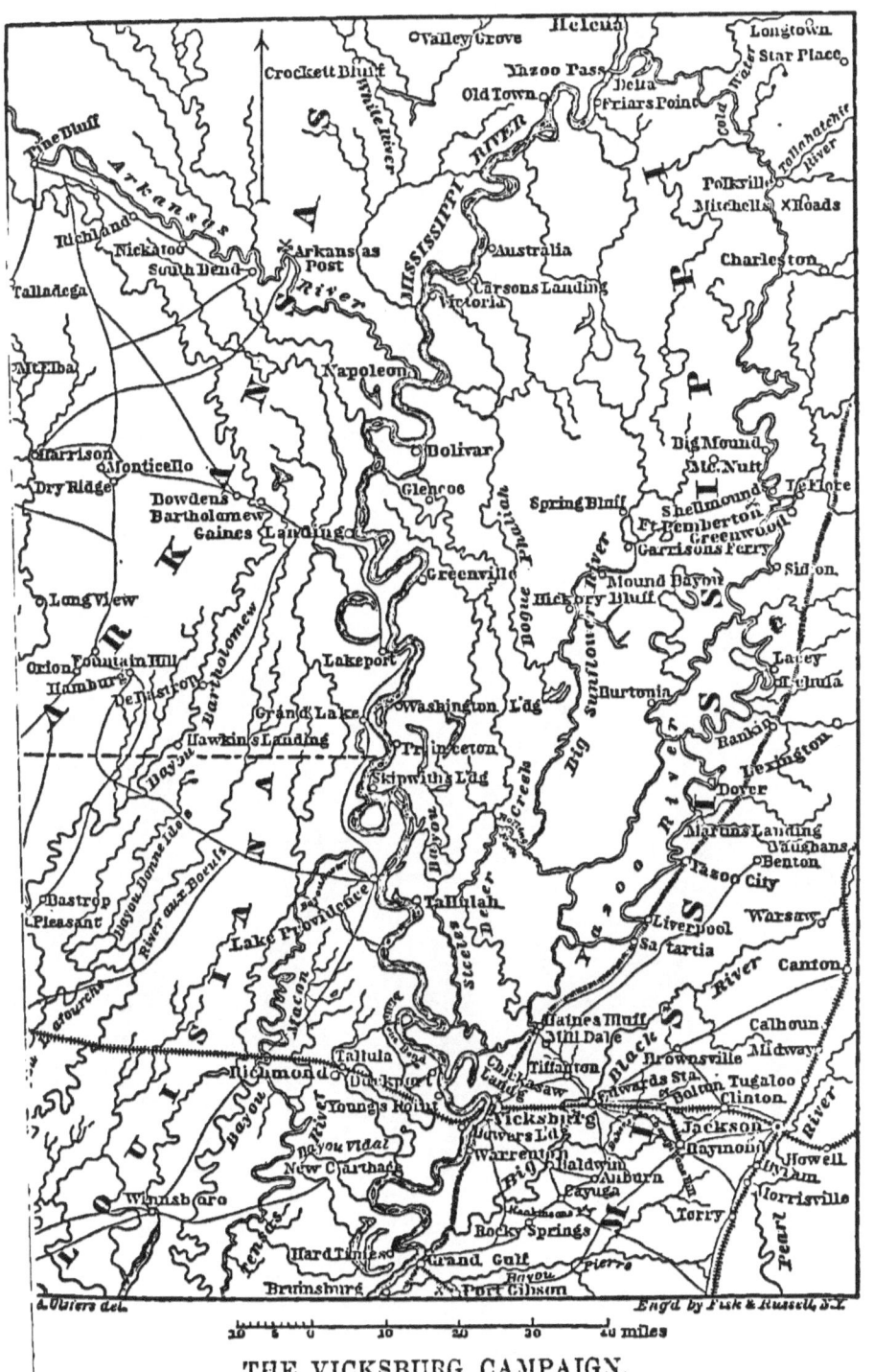

THE VICKSBURG CAMPAIGN.

and Carr made fair headway, but the rebels replied with spirit and with deadly effect. The ground was too much broken and encumbered with fallen timber and regular abattis; no order could be maintained among the troops, though every effort was made to carry them forward even in disarray; but it was impossible. The Thirteenth Regulars, Eighty-third Indiana and One Hundred and Twenty-seventh Illinois, planted their colors on the rebel parapet, but officers and men alike perceived their inability to do more, and suspended the attack.

The national loss was considerable with no adequate gain except a more advanced position and a better understanding of the ground in front of the rebel works.

The failure of this attempt did not, however, cut off all hope of carrying the place without resorting to the laborious process of a siege. The troops were permitted to rest for awhile; roads were opened along the lines of investment, and to the new bases of supplies at Chickasaw Landing and Warrenton; provisions and ammunition were brought forward, and everything was got in readiness for a new trial. At six o'clock P. M., of the 21st, Grant issued orders directing that at ten o'clock the next day a general attack should be made along the entire line, and particularly on all the roads leading into Vicksburg. In pursuance of these instructions the troops moved forward at the appointed time, but owing to the broken ground over which they were compelled to march, it was soon found to be impossible to move either in well ordered lines, or in weighty effective columns. As before, officers and men from right to left did their best. Sherman's troops reached the parapet of the works in their front, and planted their colors upon them, but could not cross. Logan's division of McPherson's corps, headed by Stevenson's brigade, made a gallant and orderly advance, but the position they assailed was the strongest part of the rebel line, and they were compelled to fall back, after losing heavily. Lawler's brigade of McClernand's corps, remembering their success at Big Black River bridge, dashed forward in handsome style, and at one time seemed about to add a new victory to the number already

9

inscribed upon their tattered colors.   Sergeant Griffith* with
a handful of men from the leading regiment, actually crossed
the rebel parapet and captured a number of prisoners, but the
regiment found it impossible to follow him.   After holding
on at the ditch of the rebel works for several hours, they were
compelled to fall back.   This partial success was magnified
by McClernand into the capture of "several points of the
enemy's entrenchments."   He, therefore, called upon Grant
for re-enforcements, expressing his confidence that with them
he could take the city.   Grant, from his head-quarters had
witnessed the attack along McClernand's front, and therefore
doubted the propriety of sending re-enforcements, but fearing
that he might underestimate the advantages which had been
gained, he reluctantly consented to send one of McPherson's
divisions, and instructed that officer accordingly.   He also
informed him and Sherman of what McClernand claimed to
have done, and directed them to renew the attack.   McPherson sent Quimby's division from his left, Boomer's brigade
leading.   The attack was renewed again, and this time with
still more disastrous results.   The gallant Boomer† was
killed, and the list of casualties throughout the army largely
increased.   Simultaneously with the land attack, Admiral
Porter attacked the river front, both from above and below,
and although he used ammunition without stint, he could not
silence the rebel guns.

It had now become apparent that the rebels could not be
dislodged, except by a siege, or starvation.   Grant therefore
determined to try both.   He sent to West Tennessee for all

---

* The gallantry of this boy—not yet eighteen years old—was greatly praised
by the entire army.   Grant promoted him at once, and subsequently obtained
for him the appointment of Cadet at West Point, where he graduated with
honor.   He is now a Lieutenant of Engineers in the regular army.

† Colonel Boomer, although only twenty-five or twenty-six years old, was
one of the most highly accomplished and promising officers in the army.   His
conduct at Champion's Hill and in the battles of West Tennessee, had
attracted the attention and won for him the regard of both Grant and
McPherson.   Had he lived, he would doubtless have risen to great distinction.

the troops that could be spared from there. Halleck, with great alacrity, gathered all that could be dispensed with in West Virginia, Kentucky and Missouri, and sent them forward. Herron's division of the Thirteenth, Lauman's of the Seventeenth, Kimball's and Sewy Smith's of the Sixteenth corps, under Washburn, and the Ninth corps under Parke, were brought forward in succession as fast as steamboats could be found to transport them; so that within a fortnight the besieging army was increased to something over seventy-five thousand effective men. In order to prevent the escape of the garrison, Grant completed the investment of the rebel lines; established batteries on the peninsula in front of the city; and stationed a force at Milliken's Bend. For the purpose of rendering his own lines secure, he caused all of the roads leading towards the Big Black to be obstructed by felling trees in them.

Sherman with a corps of observation, consisting of about twenty thousand men, drawn from the investing force, and further strengthened by the Ninth corps, was thrown out to the north-eastward for the purpose of watching the movements of Johnston, now threatening the line of the Black River with something over twenty thousand men. Sherman established a strong line of detached works, extending from near Bridgeport on the Big Black, by the way of Tiffinton and Milldale, to the Yazoo; Osterhaus kept watch over the Big Black below the railroad crossing; while Washburn established a strongly fortified camp on Sherman's left, at Haines' Bluff. During all this time the siege operations were pushed steadily forward night and day; parallels and trenches were opened at every favorable point; batteries were built and cavaliers erected; heavy guns were borrowed from the navy and mounted on commanding points; roads were made; siege materials were prepared; mines were sunk; towers for sharpshooters were built; every means that ingenuity could devise, was brought to bear upon the work in hand. Wooden mortars were made for throwing grenades and small shells; and sharpshooters were kept constantly on the watch for the luckless rebels who might show themselves above their works. So accurate and destructive was their fire that after the first four or five days every rebel gun was silenced, and when the place was finally taken, hundreds of rebels were found in the hospitals, who had been wounded in their hands and arms while raising them above the parapet to ram cartridges.

Immediately after the assault of May 22d, McClernand issued a bombastic order of congratulation to his command, claiming for them most of the honor of the campaign, and indirectly censuring Grant, and casting unjust reflections upon Sherman and McPherson. These officers protested to Grant, sending him a copy of the order which they had cut from a newspaper. This was the first information which Grant had received of the existence of such an order, McClernand having failed to directly transmit to him a copy as required by regulations. Grant enquired of McClernand if the newspaper copy was correct, and if so, why he had not complied with the rules of the service, in forwarding it to army headquarters. McClernand's answer was defiant in the extreme. Grant, therefore, relieved him from command, and assigned Ord to the Thirteenth corps. This secured entire harmony throughout the army.

McPherson's mine in front of Logan's division was exploded at four o'clock, P. M., on the 26th of June, throwing a number of rebels and a large column of earth high into the air, shaking the ground for several hundred yards like an earthquake, and leveling the salient of Fort Hill. In anticipation of this effect, Grant had issued orders for a demonstration along the lines, with an immediate assault upon that part of the rebel front, shaken by the explosion. The assault was made by John E. Smith's brigade but was unsuccessful, and after suffering severe loss the troops were withdrawn.

By this time the heads of saps at various points had been pushed close up to the rebel works, and in several instances even into the very ditches. Orders were issued that they should be widened and connected so as to permit them to be used for the protection of troops for a general and final assault.

It was known from deserters, and confirmed by voluntary information from the rebel pickets, that their provisions were nearly exhausted. Having completed all the necessary arrangements, Grant directed that the attack should be made on the morning of the 5th of July, but early on the morning of the 3d, the rebel General sent out a flag of truce with a proposition for the appointment of commissioners to arrange the terms of capitulation. Grant declined to leave the matter to commissioners or to allow any other terms than those of "unconditional surrender" and humane treatment to all prisoners of war, but signified his willingness to meet and confer with General Pemberton in regard to the arrangement of details. This meeting took place between the lines, in front of McPherson's corps, and gave rise to the following ultimatum, submitted in writing by General Grant:

"In conformity with the agreement of this afternoon, I will submit the following propositions for the surrender of the city of Vicksburg, public stores, etc. On your accepting the terms proposed, I will march in one division as a guard, and take possession at eight o'clock A. M., to-morrow. As soon as paroles can be made out and signed by the officers and men, you will be allowed to march out of our lines; the officers taking with them their regimental clothing, and staff, field, and cavalry officers one horse each. The rank and file will be allowed all their clothing, but no other property. If these conditions are accepted, any amount of rations you may deem necessary can be taken from the stores you now have, and also the necessary cooking utensils for preparing them, and thirty wagons also, counting two two-horse or mule teams as one. You will be allowed to transport such articles as cannot be carried along. The same conditions will be allowed to all sick and wounded officers and privates, as fast as they become able to travel. The paroles of these latter must be signed, however, whilst officers are present authorized to sign the roll of prisoners."

Pemberton answered as follows:

"GENERAL—I have the honor to acknowledge the receipt of your communication of this date, proposing terms for the surrender of this garrison and post. In the main, your terms are accepted; but, in justice both to the honor and spirit of my troops, manifested in the defense of Vicksburg, I have the honor to submit the following amendments; which, if acceded to by you, will perfect the agreement between us. At ten o'clock to-morrow, I propose to evacuate the works in and around Vicksburg, and to surrender the city and garrison under my command, by marching out with my colors and arms and stacking them in front of my present lines—after which you will take possession; officers to retain their side-arms and personal property, and the rights and property of citizens to be respected."

Grant rejoined declining to fetter himself by any stipulations in regard to citizens; limiting rebel officers to their private baggage, side-arms, and one horse each to mounted officers, and giving him till nine o'clock to consider the matter.

On these terms the surrender took place early on the 4th of July. By three o'clock our troops had taken possession of the city, and all public stores; the gun-boats and transports had landed at the levee; and the troops charged with keeping order had gone into their camps. The rebels were retained as prisoners for six or eight days, till their paroles could be made out and properly delivered, during which time they were glad enough to draw their subsistence from the national stores.*

Grant's losses during the entire campaign were 943 killed, 7,095 wounded, and 537 missing; total, 8,575, of whom 4,236 were killed and wounded before Vicksburg.

The rebels surrendered 21,000 effective men, and 6,000 wounded in hospital; besides over 120 guns of all calibers, with many thousand small arms.

As soon as it was known that Vicksburg would surrender, Grant reinforced Sherman, and sent him to drive off Johnston. The march was begun promptly, and pushed with celerity to Jackson, whither Johnston fled. He was dislodged from there, however, in a short time, and continued his retreat toward Meridian. Sherman did not follow him further, on account of the exceedingly hot weather, and the great scarcity of

---

* "Southern History of the War," Vol. ii. p. 74. "The statement that the garrison of Vicksburg was surrendered on account of an inexorable distress, in which the soldiers had to feed on mules, with the occasional luxury of rats, is either to be taken as a designing falsehood, or as the cruelties of that foolish newspaper romance so common in the war. In neither case does it merit refutation."

water in the country east of the Pearl River. It was also thought that the troops were too much fatigued by the hard work of the siege to venture upon a campaign of indefinite duration at that time. Grant, therefore, permitted Sherman to return to the Black River, and to go into camp with his own corps, sending the rest of his forces to their respective corps.

During the siege of Vicksburg, the rebels on the west side of the Mississippi, were very active in striving to annoy the troops along the river, and to interrupt our communications, but under the efficient command of General Hugh T. Reid, at Lake Providence, and General Dennis, at Milliken's Bend, they were foiled and finally driven back with considerable loss.

At Milliken's Bend, on the 6th of June, the colored troops fought their first battle in the West and with the assistance of the gun-boats and a small regiment of white troops, defeated a force of 2,500 or 3,000 rebels under McCulloch. Dennis' force consisted of 1,410 effective men. He lost 127 killed, 287 wounded, and 300 missing; while the rebels lost 150 killed, and 300 wounded.

On the 4th of July, Lieutenant-General Holmes, then commanding the trans-Mississippi department, with a force of about 8,000 men, under Generals Price, Parsons, Marmaduke, Fagan, McRae, and Walker, made a vigorous attack upon General Prentiss at Helena, whose garrison consisted of 3,800 effective men, behind strongly constructed and well armed earth-works. The action lasted nearly all day, but thanks to the bravery of the troops, the good management of Generals Prentiss and Solomon, and the timely assistance of the gun-boats, the rebels were defeated. Their loss amounted to 173 killed, 687 wounded, and 1,100 prisoners, total, 1,960; while Prentiss lost fewer than 250, all told.

Immediately after the fall of Vicksburg, Grant sent Herron's division to re-enforce Banks at Port Hudson, which surrendered on the 8th of July; thus giving us 10,000 more prisoners and 50 guns. These were also fruits of the great campaign which Grant had just finished, and should be credited to him almost as much as to Banks.

Ransom was sent to Natchez to break up the business of bringing cattle from Texas for the support of the rebel army. That active officer did his duty admirably, capturing some 5,000 head, 2,000 of which were sent to Banks, and the others issued to the army of the Tennessee.

It is to be regretted that the limits of this book will not permit us to go more fully into the details of the operations we have just described. The marches, skirmishes and battles of the various regiments, brigades and divisions; the bravery, constancy and devotion of officers; the patience, ingenuity and patriotism of the private soldiers, are all worthy of attention from the historian, and it is to be hoped will some day receive it.

The campaign was a vital blow to the rebel power in the South-west. It severed the Confederacy, opened the Mississippi River to New Orleans, and released a large force of national troops for operations farther to the eastward. Grant became thenceforth the central figure of our military history. The country hailed him with unfeigned delight and sincerity as the only General who was always successful. The stories against his private character, which had been so generally circulated, were now disclaimed and disbelieved, and he was justly looked upon not only as a successful and meritorious General, but as a pure and unselfish man, equally above private vices and ignoble fears. Mr. Lincoln, who seems up to this time to have regarded him with suspicion if not with absolute distrust, and to have done him injustice in thought if not in action, wrote him the letter which follows, reflecting as much credit upon the honest nature of the writer as it did justice to Grant:

"Executive Mansion, July 13, 1863.

"To Major-General Grant—*My Dear General:* I do not remember that you and I ever met personally. I write this now as a grateful acknowledgment for the almost inestimable service you have done the country. I wish to say further: when you first reached the vicinity of

Vicksburg, I thought you should do what you finally did,—march the troops across the neck, run the batteries with the transports and thus go below; and I never had any faith, except a general hope that you knew better than I, that the Yazoo Pass expedition and the like could succeed. When you got below and took Port Gibson, Grand Gulf and vicinity, I thought you should go down the river and join General Banks; and when you turned northward, east of the Big Black, I feared it was a mistake. I now wish to make a personal acknowledgment that you were right and I was wrong. Yours very truly,

"A. LINCOLN."

Grant was neither elated nor made vain by his victories. Nor did he, like some of our Generals, imagine that he had done enough, and ask to go home, or to be permitted to take a rest. He busied himself in consolidating his conquest, reorganizing his command, and aiding the poor negroes who had fled from slavery, by publishing regulations for their government and encouragement. He also issued orders authorizing furloughs to be given to the most worthy of the soldiers, and took particular care to see that they should not be required to pay unreasonable fare upon the steamboats navigating the river which they had done so much to open.

In August, a public dinner was tendered him by the loyal citizens of Memphis, which he accepted, in a letter as remarkable for its brevity as for the patriotic sentiments which it contained. He wrote: "In accepting this testimonial, which I do at great sacrifice of personal feelings, I simply desire to pay a tribute to the first public exhibition in Memphis, of loyalty to the Government which I represent in the Department of the Tennessee. I should dislike to refuse, for considerations of personal convenience, to acknowledge anywhere or in any form, the existence of sentiments which I have so long and so ardently desired to see manifested in this department. *The stability of this Government, and the unity of this nation, depend solely on the cordial support and the earnest loyalty of the people.*"

These words are not less appropriate to-day than they were then, and should be engraved deeply upon the heart of every American citizen.

CHAPTER XVI.

AT the termination of the Vicksburg campaign, military
operations in the Mississippi Valley were conducted by three
different armies: the army of the Tennessee under Grant, the
army of the Cumberland under Rosecrans, and the army of
the Ohio under Burnside. It will be remembered that in
January 1863, General Grant recommended the consolidation
of the various departments of the West into one command.
His brilliant success on the Mississippi River, followed as it
was by the bloody defeat of Rosecrans at Chickamauga, secured for that sound strategic advice, consideration which it
ought to have received months before, and which would probably have saved the national cause the disaster of Chickamauga, which was a legitimate result of Halleck's dispersive
policy. During the Vicksburg campaign, Johnston detached
a considerable force from Bragg, leaving him largely outnumbered by the force in his front. General Hurlbut, who commanded in West Tennessee, through his admirable system of

scouts, obtained timely notice of this detachment, as well as an accurate estimate of Bragg's remaining force, which he sent to Rosecrans without delay. The Government urged Rosecrans to avail himself of the chance thus given him, but he delayed till too late. When he did move, the rebels retreated rapidly, through Chattanooga.

Rosecrans pressed on with widely scattered forces, and full of exultation at the success of his plans. But Vicksburg had fallen, and Lee had been driven from Pennsylvania by the splendid victory of Gettysburg. Throwing themselves strictly on the defensive in the East and South-west, the rebel authorities availed themselves of the lull in operations elsewhere and strongly re-enforced Bragg by sending Buckner from East Tennessee, Longstreet from Virginia and Polk from Alabama. Bragg now turned suddenly upon Rosecrans with an overwhelming force and Chickamauga was the result. Had active military operations been entrusted to the administration of one judicious commander, such as Grant proved himself to be, this could not have happened, for he would have either moved the various armies at one time, in sufficient strength to make each successful, or he would have strengthened one by detachments from the others to such an extent as to have rendered its success a matter of perfect certainty; while the others in their weakened condition would have been kept on the defensive, or used subordinately to assist the grand army. As usual, however, the country and its civil administration learned this obvious lesson only after it had been printed in the bloody characters of defeat.

Shortly after the battle of Chickamauga, Grant was directed to send re-enforcements across the country to Rosecrans, and on the 10th of October, he started from Vicksburg for the purpose of receiving orders for his future movements at Cairo. At the latter place he was directed to proceed to Louisville; and at Indianapolis he was met by Mr. Stanton, the energetic and capable Secretary of War, who, after conferring fully with him, issued the following order, dated at Washington, October 16th:

" By direction of the President of the United States, the Departments of the Ohio, of the Cumberland, and of the Tennessee, will constitute the Military Division of the Mississippi. Major-General U. S. Grant, United States Army,* is placed in command of the Military Division of the Mississippi, with his head-quarters in the field."

At Grant's request Rosecrans was relieved from the command of the Department and Army of the Cumberland, and replaced by that able, unconquerable, and modest soldier, General George H. Thomas; while Sherman was assigned to the army of the Tennessee.†

The Army of the Cumberland was besieged in Chattanooga, and its supplies were almost entirely cut off, so that the tenure of that place, which had cost already so much, was regarded as exceedingly precarious. Grant, therefore, telegraphed at once to Thomas to hold on at all hazards; to which Thomas grimly replied : " We'll hold the town till we starve."   The next day Grant went forward by rail, accompanied by his old staff, to Bridgeport, and thence rode across the mountains, by a circuitous and difficult road, to Chattanooga, reaching that place on the night of the 23d, after lying out upon the mountains in a drenching rain, and receiving a severe bruise from his horse falling upon him. This bruise was rendered the more painful from the fact that he had not recovered from a serious injury received in a similar manner at New Orleans several weeks before.   With his usual directness and promptitude, he set to work at once to rescue the army from its peril, and to prepare it for final victory.   As before stated, Bragg had closely invested Chattanooga.   By taking possession of Lookout Mountain, and

* Grant was promoted to be Major-General in the regular army as a reward for his victories during the campaign of Vicksburg; his commission was dated July 4th 1863.

† The entire force now under Grant, consisted of the Fourth, Ninth, Eleventh, Twelfth, Fourteenth, Fifteenth, Sixteenth, and Seventeenth corps, commanded respectively by Generals Gordon Granger, Potter, Howard, Slocum, J. M. Palmer, Blair, Hurlbut, and McPherson.   Thomas commanded the Fourth and Fourteenth corps; Sherman the Fifteenth, Sixteenth, and Seventeenth; Hooker the Eleventh and Twelfth, from the Army of the Potomac, and Burnside the Ninth and a part of the Twenty-third under Manson

throwing a corps into Lookout Valley, he had also cut off its communication with Bridgeport and Stevenson, the base of supplies, both by rail and river. The next best line was by a poor wagon road along the north side of the Tennessee, but the river being only a few hundred yards wide, the rebels also closed this road by an effective fire from their sharpshooters. This left no other available route but two paths, for they can not be called roads, across the Cumberland mountains, the shortest of which was about fifty miles, and the other about eighty, and as the rains were now becoming frequent, they soon got to be almost entirely impassable for even empty wagons. By the 1st of November they were so bad that a first-class six mule team, could not haul more than six hundred pounds of provisions, besides the forage for the team, from Bridgeport to Chattanooga; and in many cases after getting through, the mules were too much reduced to return with the empty wagon. It is estimated by the quartermaster's department, that ten thousand mules and artillery horses died there from starvation during the months of October and November. The prospect was unpromising in the highest degree. The troops were reduced to quarter rations and very scant ones at that; but fortunately a good supply of ammunition yet remained on hand. Under these circumstances there was no salvation for the army but in opening a line by which supplies could be brought to it. Even a retreat, had it ever been thought of, could not have been made through the mountains, except by the abandonment of artillery, trains, and baggage of every sort. After a rapid but careful study of the entire situation, Grant decided to adopt the plan already partially matured by General Thomas and his Chief Engineer, General William F. Smith, having for its immediate object the repossession of Lookout Valley and the re-establishment of rail, steamboat and wagon communication, by the way of Brown's Ferry with Bridgeport.

In order to carry this plan into effect, Hooker, with the Eleventh and Twelfth corps, was directed to cross the Tennessee at Bridgeport, and to march via Shellmound and

Whiteside, across the Raccoon Mountains, to Wauhatchie and the lower end of Lookout Valley. General Palmer was sent with a division of the Fourteenth corps from Chattanooga by the north side of the river to make a demonstration, and to cross at Kelly's Ferry, for the purpose of supporting General Hooker, should it become necessary; while Smith, with eighteen hundred picked men, under the immediate command of General Hazen, was directed to embark in pontoons at Chattanooga, float under cover of darkness by the rebel lines at Lookout, land at Brown's Ferry, and there secure a bridge head for the protection of the pontoon bridge to be constructed at that place. These delicate operations were so handsomely combined as to result in perfect success. Smith seized the heights, covering the ferry, on the night of October 27th, fortified them without delay, and laid his bridge in a short time. Hooker's column, composed of Howard's corps and Geary's division of Slocum's corps, debouched into the valley early the next day, having met with no serious resistance. Communication was opened at once with Smith, and arrangements made for bringing forward supplies.

The rebels were taken completely by surprise, but were not dismayed by the success of General Grant's combinations. From the top of Lookout Mountain they looked down into Hooker's camp, which unfortunately had been somewhat widely scattered, and took the sudden resolution of falling upon him, by surprise. Accordingly after midnight of the 28th, McLaw's division of Longstreet's corps, sallied from its camp on the heights of Lookout, and after a march of two miles rushed confidently upon the camp of Geary's division at Wauhatchie. But Geary (now Governor of Pennsylvania) although surprised, formed his gallant veterans as best he could, and stood bravely to the defense of his position. The rebel onset, made with unearthly yells, was at first successful; but Howard being near at hand, pushed at once towards the firing, and between the two forces the rebels were soon repulsed, leaving their dead and wounded upon the field. The next day Hooker redistributed his forces, and began the construction of works, the better to enable them to cover the newly established supply lines. Grant directed the fortification of the passes in the Raccoon Mountains, and stationed detachments near them, so that the river from Bridgeport to Chattanooga was soon firmly under his control. Steamboats were built, old ones were repaired, the railroad bridges were replaced, pontoon bridges across the Tennessee were laid, wagons and mules were brought from the rear. With these things the hungry army soon found all its wants bountifully supplied. The depression which had followed Chickamauga, was rapidly replaced by a confident spirit of aggression. Sherman with his army of swift marching veterans, was known to be approaching by the way of Corinth, Decatur, and Stevenson, and, as if to give to our confidence the assurance of success, the rebels were about to commit a fatal error.

Burnside, with the Army of the Ohio, acting with entire independence of Rosecrans, advanced from Camp Nelson in Kentucky, by the way of Cumberland Gap, into East Tennessee, about the 1st of August. He took possession of Knoxville and the rich region lying about it as far down the valley as the line of the Hiawassee. Early in November, Bragg detached Longstreet with a strong force to drive Burnside from East Tennessee. The rebel movement had hardly begun before it became known to Grant. He at once sent the Assistant Secretary of War, who was with him, and one of his own staff officers, to Burnside, with instructions to hold on to Knoxville, disputing all the ground he could with Longstreet, and keeping him engaged as closely as possible, during the execution of movements which were to be made against Bragg. Sherman was now approaching rapidly, and it was hoped that everything would be in readiness for the final blow by the middle of the month. But bad roads, swollen streams, railroad building and the want of bridges across the streams in Northern Alabama, together with the efforts of a small force of rebels under S. D. Lee and Roddy, delayed Sherman till about the 20th. Grant had become exceedingly impatient to relieve Burnside, and fixed the 21st for the attack upon the enemy; but the Tennessee River had begun to rise rapidly, and against the greatly increased currents it became exceedingly difficult to keep the pontoon bridges in place. They were frequently swept away, but as frequently repaired. Hence the concentration of the troops was delayed. In spite of all that could be done, Osterhaus' division had to be left in Lookout Valley, thus reducing Sherman's forces to about twenty thousand men, the last of whom reached the position assigned them on the 23d, immediately after which the more active operations began.

On the 20th the rebel army occupied a position extending from Missionary Ridge across the Chattanooga Valley to Lookout Mountain, with an advanced line well up against the national defenses, but they had evidently begun to feel some apprehension for their situation. Bragg adopted the cheap and rather transparent device of sending a message to Grant in which he deemed it proper to inform him "that prudence would dictate" the early removal of the non-combatants yet remaining in Chattanooga. Grant paid no further attention to this message than to hurry his preparations. His plan of operations was to attack the rebels on both flanks at the same time, and when they should be sufficiently shaken, to throw his whole army upon them,—and finish the work with a single crushing blow. In order to accomplish this, Sherman was directed to cross the Tennessee River, just at the mouth of the South Chickamauga, by means of a pontoon bridge, and to move at once against the enemy's position along Mission Ridge. Thomas, re-enforced by Howard's corps, occupying the works of Chattanooga, was to drive back the rebel center and throwing forward his left to connect with Sherman; while Hooker, with Slocum's corps and Osterhaus' division, was directed to drive the rebels from the end of Lookout Mountain—and connecting with Thomas—to continue pressing them as long as they could be found. The entire army was provided with two days' cooked rations in haversacks, and one hundred rounds of ammunition per man. Nothing which could be done was left undone. A cavalry expedition was prepared to follow Sherman across the Tennessee, for the purpose of severing the railroad from Dalton to Knoxville, and thus cutting off the chance of withdrawing Longstreet in time for him to take part in the battle. After this plan had been fully matured, a rebel deserter came in and informed Grant that Bragg was retiring. This, in connection with the message already referred to, caused Grant to order Thomas to move out a heavy force and feel the enemy's lines. This was done on the afternoon of the 23d. Wood's division was in front, Sheridan's division of the Fourth corps, and the Fourteenth corps under Palmer supporting, Howard in reserve. The troops were drawn out with such regularity and formed with such precision, that the rebel Generals, who witnessed it from Mission Ridge and Lookout, thought they were having a general parade and review ; but they were undeceived in a few minutes, by the rapid advance of Wood's division, and a vigorous fire from the heavy guns of Fort Wood. Wood continued his regular advance to the foot of Orchard Knoll, an outlying ridge parallel to Missionary Ridge, when he ordered a charge, which was gallantly made, and resulted in the capture of that part of the enemy's advanced line, notwithstanding a determined effort to hold it. Sheridan was posted on Wood's right, while Palmer was thrown forward in echelon. Entrenchments were rapidly thrown up, and by night were strong enough to resist any attack likely to be made upon them. This was a timely movement, as it caused Bragg to recall a division which he had just started to re-enforce Longstreet, and which would have given that General a great preponderance over Burnside. While this demonstration was taking place, the materials for Sherman's bridge had been quietly collected by General Smith, now Grant's Chief Engineer, near the place intended for the crossing. The troops were concealed behind the hills, and everything in readiness. Before dawn of the 24th a large force was thrown to the opposite side of the river, and by noon, through the aid of the steamer Dunbar, under the charge of one of Grant's staff officers, two divisions had reached the south side of the river.

The bridge was constructed rapidly, and by the middle of the afternoon Sherman's entire force held possession of the northern end of Missionary Ridge, as far as the railroad crossing. A strong line of entrenchments was thrown up at once to render the position secure against all mishaps.

Hooker began his movement from Lookout Valley the same day, at four o'clock in the morning. Crossing Lookout Creek with difficulty, owing to its swollen condition, he drove back the rebel pickets, captured the rebel camps and rifle-pits, with a number of prisoners, and by noon began the ascent of Lookout Mountain. Wood (S. C.), Gross, Geary, Osterhaus, and Cruft, cheered forward their men, scrambling as best they could over the rugged and broken ground, through trees and vines, up the steep mountain's side, in face of determined resistance. By two o'clock the whole mountain-slope was carried; and by four, was so thoroughly fortified as to make its tenure certain. Communication was established at once with Thomas' right, and a bridge was built across Chattanooga Creek, by which, late in the evening, Carlin's brigade was sent to re-enforce Hooker. This brigade was posted on the extreme right of Hooker's line, relieving Geary's jaded men. Shortly after taking possession of the hastily constructed works, Carlin received a determined attack from the rebels, who were easily repelled. Seeing now that it was useless to struggle longer, they descended from the mountain-top, under cover of darkness, crossed the Chattanooga Valley, and joined Bragg on Missionary Ridge, leaving their rations and camp equipage in the hands of their assailants. Carlin's battle, after darkness had fully set in, as viewed from the town below, was one of the most interesting sights of the war.

The same afternoon, Howard moved out from Chattanooga, with one brigade of his corps, by the road nearest the river, crossed Citico Creek, and formed a junction with Sherman. Grant's entire army was thus united with its left flank in firm possession of the end of Missionary Ridge, threatening Chickamauga Station and the enemy's rear, the center holding

Orchard Knoll and the strong fortifications of Chattanooga, while Hooker, on the swinging flank, looked, menacing and secure, from the heights of Lookout. So far, not a single mishap had occurred. Every movement had been made with perfect precision, and every movement was entirely successful. Grant felt confident of the result which must follow, and issued orders for the renewal of the action at early dawn.

Sherman had the post of difficulty, as it was evident the rebels would make their best fight in his front. During the night he had strengthened his position, and gathered his forces for an early attack, upon the heavily wooded ridges before him. The rebel General had not been idle, but seeing the full measure of his danger had strongly re-enforced his right. All night long the sound of falling trees betokened his activity in the construction of breastworks and rifle trench. The ground separating Sherman from the enemy's right was heavily wooded, and much broken by tranverse ridges and ravines, almost as susceptible of defense as the front face of the main ridge itself. Sherman examined it carefully in person. It was already sunrise before his bugles sounded forward. The main attack was made by the Fortieth Illinois, Forty-sixth Ohio, and Twentieth Ohio, of Corse's brigade, Ewing's division, led by Corse in person, with his usual intrepidity; and although pressed with great determination, it was unsuccessful in breaking the enemy's line. Corse was severely wounded, and carried from the field. His place was filled by Colonel Wolcott of the Forty-sixth Ohio. Loomis' brigade on the right, Rannis' and Mathias' brigades of John E. Smith's division; Morgan L. Smith's division, Bushbeck's brigade of Howard's corps, and, in fact, Sherman's entire force, pressed forward at the same time, continuing the action hotly till the middle of the afternoon; and although they gained much ground, they could not drive the enemy from his stronghold. Artillery was freely used on both sides. Sherman pressed his attack so closely and incessantly that Bragg gradually massed the bulk of his forces for the defense of his right. Grant anxiously watched the progress of the battle from Orchard Knoll, over two miles away, waiting for the signs of success before ordering Thomas to advance. He saw plainly the continuous movement of the rebels in that direction along the crest above him, and at three o'clock witnessed the repulse of Sherman's right, under John E. Smith. Meanwhile Hooker had descended from the top of Lookout, and was well on his way towards the extreme left of Bragg's line.

The time had come for the Army of the Cumberland to be revenged for the defeat of Chickamauga. Turning to Thomas, who had also been anxiously watching the events of the battle, Grant ordered him to attack. Six guns were fired in rapid succession from Orchard Knoll as a signal for the advance, and promptly the eager troops who had so long been straining at the leash, sprang forward, arrayed in splendid order, and covered by a heavy cloud of skirmishers. Baird on the left, Wood and Sheridan * in the centre, Johnson on the right, and, still further to the right, Hooker, with Geary and Osterhaus, led their gallant volunteers intrepidly to the assault. The rebel rifle-pits, the special object of their attack, at the foot of the hill, were carried like a flash, and yet eight hundred feet above stood the main rebel line pouring forth a deadly fire of musketry and artillery. With one of those wild and unaccountable impulses originating in the native sagacity of men and officers alike, the national soldiers, by regiment, brigade and division, rushed forward to the heights, pausing only now and then to regain their breath, and then to dash on again with renewed vigor. Clambering over rocks and through bushes, lifting themselves by thrusting their bayonets into the ground, or by catching hold of limbs and twigs, they finally reached the crest and swept the rebel lines away like chaff before the whirlwind. Baird turned towards Sherman, Sheridan pressed straight forward towards the Chickamauga, and Hooker swept along the crest towards the center.

---

* During the momentary pause after carrying the rifle-pits, Sheridan rode to the front, bowed to the rebels, took out his flask, and raised it to his lips. The rebels, only a few hundred yards away, saw him plainly, ceased firing for the moment, and cheered him lustily.

Nothing could stay these converging and exultant columns. The rebels were routed and driven entirely from the field, never stopping till they had passed Chickamauga Creek. Grant seeing his gallant soldiers clambering up the mountain side, could restrain himself no longer; turning to Granger who had been wasting his time with a battery of artillery, he ordered him with energy to join his corps, and then attended by his staff galloped rapidly to the front. Ascending the ridge, he was hailed by the wounded, forgetful of their bloody faces and broken limbs, with acclamations of delight: "We've gained the day, General;" "All we wanted was a leader;" "*We are even with them now for Chickamauga!*" But Grant pressed on to the very front, exposing himself fearlessly to the heaviest fire of the enemy. He wished to see for himself that the victory was complete. Darkness soon put an end to the general pursuit, though Sheridan continued it as far as the Chickamauga, guided by the fire of his own and the enemy's rifles, taking prisoners and harassing the rebels till after midnight.

Grant informed Halleck of his success in the following terms: "Although the battle lasted from early dawn till dark this evening, I believe I am not premature in announcing a complete victory over Bragg."

The pursuit was renewed by the army at an early hour the next day; Sherman marching by the way of Chickamauga Station; Hooker and Palmer by the Rossville road towards Ringgold and Dalton. Late in the afternoon, Hooker came up with the rear guard of the rebel army under Cleburne, strongly posted in the gorge of White Oak Ridge, and along the crest of Taylor's Ridge, twenty-two miles from Chattanooga, and after a gallant attack, received a bloody check; but this was only temporary. The rebels continued their retreat as far as Dalton, where they halted, and took up a strong position. Grant's army had not yet re-established its transportation, and was too weak in the means of moving its artillery to continue the campaign. The rebels had burned the railroad bridges and withdrawn all their cars, and Grant had none nearer than Bridgeport, in Alabama, with no means of getting them across the Tennessee, or the great gorge in the Raccoon mountains at Whiteside; the country had already been stripped of its scanty supplies; it was therefore entirely out of the question to think of subsisting his army, even a day's march from Chattanooga. Then, too, Burnside was still in imminent and increasing danger. He had already been shut up in Knoxville, and had informed Grant that his supplies were limited, and that he could not possibly hold out longer than ten or twelve days. Under these circumstances Grant was reluctantly compelled to suspend further pursuit of Bragg's demoralized army, to withdraw Thomas into Chattanooga, and to send Sherman, with a larger force, to raise the siege of Knoxville.

The battle of Chattanooga, is one of the most remarkable in history, and reflects infinite credit upon Grant's generalship, as well as upon the good management of his subordinates, and the courage and endurance of the men composing the army. The precision and promptitude with which every movement was carried out, from that against the rebels in Lookout Valley to the final assault of the rebel center on Missionary Ridge, are models for future Generals to imitate. The assault of Lookout, the passage of the Tennessee, and the lodgment upon the enemy's flank,—all necessary preliminaries to the final assault,—were combined and conducted with the regularity of clock-work. Grant was nobly seconded by Sherman, Thomas, Hooker, and his own staff, as well as by a splendid array of subordinate commanders; but it is only just to add that his own capacity, courage, and magnanimity, have secured for him the chief honor of that glorious triumph.

Bragg's loss in killed and wounded, during this battle, is not known, but could not have been less than 10,000, all told, as he left 6,142 prisoners, with 7,000 small arms, 40 guns, and many colors, in the hands of the victors. Grant's losses, exclusive of Burnside's in East Tennessee, as derived from the reports of the corps commanders, were 6,804 killed, wounded and missing. As usual with the rebels, notwithstanding their great advantage in position, they claimed to have lost the battle by being largely outnumbered, but if this was true it was due again to Grant's superior generalship. There is no surer way, all other things being favorable, to conduct war successfully than by managing so as to outnumber the enemy, at the vital point during the hour of battle.

The following Table, from the Reports of General Thomas, exhibits the organization of the contending Armies at the Battle of Chattanooga

COMMANDING THE UNITED STATES FORCES, ... MAJOR-GENERAL ULYSSES S. GRANT.

COMMANDING THE ARMY OF THE CUMBERLAND, ... MAJOR-GENERAL GEORGE H. THOMAS.

Commands.	Fourth Corps.	Eleventh Corps.*	Twelfth Corps.	Fourteenth Corps.	Cavalry Corps.	Commands.	Fifteenth Corps.
		COMMANDING 11TH AND 12TH CORPS, Major-General J. HOOKER.					PART OF THE ARMY OF THE TENNESSEE, Commanding Army of the Tennessee, Major-General T. W. SHERMAN.
Commanding Corps.	Major-General Gordon Granger.	Major-General O. O. Howard.	Major-General H. W. Slocum.	Major-General J. M. Palmer.	Brigadier-General W. L. Elliott.	Commanding Corps.	Major-General F. P. Blair.
Commanding 1st Division.	Major-General D. S. Stanley.	Brigadier-General A. S. Williams.	Brigadier-General R. W. Johnston.	Colonel E. M. McCook.		Commanding 1st Division.	Brigadier-General P. J. Osterhaus. †
Commanding 2d Division.	Major-General P. H. Sheridan.	Brigadier-General A. von Steinwher.	Brigadier-General J. W. Geary.	Brigadier-General J. C. Davis.	Brigadier-General Geo. Crook.	Commanding 2d Division.	Brigadier-General M. L. Smith.
Commanding 3d Division.	Brigadier-General T. J. Wood.	Major-General C. Schurz.		Brigadier-General A. Baird.		Commanding 3d Division.	Brigadier-General J. E. Smith.
						Commanding 4th Division.	Brigadier-General Hugh Ewing.

* The 11th and the 2d Division of the 14th Corps reported to General Sherman.　　　† General Osterhaus' division reported to General Hooker.

COMMANDING REBEL ARMY, . . . GENERAL BRAXTON BRAGG.

Commanding Wings.	Right Wing, Lieutenant-General W. J. Hardee.	Left Wing, Major-General J. C. Breckenridge.	Cavalry, Maj.-Gen. J. Wheeler.
Commanding Divisions.	Major-General P. R. Cleburne.	Major-General B. F. Cheatham.	Major-General A. P. Stewart.	Major-General S. B. Buckner.	Brigadier-General J. A. Wharton.
Commanding Divisions.	Brigadier-General S. R. Gist.	Major-General C. L. Stevenson.	Brigadier-General P. Anderson.	Brigadier-General Lewis.	Brigadier-General W. Martin.

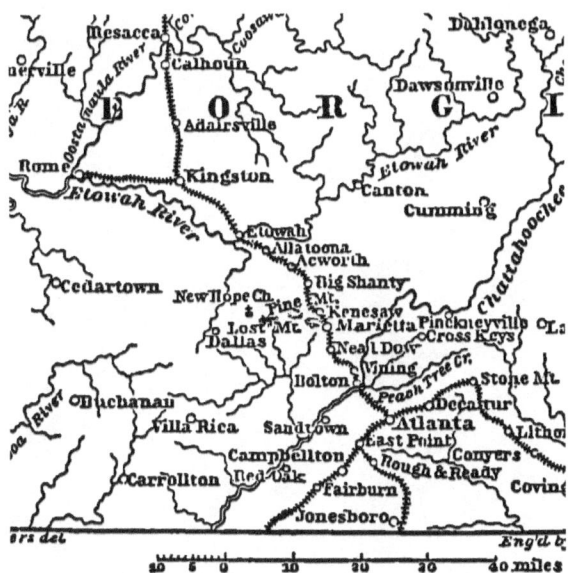

CHATTANOOGA, KNOXVILLE, ATLANTA.

CHAPTER XVII.

As before stated, Longstreet, who had been detached from
Bragg's army before the battle of Chattanooga, marched
leisurely into East Tennessee; his object being to drive out
Burnside, to repossess the fertile vallies of that region, and
to bring again under rebel sway, its patriotic and Union-
loving citizens. He crossed the Tennessee at Loudon, on
the 14th of November, and immediately took up his march
towards Knoxville. Burnside had, in the meantime, been
instructed to concentrate his forces in front of the enemy,
and retard his progress in every possible way, without jeop-
arding the safety of his own command. The main body of
his army, (not over 12,000 strong,) was then at Lenoir's
Station, a few miles above the mouth of the Holston, where,
under the direction of Lieutenant-Colonel Babcock, it had
built an excellent pontoon bridge, and was thus enabled to
move in any direction. When it became positively known
that Longstreet was advancing, Burnside ordered the destruction of the bridge, and prepared for battle; assuming
command in person, he marched from Lenoir's, and attacked
the rebel advanced forces, giving them a sharp and decided

check. He then fell back slowly along the main road to Knoxville. Selecting a strong position at Campbell's Station, he formed his little army and waited for the attack. The rebels soon closed upon him, but were again brought to a stand, suffering severe loss in every effort to dislodge him. But it was not Burnside's object to do more than delay and cripple the movements of the enemy. He had been cautioned particularly not to hazard the loss of his army, nor to jeopard the safety of Knoxville, by a decided battle in the open field; he therefore withdrew to the fortifications of the city, already prepared and provisioned as well as circumstances would permit, to receive his forces. His cavalry, under General Sanders, (a promising and zealous officer,) had anticipated the movements of the rebel cavalry under Wheeler, and by a well delivered battle, in which Sanders was mortally wounded, had frustrated the attempt to take Knoxville by a *coup de main.*

On the 17th of November, Longstreet arrived in front of the place, and on the 18th made a complete investment on the west side of the Holston, but found the city too well manned and too strongly fortified to venture at once upon an assault. After some desultory fighting, he therefore determined to starve it out. He was soon afterwards re-enforced by Jones, and one or two small commands from Virginia, and made a disposition of his forces with the view of cutting off Burnside's supplies. In this process, which required time, he was rudely interrupted by the intelligence of Bragg's defeat. He was too good a General to waste more time in perfecting the starvation process, and immediately decided to venture alone upon an assault of the fortifications. Accordingly, on the morning of the 29th, he threw three brigades of McLaw's division with terrible energy upon Fort Sanders, near the north-western angle of Burnside's works, supporting them with the rest of his force. They rushed up the heights, through the entanglements, into the ditches, and finally reached the parapet, but could go no further. The fort was held by Benjamin's regular battery of twenty-pounder parrots, supported by the Seventy-ninth New York, Twenty-ninth Massachusetts, and detachments from the Second New York and the Twentieth Michigan. Every man did his duty nobly; the double-shotted guns were served with great precision and coolness by their gallant young commander; lighted shells were thrown into the ditches as hand grenades, and the infantry poured out a deadly and incessant fire. The rebels were repulsed again and again, and finally driven from the hill entirely, leaving the ditch filled with killed and wounded, besides many who would not risk the almost certain death of retreating under the infernal fire through which they had advanced. Longstreet's repulse cost him a thousand men, and gained him nothing whatever.

Immediately after the victory at Chattanooga, Grant ordered General Gordon Granger, with the Fourth corps, and detachments from the rest of the army, sufficient to bring the strength of his command to 20,000 muskets, to march rapidly to the relief of the beleaguered garrison at Knoxville; but that officer, who had been selected out of compliment to his behavior at the battle of Chickamauga, raised so many objections, and lost so much time in preparations, that Grant, in order to make sure, also directed Sherman to go with the Eleventh and Fifteenth corps. Elliott, commanding Thomas' cavalry in Central Tennessee, was instructed at the same time to march rapidly into East Tennessee by the nearest route. Sherman, who was then at Cleveland, pushed forward with great celerity by the way of Philadelphia, Morgantown and Marysville, repairing the railroad bridge across the Hiawassee, and bridging the little Tennessee in two places. One of these bridges, two hundred and fifty yards in length, was constructed of timber obtained by tearing down houses in Morgantown, while the other was made by running wagons into the river, and building a roadway resting upon them. In the meantime, however, as has been seen, Longstreet had been repulsed, and hearing of Sherman's and Granger's movements, there was nothing left for him but to retire as rapidly as possible, marching towards Western Virginia.

Sherman's advance arrived at Knoxville on the morning of December 4th, and Sherman himself was there on the 5th, leaving his army in the neighborhood of Marysville. Granger arrived shortly afterwards. Grant's instructions required the total destruction of Longstreet's force, or that he should be expelled at once and for good from East Tennessee. Burnside, however, being in command of the Department, Sherman submitted the whole matter for his disposition, offering his troops and volunteering to go wherever it might be thought necessary. The former felt himself amply strong enough, with Granger's corps, to do all the remaining work of the campaign, and therefore permitted Sherman to return towards Chattanooga. A few days thereafter, Burnside was relieved by order of General Halleck, the General-in-Chief, and General J. G. Foster took his place. Cold weather set in shortly afterwards, and many of the troops being almost barefoot and poorly clad, the movement was suspended, in the neigborhood of Strawberry Plains and Dandridge. No serious fighting took place in that region during winter. Longstreet rejoined the army under Lee, in the spring.

Sherman, withdrawing by slow marches from East Tennessee, passed through Chattanooga, and was for awhile charged with the defense of the frontier, extending from that place towards Huntsville, in Northern Alabama. Late in January, 1864, Grant sent him to Vicksburg, for the purpose of making an expedition from that point towards Meridian and Mobile. Thomas was charged with watching the rebel army at Dalton, now temporarily under Hardee, and with the re-equipment of his own army, for the spring campaign.

The news of the splendid victory at Chattanooga, followed as it was by that at Knoxville, filled the loyal States with rejoicing. Mr. Lincoln appointed a day of thanksgiving "for this great advancement of the national cause;" while Congress, in grateful appreciation of the glorious victories he had gained, passed a joint resolution of thanks to General Grant and the troops which had fought under him. They also ordered a gold medal, with suitable emblems and devices, to be struck and presented to him, and Legislatures of various States presented him with a vote of thanks. But, better than all this, a movement was at once set on foot by the Hon. E. B. Washburne, Member of Congress from Illinois, to revive the grade of Lieutenant-General, and to call General Grant to the chief command of all the armies of the United States. This measure did not pass at once, but it was founded upon a just appreciation of what the exigency in military affairs required.

The careful student of history will have seen how great victories had been won in the South-west by the concentration of great armies, and by bringing them to operate in concert and under the leadership of one clear-headed, fearless, and faithful commander. Hitherto the Government had not found a military chieftain by whose counsels it was willing to be guided. McClellan had promised much and accomplished little. Halleck, who was called to his place, was well meaning, but incapable. The President was earnest, thoughtful, sagacious and far-reaching in his judgment; but he was too cautious to entrust the unlimited control of military operation to the hands of those about him. None of his subordinates, except Grant, had yet been so uniformly successful as to become entitled to unquestioning confidence. Neither had the President learned that the true province of the civil government was to provide the sinews of war—to select the ablest General, and to leave him free to control the armies, according to the true principles of warfare. Mr. Stanton, the able Secretary of War, appreciated this truth at an early day, and bent all his wonderful energy to carrying it into effect; but to Mr. Washburne, more than to any one else in high position, is due the credit of bringing the Government to its final adoption. Fortunately he persisted in the advocacy of the bill reviving the grade of Lieutenant-General, until Congress, as well as the entire country, became convinced that nothing else but that measure, or its equivalent,—the placing of Grant in supreme control of the army, subject only to the President, his constitutional commander,—could carry the war for the stability of the Union to a successful termination.

CHAPTER XVIII.

As soon as the Chattanooga campaign was terminated,
Grant set about acquiring a thorough knowledge of his
vast military division extending from the Mississippi River
on the west, and the Ohio on the north, to the borders of
Virginia, the Carolinas and Georgia on the east, and as far
southward as he might be able to carry his armies. His
first task was to supply and consolidate his forces, so as to
make sure of all that had been gained, and to prepare for
new conquests. Early in December, he went to Nashville
to inspect and perfect the arrangements for forwarding supplies. The army in Northern Georgia depended entirely
upon the railroads leading southward through Tennessee for
the transportation of its military stores. The Louisville and
Nashville Railroad was also a necessary link in his communications with the North, and as it had fallen into bad management, a thorough reorganization became necessary. It was
claimed by the persons controlling the roads, that they were
already taxed to their utmost, but this was not true. Grant
removed the military superintendent, and replaced him by an
abler man. He also directed General Thomas to have the
Nashville and Decatur road repaired to Decatur, and the

Memphis and Charleston road, from Decatur to Stevenson; thus giving two lines instead of one from Nashville to Bridgeport. The roads in East Tennessee were likewise rebuilt, and every encouragement was given to the authorities charged with the completion of the Nashville and Johnsonville road. But the process of building bridges, of which there were many, some of them very extensive, and of repairing tracks and gathering locomotives and cars, was by no means an easy or rapid one. Having done all he could to get these matters into proper hands, in the latter part of December, Grant returned to Chattanooga, where he was chagrined to learn that operations against Longstreet in East Tennessee had been suspended, and that instead of being far up the valley towards Virginia, Granger was in Knoxville, boasting that he could hold that place against all sorts of impossible combinations, natural and supernatural. As a matter of course, Grant lost no time in hurrying to Knoxville. Accompanied by his staff and a few orderlies, he took passage to Loudon on a steamboat, which had been built by the soldiers. From Loudon he went to Knoxville by rail, arriving there on the 4th of January. After an interview with General Foster, whom he found suffering from an old wound received in Mexico, he went on to Strawberry Plains. In the meantime, intensely cold weather had set in, and as the troops had not yet been properly supplied with clothing and shoes, owing to the fact that communication with Kentucky by wagon was almost entirely out of the question, and railroad communication by the way of Chattanooga had not yet been re-established, it was apparent that active operations could not be resumed without inflicting great suffering on the army. The rebel cavalry were making occasional dashes upon the outposts, and some desultory fighting took place at intervals, as the weather would permit; but seeing that no general engagement could be fought, Grant left instructions for the government of the department, and proceeded on horseback to Cumberland Gap. After inspecting that place, he crossed the mountains, and rode rapidly to Lexington, Kentucky. The journey made in mid-winter was one of great hardship and danger, the passage of the Cumberland and Wild Cat Mountains, covered with snow and ice, being especially difficult and perilous. The cold for several days was ten degrees below zero. It was impossible to ride down the ice-covered slopes of the mountain; so Grant and his party were compelled to lead their horses and walk. The General, in advance, had many falls but suffered no serious injury. At Lexington and Frankfort he was received with acclamations of joy, and urgent offers of hospitality, but he refused to stop, and taking the cars hastened to Louisville, and thence back to Nashville, where he established the head-quarters of the Military Division. He was soon afterwards called to St. Louis for a few days, by the dangerous illness of one of his children. Hurrying through the country in the modest dress of a citizen, he studiously avoided all public ovations and display, and as soon as the danger which threatened his son had passed, returned in the same manner to his head-quarters. He did not allow himself to be idle for a day, but bent all his energies and ability to caring for his command and devising new plans of warfare against the insurgent forces. Hitherto military operations in the West and South-west had been connected independently of those in the East; but since the rebel Teritory had been cut in twain along the line of the Mississippi, and the rebel forces had been pressed back into the interior of Alabama and Georgia, and to the east side of the Blue Ridge, it became a matter of vital importance that there should henceforth be a unity of plan, and effective co-operation between the armies under Grant and the Army of the Potomac. To this end he studied the military situation in all its aspects with profound attention, making such suggestions to the Government as circumstances seemed to justify. It was about this time that the idea of severing the rebel territory again, by conducting a campaign from Chattanooga to the sea-coast first presented itself to his mind. But before putting it into execution, he thought it necessary to thoroughly repossess Alabama, particularly Mobile and Montgomery. Sherman was, therefore, sent to Vicksburg for the purpose of organizing an expedition to be composed of the forces serving along the Mississippi River, with which to operate towards Meridian, while Halleck was counseled to send Banks with all his forces against Mobile.

In pursuance of this general plan, and also for the better protection of the various important points along the Mississippi River, Sherman moved from Vicksburg, on the 3d of February, with two divisions of the Sixteenth corps, under Hurlbut, two of the Seventeenth corps, under McPherson, and a brigade of cavalry under Colonel Winslow, of the Fourth Iowa Cavalry. General William Sewy Smith, Grant's Chief of Cavalry, was also ordered to assemble all the available troops of that arm in West Tennessee, and to march from Memphis at the same time, sweeping down through Northern Mississippi, and joining Sherman in the neighborhood of Meridian. Sherman moved in two columns, and although confronted by Loring, French, and S. D. Lee, with a considerable force of infantry and cavalry, he drove them rapidly back, entered Jackson on the evening of the 5th, crossed the Pearl River the next day, and continued his rapid march towards Meridian, pausing only to build bridges or remove obstructions from the roads, and to destroy the railroad. He entered Meridian on the 14th, that place having been evacuated the night before by the Confederate troops under Polk in person. Sherman now halted his command, and after two day's rest, sent it out in all directions for the purpose of breaking up the railroads crossing at that place: "The depots, store-houses, arsenals, officers' hospitals, hotels, and cantonments in the town, were burned; and during the next five days, with axes, sledges, crow-bars, claw-bars, and fire, Hurlbut's corps destroyed, on the north and east, 60 miles of ties and iron, 1 locomotive, and 8 bridges; and McPherson's corps, on the south and west, 55 miles of railroad, 53 bridges, 6,075 feet of trestle-work, 19 locomotives, 28 steam cars, and 3 saw-mills. Thus was completed the destruction of the railways for one hundred miles from Jackson to Merid-

11

ian, and for twenty miles around the latter place, in so effect-
ual a manner that they could not be used against us in the
approaching campaigns."* The rebels, in the meantime, had
received re-enforcements, and on the 17th recrossed the Tom-
bigbee, moving towards Meridian. Sherman at once concentrated his command, and as Smith with the cavalry had not
yet made his appearance, he thought it prudent to withdraw.
This he did on the 20th, sending McPherson on the direct
road to Jackson, and with Hurlbut and Winslow moved
towards the North for the purpose of looking for the cavalry.
Making a wide detour without finding it, he recrossed the
Pearl River and concentrated his forces at Canton.

Smith did not leave Memphis till the 11th of February;
and although he had a force of eight thousand well mounted
and equipped cavalry, he succeeded in getting no farther
towards Meridian than West Point, in Mississippi, from which
place he rapidly retreated, closely followed by Forrest, on the
22d. Banks had not been allowed, as Grant recommended,
to operate against Mobile; but in pursuance of a mistaken
policy on the part of the Government, was shortly afterwards
sent against the rebels west of the Mississippi. Sherman's
campaign, therefore, became nothing but an extensive raid instead of being made, as it should have been, the means of
taking Mobile and re-establishing the national control over
both Mississippi and Alabama.

With this raid, Grant's immediate supervision of military
operations in the South-west terminated. He was shortly
afterwards called to the command of all the armies of the
United States, with ample authority to carry on the war in
accordance with the principle which had so far given us our
only substantial victories, namely: that of concentration
against the detachments of the enemy.

* "Sherman and his Campaigns," p. 161.

CHAPTER XIX.

On the 1st of March, 1864, the bill reviving the grade of Lieutenant-General in the armies of the United States, became a law, by the approval of Mr. Lincoln. As has been shown, it had its origin in the desire expressed by far-seeing statesmen, to confer the actual control of military operations solely upon General Grant; and it received its warmest support from those who believed that nothing less than this measure would enable the Government to make successful head against the insurgent Southerners. Grant had so far been the most successful General, and it was believed that his elevation to a grade above all the rest, would give him a power for good, which he could not otherwise exert. In order to make sure that neither Halleck nor any one else should be called by the President to fill the new office, it was moved in Congress that it should be expressly conferred upon Grant; but that body was so confident that no one else would be selected, that it declined to accept an amendment to the act, in any way limiting the President's power of nomination, though a resolution requesting Mr. Lincoln to appoint Grant, was promptly passed. This confidence was not misplaced, for, on the next day, Mr. Lincoln sent to the Senate the nomination of Ulysses S. Grant, to be Lieutenant-General. The nomination was confirmed at once, and an order was sent directing Grant to repair to Washington for the purpose of receiving his commission. Before leaving Nashville he wrote to Sherman, his faithful Lieutenant:

" Whilst I have been eminently successful in this war, in at least gaining the confidence of the public, no one feels more than I do how much of this success is due to the energy, skill, and the harmonious putting forth of that energy and skill, of those whom it has been my good fortune to have occupying subordinate positions under me. There are many officers to whom these remarks are applicable to a greater or less degree, proportionate to their ability as soldiers; but what I want, is to express my thanks to you and McPherson as the men to whom, above all others, I feel indebted for whatever I have had of success. How far your advice and assistance have been of help to me, you know; how far your execution of whatever has been given you to do entitles you to the reward I am receiving, you can not know as well as I. I feel all the gratitude this letter would express, giving it the most flattering construction." *

This letter was intended as much for McPherson as for Sherman, and while it reflects the highest credit upon the magnanimous heart of the writer, it does those able and gallant Generals no more than simple justice. Grant had that about him which drew true men irresistibly towards him, causing them to cheerfully exert their entire strength in the performance of the duties assigned them. No man was ever more devotedly or worthily served by those who came within his immediate influence, and no man ever rewarded merit more unselfishly or promptly.

Sherman, in replying to Grant's letter, says:

" You do yourself injustice, and us too much honor, in assigning to us too large a share of the merits which have led to your high advancement. I know you approve the friendship I have ever professed to you, and will permit me to continue as heretofore, to manifest it on all proper occasions.

" You are now Washington's legitimate successor, and occupy a position of almost dangerous elevation; but if you can continue as heretofore, to be yourself, simple, honest and unpretending, you will enjoy through

* " Sherman and his Campaigns, p. 166."

life the respect and love of friends and the homage of millions of human beings, that will award you a large share in securing to them and their descendants a government of law and stability.

"I repeat, you do McPherson and myself too much honor. At Belmont you manifested your traits,—neither of us being near. At Donelson, also, you illustrated your whole character. I was not near, and McPherson in too subordinate a capacity to influence you.

"Until you had won Donelson, I confess I was almost cowed by the terrible array of anarchical elements that presented themselves at every point; but that admitted a ray of light, which I have followed since.

"I believe you are as brave, patriotic and just as the great prototype, Washington; as unselfish, kind-hearted and honest as a man should be; but the chief characteristic is the simple faith in success you have always manifested, which I can liken to nothing else than the faith the Christian has in the Saviour.

"This faith gave you victory at Shiloh and Vicksburg. Also, when you have completed your best preparations, you go into battle without hesitation, as at Chattanooga,—no doubts, no answers,—and I tell you, it was this that made us act with confidence. I knew wherever I was, that you thought of me; and if I got in a tight place you would help me out if alive.

"My only point of doubt was in your knowledge of grand strategy, and of books of science and history; but I confess your common sense seems to have supplied all these.

"Now as to the future. Don't stay in Washington. Come West; take to yourself the whole Mississippi Valley. Let us make it dead sure; and I tell you the Atlantic slopes and Pacific shores will follow its destiny as sure as the limbs of a tree live or die with the main trunk. We have done much, but still much remains. Time and time's influences are with us. We could almost afford to sit still and let these influences work. Here lies the seat of coming empire; and from the West, where our task is done, we will make short work of Charleston and Richmond, and the impoverished coast of the Atlantic." *

But Grant had gone to Washington, and for reasons which will be explained hereafter, he wisely chose to cast his future fortunes with those of the national cause in the East.

On the 8th of March he arrived at the capital, and the next day, at one o'clock, he was received by the President in the Cabinet Chamber. The different Cabinet officers, General Halleck, and a few other persons were there by the

* "Sherman and his Campaigns."

President's invitation.   General Grant was accompanied by
an aid-de-camp, Colonel Comstock, and General Rawlins, his
able and devoted Chief-of-Staff, and after being introduced to
the Cabinet was addressed as follows, by the President:

" GENERAL GRANT :—The expression of the nation's approbation of
what you have already done, and its reliance on you for what remains
to be done in the existing great struggle, are now presented with this
commission, constituting you Lieutenant-General in the Army of the
United States. With this high honor, devolves on you an additional
responsibility. As the country herein trusts you, so, under God, it will
sustain you. I scarcely need to add, that with what I here speak for
the nation, goes my own hearty personal concurrence."

General Grant replied with feeling:

" MR. PRESIDENT :—I accept the commission with gratitude for the
high honor conferred. With the aid of the noble armies that have
fought on so many battle-fields for our common country, it will be my
earnest endeavor not to disappoint your expectations. I feel the full
weight of the responsibilities now devolving on me ; and I know that
if they are met, it will be due to those armies, and, above all, to the
favor of that Providence which leads both nations and men."

The next day, as had been expected, the President assigned
the new Lieutenant-General to the command of all the armies,
with his head-quarters in the field.   Grant made a hurried
trip to the Army of the Potomac at Culpeper Court House,
to confer with General Meade, and then returned to Nashville
for the purpose of making arrangements to enter upon the
performance of the duties of his new position.   Here, on the
17th day of March, he issued his order assuming command
of the armies of the United States, and announced that till
further notice his head-quarters would be with the Army of
the Potomac.   At his request the Secretary of War had already assigned Sherman to the Military Division of the Mississippi, including the Department of Arkansas in addition to
those departments already within it ; McPherson succeeded
Sherman in the command of the Department of the Tennessee ; and, as a matter of course, Halleck, who had so long
filled the place of General-in-Chief, was relieved from that
position.   He was, however, soon afterwards assigned to duty

in Washington by General Grant as Chief-of-Staff of the Army, for which position, charged with the details of military administration, it was thought, his capacities peculiarly fitted him.

On the 23d of March, Grant, accompanied by his family and the members of his personal staff, arrived at Washington, and on the next day he took actual command,—his first act being to reorganize the Army of the Potomac by consolidating it into three corps,—to be known thereafter as the Second, Fifth, and Sixth, to be commanded respectively by Major-Generals Hancock, Warren, and Sedgwick. The Ninth corps, under Burnside, lately from East Tennessee, had been reorganized at Annapolis, and was added to the Army of the Potomac, but acted for a time independently of Meade, on account of Burnside's older commission. Generals Barlow, Gibbon, Birney, J. B. Carr, Wadsworth, Crawford, Robinson, Griffin, Wright, and Prince, commanded divisions. The cavalry of the army was consolidated into a corps under General Sheridan, with Generals Gregg, Torbert, and Wilson, commanding divisions. These officers had all distinguished themselves in the war and were selected for their services and their zeal in the national cause.

The staff organization of the Army of the Potomac remained unchanged with Brigadier-General H. J. Hunt, as Chief of Artillery; Major J. C. Duane, Chief of Engineers; Brigadier-General Rufus Ingalls, Chief Quartermaster. Major-General A. A. Humphreys, an able officer of Engineers, distinguished also as a division commander, was Chief-of-Staff; while Brigadier-General Seth Williams was Adjutant-General.

The law creating the grade of Lieutenant-General, enabled Grant to reorganize his own staff also. General Rawlins, his constant companion from the beginning of the war, was retained as Chief-of-Staff, and Colonel T. S. Bowers as Adjutant-General; Colonel Wilson, his Inspector-General, who had been promoted to be Brigadier-General after Chattanooga, and had been ordered to Washington for the purpose of reorganizing the Cavalry Bureau, was assigned to the command of a division under Sheridan. His place on the staff was filled by Colonel Comstock of the Engineer corps; Colonel Horace Porter and Colonel O. E. Babcock, two young officers of the regular army, who had already given great promise of usefulness and ability, were designated as Aids-de-Camp; while Colonels Adam Badeau, and Ely S. Parker (a hereditary chief of the Six Nations), were assigned as Military Secretaries. These officers were all young in years, but old in experience, having served with marked distinction from the beginning of the rebellion. Grant had always had great faith in young men for war, and therefore carefully avoided the selection of old or middle aged officers for service near him.

The conduct of Grant in assuming command of the Army of the Potomac against the advice of such friends as Sherman, had a deeper and more chivalric significance than is apparent at the first glance; for while it was "of itself a recognition of that primacy of interest and importance which belonged to that army, but which appeared for awhile to have passed from it to its more fortunate rival in the western theatre of operations," * he saw with the intuitive and unerring perception of a heroic and loyal nature, that his acceptance of the Lieutenant-Generalship carried with it the inevitable duty of undertaking to "overwhelm the foremost army of the Confederacy under the Confederacy's foremost leader." He must have felt that Congress had bestowed upon him the high rank of Lieutenant-General, and clothed him with its ample powers, the better to prepare him for a trial of prowess with Lee and the army under his command. Lee's soldiers had defeated McClellan, Hooker and Burnside. They had baffled every effort on the part of Meade, and so long as they remained to bar the road to Richmond and to uphold the rebel cause, so long would rebellion continue and the country remain divided against itself. Grant saw this as plainly as any man could see it, and knew that he could no more decline the trial with Lee, without injuring his fame and weakening his power

* "Campaigns of the Army of the Potomac," p. 405.

to command, than the country could afford to allow its life-blood and treasure to be fruitlessly wasted at the hands of incompetent and irresolute Generals. He realized too truly the significance of his new rank, and the task imposed upon him by his countrymen, to permit himself to be turned from this duty either by the difficulties and dangers attending it, or the solicitations of devoted but misjudging friends.

CHAPTER XX.

No clearer statement of the situation of military affairs, or of the plan of operations adopted for the future conduct of the war, can be made, than that given in General Grant's own words:

" From an early period in the rebellion," he says in his comprehensive and admirable report,* " I had been impressed with the idea that active and continuous operations of all the troops that could be brought into the field, regardless of season and weather, were necessary to a speedy termination of the war. The resources of the enemy, and his numerical strength, were far inferior to ours; but, as an offset to this, we had a vast territory, with a population hostile to the Government, to garrison, and long lines of river and railroad communications to protect, to enable us to supply the operating armies.

" The armies in the East and West acted independently, and without concert, like a balky team,—no two ever pulling together,—enabling the enemy to use to great advantage his interior lines of communication for transporting troops from East to West, re-enforcing the army most vigorously pressed, and to furlough large numbers, during seasons of inactivity on our part, to go to their homes and do the work of providing for the support of their armies. It was a question whether our numerical strength and resources were not more than balanced by these disadvantages and the enemy's superior position.

" From the first, I was firm in the conviction that no peace could be

* Report of Lieutenant-General U. S. Grant, of the Armies of the United States, dated Head-quarters Armies of the United States, Washington, D. C., July 22, 1865.

had that would be stable and conducive to the happiness of the people, both North and South, until the military power of the rebellion was entirely broken.

" I therefore determined, first, to use the greatest number of troops practicable against the armed force of the enemy, preventing him from using the same force at different seasons against first one and then another of our armies, and the possibility of repose for refitting and producing necessary supplies for carrying on resistance; second, to hammer continuously against the armed force of the enemy and his resources, until, by mere attrition, if in no other way, there should be nothing left to him but an equal submission with the loyal sections of our common country to the Constitution and Laws of the land.

" These views have been kept constantly in mind, and orders given and campaigns made to carry them out. Whether they might have been better in conception and execution is for the people, who mourn the loss of friends fallen, and who have to pay the pecuniary cost, to say. All I can say is, that what I have done has been done conscientiously, to the best of my ability, and in what I conceived to be for the best interests of the whole country.

" At the date when this report begins, the situation of the contending forces was about as follows: The Mississippi River was strongly garrisoned by Federal troops from St. Louis, Mo., to its mouth. The line of the Arkansas was also held, thus giving us armed possession of all west of the Mississippi north of that stream. A few points in Southern Louisiana, not remote from the river, were held by us, together with a small garrison at and near the mouth of the Rio Grande. All the balance of the vast territory of Arkansas, Louisiana, and Texas, was in the almost undisputed possession of the enemy, with an army of probably not less than 80,000 effective men that could have been brought into the field, had there been sufficient opposition to have brought them out. The *let-alone-policy* had demoralized this force so that probably but little more than one-half of it was ever present in garrison at any one time. But the one-half, or 40,000 men, with the bands of guerrillas scattered through Missouri, Arkansas, and along the Mississippi River, and the disloyal character of much of the population, compelled the use of a large number of troops to keep navigation open on the river, and to protect the loyal people to the west of it. To the east of the Mississippi we held substantially with the line of the Tennessee and Holston Rivers, running eastward to include nearly all of the State of Tennessee. South of Chattanooga a small foothold had been obtained in Georgia, sufficient to protect East Tennessee from incursions from the enemy's force at Dalton, Georgia. West Virginia was substantially within our lines. Virginia, with the exception of the northern border, the Potomac River, a small area about the mouth of

James River covered by the troops at Norfolk and Fort Monroe, and the territory covered by the Army of the Potomac lying along the Rapidan, was in the possession of the enemy. Along the sea-coast, footholds had been obtained at Plymouth, Washington, and Newbern, in North Carolina; Beaufort, Folly, and Morris Islands, Hilton Head, Fort Pulaski, and Port Royal, in South Carolina; Fernandina and St. Augustine, in Florida. Key West and Pensacola were also in our possession, while all the important ports were blockaded by the navy. The accompanying map, a copy of which was sent to General Sherman and other commanders in March, 1864, shows by red lines the territory occupied by us at the beginning of the rebellion, and at the opening of the campaign of 1864, while those in blue are the lines which it was proposed to occupy.

"Behind the Union lines there were many bands of guerrillas, and a large population disloyal to the Government, making it necessary to guard every foot of road or river used in supplying our armies. In the South, a reign of military despotism prevailed, which made every man and boy capable of bearing arms a soldier, and those who could not bear arms in the field acted as provosts for collecting deserters and returning them. This enabled the enemy to bring almost his entire strength into the field.

"The enemy had concentrated the bulk of his forces east of the Mississippi into two armies, commanded by Generals R. E. Lee and J. E. Johnston, his ablest and best Generals. The army commanded by Lee occupied the south bank of the Rapidan, extending from Mine Run westward, strongly intrenched in position at Dalton, Ga., covering and defending Atlanta, Ga., a place of great importance as a railroad center, against the armies under Major-General W. T. Sherman. In addition to these armies, he had a large cavalry force under Forrest, in North-east Mississippi; a considerable force, of all arms, in the Shenandoah Valley, and in the western part of Virginia and extreme eastern part of Tennessee; and also confronting our sea-coast garrisons, and holding blockaded ports where we had no foothold upon land.

"These two armies, and the cities covered and defended by them, were the main objective points of the campaign.

"Major-General W. T. Sherman, who was appointed to the command of the Military Division of the Mississippi, embracing all the armies and territory east of the Mississippi River to the Alleghanies, and the Department of Arkansas, west of the Mississippi, had the immediate command of the armies operating against Johnston.

"Major-General George G. Meade had the immediate command of the Army of the Potomac, from where I exercised general supervision of the movements of all our armies.

"General Sherman was instructed to move against Johnston's army, to break it up, and to go into the interior of the enemy's country as far as he could, inflicting all the damage he could upon their war resources. If the enemy in his front showed signs of joining Lee, to follow him up to the full extent of his ability, while I would prevent the concentration of Lee upon him if it was in the power of the Army of the Potomac to do so. More specific written instructions were not given, for the reason that I had talked over with him the plans of the campaign, and was satisfied that he understood them and would execute them to the fullest extent possible.

"Major-General N. P. Banks, then on an expedition up Red River against Shreveport, Louisiana, (which had been organized previous to my appointment to command), was notified by me, on the 15th of March, of the importance it was that Shreveport should be taken at the earliest possible day, and that if he found that the taking of it would occupy from ten to fifteen days' more time than General Sherman had given his troops to be absent from their command, he would send them back at the time specified by General Sherman, even if it led to the abandonment of the main object of the Red River expedition, for this force was necessary to movements east of the Mississippi; that should his expedition prove successful, he would hold Shreveport and the Red River with such force as he might deem necessary, and return the balance of his troops to the neighborhood of New Orleans, commencing no move for the further acquisition of territory unless it was to make that then held by him more easily held; that it might be a part of the spring campaign to move against Mobile; that it certainly would be if troops enough could be obtained to make it without embarrassing other movements; that New Orleans would be the point of departure for such an expedition; also, that I had directed General Steele to make a real move from Arkansas, as suggested by him (General Banks), instead of a demonstration, as Steele thought advisable.

"On the 21st of March, in addition to the foregoing notification and directions, he was instructed as follows:

"'1. If successful in your expedition against Shreveport, that you turn over the defense of the Red River to General Steele and the navy.

"'2. That you abandon Texas entirely, with the exception of your hold upon the Rio Grande. This can be held with 4,000 men, if they will turn their attention immediately to fortifying their positions. At least one-half of the force required for this service might be taken from the colored troops.

"'3. By properly fortifying on the Mississippi River, the force to guard it from Port Hudson to New Orleans can be reduced to 10,000 men, if not to a less number; 6,000 more would then hold all the rest of the territory necessary to hold until active operations can be resumed west of the river. According to your last return, this would give you a force of over 30,000 effective men with which to move against Mobile. To this I expect to add

5,000 men from Missouri. If, however, you think the force here stated too small to hold the territory regarded as necessary to hold possession of, I would say, concentrate at least 25,000 men of your present command for operations against Mobile. With these, and such additions as I can give you from elsewhere, lose no time in making a demonstration, to be followed by an attack upon Mobile. Two or more iron-clads will be ordered to report to Admiral Farragut. This gives him a strong naval fleet with which to co-operate. You can make your own arrangements with the Admiral for his co-operation, and select your own line of approach. My own idea of the matter is, that Pascagoula should be your base; but, from your long service in the Gulf Department, you will know best about the matter. It is intended that your movements shall be co-operative with movements elsewhere, and you can not now start too soon. All I would now add is, that you commence the concentration of your forces at once. Preserve a profound secrecy of what you intend doing, and start at the earliest possible moment.'

" Major-General Meade was instructed that Lee's army would be his objective point; that wherever Lee went he would go also. For his movement two plans presented themselves:—one to cross the Rapidan below Lee, moving by his right flank; the other above, moving by his left. Each presented advantages over the other, with corresponding objections. By crossing above, Lee would be cut off from all chance of ignoring Richmond or going North on a raid. But if we took this route, all we did would have to be done whilst the rations we started with held out; besides it separated us from Butler, so that he could not be directed how to co-operate. If we took the other route, Brandy Station could be used as a base of supplies until another was secured on the York or James Rivers. Of these, however, it was decided to take the lower route.

" The following letter of instructions was addressed to Major-General B. F. Butler:

"'FORT MONROE, VA., April 2, 1864.

"'GENERAL—In the spring campaign, which it is desirable shall commence at as early a day as practicable, it is proposed to have co-operative action of all the armies in the field, as far as this object can be accomplished.

"'It will not be possible to unite our armies into two or three large ones, to act as so many units, owing to the absolute necessity of holding on to the territory already taken from the enemy. But, generally speaking, concentration can be practically effected by armies moving to the interior of the enemy's country from the territory they have to guard. By such movement they interpose themselves between the enemy and the country to be guarded, thereby reducing the number necessary to guard important points, or at least occupy the attention of a part of the enemy's force, if no greater object is gained. Lee's army and Richmond being the greater objects towards which our attention must be directed in the next campaign, it is desirable to unite all the force we can against them. The necessity of covering Washington with the Army of the Potomac, and of covering your Department with your army, makes it impossible to unite these forces at the beginning of any move. I propose, therefore, what comes nearest this of any thing that seems practicable : The Army of the Potomac will act from its present base, Lee's army being the objective point. You will collect all the forces from your command that can be spared from garrison duty,—I should say not less than 20,000 effective men,—to operate on the south side of James River, Richmond being your objective point. To the force you already have will be added about 10,000 men from South Carolina, under Major-General Gilmore, who will command them in person. Major-General W. F. Smith is ordered to report to you, to command the troops sent into the field from your own Department.

"'General Gilmore will be ordered to report to you at Fortress Monroe, with all the troops on transports, by the 18th instant, or as soon thereafter as practicable. Should you not receive notice by that time to move, you will make such disposition of them and your other forces as you may deem best calculated to deceive the enemy as to the real move to be made.

"'When you are notified to move, take City Point with as much force as possible. Fortify, or rather intrench at once, and concentrate all your troops for the field there as rapidly as you can. From City Point, directions can not be given at this time for your further movements.

"'The fact that has already been stated,—that is, that Richmond is to be your objective point, and that there is to be co-operation between your force and the Army of the Potomac,—must be your guide. This indicates the necessity of your holding close to the south bank of the James River as you advance. Then, should the enemy be forced into his intrenchments in Richmond, the Army of the Potomac would follow, and, by means of transports the two armies would be a unit.

"'All the minor details of your advance are left entirely to your direction. If, however, you think it practicable to use your cavalry south of you, so as to cut the railroad about Hick's Ford about the time of the general advance, it would be of immense advantage.

"'You will please forward, for my information, at the earliest practicable day, all orders, details, and instructions you may give for the execution of this order.'

"On the 16th, these instructions were substantially reiterated. On the 19th, in order to secure full co-operation between his army and that of General Meade, he was informed that I expected him to move from Fort Monroe the same day that General Meade moved from Culpepper. The exact time I was to telegraph him as soon as it was fixed, and that it would not be earlier than the 27th of April; that it was my intention to fight Lee between Culpepper and Richmond if he would stand. Should he, however, fall back into Richmond, I would follow up, and make a junction with his (General Butler's) army on the James River; that, could I be certain he would be able to invest Richmond on the south side so as to have his left resting on the James, above the city, I would form a junction there; that circumstances might make this course advisable anyhow; that he should use every exertion to secure footing as far up the south side of the river as he could, and as soon as possible, after the receipt of orders, to move; that if he could not carry the city, he should at least detain as large a force as possible.

"In co-operation with the main movements against Lee and Johnston, I was desirous of using all other troops necessarily kept in departments remote from the fields of immediate operations, and also those kept in the background for the protection of our extended lines between the loyal States and the armies operating against them.

"A very considerable force, under command of Major-Generel Sigel, was so held for the protection of West Virginia, and the frontiers of Maryland and Pennsylvania. Whilst these troops could not be withdrawn to distant fields without exposing the North to invasion by comparatively small bodies of the enemy, they could act directly to their front and give better protection than if lying idle in garrison. By such movement they would either compel the enemy to detach largely for the protection of his supplies and lines of communication, or he would lose them.

"General Sigel was therefore directed to organize all his available force into two expeditions, to move from Beverly and Charleston, under command of Generals Ord and Crook, against the East Tennessee and Virginia railroad. Subsequently, General Ord having been relieved at his own request, General Sigel was instructed, at his own suggestion, to give up the expedition by Beverly, and to form two columns, one under General Crook, on the Kanawha, numbering about 10,000 men, and one on the Shenandoah, numbering about 7,000 men, the one on the Shenandoah to assemble between Cumberland and the Shenandoah, and the infantry and artillery advanced to Cedar Creek, with such cavalry as could be made available at the moment, to threaten the enemy in the Shenandoah Valley, and advance as far as possible; while General Crook would take possession of Lewisburg with part of his force and move down the Tennessee railroad, doing as much damage as he could, destroying the New River bridge and the salt-works at Saltville, Virginia.

"Owing to the weather and bad condition of the roads, operations were delayed until the 1st of May, when, everything being in readiness and the roads favorable, orders were given for a general movement of all the armies not later than the 4th of May.

"My first object being to break the military power of the rebellion, and capture the enemy's important strongholds, made me desirous that General Butler should succeed in his movement against Richmond, as that would tend more than anything else, unless it were the capture of Lee's army, to accomplish this desired result in the East. If he failed, it was my determination, by hard fighting, either to compel Lee to retreat, or to so cripple him that he could not detach a large force to go North, and still retain enough for the defense of Richmond. It was well understood, by both Generals Butler and Meade, before starting on the campaign, that it was my intention to put both their armies south of the James River; in case of failure to destroy Lee without it.

"Before giving General Butler his instructions, I visited him at Fort Monroe, and, in conversation, pointed out the apparent importance of getting possession of Petersburg, and destroying railroad communication as far south as possible. Believing, however, in the practicability of capturing Richmond, unless it was re-enforced, I made that the objective point of his operations. As the Army of the Potomac was to move simultaneously with him, Lee could not detach from his army with safety, and the enemy did not have troops elsewhere to bring to the defense of the city in time to meet a rapid movement from the north of James River.

"I may here state that, commanding all the armies as I did, I tried, as far as possible, to leave General Meade in independent command of the Army of the Potomac. My instructions for that army were all through him, and were general in their nature, leaving all the details and the execution to him."

The particular plan of operations for the Army of the Potomac has been severely criticised by various writers upon the war; apparently with the object of detracting from Grant's reputation as a General,[*] but in their eagerness to exhibit superior knowledge of strategy, they lose sight, in the outset, of the first principle applicable to the problem which presented itself for solution at that stage of the war. It is a matter of some importance, for the sake of history, that this question should be carefully examined. It will be remembered that Grant's primary object was not the capture of Richmond, nor the conquest of hostile territory, as has been falsely assumed, but the absolute destruction of the insurgent armies. From the first he was "firm in the conviction that no peace could be had that would be stable and conducive to the happiness of the people, both North and South, until the military power of the rebellion was entirely broken." How he expected to break this military power is

[*] See particularly "Campaigns of the Army of the Potomac," by William Swinton.

stated with clearness, and is based upon the soundest military principles:

"I therefore determined, first to use the greatest number of troops practicable against the armed force of the enemy, preventing him from using the same force at different seasons against first one and then another of our armies;" and, "second, to hammer continuously against the armed force of the enemy and his resources, until by mere attrition if in no other way, there should be nothing left to him but an equal submission with the loyal section of our common country, to the Constitution and the laws of the land."

It will be observed that he says nothing here in reference to strategic points; converging or diverging lines of operations, but has steadily kept in view only the armed forces of the enemy. But as if to leave no room for doubt on this point, he instructed Meade that Lee's army, the very head and front of the rebel cause, "would be his objective point; that wherever Lee went, he would go also." In the entire range of all that has ever been said, either by the writers or the fighters, there can not be found a more comprehensive plan of a great war, nor a more judicious statement of the principles upon which it should be conducted. If it be true, as has been stated, that the General who conceived and carried this plan into execution, although educated as a soldier, never read a treatise on grand tactics or strategy, and, like Bagration, knew nothing of those sciences, except what he learned from his own experience and reflection, his countrymen may justly ascribe to him the possession of military genius of the highest order.

The position of Lee's army was as well known as that of the Army of the Potomac, when Grant moved his head-quarters to Culpepper Court House; but even if there had been a reasonable doubt on this point, past experience had shown that the national forces would not be permitted to go far in the right direction without obtaining the desired information. This fact alone, ought to have settled, as it did, all questions in reference to the line of operations to be pursued in the coming campaign; and yet it is claimed that Grant should have withdrawn from Lee's front, marched to Washington or

Acquia Creek, transported his army to the James, and there begun his campaign, by moving directly upon Richmond or its communications. It is asserted, in support of this plan, that Grant himself, before being called to the command of all the armies, wrote a letter to Halleck recommending a plan similar to that devised by Generals Franklin and Smith. But without entering into the details of these plans, or the circumstances under which they were submitted, it is enough for present purposes to assert that the country has good reason to be thankful that Grant, when he became charged with the actual responsibility of making and executing a plan for the Army of the Potomac, saw sufficient reason, after careful investigation and study, to change his views, and adopt a plan more strictly in accordance with the principles of war. The Army of the Potomac had already tried the Peninsula route to its sore cost. The long array of unfortunate events, beginning with the seven days' battle, including the closing events of Pope's well-managed but disastrous campaign; the indecisive battle of Antietam; the bloody disaster of Fredericksburg; the inglorious failure of Chancellorsville, scarcely counterbalanced by the expulsion of Lee from Pennsylvania by the uncompleted victory of Gettysburg, the Mine Run campaign, followed by the rapid retreat on Washington, had their beginning in the attempt to take Richmond by advancing upon it by the way of the Peninsula. And although it may be true that misfortune, privation, and misery are the school of good soldiers, it can scarcely be claimed that two years of such schooling, unvaried by a single decisive victory, had improved the *morale* of the army. Its ranks had been decimated by battle and disease, its hope wasted by continual delay, and although discipline had not yet been subverted, and that soul of armies, the spirit of a great people, still animated its ranks, it was not then the splendid organization it once had been, or that it would have been had victory rested permanently upon its banners.

By an examination of the map it will be seen that the eastern theater of operations is mainly a narrow strip of country from thirty to sixty miles wide, and one hundred and twenty in length, lying between the Blue Ridge, on the west, and the coast of Chesapeake Bay on the east, limited on the north by the Potomac, and intersected at intervals rarely greater than ten miles by rivers of various sizes, but none of them impassable by the various means usually commanded by armies. The uniform failure which had attended the campaigns of Pope, Hooker, Burnside and Meade, through this region was not due so much to the difficulty of passing the rivers or overcoming the natural obstacles, as to faulty combinations and indecisive generalship. Had either of these Generals been permitted to unite the forces available for active operations, and moved them with energy and decision upon the enemy's lines, the result must have been in his favor, notwithstanding the natural and artificial difficulties encountered, or the length of the lines which he would have been compelled to maintain. The student of military history will find Grant's overland campaign a model in this respect. The difficulties surmounted in passing the various rivers and creeks, and in overcoming all the other obstacles, except the Wilderness, peculiar to this line, were not unusually destructive of life ; and no army was ever more abundantly or more promptly provided with supplies of all kinds necessary to its efficiency. The passage of the Rapidan, North Anna, Pamunky, Chickahominy and James Rivers, was effected with the loss of scarcely a single man. Lee made no defense of those streams ; but this was to have been anticipated ; for had he tried to hold any one of them, he must have been compelled to disseminate his troops in such a manner, to watch the various points available for crossing, that Grant could easily have caught him at such disadvantage as to render victory certain.

It was only by holding his army well in hand, compact and alert, that Lee was enabled to plant himself with such address across Grant's line of march, in time to prepare those entrenched positions which covered him almost as effectively as the regular entrenchments of Richmond could have done.   It

was this and not the physical features of the theatre of operations which gave the overland campaign its destructive
peculiarities,—making it "a kind of running siege" instead
of a campaign subject to the ordinary rules of warfare. This
peculiarity characterized all the later campaigns in the war,
and would have been just as certainly encountered had the
final campaign been made from Fortress Monroe instead of
from the Rapidan. In fact, the Peninsula route presents all
the difficulties which were encountered in the overland campaign, besides others still more formidable. The distance
from Fortress Monroe to Richmond, by the way of Williamsburg, is about eighty-five miles, and as the Peninsula is only
from five to ten miles in width, occasionally narrowing, as at
Yorktown and Williamsburg, to a defile not over two miles
wide, it is evident that, by the system of rapid fortification
which can be adapted with at least as much advantage to a
level country as to a broken one, Lee could have made as
stubborn a defense on that line as on any other. Indeed, the
battle of Cold Harbor, the bloodiest of the entire campaign,
was fought on the Peninsula, at the point where the overland
route intersects it. To be sure, Lee's position at any place
on the Peninsula might have been turned by a double passage
of either the James or the York River, but such a maneuver
would have been attended by a great deal more danger to the
invading army than any ordinary turning movement in the
open country. If undertaken, it would have presented to Lee
even a better opportunity than that of which he availed himself to deal McClellan the staggering blow at Gaines' Mill.
A route south of the James would have been, if anything,
still more disadvantageous. The experience of McClellan,
who was delayed by an insignificant* force of rebels at Yorktown nearly a month, and finally defeated by being caught

---

* "It is almost incredible, but it was nevertheless true, that an army of
58,000 men and 100 guns had been repulsed by 5000 men, and forced to resort
to the tedious delay of a siege. Had General McClellan massed his troops,
and made a bold and determined dash at any part of the Southern line on
the 5th, 6th or 7th of April, he could have broken through it."—"*Life of R.
E. Lee,*" p. 83.

with his army astride of the Chickahominy, may be justly
regarded as a warning not to be neglected by a General of
ordinary capacity. Most people of sound judgment when
they consider these arguments, will not only hold Grant
blameless, but will regard him as having shown the highest
qualities of a General in preferring the direct route to Lee's
position, where he could always defend Washington, and have
ample room for manœuvering either to the right or the left.

The case does not require further discussion; but let it be
supposed that Grant had decided differently, and after leaving 30,000 or 40,000 good troops to cover Washington, had
transferred the bulk of his army by water to Bermuda Hundred or West Point. What would have been the probable
course of events? It is not likely at that stage of the war
that Lee could have been kept ignorant of such a movement
longer than a few hours, and still less likely that he would
have remained quiescent during the month or six weeks which,
at the lowest calculation, must have intervened before the
army could have been assembled at either place. When
McClellan determined to transfer the Army of the Potomac
to the lower Chesapeake, he gave the order for collecting the
transports on the 17th of February and began his movement
from Washington on the 17th of March, and his advance
reached the vicinity of Yorktown on the 5th of April, fifty-
one days from the date of the first order, and twenty from
the actual commencement of the transfer. It is not to be
supposed that Grant, confronting the enemy on the Rapidan,
could have either withdrawn so readily, or made the movement in so short a time, even if he had decided to do so silly
a thing as to move his army by land and water three hundred
miles for the purpose of finding an enemy whom he could
reach any time in a half day's march. Had he really put
this absurd proposition into practice, how many chances would
he have had thereby, more than on the Rapidan, of finding
and beating the enemy? It is not probable that a General of
Lee's capacity would have thrown away the advantage of his
interior lines of railway communication, and stood idly wait-

ing to see where the blow would fall. During the twenty
days upon which he could have surely counted, his army could
have marched four hundred miles, or from his position at
Orange Court House to Washington, back to Richmond, then
to Washington, and back to Orange Court House again. In
all human probability he would have put into operation his
long contemplated game of "swapping queens," and when
Grant had left Washington with his army, would have overwhelmed the covering force of 30,000 or 40,000 men, and
made a detachment to take possession of the National Capitol,
while he moved with the bulk of his force upon Baltimore
and Philadelphia; or, better still, while he marched to Richmond or Petersburg, or wherever else it might be necessary
in order to meet the expeditionary force threatening him. In
this aspect of the case, the dangers of which are by no means
overstated, General Grant may well congratulate himself, as
well as the country, that he chose the overland route to find
the enemy, rather than going by water to the Peninsula, or
to the south side of the James. His fame as a strategist and
far-seeing commander needs no better foundation.

Grant has been also severely criticised for permitting Butler to advance from Fortress Monroe, and Sigel from West
Virginia, instead of uniting them with Meade before the campaign began; but it must not be forgotten that Butler was
united with Meade before the army reached Richmond, and
that Sigel's advance from West Virginia was made with
troops "which, under no circumstances, could be withdrawn
to distant fields, without exposing the North to invasion."
It was hoped, too, that the latter command, if it did not
succeed in breaking up important railroad communications,
would at least neutralize the large force which must necessarily be detached by Lee for their protection. Its success
in the latter respect was sufficiently realized in the earlier
stages of the campaign, as well as subsequently when, under
Crook, it formed a part of Sheridan's army in the Shenandoah
Valley. General Grant's plan, instead of being the concen-
tric movement of three independent and equal armies, was

really in the nature of an advance by one grand army, with two converging but important and indispensable detachments; and even if success had not given it sufficient approval, the example of Napoleon the Great, master of modern warfare, on many similar occasions, relieves the General from any culpability which may be charged upon him by over-captious critics.

It is much to be regretted that he could not have had, in some places, the assistance of men better able to comprehend and perform the duty allotted them; for it is safe to say that whenever Grant's plans failed, it was due more to faults in the details and execution than to defects in the plans themselves. No fairer opportunity was ever lost than Butler had after landing at Bermuda Hundred. Had that General been adequate to the part assigned him, he would have marched instantly against the communications of Richmond, and the rebel troops from the Carolinas hastening to its defense. He would not have disobeyed his orders to fortify at City Point, but would have left that duty to a detachment, and, in emulation of Grant's example, the year before in the interior of Mississippi, would have seized Petersburg with the bulk of his troops, broken the railroads to the South and West, scattered the forces under Beauregard, and then essayed a movement against Richmond itself. Such a campaign as this must have resulted in the capture of the rebel capitol, or at least in compelling Lee to send a strong detachment for its defense. To claim that Grant's orders did not contemplate such a campaign, is as unreasonable as to say that, when he landed at Bruinsburg, he had only Vicksburg in view, and did not contemplate making any movement whatever towards the interior, or giving battle at Port Gibson, Raymond, Jackson, or Champion's Hill, or even the necessity of breaking up the railroad between Jackson and Vicksburg, before securing a base on the Yazoo, and beginning the final operations of the siege.

It is a well established fact that throughout his career, Grant has studiously avoided giving detailed instructions to

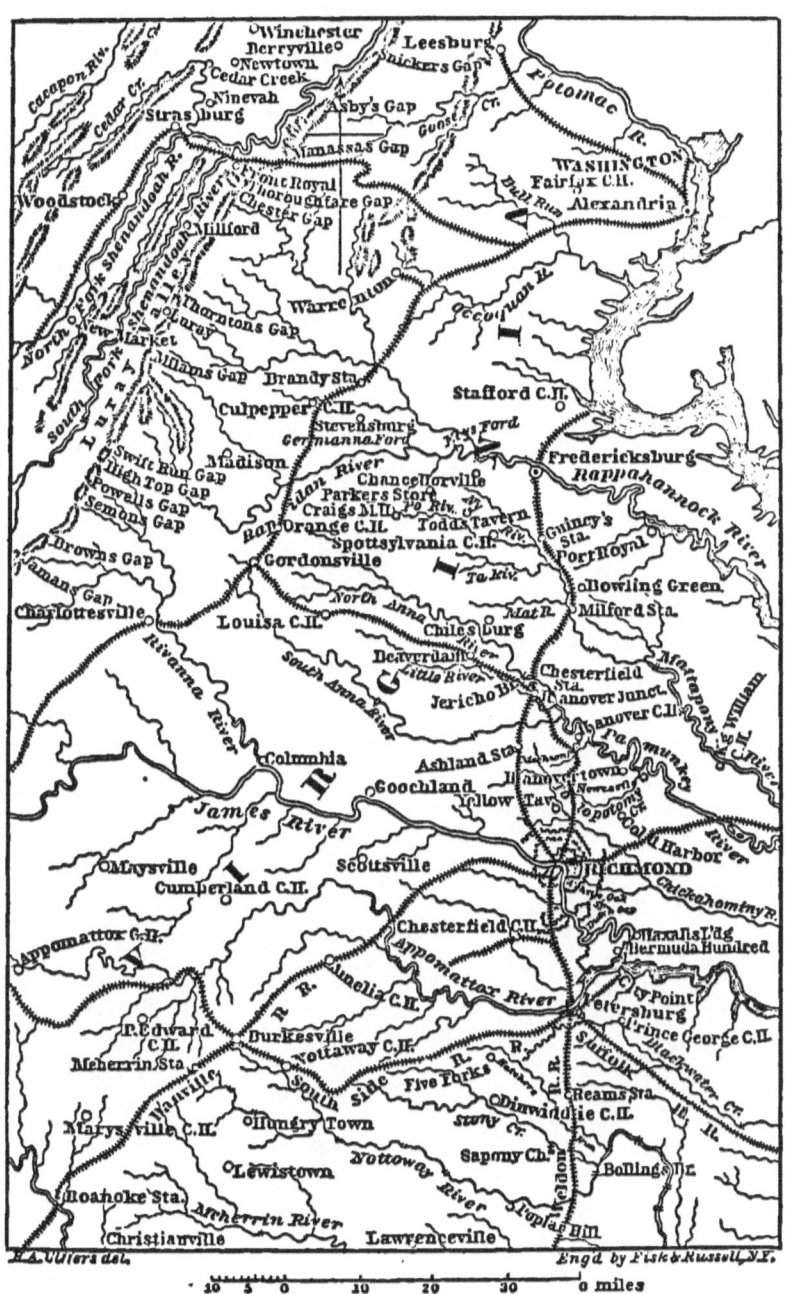

THE WILDERNESS, RICHMOND, PETERSBURG.

his subordinates. His habits in this respect were very peculiar. His greatest care seems to have been directed to the selection of subordinates who would know how to make their own orders in emergencies. With Sherman, McPherson, and Sheridan, he always regarded it as sufficient to indicate what he wished to have done, leaving them to accomplish it in whatever way circumstances might seem to require. He had the sagacity to understand that, all other things being equal, even such Generals as these would work more energetically to carry out their own plans than 'his. This indicates no servility or poverty of mind on the part of the General, but shows the keenest insight into the mysteries of human nature, and accounts, in a great degree, for some of his best generalship.

In regard to the control of events under his immediate supervision, the rule not to interfere with details appears to have been seldom departed from. He says: "Commanding all the armies as I did, I tried as far as possible to leave General Meade in independent command of the Army of the Potomac. *My instructions for that army were general in their nature, leaving all the details and the execution to him.*"* In the face of this clear statement, Grant has been held responsible for the blunder of every division, corps or army commander. No one at that period realized more clearly than the Lieutenant-General that he was engaged in a war *à l'outrance*, and while he believed in the virtues of continuous fighting, it is safe to say that he never ordered an assault, or consented to one, against the expressed judgment of the General charged with arranging the details.

When Grant took command of the Army of the Potomac, as has been stated, it was not what it had once been. The different corps could never be made to act in vigorous concert either on the march or in battle. To use the celebrated figure of the balky team, "no two of them would work together." Changes were made for the sake of harmony and to promote zeal and good feeling; but no efforts of this sort were ever

* Official Report.

entirely successful.   There always remained a faction that believed in the superiority of McClellan, and looked upon Grant
with cynical distrust.   They were not positively insubordinate, but were even more dangerous than if they had been ;
ever ready to criticise this movement or that, and to lay all
blunders at his door.   They reasoned from Grant's ante-
cedents that he was fortunate rather than able ; that he had
been always victorious because he had not yet contended
either with the best armies or the best Generals.   They could
not believe it possible that a man who had taken only a medium stand in his class at West Point, and had chosen the
infantry service, should be great in anything, and it was
thought that when he should encounter Lee and his army, he
might possibly learn something about real warfare.   It is but
just to state that these sentiments were neither general nor
powerful ; but, joined with the other difficulties of the situation, they materially complicated the solution of the problem
presented at that stage of the contest.   But for the fact that
the rank of Lieutenant-General, and the general command of
all the national forces, carried with it the power to make and
unmake whom he pleased, it is more than doubtful if even
Grant, with all his courage and generalship, could have led
the army through the first three days of the Wilderness, much
less maintained its constancy till the end.   But if there were
doubters like the faction to which we have referred, the cause
had its champions as well, who, like Lincoln and Stanton, in
the Cabinet, with Sherman, Thomas, Sheridan and a host of
gallant officers and men, in the field, inspired by the loyal
spirit of the people, gave their whole strength to the support
of the General into whose hands they had committed the destiny of the national cause.

When the complete history of all this shall be recorded, it
will be seen as not the least among the glories of our country,
that it produced its leader, as it were, out of its own virtues ;
pure, unselfish, and just ; courageous, constant and self-reliant ; watchful, patient, and full of hope ; clear-sighted,
truthful, and magnanimous.

CHAPTER XXI.

THE defensive line occupied by Lee at Orange Court House,
was well selected and thoroughly strengthened. Covered by
the Rapidan, a stream of considerable size with steep banks
and difficult fords, flanked on the east by the Wilderness, and
on the west by the foot-hills of the Blue Ridge, a direct attack
was entirely out of the question, and to turn it was exceedingly difficult. But Grant was not the man to remain long in
doubt as to what policy to pursue. A turning movement towards his right, avoiding the Wilderness, throwing him into
the open country, and more directly upon the rebel lines of
communication, seemed to promise better results in case of
immediate success; but on the other hand it would carry him
away from his own communications and leave him in greater
danger in case of a drawn battle, or a counter attack from
the enemy. He hoped to be able to crush Lee at a single
blow or at most in a few days, but he was too sagacious to
count certainly upon this. He therefore determined to move
by the left flank, crossing the Rapidan by the lower fords and

pushing through the Wilderness towards the open country in the direction of Spottsylvania. Accordingly on the 3d of May all arrangements having been perfected, the troops fully equipped, armed, and supplied with three days' cooked rations, the cavalry and artillery horses newly shod and the army concentrated in the neighborhood of Culpepper and Brandy Station, he issued his instructions to Meade for the movement to begin. That officer arranged the details as follows: Wilson, with the Third cavalry division, about 3,000 strong, was ordered to move from his camp near Stevensburg at one o'clock, on the morning of Thursday, May 4th, and to cross the Rapidan at Germania Ford, covering the construction of a pontoon bridge at that place and clearing the way for the infantry of Warren's corps, which was directed to follow close upon him. As soon as Warren's advanced division had crossed the river, Wilson was to move out by the old Wilderness Tavern and take the road to Parker's store, scouting the country in all directions and keeping the infantry informed of rebel movements. Sedgwick was directed to follow Warren, keeping close up. Gregg, with the Second cavalry division, about 3,500 strong, was ordered to move at the same time to Ely's Ford, still lower down the river, covering the march and clearing the way for Hancock's corps towards Chancellorsville. Torbert with the first cavalry division, about 3,500 strong, was to cover the trains and the rear of the army; strongly picketing the river from Rapidan Station to Germania Ford, and holding the line from Mitchell's Station to Culpepper; as soon as the crossing should be secured he was directed to rejoin Sheridan at Chancellorsville.

Precisely at midnight the movement began. Wilson's advanced guard crossed the river at 3.50, A. M., driving back the rebel pickets, and by six o'clock the bridge was laid and his division formed in line, a mile in advance of the ford.*

---

* Swinton incorrectly states that the passage of the cavalry began at six o'clock, whereas the last man had crossed ten minutes before six. See General Wilson's official report.

Warren began crossing soon afterwards, and by noon his advanced division, covered by the cavalry, had reached Wilderness Tavern, at the crossing of the Orange Turnpike and the Germania Ford roads, where he bivouacked for the night. Sedgwick kept well closed up, crossed the bridge during the afternoon, and encamped before dark about a mile beyond the ford. Hancock's corps reached the river also at an early hour in the morning, found the cavalry across and the bridge ready, and therefore lost but little time in following, camping for the night on Hooker's old battle-ground. Neither column had encountered the enemy, except the small force of pickets which had been watching the river. These were rapidly driven back by Wilson's advance, and were pursued by a small force as far as Mine Run. The country was thoroughly scouted along all the roads leading towards the stream, without encountering Lee's forces in any strength. The crossing was evidently a surprise, but the rebel General was in no manner cast down by it. He knew that he could not hold the line of the Rapidan, a fordable river, so strongly as to keep it intact, and therefore wisely held his army concentrated in an advantageous position, ready to strike in whatever direction circumstances might require. His pickets gave him timely notice, and with ready determination he moved to the attack.

On the morning of the 5th of May, Grant's army, between 90,000 and 100,000 strong, lay in the Wilderness in the following order: Wilson at Parker's store, Warren and Sedgwick on the road from Germania Ford to Wilderness Tavern, Hancock at Chancellorsville, Sheridan with Gregg and Torbert near by. The orders of the day did not contemplate a battle, although the troops were disposed in such a manner as to be prepared for attack. Wilson was directed to move at five o'clock A. M. to Craig's meeting-house on the Catharpen road, keeping out parties on the Orange Court House pike and plank-road, and sending scouts well out on all the roads to the south and west. Warren was directed to move at the same hour to Parker's store, extending his right towards

Sedgwick, who was to move to old Wilderness Tavern as soon as the roads were clear. Hancock was to march towards Shady Grove Church, extending his right towards Warren's left at Parker's store. Sheridan, with Gregg and Torbert, was directed against the enemy's cavalry at Hamilton Crossing. Wilson moved promptly at the hour designated, leaving the Fifth New York cavalry, Colonel John Hammond commanding, to hold Parker's store till relieved by Warren's advance; but by dawn this gallant regiment was hotly attacked, of which due notice was given to the troops in the rear.

Lee had taken his determination to fall upon Grant while still entangled in the Wilderness, and during the night put his entire army in motion by the two roads leading from his position to Fredericksburg, intersecting the roads from the Rapidan to Richmond at right angles. Ewell's corps was thrown forward on the old turnpike, and Hill's on the plank-road, while Longstreet's corps, which had occupied the extreme left of Lee's line, was rapidly withdrawn from Gordonsville, and ordered to the front. The two armies had bivouacked within five or six miles of each other, and both were on the alert at an early hour.

Griffin's division of Warren's corps had been thrown to the right of old Wilderness Tavern on the turnpike, the evening before, relieving the cavalry, and posting its own pickets well out.

Warren had hardly got his column in motion when his covering division was attacked with great vehemence, his pickets falling back rapidly. His orders to Crawford, commanding his advance division, were to push forward to Parker's as rapidly as possible, but that officer, although informed by Colonel McIntosh, who commanded a brigade of Wilson's division, and had just joined Hammond's hard pressed regiment, that the rebel infantry were advancing in force, moved with great deliberation, and did not reach Parker's at all. The intensity of the rebel attack in the meantime had increased to such a pitch, that a general battle was now certain. Warren lost no time in deploying Wadsworth's division abreast of, and to the left of Griffin's on the plank-road. Robinson's division was held in reserve, with one brigade in line on Wadsworth's left. Wright's division of the Sixth corps, was also ordered into position on the right of this line. With this force, a vigorous attack was made upon the advancing rebels, driving them back rapidly and in confusion; the heaviest of the fighting being done by Ayers' and Bartlett's brigades. But Ewell's leading division was soon supported by the rest of his corps, and in turn drove back Warren's entire line. The woods were so tangled and thick that the alignment could not be kept; Crawford's division was separated from Wadsworth, and the latter from the main force arrived on the turnpike; while Wright, for a similar reason, found it impossible to bring his division properly to Warren's support. Under such circumstances; these subdivisions of his command were unable to make head against the force bearing down upon them, although they struggled gallantly.

Warren had, therefore, nothing to do but to withdraw his troops to a new line somewhat to the rear but still in front of Wilderness Run. Had his attack been properly supported, Ewell must have been routed before assistance could have reached him; but this was a matter of detail which Grant could not, in person, take the time to regulate. As it was, the force of Lee's onset was broken, and his object discovered. It was now certain that the bulk of the rebel army was in our front, bent upon cutting the Army of the Potomac in two, and, if possible, driving it to the north side of the Rapidan.

Grant therefore directed Meade to recall Hancock's column, which had moved at the appointed time, southward by the way of Todd's Tavern. It was ordered to countermarch by the Brock road, and take position on Warren's left. In the meantime, Hill's corps moving on the Orange plank-road, had encountered Hammond's regiment, and, after a severe engagement, in which Colonels Hammond and McIntosh behaved with great gallantry, had driven it from Parker's, but not till Getty's division of the Sixth corps had reached the cross-roads, four miles to the eastward, and put itself in position to check Hill's advance. The intention of the latter was evidently to march down the Orange plank-road till he reached the Brock road, and then turning to the northward to throw himself upon what he supposed to be the flank of Grant's army. Fortunately this purpose was counteracted by the immovable stand made by Getty at the intersection of the roads. Hancock reached this position at three o'clock, and after beginning the construction of a line of breastworks along the Brock road, he was ordered to advance against Hill and if possible drive him beyond the position at Parker's store. A few minutes past four o'clock the attack was made in fine style by Getty's division, which encountered the rebels in great strength only a few hundred yards to the front. Hancock went to his support with Birney's and Mott's divisions, and soon afterwards the greater part of Gibbon's and Barlow's divisions, with all the artillery, became engaged, pressing forward with great ardor; but our troops could not carry the rebel position, or break the rebel lines, although they did not relinquish the effort until after nightfall.

In order to relieve the pressure on Hancock's front, and to strike Hill on the flank, Warren was directed to send a force from his left towards Parker's store. Wadsworth's division and Baxter's brigade were selected, and began the movement at about four o'clock, but they experienced such difficulty in penetrating the tangled forest that it was dark before Wadsworth could make himself felt by the enemy. Wilson's division, in the meantime, reached Craig's meeting-house at an early hour in the morning, and just beyond there encountered the rebel cavalry under Stuart, driving it rapidly back more than a mile. His ammunition becoming exhausted, he was in turn repulsed, and shortly afterwards ascertained that the rebel infantry had dislodged his regiment from Parker's store, and interposed between him the main army. Uniting his division as rapidly as possible, he struck across the country, and, after severe fighting, succeeded in forming a junction with Gregg's division at Todd's Tavern. Sheridan, having learned early in the day that the rebel cavalry at Hamilton Crossing had rejoined Lee, concentrated his corps on the left of the army, confronting the rebel cavalry under Stuart, defeating all his attempts to reach our trains, and holding all the country from Hancock's left, by the way of Todd's Tavern, to Piney Branch Church. The Ninth corps, under Burnside, had been instructed to hold a position on the north side of the Rapidan for twenty-four hours after the army had crossed. It was now ordered to the front, and, after a long and fatiguing march, reached the field on the morning of the 6th, where it was assigned a position between Warren and Hancock. Longstreet was also hastening to re-enforce Lee.

The operations of the 5th, as has been seen, were of somewhat desultory character, the principal efforts of both armies being to secure a position for delivering battle favorably. It has been said that Grant's moving columns were surprised and caught in flank, but this is not so; for although he had hoped to get through the Wilderness before encountering Lee, he had disposed of his forces to the best possible advantage, in anticipation of a battle. It has been shown that the first, and even the second, decided attacks were made by Grant's forces, and not by Lee's.

The field upon which the contending armies were concentrated, is one of the most remarkable ever known. It is a wilderness of low and bristling pines, intermingled with scrub oaks and hazels, whose sombre shade is relieved only at distant intervals by scanty clearings and scrubby openings. The face of the country is gently undulating, though here and there cut deeply by winding brooks which flow into old Wilderness Run. The roads are narrow and poor and very few. Infantry could scarcely force its way through the tangled underbrush, while artillery and cavalry were entirely out of the question, except when opportunity occurred to move them by the roads. No tactics, except those of the skirmisher, could avail. Maneuvering was impossible. Neither officers nor men could see fifty paces beyond them. The

13

Union Generals were compelled to rely exclusively upon the valor of their men, and to direct the battle by the ear or compass. Lee, on the other hand, having fought over the same ground, was familiar with its peculiarities.

Grant, with his usual aggressive determination, decided to be the attacking party on the 6th, and gave his instructions to Meade accordingly. Lee had also taken the resolution to be beforehand with offensive movements, but owing to the delay of Longstreet in joining him, he was compelled to defer his attack upon Grant's left, and occupied the first hour of the morning in making a threatening demonstration along the front of Sedgwick's corps, beginning some fifteen or twenty minutes before the time set by Grant for the general advance. It will be remembered that Sedgwick held the right, Warren and Burnside the centre, and Hancock the left, covered and supported on the extreme left and rear by Sheridan's cavalry. In this order the Union troops moved to the attack. Seymour's brigade and Rickett's division repulsed the rebel demonstration readily, while the rest of Sedgwick's corps advanced its lines some two or three hundred yards without much serious opposition; but the action soon became hot, and raged with desperation at intervals throughout the day. Sedgwick and his officers did all in their power; but the rebels, who had fortified their position during the day and night previous, could not be dislodged, while Warren's corps, which lay across the Orange Turnpike, having been called upon at an early hour to send two divisions to assist Hancock, could give Sedgwick little effective help. Lee, it seems, had conceived the idea of crushing Grant's left by an early and overwhelming attack, but before he could make his disposition for carrying this plan into effect, Hancock promptly at five o'clock in the morning, advanced with his two right divisions, and Getty's division of the Sixth corps, along both sides of the Orange plank-road, striking the rebels within a few hundred paces, and sweeping them rapidly back in the direction of Parker's store. Wadsworth led his division of the Fifth corps forward at the same time.

After an hour's most desperate fighting, the whole rebel position in Hancock's front was carried. The right of Hill's corps was driven back nearly two miles, through the heavy woods; his artillery and trains were in sight of the triumphant soldiers of the Union, and fortune seemed about to reward their courage and endurance with a complete and overwhelming victory; when Hancock unwisely called a halt for the purpose of reforming his scattered but exultant battalions. Two precious hours were irrevocably lost, and although Hancock in the interval was re-enforced by Frank's brigade of Barlow's division, Wadsworth's division of the Fifth and Stevenson's division of the Ninth corps, when he again assayed to advance and complete the work so fortunately begun, he met with most bitter opposition. The rebel leader had strengthened his imperilled right by advancing Anderson's division; he had also despatched most urgent orders to Longstreet to quicken his already rapid march. The latter had been previously directed to throw himself strongly against Hancock's left, but was now ordered to hurry to the support of Hill. Never a laggard in battle, he arrived upon the field before the onset was renewed, and, taking position on the extreme right of the rebel line, succeeded in retrieving the disasters of the morning.

Gibbon had been left with his own and Barlow's division to hold the intersection of the Brock and plank-roads, and to cover the flank of the assailing force from any turning movement on the part of the enemy; but when Hancock found himself so far advanced on the right, and the two wings of his corps separated by such a wide interval, he ordered Gibbon also to advance. That officer, apprehensive of the flank movement against which he had been warned, sent only one brigade to strengthen the advanced line. A part of Lee's plan was for Stuart to advance along the Catharpen road, and to fall upon Grant's extreme left. This movement began at an early hour, but was frustrated by Sheridan in a gallant fight at Todd's Tavern, the sound of which, however, was borne to the ears of Gibbon and Hancock, and increased their apprehensions. Under these circumstances, almost one-half of Hancock's best troops were paralyzed, instead of being thrown with crushing violence upon the already shattered lines of Hill's corps.

This apprehension for the left seems to have been fully shared by General Meade; for at one o'clock he notified to Sheridan that Hancock had been heavily pressed and his left turned,[*] and directed that the cavalry should be "drawn in" to protect the trains. Sheridan complied with this order by moving in towards Chancellorsville, while the enemy immediately occupied Todd's Tavern, Piney Branch Church, and the Furnaces. This withdrawal was founded upon a false report; but it nevertheless gave the rebels a terrible advantage, and threw the entire army into imminent jeopardy. On the other hand, had Hancock's success of the morning been properly supported and pushed forward, or had his advanced position been strengthened by properly constructed entrenchments, the advantages of the day must have been greatly in our favor, if they had not ended in a complete victory.

During the entire forenoon Longstreet's corps continued to arrive upon the field. His leading division had enabled Hill to withstand the renewal of Hancock's advance; and now it became the rebel turn to press forward under the inspiring effect of success. The attack fell at first upon Frank's brigade, the extreme left of Hancock's advanced line, which, after making the best resistance possible, was completely overrun. Mott's division then received the shock of the rebel onset, then Getty's, and, in time, the entire line under Hancock's personal supervision, including Wadsworth's division of Warren's corps. One of the most determined and bloody struggles of the war ensued; but the national divisions, in spite of the heroic efforts of men and officers, were gradually pressed back to the position from which they had advanced at dawn. In the midst of the struggle, the gallant and patriotic Wadsworth was mortally wounded, and fell into the

---

[*] Report of Major-General Sheridan, Conduct of the War, Supplement, vol. ii., p. 19.

hands of the enemy. The rebel leaders seemed to be inspired with a perfect frenzy of determination, and exposed themselves fearlessly wherever the action was hottest. Longstreet was severely wounded and carried from the field while in the act of completing his dispositions for crushing Hancock's left. Lee succeeded him in the personal supervision of the attack, and again hurled Hill's and Longstreet's corps against Hancock's sorely tried divisions, now fortunately covered by the entrenchments along the Brock road. The left had been thrown back across that road, fortified and strongly re-enforced; and had the woods not taken fire in front of the line during the final assault, the rebels must have been easily repulsed. As it was, they dashed through the flames and smoke, and a few of the more adventurous succeeded in crossing the breastworks, the defenders of which fled towards Chancellorsville.

This success was short, for Carroll's brigade, then in reserve, dashed forward in gallant style, and re-established the line. Night closing in, the battle on the outer flank was suspended; but the enemy, massing swiftly on his left under Gordon, unexpectedly assailed Sedgwick's corps in front and flank, with great fury, overthrowing Seymour's and Shaler's brigades, and taking with those Generals nearly 4,000 prisoners. For a few minutes it seemed that nothing but a miracle could save the army; but the gallant and imperturbable Sedgwick lost no time in throwing back his right and re-establishing his corps against the impetuous but disorderly onset of the rebels. The darkness of night, deepened by the impenetrable shades of the Wilderness, put an end to the second days' battle. The loss on both sides had been unusually heavy, though the advantages gained were greatly in favor of the national army. Lee had chosen his own line of attack, and made his plan of battle with the intention of forcing Grant back upon the Rapidan; but before the first movement could be made he was foiled by Grant, who forced the fighting with such determination as to seriously threaten the complete destruction of Lee's army before noon. The sudden and overwhelming onset of Hancock, threw Lee essentially upon the defensive, in which attitude he remained during the remainder of the campaign, notwithstanding the fact that he resolutely availed himself of every opportunity to make an offensive return, and to re-establish his lines whenever broken. The actual result of Gordon's attack upon Sedgwick was insignificant, with the exception of the damage inflicted upon Grant's army by the loss of prisoners and the exaggerated influence it produced in the minds of such persons as had a longing desire for an encampment on the north side of the Rapidan. Grant himself was not shaken in his purpose. He knew that if he had not defeated Lee, he had at least not suffered defeat; and as it had never been his custom to rest content with a drawn battle, it did not occur to him that there was anything else to be done but to go ahead.

In most accounts of the two days in the Wilderness, Sheridan's operations are hardly mentioned, although it has been seen that they had an important influence upon the course of events. Had not the march of the rebel infantry along the Orange plank-road been checked at Parker's store by McIntosh, and had not the movement of the rebel cavalry under Stuart on the Catharpen road been foiled by the actions at Craig's meeting-house and Todd's Tavern, under Wilson and Gregg, the result of the second day's battle might have been entirely different. Stuart would have turned the left of Hancock's line, fallen upon our trains and rear, and, in some degree, accomplished what Longstreet aimed at by his movement against the Brock road. The most prominent feature, however, of the actions in the Wilderness, was the overthrow of the rebel right by Hancock, Getty, and Wadsworth, the loss of the advantage due to this fortunate movement by an apprehension for our left and the great difficulty of maintaining a close and orderly array. The return of the rebels re-enforced by Longstreet, and the assault upon Sedgwick's right, were subordinate incidents, grave enough in their character, and, to a General of less resolute temper, or duller perception than Grant, might have been looked upon as a sufficient reason for relinquishing the campaign in its outset.

It has been asserted that in this battle Grant made little account of those arts that accomplish results by the direction and combination of forces, and that he avowedly despised manœuvering at that period, relying exclusively on the application of brute masses in rapid and remorseless blows ; * but when it is remembered that the dense forest in which he was compelled to give battle, was an unknown region through which no vision could penetrate, and in which no tactical or strategic skill could be made available, it will be sufficiently understood why he was unable to avail himself of the successes which followed his first combinations. But this battle is not to be judged by ordinary rules. It was probably the strangest ever fought. The manœuvers by which it was introduced, and the direction of the forces as they plunged into the Wilderness, could not have been more advantageously or brilliantly combined; and without referring to the strategy of Vicksburg and Chattanooga, they are a sufficient answer to the criticism just mentioned. General Grant may indeed have said, as alleged, that he never manœuvered ; but if so, it may fairly be assumed that the remark was intended as a rebuke to the empty spirit of pedantry at one time so common in that army, and under the influence of which it had too frequently striven to avoid battle, or had lost opportunities which, with more action and less theory, might have led to victory and to good fortune. It is well known, however, that in the Wilderness, as everywhere else during the overland campaign, the tactics, whatever may have been their merit or demerit, were Meade's ; while the heroic resolution which carried the army through " the region of gloom and the shadow of death," was Grant's. It was no blind faith in the policy of " hammering continuously," nor lack of faith in judicious combinations, which saved the army from the perils that beset it in that " battle which no man could see." Grant knew that the battle had not been fought through, and was confident that, uncovered by breastworks, upon a fair field, his army was superior to Lee's, and he was morally certain that it had suf-

* Swinton's " Army of the Potomac."

fered proportionally no more than Lee's in the two days' death-grapple which it had passed through. But, more than all, he felt that the country stood in absolute need of victory, and, like a true citizen, he determined that it should not be disappointed, no matter what the cost. To prove that Grant did not miscalculate, it is only necessary to point to the result. At no time after the battle of the Wilderness did Lee show the boldness which had previously characterized him; for he had learned a lesson in the preliminary struggle that he could never forget. He had found his superior in pluck and generalship, and ever afterwards played his game as warily as if he felt a prophetic certainty that defeat must eventually overtake him as well as the cause he was upholding. The days of rapid maneuvering in which he commanded both armies, had passed, and there was nothing left him but to conform to the irrevocable decrees of fate.

The Army of the Potomac had at last found its hero, who, clear of head, stout of heart, loyal, true, and brave, was destined to hold it to the work of National salvation till the rebel power should be broken and destroyed, and Richmond, like another Vicksburg, should fall before his unrelenting blows. There are many who well remember the night of the 6th of May, when a terrible disaster seemed about to overwhelm us, and it was whispered with bated breath that we should be compelled to retreat by obscure roads and difficult fords to the north side of the Rapidan. The turning of the Sixth corps introduced one of those crises calculated to shake the fortitude of the stoutest heart, and upon which, it is not too much to assert, the success of our cause depended with tremulous uncertainty. A single blunder, or a moment's hesitation, would have covered the army with disgrace. The situation was such as to demand every heroic quality in the commander whose shoulders were required to bear the burthen of that perilous emergency; and when Grant, surpassing the steadiness indicated by the hereditary motto of his clan,— "Stand fast: Craig Ellachie!"—with that restrained but indomitable resolution which has never failed him, gave utter-

ance to the order: "Forward to Spottsylvania!" there was not
a heroic nature in all that host but felt its troubles lightened.
Every true soldier knew by instinct that the greatest danger
had past.   The Army of the Potomac from that moment entered upon a new career; hitherto it had in no single instance
fought its battle through, or reaped the legitimate fruits of
the contest; but henceforth it was destined never to turn
back, or to rest in the struggle till crowned with the laurels of
victory.   From that day forth, although baffled, delayed, and
staggered, it held its way onward through the terrible times of
Spottsylvania, North Anna, Tolopotomoy, Cold Harbor, and
the investment of Petersburg, sternly and courageously for a
whole year, meeting the enemy in almost daily battle.   It is
true that the wisest sometimes doubted, and the hearts of the
bravest occasionally grew faint and despondent,—but the army
gloriously responded to the call of duty; and yet it is not too
much to say that without a greater quality than the discipline
and organization for which it has been so justly lauded, even
Grant himself could not have led it through such a campaign
to its final triumph.   The spirit of the people living in its
ranks, answered the call of its leader, and carried it still
onward, when discipline alone was powerless.

CHAPTER XXII.

At an early hour on the 7th of May, Grant threw forward
his skirmishers to ascertain the movements of the enemy;
while Sheridan dispatched Wilson's division from Chancellorsville towards Germania Ford, for the purpose of ascertaining whether any part of the insurgent force had interposed
itself between Sedgwick and the river. By these means it
was soon ascertained that the rebels had retired to their fortified line, and no longer courted battle. The trains, in the
meantime, had been collected in the neighborhood of Chancellorsville, and at an early hour were ordered to move to
Piney Branch Church; but as this point and Todd's Tavern
were both held by the rebel cavalry, Sheridan parked the
trains on the road toward Fredericksburg, and proceeded
with Gregg's and Merritt's* divisions to drive back Stuart's
horse, which he succeeded in doing after a severe engagement
at Todd's Tavern. At three o'clock P. M., Meade issued the
detailed orders for the movement of the army towards Spottsylvania, beginning after nightfall, Warren withdrawing first,
moving by the Brock road and Todd's Tavern, followed closely
by Hancock; while Sedgwick and Burnside were ordered to
move by Chancellorsville and Piney Branch Church. Sheri-

* The latter temporarily commanded by General Torbert.

dan was instructed to keep a proper force well out in front of the exposed flank of the army. It was hoped that this movement would be made with such rapidity as to concentrate the army at Spottsylvania by an early hour in the morning; but for a variety of reasons this expectation was not realized. The average distance to be marched did not exceed twelve miles; but the troops never marched more slowly. Warren was delayed by General Meade's escort, and finally, it is claimed, by Merritt, with the first cavalry division; but no such excuse can be given for the failure of the left column to reach the designated point upon which it was directed. Sheridan ordered Wilson to march at five o'clock A. M., by the way of Alsop's to the Fredericksburg road, to cross the Ny River, and then to push forward to Spottsylvania Court House, forming a junction with Gregg and Merritt at Snell's Bridge.* It was understood, and Wilson was informed, that Burnside would follow closely upon the same route. The former, therefore, marched with great celerity, meeting with no resistance till he reached the crossing of the Ny, where he found a cavalry picket; but, brushing it promptly out of the way, he dashed across the stream, and pushed rapidly towards the Court House, where he encountered and dispersed Wickhams brigade of cavalry. Hearing heavy musketry to the northward on the roads to Todd's Tavern and Piney Branch Church, he held the cross-roads at the Court House with one brigade, and marched in the direction of the fighting with

* NOTE.—"Had these movements been carried out successfully, it would probably have sufficiently delayed the march of the enemy to Spottsylvania Court House as to enable our infantry to reach that point first, and the battles fought there would have probably occurred elsewhere; but upon the arrival of General Meade at Todd's Tavern the orders were changed, and Gregg was simply directed by him to hold Corbin's Bridge, and Merritt's division ordered in front of the infantry column, marching on the road to Spottsylvania. In the darkness of the night, the cavalry and infantry becoming entangled in the advance. caused much confusion and delay. I was not duly advised of these changes, and for a time had fears for the safety of General Wilson's command, which had proceeded, in accordance with my instructions, to Spottsylvania, capturing and holding it till driven out by the advance of Longstreet's corps." *Report of Major-General Sheridan, Supplemental Report on the Conduct of the War,* vol. ii., p. 19.

the other, but had not proceeded more than a half or three quarters of a mile before his advance found itself behind a line of the rebel infantry, which it assailed, capturing prisoners from two divisions of Longstreet's corps, and recapturing some of Warren's men who had just been taken. At this juncture of affairs, the arrival of one of Burnside's divisions would have given Grant firm possession of Spottsylvania, besides enabling him to crush Longstreet by an attack front and rear; but, for some reason not sufficiently explained, Meade had, in the meantime, suspended the entire movement. Upon learning this, Sheridan ordered Wilson to withdraw from Spottsylvania, and to rejoin the army on the north side of the Ny.

The column on the Brock road led by Merritt's division was strongly resisted by Stuart's cavalry, which had been driven back several miles the day before, but which still maintained a determined front. Merritt, weakened by the detachment of Gregg, made but slow progress in advancing through the heavily wooded country, and after several hours' hard work was relieved by Warren's leading division, under Robinson. The rebel cavalry in falling back had taken the precaution to barricade the roads, so that Robinson's advance was not made with any remarkable rapidity. However, about eight o'clock, A. M., it reached an open field nearly two miles north of the Court House, with rising, heavily wooded ground beyond, upon which the enemy was seen to be in considerable force. Hastily forming his troops, Robinson, assisted by Warren in person, advanced to the attack, but had not succeeded in crossing half the open space before he received a terrible fire of musketry, which threw the entire division into great confusion; General Robinson was severely wounded. Neither officers nor men expected to be met so soon by their old antagonists of the Wilderness, and hence fell back without delay to the woods from which they had advanced, and where it was difficult to halt and reform them. Griffin's division, which had been thrown forward on Robinson's right, received the same unexpected greeting, and also fell back.

Crawford's division and Cutler's (formerly Wadsworth's), were hurried forward, and succeeded, after some sharp fighting, in carrying a part of the rebel position, thus relieving the pressure against Robinson and Griffin.

The corps was now developed, and involuntarily fell to entrenching. The force which had thus checked Warren and paralyzed the entire movement against Spottsylvania, was the advanced division of Longstreet's corps, which had just arrived. It was not till some hours afterwards that Lee fully discovered the extent and scope of Grant's southward march, and not till night that he had succeeded in concentrating his army in front of Spottsylvania. In the meantime, Meade had become alarmed for his right flank and rear, and had halted Hancock at Todd's Tavern for the purpose of resisting any movement along the Catharpen road. Sedgwick, who had closed upon Warren and put a part of his corps into position facing the new rebel front, late in the afternoon decided to make an attack, and gave orders to that effect; but the attack was made by an insufficient force, consisting of the New Jersey brigade and Crawford's division. The former was repulsed, but the latter caught a part of Ewell's corps in flank, and drove it rapidly for some distance, capturing a hundred prisoners and one flag. Burnside and Hancock did no fighting whatever, so that between fortifying in front and watching for the rebels in flank and rear, Lee was quietly suffered to march by the nearest route, and put his army directly in the road along which Grant wished to march. The rebel commander showed no desire to take the offensive in any manner whatever, but fell to work rapidly and silently to fortify the ridges lying about Spottsylvania, which were to become his new bulwark of defense. Fortune, and the slow marching of the national troops, had favored him more than he ought to have expected; the shovels, picks, and axes of his men did the rest towards preparing Spottsylvania for the desperate struggle about to burst upon its quiet and hitherto peaceful surroundings.

On Monday, the 9th of May, Sheridan, with all the cavalry,

was despatched upon a movement towards Richmond in quest of the rebel horse, and for the purpose of breaking Lee's communications with the rear; while the four corps of infantry took up their position in the general line already determined by the events of the preceding day. Hancock, marching to the field by the road from Todd's Tavern, went to Warren's right, and formed the right of the Union line on high ground overlooking the valley of the Po. Sedgwick was already on Warren's left, and Burnside, crossing the Ny, near the road upon which he was originally expected to move, formed the left of the line, on a ridge conforming to one of the branches of the Ny. Lee had formed his army along the irregular ridge separating the vallies of the Ny and Po, and sweeping around Spottsylvania on the arc of a circle, covering all the roads centering at that place. Longstreet held the left, Ewell the center, and Hill the right. The contending lines were drawn so closely to each other that no advance could take place on either side without bringing on a battle. Neither army lost time in fortifying its position, but with the exception of the usual fusillade kept up by the skirmishers, no fighting took place during the day. Lee rested content with holding himself ready to repel attack, while Grant and his subordinates were eagerly seeking for a flaw or a weak point in the enemy's well established lines, through which an effective blow might be struck. During the afternoon, while engaged in examining the rebel lines from an advanced part of his own, General Sedgwick, commanding the Sixth corps, was killed by a rebel rifle shot, which struck him full in the face. He had just been bantering the men near him for seeking cover behind their parapets, as the rebel bullets were whistling over them, when he received the fatal blow. This unfortunate event caused the most profound grief throughout the army, as well as in his own corps, for he was not only regarded as one of the best, bravest, and most discreet commanders, but was generally beloved for his rare personal qualities. He was justly respected as the Thomas of the Eastern armies; endowed with every manly and soldierly quality, ripe in experience, brave and skillful in battle, patient and regular on the march, and full of ardent zeal for the cause of his country. His death was looked upon by Grant as a greater disaster than the loss of an entire division of troops would have been. He was succeeded in command of the Sixth corps, by General H. G. Wright, an officer of experience and ability.

During the afternoon, a rebel wagon train was observed moving southward towards Spottsylvania; and as the road was not far from Hancock's right, he was directed to cross the Po, and after capturing the train, to try that flank of the rebel line. The movement began at once; and although the stream was crossed without any material difficulty or delay, night set in before a blow could be struck. In the meantime the wagon train escaped, but at an early hour the next day the movement against the rebel left was continued. The entire army was now in position, and batteries were established, and the lines well entrenched. Hancock had not gone far before he found himself stopped by the deep vallies of an affluent of the Po, beyond which the enemy was posted in great strength. Throwing forward Brooks' brigade still farther to the right, he crossed, and began an attempt to develop the rebel position and strength. In the meantime it had also been decided to make an assault upon the rebel works in front of the Fifth and Sixth corps. Hancock's movement was accordingly suspended, and two divisions of his corps were ordered to recross the Po, for the purpose of joining in the assault. In obedience to this order, Gibbon and Birney were withdrawn, leaving Barlow to hold the advanced position already gained, and to cover the retrograde movement. The rebels, however, were not slow to perceive this withdrawal, and therefore hastened to attack the rear of Birney's column. Fearing to isolate any part of his corps, Hancock then decided to withdraw Barlow also, whose skirmishers had already been attacked and pressed back. The rebels seemed to be inspired by what they looked upon as a forced retreat of the troops confronting them, and made a decided attack upon this division, but met with a severe and

bloody repulse. The woods taking fire complicated the difficulties surrounding Hancock's rear, but the withdrawal was
finally effected in good order, though many of the wounded
were left behind, to perish in the flames or to languish in
rebel hospitals.

The principal point of attack in Warren's front, was a
densely wooded ridge which the rebels had occupied and
strongly fortified. During the morning, Gibbon's division of
Hancock's corps had this position, but was repulsed with
severe loss. At three o'clock P. M., Crawford's and Cutler's
divisions of Warren's corps made a strong demonstration
against the same point, but with no better fortune. So far
the operations of the day had resulted in no substantial advantage to the national arms except a tolerable understanding
of the rebel position and its capability of defense. A weak
point had been discovered in front of Russell's division of the
Sixth corps, and a column of twelve picked regiments, under
command of Colonel Emory Upton, of the One Hundred and
Twentieth New York, an exceedingly able and intrepid young
officer of the regular army, was formed for the purpose of
assaulting this part of the rebel line ; Hancock and Warren
were informed that this assault would be made, and were directed to support it with their entire corps. The remainder
of the Sixth corps had similar orders. Upton made his dispositions with great care and discretion—instructed his officers
and men minutely in the course they were to pursue during
the charge, and also after the works should be carried, formed
his battalions in column, and about five o'clock led them
gallantly to the attack.

So carefully had all his plans been made, and so suddenly
and coherently were they carried into effect, that the rebel
lines were completely broken, and several guns and nearly a
thousand prisoners were taken. The success of the attack was
all that could be wished, but the intrepid young commander
was not satisfied with holding the works he had captured.
He knew too well that the rebels would fall upon him in
tremendous force if he allowed them time to reform their dis-

ordered ranks; he therefore turned at once to the right and left along their entrenchments, wrapping up and driving back the rebels holding them. The operation seemed to promise a complete victory, but unfortunately the Generals whose business it was to support the movement, did not lead their divisions forward until it was too late. Nobody but Grant and Upton appeared to have any confidence that the rebel works could be carried, and therefore nobody but Upton was ready for the part assigned him. The balky team could not be made to pull together, and hence Upton, after holding what he had gained till dark, was finally compelled to fall back to his own works. Thus a splendid opportunity was lost. Shortly afterwards, Hancock and Warren both led their corps bravely forward upon other and unshaken sections of the rebel line, and although the men did all in their power to carry their standards into the rebel stronghold, they were compelled to relinquish the attempt, after having suffered heavily in killed and wounded, Generals J. C. Rice and T. G. Stevenson being among the former. The assaults were renewed an hour later, in the vain hope that they might be simultaneous, and result in victory, but this was not to be. The close of the day's fighting found the two hosts holding substantially the same positions they held in the morning, but Grant's confidence, although sorely tried, remained unshaken. He saw that the rebel lines when properly attacked could be broken, that the men composing the army, whenever well led, acquitted themselves with courage and resolution, and he therefore felt confident that success must ultimately crown their exertions. At eight o'clock, on the 11th of May, he sent to the War Department the following characteristic bulletin: "We have ended the sixth day of very heavy fighting. The result to this time is much in our favor. Our losses have been heavy, as well as those of the enemy. I think the loss of the enemy must be greater. We have taken 5,000 prisoners by battle, whilst he has taken from us but few except stragglers. *I propose to fight it out on this line if it takes all summer.*"

14

Fight it out he did, bravely, persistently, and patiently, against opposition and resistance which might well have shaken even his iron determination.

On the 11th there was no general engagement, but continuous skirmishing was kept up and much time was devoted to reconnoitering the enemy's lines in the hope of finding a weak place in them. Hitherto the attack had been principally against Lee's left and left centre, but it was now determined to attack farther towards his right, where his lines made a strong salient. During the dark and stormy night of the 11th, Hancock's corps drew out from its old entrenchments, and passing in rear of the Sixth corps went into position about midway between the Piney branch and Fredericksburg roads, some twelve hundred yards in front of the rebel works which it was required to storm. Hancock massed his corps as follows: Barlow's division, formed by brigade in regimental columns, doubled on the center, with Birney's division deployed in double lines, constituted the front of attack; Mott's division supported Birney, while Gibbon's division was held in reserve. The direction was given by the point of the compass, and at dawn on the morning of May 12th, the advancing columns emerged from the woods and without stopping to fire a shot marched at quick time against the enemy. When nearly half way towards the hostile line, the gallant veterans of the Second corps burst forth with a thundering cheer, and taking the double quick, pushed rapidly forward to the abattis, tearing it away, and rolling across the entrenchments beyond with an irresistible impulse. The rebels were taken by surprise but they rushed to their arms and made a gallant but ineffectual defense. Birney and Barlow crossed their works almost simultaneously, and after a desperate battle with bayonet, clubbed musket, and rifle shot, established themselves firmly in the rebel stronghold. They captured thirty field guns, two rebel Generals, and something over 3,000 prisoners. Hancock, after apprising Grant of his success, pushed forward in the hope of cutting the rebel army entirely in two, and completing the victory. He had struck Lee a staggering blow and another such would annihilate the rebel army of North Virginia. But the surprise was now over; and although the victors were inspired by success and pushing forward with determination, they were soon checked by a steady and well directed fire from an interior line of works, nearly a half mile beyond the line they had already carried.

This checked the advance, and as the supporting corps were not at hand, the rebel commander was enabled to re-enforce his center by drawing troops from his flanks, and after a sharp fight drove Hancock back to the first position carried. Grant had foreseen the emergency, and hurried Wright's corps to aid Hancock, while Burnside and Warren were directed to attack along their fronts for the purpose of preventing an overwhelming assembly of rebels in front of the captured salient. Meade received orders to this effect in ample time, but his execution of them was too slow by twenty minutes or a half-hour. If Wright had followed closely after Hancock, with his forces well in hand ready to hurl them upon the broken lines of the enemy before they were able to reform, a complete victory might have been won, but opportunities of this kind with a well-disciplined army rarely last more than five or ten minutes, so that when Wright did arrive, which was at six o'clock, he found Hancock closely beset by Lee, who was now exerting himself to the utmost to re-establish his broken lines. Wright at once relieved that part of Hancock's line holding the rebel works to the right of the salient, while Hancock concentrated his corps on the left. Warren and Burnside assaulted about eight o'clock, but made no perceptible impression. The fight now became general all along the line. Lee made five furious assaults in quick succession with the intention of dislodging our men from the dearly bought works; and although the rebels fought with great fury, planting their flags in some instances in the very midst of the Union troops, they were repulsed each time with great loss. Finding that Warren could not carry the works in his front, Cutler's and Griffin's divisions were sent to support Hancock and Wright, and render their tenure of the salient as certain as it could be made. It was hoped, too, that a new movement might be conducted from this place, but our troops were unable to advance, though they ultimately succeeded in getting off twenty of the captured guns, and continued to hold firm possession of the salient which they had won at such a terrible cost. Lee fortified and held a line only a few paces to the front, so that his position became as secure as ever.

The fighting of this day was as severe as any during the war, and it is to be doubted if musketry firing was ever kept up so incessantly as it was by the contending troops near the captured salient. The whole forest within range was blighted by it, and one tree eighteen inches in diameter was actually cut in two by the leaden bullets which struck it. The loss on both sides was great, but, the advantages gained by the Union army confirmed Grant in his plans, and reassured the army in its own prowess.

The terrific battle of the 12th, having resulted in Lee's retiring to his inner line, Grant soon decided to undertake a movement against his right flank. With this view, the Fifth corps was withdrawn from its old position, on the right, and directed to move by the rear of the army to the extreme left. The march began at ten o'clock on the night of the 13th, but owing to the heavy rain which had fallen the day before, and to the dense fog which arose during the night, the troops moved with great difficulty, and although fires had been lighted to guide them through the trackless woods, they did not reach the left of the line till daylight, and then in such a jaded condition as to deprive them of all hope of making a successful attack. The Sixth corps followed close upon the Fifth, and was followed in turn by the Second, and after much skirmishing with several sharp combats, intermitted by maneuvers and marches for position, hard work upon roads and a change of base to Acquia Creek, Grant formed his army on the 18th, facing nearly east, with its left flank at Massaponax Church, and the right on the Fredericksburg road. Lee had gradually extended his lines in the same direction, covering himself wherever it was possible by rifle-trench and impenetrable slashings. By dawn of this day, the army was in position for an assault. It was hoped that by throwing a part of Hancock's corps rapidly back to the ground of its former victory, the enemy might be caught napping. Accordingly the divisions of Gibbon and Barlow, supported by Birney, and Tyler's division of heavy artillery, drawn from the defenses of Washington, were selected for this purpose, and moved to the attack in two lines, but they were met by the enemy before they had advanced a quarter of a mile; after suffering severe loss in trying to force their way through the slashing that encumbered the ground, they were forced to retire.

Grant had, in the meantime, determined to carry the army forward by a turning movement towards the south. Prepara-tions for putting this plan into effect were begun on the after-noon of the 19th, but the enemy perceiving something of Grant's intention, made a bold demonstration against his ex-treme right, now held by the heavy artillery division under Tyler. Ewell sallied out from his works, crossed the Ny above Tyler's position, and swung in behind him striking the Fredericksburg road and taking possession of an ammunition train then marching to join the army. Tyler met this move-ment promptly and vigorously, driving the rebels quickly from the road and into the woods beyond. His men were unused to battle, although they had been in service nearly two years, but they fought like veterans, or even better and much more recklessly. Shortly after the action began, the Second and Fifth corps, were sent to Tyler's support and with him drove Ewell back into his works, taking several hundred prisoners. This threw Lee again upon the defensive, and enabled Grant to renew his southward march on the night of the 21st, direct-ing his columns by the way of Milford Station, and Chester-field towards the North Anna River. Lee, however, had again the shorter line and lost no time in hurrying his army towards Richmond for the purpose of intercepting his relent-less adversary.

On emerging from the Wilderness, Grant had despatched
Sheridan with the cavalry, led by Merritt, Gregg, and Wilson,
on a raid, with orders to engage the rebel cavalry, break up
Lee's communications, and then to threaten Richmond, and
eventually communicate with Butler on the James River.
Making a detour in the direction of Fredericksburg, and then
moving directly southward, Sheridan crossed the North Anna
on the 10th, and struck the Virginia Central Railroad at Beaver
Dam Station, destroying ten miles of track, two locomotives,
three trains of cars, and a million and a half of rations. He
also liberated four hundred prisoners, taken in the Wilderness
and now on the road to captivity in Libby prison. The march
had hardly begun before Lee's scouts informed him of it. As
was expected, Stuart with the mass of rebel cavalry, started
at once in pursuit, and came up with Sheridan's rear on the
North Anna, but was easily repulsed. Sheridan crossed the
South Anna at Ground Squirrel Bridge and pushed on towards Richmond with Merritt and Wilson, but sent Gregg to
the left for the purpose of striking the railroad at Ashland
Station. Moving rapidly, Gregg reached the station just after
daylight, and destroyed one train of cars, a large lot of army
supplies and six miles of track. While engaged in this work, his
rear brigade was attacked by Stuart, but after a sharp fight,
succeeded in driving him off. Sheridan moving down the direct turnpike towards Richmond, found the main part of the
rebel cavalry in position near the Yellow Tavern, where a
sharp fight ensued, in which Custer's brigade of Merritt's division, and Wilson's division took the principal part. The
rebels were quickly routed, losing three guns and a number
of prisoners, besides General Stuart and J. B. Gordon mortally wounded.

After this action a demonstration was made in the direction
of Richmond, but the works of that place were thought to be
too strong and too strongly manned, to be attacked with a
reasonable hope of success. Sheridan therefore halted his
command till nearly midnight, at which time he resumed the
march, Wilson in advance, for the purpose of penetrating be-

tween the Chickahominy and the Richmond defences to Fair
Oaks and thence to the James River. The marching columns were undisturbed except by the bursting of an occasional torpedo, which the rebels had planted in the roads, till
the advanced guard had reached the Mechanicsville pike,
where a halt was called and the advanced division massed.
This delay arose from the necessity of finding a new guide,
and looking out the road which could be no longer seen on
account of darkness ; but the halt had hardly been called when
the heavy guns of the rebel works, not over two hundred
yards distant opened upon the unsuspecting troopers, throwing them momentarily into considerable confusion. Wilson
however, deployed both brigades of his division promptly, and
drove the rebel skirmishers back into their works. Shortly
afterwards daylight appeared and revealed the true situation
of affairs, showing the rebel works resting upon the bluffs of
the Chickahominy so closely as to preclude all idea of continuing the march any farther towards Fair Oaks. By this
time Gregg with the rear division had also been attacked.
The whole command was now wedged in between the rebel
works in front, and the swamps of the Chickahominy in rear.
Sheridan, however, was not long in finding a way out. Ordering Wilson and Gregg to hold their position at all hazards,
he directed Merritt to force a crossing of the Chickahominy,
driving away the rebel cavalry, and to repair the bridge
which the rebels had destroyed a few days before. This was
done in handsome style, after Custer had essayed a crossing
and failed ; and although the rebel force continued to press
Wilson and Gregg, the command was withdrawn without serious loss. The march was then resumed by the way of Pole
Green Church to Gaines' Mill, where the entire corps encamped for the night. The next day it recrossed the Chickahominy by fording, at the bottom bridges, and continued the
march by the way of White Oak Swamp and Malvern Hill,
to Haxall's Landing, where Sheridan communicated with
Butler at Bermuda Hundred.

This raid was a success in one essential particular, leading

to the victory at Yellow Tavern, which was complete, in so
far as it put an end to the fancied superiority of the rebel
cavalry.   It was observed always afterwards that they could
not make head successfully against the national horse, unless
supported and re-enforced by infantry.   Sheridan's troopers
were correspondingly improved by their achievements.

CHAPTER XXIII.

An important part of Grant's plan of operations was the
movement of Butler's column from Fortress Monroe. A considerable force hitherto engaged in profitless coastwise expeditions had been concentrated at that place under Gillmore
and W. F. Smith,—the former commanding the Tenth,[*] and
the latter the Eighteenth corps,—in all, not far from 30,000
men. This force, with the exception of a small division of
horse under Kautz, stationed at Norfolk and Portsmouth,
was assembled at Yorktown and Gloucester Point. Butler
was, therefore, in position to move by the Peninsular route
directly upon Richmond, or to throw his force suddenly by
transports to some convenient point on the James, threatening
the rebel capital from the south side. The latter was the real
plan in view, but with the intention of misleading the rebels,
Butler on the 1st of May made a feint of striking from the
York River as well as along the Peninsula. Kautz, with his
mounted division, also moved forward from Suffolk. Hav-

---

[*] The Tenth corps was composed of three divisions under Terry, Ames and
Turner; the Eighteenth, of two divisions under Weitzel and Brooks, with a
brigade of colored troops under Hinks.

ing pushed a small force to within a few miles of Richmond, he withdrew rapidly and embarked his entire force on board the transports on the night of the 4th, and steamed down the York and up the James, convoyed by a fleet of gun-boats under Admiral Lee.   The next day he landed detachments of his force at Wilson's wharf, Fort Powhattan, and the main body of his army at City Point and Bermuda Hundred, two miles above the mouth of the Appomattox.   This point was selected as being susceptible of easy defense, and also affording a good base for operations against either Petersburg or Richmond as well as the railroad connecting them.   The landing was made without resistance, and on the next day Smith moved out towards the Petersburg and Richmond road, but failed to reach it.   On the 7th he was re-enforced by a part of Gillmore's corps, struck the railroad near Walthall Junction, and immediately began the work of destruction, pushing towards Petersburg.   During these operations he encountered and drove back the rebels under D. H. Hill, and made rapid progress in the task assigned to him.   While this was going on, Butler, with the rest of his troops, was engaged in establishing a strong defensive line across the neck at Bermuda Hundred, and in concentrating the detachments of his command.   About this time he heard of Lee's retrograde movement towards Richmond, closely pursued by the Army of the Potomac ; he therefore withdrew Smith who had reached Swift Creek, three miles from Petersburg, concentrated his available force on the railroad, and turned his face towards Richmond, with the intention of getting there before Grant. Pushing northward he drove the rebel force of observation beyond Proctor's Creek, into their entrenched position' near Drury's Bluff, and by the 15th, made his arrangements to assault and drive them from that fortification.

But in the meantime the Richmond authorities were not idle.   As soon as Butler's movement had developed itself, they summoned Beauregard from Charleston with all the troops that could be gathered in Georgia, and North and South Carolina.   This force, together with the local militia and the garrison of Richmond, amounted to something like 20,000 men; and instead of being divided by the operations against the railroad as had been supposed, they were assembled in the works extending from the railroad to Drury's Bluff. On the morning of the 16th of May, Beauregard assumed the offensive and under cover of a heavy fog made a general attack upon Butler's long and attenuated line. The rebel commander had left Whiting's division in the neighborhood of Petersburg, and his plan was for this division to advance and seize Butler's line of retreat, while the main force interposed itself between his right flank and the James River. The attack was made with unusual vigor, and being favored by the darkness of the morning was at first almost entirely successful. Smith's right brigade under Heckman was swept away, and routed; but just at this juncture General Ames threw forward three regiments of his division, which had been placed in reserve to support Smith, and happily succeeded in checking the advancing rebels just as they were about to seize the road to Bermuda Hundred. While this turning movement was in progress Beauregard attacked Weitzel's and Brook's divisions of Smith's corps, with great fury, but was easily repulsed.

This fortunate result was partially due to the ingenuity of General Smith, who had made an entanglement of telegraph wire, covering a part of his front. Being checked on all sides, the advantage of Beauregard's offensive was lost, but he now determined to renew his turning movement against the Union right, by marching to the southward, by a route nearer to the James. This caused Smith to fall back so as to protect the trains and to cover the roads leading to the depots at Bermuda Hundred. His front was too much extended already for a defensive battle and an offensive one with such a leader as Butler, was then out of the question. Gillmore's position was not seriously attacked. His right brigade felt the shock of the assault against Smith, but the left of his line did not fire a shot. This may have been due to the darkness of the day which rendered it impossible to discover the rebel movements, and also to the inexplicable tardiness on the part of Whiting. Had Butler thrown Gillmore forward promptly against the rebel right, it must have relieved the pressure against Smith, and enabled the army to hold its position if not to inflict an overwhelming defeat upon the rebels. But instead of doing this, he caused Gillmore to conform to Smith's retrograde movement and finally allowed himself to be shut up in the *cul de sac* at Bermuda Hundred, not to emerge from there again permanently for an entire year.

It was a great misfortune to the national cause, that Butler did not pursue a vigorous and determined policy, immediately after landing his army on the south side of the James; but he seems to have had no perception of the strategic importance of his operations, or of the relative value of the points before him. He should have marched with all possible celerity upon Petersburg with his entire force, except the few men required to mark out and occupy the lines of defense at Bermuda Hundred or City Point; but instead of doing this he seems to have had no well defined plan. He neither marched rapidly nor fought vigorously in any direction, and hence did no serious damage to the enemy. It is claimed as a justification of his course, that his orders from Grant were vague, and uncertain in their tenor, but this is a poor excuse. Grant indicated his wishes in general terms, told him to fortify at Bermuda Hundred, to break up railroads, and to make Richmond the objective point of his campaign, but the details of the various operations necessary, were left entirely to Butler and his able subordinates. Even if these details, as they were afterwards developed, had been specifically sanctioned by the Lieutenant-General, Butler would not have been justified; for being on the ground in person and fully informed of the rebel movements, it was his duty to arrange his details to suit the actual condition of affairs. Whatever may have been the precise import of Grant's written and verbal instructions, there seems to have been little doubt as to his expectations, and there is less as to what should have been done. The convictions of most sensible persons upon the merits of this question are fixed, and no amount of vagueness in the official directions, can justify Butler for failing to thoroughly break the railroads, scatter the inferior forces of Beauregard, and secure Petersburg at least.

The small army in West Virginia, formed the second co-operating column, in aid of Grant's general movement with the Army of the Potomac. Sigel divided it into two detachments, one composed of a division of infantry and Averill's cavalry operating through the valley of the Kanawha against the East Tennessee and Virginia Railroad, while the other under Sigel's immediate command, marched up the Shenandoah towards Staunton and Lynchburg. These movements began on the 1st of May, but on the 15th, Sigel encountered the rebels under Breckenridge at New Market, and after a severe engagement with considerable loss, was repulsed, and fell back beyond Cedar Creek. He was at once relieved by that zealous and gallant, though not fortunate officer, General Hunter, who assumed the offensive without delay. Hunter was instructed to march upon Staunton, and after capturing that place and breaking up the railroad towards Charlottesville, to move rapidly to Lynchburg. He encountered the rebels at Piedmont, on the 5th of June, and after a severe engagement of four or five hours, drove them from the field, capturing 1500 prisoners and 3 field guns. On the 8th, Hunter formed a junction with Crook and Averill at Staunton, and then directed his march by the way of Lexington towards Lynchburg, without encountering any decided resistance, and made his arrangements for an attack; but meanwhile the Richmond authorities had become alarmed for the safety of that important place, and directed Lee to detach a force for its defense. These troops had begun to arrive before Hunter reached the neighborhood of the city, and as his ammunition was nearly exhausted, he determined not to hazard an attack, but to retire by the line of the Kanawha, choosing this line because he deemed it safe from interruption by a force moving from Richmond by the way of Charlottesville, and also for the reason that it promised to bring him to supplies in a much shorter time. A depot of military stores had been left by Crook at Charlestown, a few days before, under charge of two regiments of hundred day men, but unfortunately for Hunter these troops allowed themselves to be stampeded by guerrillas, and after burning most of the stores removed the remainder farther down the river.

The line of march, lying in the desolate mountain region of West Virginia, Hunter found great difficulty in sustaining the strength and resolution of his forces, but after a wearisome march and much suffering, he reached the Ohio River at Wheeling, whence he returned to Martinsburg by rail. He committed a grave mistake in retreating by such a circuitous and eccentric line; for it left the entire Shenandoah Valley open to rebel incursions, and ultimately enabled Early to cross the Potomac and threaten Washington. Grant's main object in sending him towards Lynchburg was to obtain possession of the railroads at that point, and to cut off the supplies of grain and meat drawn from South-west Virginia for the support of the troops defending the rebel capital. After the Army of the Potomac had crossed the James, Grant detached Sheridan with Gregg's and Torbert's divisions to march through the country by the way of Charlottesville, for the purpose of completing the destruction of all the railroad lines north of Richmond, and then to join Hunter somewhere between Staunton and Petersburg. These operations, it was hoped, would render it impossible for Lee to make an offensive return towards Washington with a large force, but Sheridan did not succeed in getting farther than Trevillian Station where he had a bloody and obstinate battle with the rebel cavalry under Hampton.

CHAPTER XXIV.

IN pursuance of his determination to fight it out on that line, Grant continued his march towards Richmond, in the hope of catching Lee in a disadvantageous position, and dealing him a crushing blow. Flanking operations in the presence of the enemy are usually regarded as being extremely hazardous, affording him good and frequent opportunity for sudden and effective return; but in the case of the southward march of the Army of the Potomac from Spottsylvania, so great were the skill and precision of every movement, that Lee made no effort to interfere; but holding high ground which covered the direct road to Richmond, and seeing all that was done, he hastened southward also, and took up a strong position on the south side of the North Anna. Grant, on the other hand, had to make a considerable detour, and to move by poor and devious roads, so that when he reached the North Anna near the railroad crossing, on the 23d of May, he found his wily antagonist already in position, covering the railroad junction, and ready to dispute his farther progress.

The prospect seemed uninviting enough, but Grant was not the person to take appearances for well-assured facts; he therefore ordered Warren, whose corps was on the right, to cross the river at Jericho, and to try the enemy's position. The crossing was made in handsome style, and the rebels were driven back nearly to the Virginia Central Railroad. Warren's corps was formed as follows: Cutler on the right, Griffin in the center, and Crawford on the left.

Lee at once threw forward the divisions of Wilcox and Heth to drive Warren into the river, but they were repulsed with heavy loss by Griffin. The rebel commander then detached three brigades under Brown for the purpose of assailing the right flank of Warren's line. Marching rapidly along the railroad till a sufficient distance had been gained, Brown moved his command by the right flank, falling upon Cutler, not yet fairly in position, swept his left back, and threw the entire division into confusion. Griffin became again involved, and for a few minutes was in considerable jeopardy. But at this critical juncture, the Eighty-third Pennsylvania, Lieutenant-Colonel McCoy commanding, hastening forward to fill the gap in the line, made an effective charge, striking Brown's regiments in flank, and driving them rapidly back. Reassured by this favorable turn in the progress of the contest, the lines of the shaken divisions were soon re-established, and the rebels completely driven off, leaving 1,000 prisoners in Warren's possession. His lines were rapidly intrenched, and rendered safe against all direct attacks. Hancock struck the river at the County Bridge, a mile west of the railroad crossing; but the rebels had constructed a *tête-de-pont* covering this bridge, overlooked by a heavy line of entrenchments on the south side of the river, and it was necessary to capture these works in order to effect a passage. Birney's division of the Second corps was charged with this perilous duty, and about an hour before sundown, under the cover of a heavy fire from the corps of artillery placed in position under Colonel Tidball, the assault was made, the brigades of Egan and Pierce bearing the brunt of the fight. Advancing at a double-quick, those gallant veterans carried the bridge head in the handsomest manner, capturing some 30 or 40 prisoners, who were left in the trench by their flying companions. Early the next morning the Second corps pushed across the bridge and took up a position on the south side of the river the rebels having drawn back their line during the night.

The Sixth corps crossed at Jericho. Thus three corps were safely on the south side confronting Lee once more; but it was soon discovered that they could not communicate with each other, on account of a strong salient in the rebel lines resting on the bank of the river between the two points of passage. It seems that Lee had formed the left half of his army across the neck of land lying between Little River and the North Anna, the extreme left resting on the former, and the center on the latter, while the right wing was thrown back at an obtuse angle with the left. In order to establish communication between the right and left wings of the Army of the Potomac, Grant ordered Burnside to make a crossing between the points at which Warren and Hancock had crossed, but this order could not be carried out. Crittenden's division, which was charged with its execution, was repulsed with heavy loss; while Crawford's division, which made a demonstration from Warren's front towards the new point of crossing, was thrust back upon the river and compelled to return to its works, narrowly escaping a serious disaster. In spite of all that could be done, Lee succeeded in maintaining his center in its salient position, and therefore in keeping the Army of the Potomac so divided as to render it incapable of advancing except at the imminent risk of having either wing overwhelmed before it could receive succor from the other. Grant examined the situation with great care, but the rebel position was found to be impregnable; he therefore did not hesitate to throw away the advantage which he had already gained by his brilliant double passage of the river, and issued orders for the army to withdraw to the north side preparatory to a new turning movement.

15

In the meantime, Sheridan with the cavalry had rejoined the Army of the Potomac, having marched northward by the way of the White House and Aylett's, on the Mattapony. On the 25th, Wilson's division crossed the North Anna at Jericho, and made a demonstration of crossing Little River on the extreme right of the army ; but that stream was found impassable.   He was, however, directed to make a vigorous show of crossing, and did so, with the view of attracting Lee's attention in that direction while the army was withdrawing in another.   Torbert's and Gregg's divisions, supported by Russell's division of the Sixth corps, the next day moved down the North Anna, for the purpose of seizing the crossings of the Pamunky.   Torbert was sent to Taylor's Ford with orders to make a demonstration of crossing there till after dark.   Gregg was ordered to Littlepage's Ford, with similar instructions.   After leaving detachments at these fords to keep up the feint, both divisions were to march rapidly under cover of darkness to the ford at Hanovertown, and to cross without delay.   These movements were admirably and rapidly executed, and early on the morning of the 27th, Torbert's leading brigade forced a passage, driving back a strong cavalry picket and capturing some 30 or 40 prisoners.   Torbert followed quickly with the rest of the division, driving Gordon's cavalry brigade from Hanovertown and pursuing it to Cramp's Creek.   Gregg joined Torbert at this place, and Russell encamped near the crossing of the river, covering all approaches to it.   By this skillful and rapid handling of the cavalry, Grant completely masked his plans till their execution had been made certain.   On the night of the 26th the Second, Fifth and Sixth corps retired silently to the north side of the river, by different bridges, and the next day headed towards the new crossing of the Pamunky, reaching and crossing that stream without molestation or difficulty.   The Sixth corps led the van, followed closely by the Fifth, Ninth and Second corps in their order,—the whole covered in flank and rear by the march of Wilson's horse.   The Second corps, however, crossed four miles further up the river.   Thus by the night of the 27th, the whole army stood intact on the south side of the Pamunky. This stream is made by the union of the North and South Anna, and with the Mattapony forms the York, at the head of which is situated West Point, now become the base of supplies.

It will be seen that by this single passage, Grant compelled Lee to pass two rivers, the last remaining barriers of importance which obstructed the march of the Union soldiers. While the Army of the Potomac was on the North Anna, its base was shifted from Fredericksburg to Port Royal, on the Rappahannock. Those who have doubted Grant's capacity to maneuver should study carefully the details of the combinations just related. Nothing could have been more admirable than the regularity with which the different subdivisions of the army, performed the marches assigned them, nor more profound than the judgment displayed by the Lieutenant-General in the calculations and instructions upon which these marches were based. As a matter of course, Lee was not long kept in ignorance of Grant's real designs, and having the inside line, less than half as long as the detour made by the Army of the Potomac, it was not remarkable that he should again interpose himself between the invaders and the Chickahominy, covering the rebel capital. His line of battle was formed facing north-east, and was far enough advanced to cover the railroads running northward from Richmond. Grant was therefore compelled to force him back before trying to pass the Chickahominy. With this object in view, Sheridan was pushed out towards Hawes' shop, where, on the afternoon of the 28th, he encountered the rebel cavalry under Hampton, the successor of Stuart. A long and severely-contested battle ensued in which the dismounted troopers of Davies, Gregg and Custer took the principal part. Sheridan succeeded in holding the junction of the roads for which he had fought, and in driving the rebels from the field with a loss of over 800 men killed, wounded, and prisoners. Grant threw forward the army at once, and assumed a position in front of that place. Lee was therefore compelled to move rearward by the right flank, taking up a new line across the head of the Tolopotomy, though his exact position was not known. Strong reconnoissances were made in all directions, and a gradual tendency of the enemy towards the left was manifested. On the 29th of May, Hardin's reserve brigade of Crawford's division was struck in flank at Bethesda Church, by Rhodes' division of Ewell's corps, and driven back to the Shady Grove road.

At this place new troops were brought into action, in turn driving the rebels back, and enabling Warren to establish his corps firmly on the Mechanicsville road. Hancock, advancing towards Hanover Court House, was checked at the Tolopotomy, a swampy and difficult stream emptying into the Pamunky, and behind which the enemy were too strongly posted to be successfully assailed. Hancock was supported by Burnside on his left and Wright on his right; and although there was, of necessity, a good deal of heavy skirmishing, it was evident that the rebel position was too strong to warrant a battle at that place. The only course open to Grant was to prolong his line in the direction of Cold Harbor, which Sheridan had already occupied. The Sixth corps was therefore withdrawn from the right, and directed to move by the rear of the army to that place. Marching nearly all night, it arrived at the designated point early on the morning of June 1st, and was shortly afterwards joined by General W. F. Smith, with four small divisions from the Tenth and Eighteenth corps, which Grant had detached from Butler at Bermuda Hundred, and brought around by steamer to the White House. These troops took position on the right of the Sixth corps, and were at once ordered forward by Meade to break the enemy's line in their front, and to force a crossing of the Chickahominy. These orders were given under the impression that they could be executed before Lee could interpose his infantry to counteract it; but he had perceived the withdrawal of the Sixth corps, and, suspecting where it would turn up, had detached Longstreet's corps from the rebel left, and by a similar march threw it to his extreme right. Smith and Wright were therefore unable to carry out their orders literally, but after a careful and judicious disposition of their force, late in the afternoon they made a spirited advance, capturing the first line of rifle-trench already prepared by the rebels, together with 600 or 700 prisoners. They put forth a vigorous and determined effort to carry the second, and only desisted after they had lost nearly 2,000 men, and were forced to acknowledge the task impracticable. Had it been possible to make their assault early in the forenoon, better results might have been obtained ; but both Smith's and Wright's men were much jaded, and could not be brought into action sooner.

Grant's aversion to sacrificing the lives of his men was well exemplified when he declined to attack Lee's position on the North Anna; he would gladly have done so again, had he been able to find any alternative, but it was plain to the newest lieutenant in the army, that nothing but hard fighting could secure the advantages which were requisite at Cold Harbor. The losses in Smith's and Wright's corps in these preliminary essays were heavy ; but the battle secured us a firm hold upon a position, without which the army could hardly have carried out the plan formed for it. On the night after this introductory engagement, Hancock, who now held the extreme right, was directed to march by the left flank and take post on the left of the Sixth corps. The right of Warren's corps still continued near Bethesda Church, while his left was extended well towards Smith's right, and Burnside was ordered to withdraw from the front line and mass in rear of Warren. While executing this movement on the afternoon of June 2d, the enemy followed him up, captured a number of his skirmishers, and struck the left of Warren's line, arresting its extension towards Cold Harbor, and compelling him to assume a more compact formation. Bartlett's brigade was thrown forward promptly and checked the hostile advance, after which new dispositions were ordered. Before they were carried into effect, Wilson was directed to cross the Tolopotomy, drive the rebel cavalry from Hawes' shop, and

then recross the Tolopotomy near its head, striking the rebel
infantry in the rear.   The movements were made with despatch and success, resulting in a sharp fight at Hawes' shop,
in which Colonel Preston, of the First Vermont cavalry, was
killed, after he had driven the rebels from their works.   Just
at sunset the rebel left and rear were attacked under cover
of the horse artillery, at Via's house, and compelled to relinquish their advanced position in front of Burnside, with the
loss of some prisoners.

On the 3d of June, the two armies held positions nearly
similar to those held by Porter's corps, and Jackson's turning
column on the day of the battle of Gaines' Mill, though in
the contest about to be opened the rebels were this time to be
assailed, instead of assailing.   Grant's troops were well in
hand.   Sheridan, with Gregg and Torbert, held the left and
rear, while Wilson held the extreme right of our line.   The
situation of the latter had been one of extreme danger, for
soon after crossing the Pamunky, which he did immediately
after the infantry had all crossed, he was sent to the extreme
right, defeating the rebel cavalry under W. H. F. Lee, in a
night fight at Hanover Court House, and then proceeding to
break up the two railroads running North, and to burn the
bridges over the South Anna.   This work was promptly and
efficiently done, but while engaged in covering it, McIntosh's
brigade was attacked by three brigades of cavalry at Ashland
Station, and after a desperate fight was compelled to retire.
Just at this juncture, Wilson fell upon the rebel rear with
the First Vermont cavalry, and succeeded in extricating his
command from its perilous strait.   Having accomplished the
task assigned him, he withdrew through Hanover Court
House, and rejoined the army, beyond the Tolopotomy, after
three days of ceaseless fighting, marching and hard labor, in
the destruction of railroads and bridges, for the purpose of
isolating the rebel capital.

Lee had disposed of his army about New Cold Harbor,
covering the approaches of Richmond, while Grant confronted
him with lines encircling Old Cold Harbor.   The positions

occupied by both were naturally strong for a defensive battle, but they had been strengthened immensely by slashings and rifle-trench. The Union forces were arranged in the following order:—Hancock's corps on the extreme left, resting on the road to Despatch Station; then Wright, then Smith's division, then Warren, and finally Burnside. Sheridan, with two divisions of horse, was watching the lower crossing of the Chickahominy and covering the base of supplies at the White House, while Wilson was watching the right. Grant had ordered the attack to be made by corps, and to begin at half-past four o'clock on the morning of June 3d. Every officer and man seemed to realize the necessity of promptitude, and within a few minutes of the time specified, the entire army was bearing its tattered standards towards the rebel lines. Silently and devotedly it rushed forward into the jaws of death, against the bristling and well-manned intrenchments. Every corps commander had been left to select his own point of attack, and to form his divisions as circumstances might determine. It was entirely impossible for Grant to regulate such details for so vast an army, even had he been so minded; his staff being too small to gather the specific information which must have been gained before specific orders could be made. Enough was known through the reports of subordinates to assure him that Lee had used the ground to the best advantage; but where the lines were the weakest could not be determined, except by actual attack. The country being generally level, and only slightly undulating, the sharpest eye could perceive through the woods and fields, nothing but faint lines of rifle-trench, bristling with rebel bayonets, and topped by the dirty gray of rebel uniforms. The order of battle, was therefore simple: a general attack by each corps, but there was nothing in this order forbidding, limiting, or in any way discouraging the different subordinates. They were left entirely free, as before stated, to form their columns, and to direct them according to their own judgment.

Hancock, holding the extreme left, sent Barlow and Gibbon forward, supporting them with Birney. The advance was made in handsome style, and resulted in driving the rebels from a sunken road into their works, from which they were also driven, leaving several hundred prisoners and three guns in the hands of the victors. Barlow pressed his advantage, turning the captured guns upon the enemy, but not being promptly supported by Birney, he was driven back by the rallying rebels, and after a determined effort to hold what he had captured, was finally compelled to abandon the rebel works, though he managed to hold on and entrench himself just outside of them.   Gibbon had advanced at the same time with Barlow, but the coherence of his attack was broken by a swamp, cutting his division into unequal fragments, neither of which was strong enough to produce a decided impression, though several regiments reached the enemy's works and planted their colors on them.   In spite of the great disadvantages under which they labored, Gibbon's men behaved with great gallantry.   Many of his best officers, including Colonels McMahon, Porter, Morris, McKeen, and Haskel, were killed; while General Tyler was wounded.   Wright and Smith advanced at the same time; but having already had a taste of what they might expect in a death-grapple with the defenders of the hostile entrenchments, they did not push their attack with such decided vigor as Hancock.   They were readily repulsed, loosing very heavily, and gaining nothing in return.

Warren, holding a long thin line, did not feel himself strong enough to risk a concentrated attack, and knowing that one with thinly scattered battalions could not possibly win, maintained a silent defensive, with everything except his artillery. Burnside did not advance at the designated hour, but towards noon he threw forward his right flank, and succeeded in reaching a position from which the rebel left could be advantageously assailed, but the action had already been decided against us.   It did not last an hour all told, but in this brief space of time the loss was very heavy.   Notwithstanding this severe intimation of the hopelessness of the task, later in the day Meade sent orders to each corps commander to renew the attack without reference to the troops on his right or left. The order was issued through these officers to their subordinates, and from them descended through the usual channels to the troops, but it was silently disobeyed. The morning's work had convinced the army that it was hopeless to tempt fortune further in that direction.

Grant has been severely criticised for the details of this battle, and it is possible that it should not have been fought at all; but it ought to be remembered that Grant could give only general directions, and that it was Meade's special function to see that the actual dispositions of the troops were made in such a manner as to secure the greatest possible advantage in direction as well as in tactical execution, while it was the privilege and duty of each corps commander, upon that occasion as well as upon all others, to use his discretion in forming his troops for attack, and in selecting or at least suggesting that point in his own front, upon which his efforts should be directed. It seems to be well established, however, that Meade gave his orders in the same general terms as they were couched in when they reached him, and finally ordered the different corps commanders to attack without regard to each other. It was not in the character of General Grant, any more than in the necessities of the case, that he should depart from his well established and judicious practice in such matters; nor was it possible for him to become acquainted so thoroughly with the varied features of the extended battle-field as to be able to designate to the subordinate commanders the points upon which they should move.

It does not appear from any official report or statement yet published, that either Meade or any of the corps commanders, ever proposed a meritorious plan of attack or pointed out a weak place in the enemy's line, without being encouraged by the Lieutenant-General to avail himself of it. Neither does it appear in any official paper, or in any authentic record of military events that General Grant ever ordered an assault or permitted one, either against troops in the open field, or behind breastworks, in opposition to the expressed judgment of

Meade or any one of his corps commanders. Those who know him best are well aware of the fact that while he believes celerity and hard fighting to be essential elements in warfare, there is no commander more opposed to hammering without an object, or whose humane heart is more deeply afflicted by the unnecessary effusion' of blood. On the other hand it would be injustice to him and an outrage upon common sense to assert that he is a believer in partial or irresolute measures. He knows as well as any man that war can not be made affectionately; nor can it be made successfully, without loss of human life.

CHAPTER XXV.

THE battle of Cold Harbor demonstrated the impractica-
bility of forcing Lee to give battle north of Richmond, beyond the cover of entrenchments, and also that he could not
be dislodged by direct attack from his well chosen position
in front of the Chickahominy. There remained nothing for
Grant to do, but to resort to a siege, or to cross the Chickahominy and the James, and place his army where it would
break the lines connecting the rebel capital with the South,
and thus isolate it completely from the confederacy. In this
case Lee would be compelled to abandon Richmond or to give
battle at a great disadvantage. This plan, it will be observed,
involved the necessity of uncovering Washington, with the
main body of the army, but the principal danger which was
originally apprehended in such an event was necessarily removed by the proximity of the national army to the rebel
capital. In other words, Grant in his overland campaign
had effectually protected the national capital, by keeping it
constantly behind him, and the enemy constantly engaged.
There was no time during the entire month spent in march-

ing and fighting from the Rapidan to the Chickahominy at which Lee could have afforded to make any detachments whatever ; but had Grant chosen to go to the James River or to the lower Chesapeake by water, Lee would have had a rare opportunity for striking a telling blow in the direction of the Potomac. Moreover, Grant was now in a position to gain all the advantages that could have been gained at any previous time by operating south of the James, and from his proximity to Richmond and the vital lines of supply upon which Lee had to depend, it was morally certain that Lee would find a greater need than ever of keeping his forces concentrated. Should he lose either the supply lines or the city, his army would be in great jeopardy, while the movement of a detachment to threaten Washington could be readily counteracted by a detachment from the Army of the Potomac for its defence.

In connection with this discussion, it should also be remembered that Lee was so close to the defences of Richmond that it was impossible, by any flank movement, to interpose between him and the city. General Grant says :

" I was still in a condition to either move by his left flank and to invest Richmond from the north side, or continue my move by his right flank to the south side of the James. While the former might have been better as a covering for Washington, yet a full survey of all the ground satisfied me that it would be impracticable to hold a line north and east of Richmond that would protect the Fredericksburg Railroad—a long, vulnerable line, which would exhaust much of our strength to guard, and that would have to be protected to supply the army, and would leave open to the enemy all his lines of communication on the south side of the James. *My idea from the start, had been to beat Lee's army north of Richmond if possible. Then, after destroying his lines of communication north of the James River, to transfer the army to the south side and besiege Lee in Richmond, or follow him south if he should retreat.* After the battle of the Wilderness, it was evident that the enemy deemed it of the first importance to run no risks with the army he then had. He acted purely on the defensive behind breastworks, or feebly on the offensive immediately in front of them, and when in case of repulse, he could easily retire behind them. Without a greater sacrifice of life than I was willing to make, all could not be accomplished that I had designed north of Richmond. I therefore determined to continue to hold substantially the ground we then occupied, taking advantage of any favorable circumstances that might present themselves, until cavalry could be sent to Charlottesville and Gordonsville to effectually break up the railroad connection between Richmond and the Shenandoah Valley and Lynchburg; and, when the cavalry got well off, to move the army to the south side of the James River, by the enemy's right flank, when I felt I could cut off all his sources of supplies except by canal."

In pursuance of this plan, Sheridan proceeded on the 7th of June, with the divisions of Torbert and Gregg to Charlottesville, for the purpose of cutting the Virginia Central Railroad, and meeting at that place the forces under Hunter, with whom he was expected to return to the Army of the Potomac. It was also anticipated that this movement would cause Lee to detach his cavalry, and thereby reduce his power to prevent the passage of the Chickahominy and James by the Army of the Potomac. This expectation was fully realized; for when Sheridan's advance under Torbert arrived at Trevillian's Station on the 11th, it met Hampton's division of cavalry, while Gregg encountered Fitzhugh Lee's division on the Louisa Court House road. A series of brilliant maneuvers and sharp combats ensued, in which Sheridan captured about 500 prisoners; but hearing that Hunter had passed on towards Lynchburg without turning towards Charlottesville; that Ewell was marching towards the same place, and that Breckenridge had gone to Gordonsville with a considerable force, Sheridan gave up the attempt to join the national force in the valley, and decided to return. On the 12th, while Gregg was tearing up railroads, Torbert was attacked by a strong force of the enemy, with whom he was hotly engaged nearly all day. By this time Sheridan had become encumbered with a large number of wounded and prisoners, and had expended most of his ammunition, and therefore set out to return to the army, making a detour through Spottsylvania, Walkerton, and King and Queen Court House to the White House.

In the interval, by Grant's directions, Butler sent a force of the infantry and cavalry under Gillmore and Kautz, from Ber-

muda Hundred, with orders to capture Petersburg if possible
and to break up the railroads and bridges crossing the Appomattox. Kautz moving rapidly and acting with commend-
able boldness, drove back the local militia, captured the works
on the south side and reached the suburbs of the town, but
encountering sharp resistance from better troops, he was soon
driven out. Gillmore found the works on his side very strong,
and thinking it useless to attack them with so small a force, he
decided not to do so, and returned to Bermuda Hundred.
Grant attaching great importance to the possession of Petersburg, had sent Smith's troops to the White House, and thence
rapidly to City Point by steam transports. The express purpose of this movement was to concentrate a sufficient force
under Butler, to render the capture of Petersburg a matter
of certainty before the enemy, divining his intention, could
re-enforce the place sufficiently to resist him. While this-
concentration was in progress, Grant had perfected arrangements for the passage of the Chickahominy and the James.

Immediately after the battle of Cold Harbor, the Ninth
corps was withdrawn from its place on the extreme right of
the line, and put into position between Warren and Smith.
On the next day the Fifth corps was withdrawn, and massed
in rear of the works, leaving the Ninth corps again on the
right. The Second corps then extended itself towards the
Chickahominy, while the Fifth corps was a short time afterwards posted on the extreme left, extending that flank to
Despatch Station, on the York River Railroad. Sheridan
having been detached, as before related, Wilson was ordered
to send one brigade of his division to picket the lower Chickahominy. By these gradual extensions of the different corps
towards the left, the army was brought into position near the
lower crossings of the Chickahominy, and by the night of the
12th of June, everything was in readiness to push forward in
quest of better fortune than had yet cheered the gallant but
sorely tried veterans. Wilson, with Chapman's brigade, forced
a passage at Long Bridge; under cover of darkness, the dismounted troopers struggled through the swamps, clambered

over drift-logs, and finally crossed the stream by using the limbs of the overlapping trees as a bridge. As soon as the leading detachment had gained a footing on the west side of the stream, the rebel force of observation fled. The pontoon bridge was rapidly laid, and shortly after midnight the brigade of troopers had all crossed and pushed out towards Richmond by the road striking White Oak Swamp, followed closely by Warren's corps.

At dawn the rebel cavalry was encountered in some force, but by eight o'clock Chapman had driven it across White Oak Swamp on the road leading from Malvern Hill towards the rear of Lee's old position in front of Cold Harbor. Crawford's division relieved the cavalry at this crossing, and thus enabled it to make a strong demonstration in the direction of Richmond. A sharp fight ensued at Riddle's shop, near the junction of several roads all leading towards the city, and the enemy were routed. Meanwhile Hancock's and the rest of Warren's corps were filing rapidly across the bridge, and moving towards Wilcox's Landing on the James. Wright and Burnside following another route, crossed at Jones' Bridge and marched to Charles City; while the trains crossed still farther down at Cole's Ferry. McIntosh's brigade of cavalry which had been left on the right, interposed itself between the rear brigade and the rebel infantry, and by ceaseless activity during two days and nights, succeeded in bringing up the last of our forces without the loss of a man. By the morning of the 15th, the entire army stood upon the north bank of the James, having marched fifty-five miles in two days. Lee was completely deceived in regard to Grant's intentions, for although he soon discovered the passage of the Chickahominy, he supposed a direct advance upon Richmond to be the object in view. He therefore moved out of his lines at Cold Harbor, and marched towards the junction of roads at Riddle's shop. His leading divisions reached there late in the afternoon of the 13th, and passing across Wilson's front, proceeded at once to entrench themselves in a position covering the main approaches to the city.

After nightfall, Crawford seeing evidence of activity on the part of the rebels, proceeded to rejoin his corps in the direction of Harrison's Landing; leaving Wilson to make head as best he might against the advance of the rebel infantry. After holding on till nearly midnight, the latter fell back as far as Nancy's shop. The next day the arrival of McIntosh's brigade united his division, and enabled him to thoroughly patrol the country between White Oak Swamp and Malvern Hill, and to make effective demonstrations upon the enemy. These feints and dashes secured the movements of the army and enabled it to lay bridges and make all arrangements for the final passage to the south side of the James before Lee had fully discovered its intentions. This in a great measure neutralized the immense advantage which Lee again had in moving upon a short chord, while Grant was compelled to march almost around the circle. Grant's calculations were all made with great precision and certainty. The orders for moving the army were admirable. The long pontoon bridge across the James, constructed by Major Duane, was a marvel of its kind. Leaving these details to General Meade, Grant in person lost no time after reaching the James River in proceeding by steamer to Bermuda Hundred, for the purpose of giving the necessary instructions for the capture of Petersburg. Smith having already arrived, was put in charge of all the available troops which Butler could give him, and on the night of the 14th, began his movement upon the town in accordance with Grant's verbal instructions.

He made a rapid march, and by daylight of the 15th, was confronting the rebel forces near Petersburg. His advance was made in three columns, composed of Kautz's cavalry and the infantry divisions of Hinks, Brooks, and Martindale. Skirmishing began at an early hour, resulting in driving the rebels into the works about Petersburg, with the loss of one gun. It was noon, however, before all the troops were brought up, and nearly sundown before the final dispositions for the attack had been perfected. Smith being an able engineer and a General of fine judgment, did everything with deliberation

and precision ; his cavalry was posted well out upon the exposed flank, his batteries occupied commanding positions,
while his infantry divisions were formed in long but mutually
supporting line. At seven o'clock, when it had begun to grow
dusk, the troops, both white and colored, deployed in a heavy
line of skirmishers, advanced rapidly to the attack, carrying
everything before them, capturing two and a half miles of
redoubt and rifle-pits, with 15 pieces of artillery, and taking
300 prisoners. It was an auspicious beginning ; Lee had not
yet arrived, and the local militia were a different sort of
soldiery from that which had been encountered at Cold
Harbor ; but darkness having set in, Smith suspended further
operations in order to reform his troops, although, says Grant :
" Between the line thus captured and Petersburg, there were
no other works, and there was no evidence that the enemy
had re-enforced Petersburg with a single brigade from any
source. The night was clear, the moon shining brightly, and
favorable to further operations. General Hancock, with two
divisions of the Second corps, reached Smith just after dark,
and offered the service of these troops, as he (Smith) might
wish, waving rank to the named commander, who he naturally
supposed, knew best the position of affairs, and what to do
with the troops. But instead of taking these troops, and
pushing at once into Petersburg, he requested General Hancock to relieve a part of his line in the captured works, which
was done before midnight." * The opportunity was deferred,
and Petersburg was lost. That night Lee's advance reached
the city, and by the next day its enclosing lines were bristling with rebel bayonets. Fortifications arose on every available spot. Grant who had returned to the Army of the
Potomac for the purpose of hurrying it forward, joined Smith
at an early hour on the 16th, and was chagrined to see that
nothing could be done with the force then at hand. Burnside
and the rest of Hancock's corps were hastened forward, and
at six o'clock in the afternoon, an attack was made, continuing
with intermissions and varying success till six o'clock the next

* Grant's Official Report.

10

morning. Several more of the enemy's redoubts to the left of Smith were taken, together with several pieces of artillery and about 400 prisoners. On the 17th, the Fifth corps arrived, and during that and the succeeding day, the fighting was renewed, but only forced the enemy to contract his lines, leaving the investing army in possession of much advantageous ground.

The reader will have perceived from the foregoing precise statement of facts, that in the movement upon Petersburg, Grant had clearly outwitted Lee, and had beaten him on the march to the town by an entire day, but through the delay in making the attack, and its untimely suspension by General Smith, the ripest fruits of this superior generalship had not been gathered. A contemporary writer, in discussing this operation has not hesitated to say: "There can be no question as to who is responsible for the failure to take Petersburg. This is no other than the Lieutenant-General himself.*" To support this assertion he quotes from a paper said to be on file in the archives of the army, and upon which General Meade has made the following endorsement: "Had Hancock or myself known Petersburg was to be attacked Petersburg would have fallen." It is hard to believe that General Meade could have written such a sentence, for on the day previous to Smith's movement, he was personally directed by General Grant to order Hancock to march directly for Petersburg by the shortest road in order to support the attack to be made there by Smith.

But independent of these orders which were given to him verbally by the Lieutenant-General, as were many of the most important orders up to that epoch of the campaign, both Meade and Hancock must have known that the army landing where it did, must necessarily take possession of and march through Petersburg in order to reach Richmond, or to secure a safe base of operations against the enemy in the field. In truth there was not a lieutenant in the army but knew that the rules of strategy required as much; but the

* Swinton's "Army of the Potomac," p., 506.

fact that Meade had specific orders from General Grant, and the additional fact that two divisions of Hancock's corps actually joined Smith at Petersburg, settle all discussion upon this point. The failure of Smith to reap the full advantage of the brilliant maneuver by which he carried the outer line of the Petersburg defenses, was a matter which Grant could not possibly control. He had perfect confidence in the judgment and generalship of that officer, but they were both at fault upon this occasion. Without wasting time in vain regrets, Grant set about arranging a plan by which the same or equal advantages might be otherwise obtained. He had sent Wright with a part of the Sixth corps to Bermuda Hundred, to re-enforce Butler, who had moved out and occupied the rebel works on the railroad, which had been abandoned in order to re-enforce Petersburg. Grant directed that General to strengthen his advance and secure his hold upon the railroad, but instead of doing so with the combined forces at his disposal, he allowed Wright to halt near the outer lines. As soon as the pressure against Petersburg was relieved, the rebels returned to Butler's front, and before he could take effective measures to avert it drove him back into his fortified line which encircled his camps at Bermuda Hundred.

The railroad was not seriously damaged, but had this movement been successful in securing a firm hold upon it, Petersburg must have fallen, for Lee would have been compelled to weaken it so much in trying to dislodge Butler, that Grant's vigorous attacks on the 16th, 17th, and 18th, must have been successful, notwithstanding Smith's well-meant but ill-timed suspension of a successful advance, because of coming darkness, or for the purpose of fixing his flanks and straightening his lines. No attempt to show that either Meade or Hancock did not know what he was expected to do, is sufficient to remove the responsibility for the failure to take Petersburg, from the shoulders which should bear it. During the whole year which followed, those officers had abundant opportunities to exert an untrammeled influence in accomplishing the object which the country had so much at heart, but notwithstanding their great merits and untiring zeal, it will be shown that Petersburg did not fall till *Grant ceased to trust them exclusively with the management of details, and took the control of the army directly into his own hands.*

CHAPTER XXVI.

THE failure of Grant's preliminary but well-planned attempts against Petersburg, made it certain that he would now
be compelled to gain by hard fighting and superior endurance,
the vantage ground that he had reasonably hoped to secure
by judicious combinations and rapid marching. With the
view of distracting the enemy's attention, and menacing Richmond, he ordered Butler to lay a bridge across the James,
connecting his camp with Deep Bottom, and to establish at

that place at least one brigade of his command. This order
was carried into effect during the night of the 20th and the
morning of the next day, thus extending Grant's lines across
both the James and Appomattox, and giving him the means
of communicating rapidly with all parts of his command.

The base of supplies was brought permanently to City
Point, wharves and storehouses were built, and in a short
time they were covered with the multifarious articles required
by the army. Hospitals and bakeries were established, transports crowded the landings, ammunition of all kinds, entrenching tools, and the ample stores of the Christian and Sanitary
Commissions were brought forward in boundless profusion.
A close investment of Petersburg had now become necessary,
and in order that it should be successfully made, the army was
required to entrench its position systematically. So ready
had it become in this art that by the 20th, the entrenchments
were in such shape as to permit the extension of the army
towards the left, as far as the Weldon Road. On the next
day the Second corps moved out and took position to the left
and rear of Hancock. Wilson's cavalry, as soon as the army
had all crossed the James, was thrown forward to Prince
George Court-house, for the purpose of watching and covering the left of the army as far round as the Blackwater. In
order to make the investment complete it had been determined
to extend the infantry by successive movements till the investing line should cross all the railroads, and its left rest upon
the Appomattox. To relieve these movements of a part of
their danger, and to effectually isolate Petersburg from the
rest of the rebel territory, Grant directed that all the cavalry
force then with the army should be sent out to break up the
Danville and Southside Railroad, with authority to join Hunter
in the neighborhood of Lynchburg, to cross the Roanoke and
march to the North Carolina sea-board, or to push on and
join Sherman in Northern Georgia, as should be found most
practicable.

Accordingly at an early hour on the 22d, General Wilson,
with his own division of cavalry, re-enforced by Kautz's di-

vision, belonging to the Army of the James, marched rapidly towards the interior, crossing the Weldon Road at Ream's Station, destroying the depot and tearing up the track for some distance; then bearing more to the northward he struck the Danville Road, at a point fifteen miles from Petersburg. He was followed by one division of rebel cavalry, but disposing his rear brigade under Chapman to cover the working parties, he pursued his way along the railroad, tearing up the track, burning the stations, ties, wood-piles, saw-mills and tanks, and dispersing the detachments of militia which were encountered. Near Notaway Court House, having lost an hour or two by being misled through the carelessness of the advanced guard, he was overtaken by W. H. F. Lee, and after a sharp combat of several hours, in which Chapman's brigade did the principal fighting, he repulsed the force confronting him and proceeded to Meherrin Station where he formed a junction with Kautz, who had been sent to seize and destroy the junction at Burksville. From the latter place to the Roanoke Bridge the Danville Road was completely destroyed, but finding the rebel militia strongly entrenched at the bridge, and being closely followed by Lee's cavalry, after an ineffectual effort to burn the bridge, he set out to return to the Army on the James River.

Marching rapidly south-eastward and then northward, crossing the Meherrin and Notaway Rivers, he took the road towards Prince George Court House, but did not succeed in passing Stony Creek before he encountered the whole of Hampton's cavalry, occupying a strong position at Sappony Church. The bulk of this force, when the raid began, was known to be on the north side of the James, engaged in a campaign against Sheridan, and it was confidently expected that it would be kept too busy to pay any attention to Wilson. But as it had repassed the James and now barred the roads towards Petersburg, a determined and bloody engagement ensued, lasting from late in the afternoon, till daylight the next day. Wilson, finding that it was impossible to force a crossing of Stony Creek, in the face of such odds, made a detour from his left with the view of crossing higher up and reaching the army in the neighborhood of Ream's Station; but on arriving at that place, instead of finding the Army of the Potomac, he met the rebel infantry, ready to dispute his further progress. His command was jaded with constant marching and fighting, and encumbered by wounded men, of whom he had two hundred and eighty in all kinds of vehicles. A rapid survey of the situation convinced him that it would be madness to undertake to break the serried lines of infantry in his front, and that there was nothing left to be done but to run for it, unless succor should soon arrive. A staff officer had been sent at an early hour with a squadron to break his way through, and report to Meade for assistance. After waiting as long as it was safe, replenishing ammunition, and parking the ambulance and ammunition train, which it was necessary to abandon, Wilson began his retrograde movement. In withdrawing, his rear guard and artillery were caught in flank and driven off the road, and the latter while crossing Hatcher's Run had to be abandoned. Kautz worked his way through the woods and succeeded in reaching the army that night, while Wilson crossed the Notaway twice, and the Blackwater once, reaching the army in safety after a march of one hundred and thirty miles in eighty hours, during the whole of which, except six hours, his command was engaged either in marching or fighting. This raid had been eminently successful till it reached Stony Creek on its return. The rail-road was broken so that the rebels were unable to use it for something over two months, and had the army succeeded in covering the southern approaches to Petersburg, as General Meade informed Wilson that it intended to do, or had Meade looked out properly to prevent Hampton from dropping Sheridan and falling upon Wilson, all danger to the latter in returning would have been averted.* As it was, General Grant avers in his report, that the danger inflicted upon the enemy by this expedition more than compensated for the loss it sustained.

* See Sheridan's Report, "Conduct of the War," vol. ii., Supplement.

As before stated, it had been designed to extend the left of the infantry so as to completely encircle Petersburg on the south side, but at the first movement toward the Weldon Road, the enemy manifested great determination to prevent it. To the Second corps was assigned the task of making the first advance, but it had not got fairly under way before it was compelled to halt. The general movement was then suspended and converted into an attempt to envelope the right flank of the rebel lines. For this purpose the left wing of the Second corps, consisting of the divisions of Mott and Barlow, was thrown forward, but as the maneuver was executed without any regard to the Sixth corps, and was so directed as to leave a constantly increasing gap between the two corps, the enemy as a matter of course, availed himself of this chance, pushed forward into the opening, driving back the flanks of both the Sixth and Second corps, sweeping away Barlow's and Mott's divisions like leaves before an autumn wind. Pressing on he struck Gibbon's division in the left flank and rear, rolling it up like a scroll, and capturing entrenchments, guns and standards, besides 2,500 prisoners. This vigorous and unexpected swoop caused a rapid contraction of the national left, and resulted in throwing it upon the defensive for several weeks thereafter. The plan of this day's operations could not have been more faultily carried out; for all the fighting which followed, it resulted in no advantage whatever to the Union army, but was the cause of severe loss and many troubles.

Both armies now for awhile abandoned the aggressive policy, and set about strengthening their lines. The rebels forthwith developed their rifle-trench into a formidable chain of redans, connected by parapets of strong profile, covered by ditches, abattis and entanglements. Beginning in front of Butler, their line crossed the Appomattox below Petersburg, encircling that place completely beyond the reach of the Union artillery. The southern or western end of these works was thrown forward to cover as much as possible, the system of communication with the South and South-west. The railroads being broken, Lee was compelled to supply his army by hauling his stores from Stony Creek depot with wagons. In order to protect them, great vigilance and a determined front on his outer flank were necessary.

Grant now allowed his army to rest from fighting, but put it to work in rendering its position entirely secure. The entrenchments were strengthened, by all the means available, artillery of larger calibre was brought forward, and every effort was made to consolidate the army and render it efficient. No systematic siege operations were undertaken, but whenever opportunity offered, our lines were advanced and new fortifications were built. Burnside's corps contained a regiment of Pennsylvania miners, commanded by Colonel Pleasants, an active and enterprising officer, who asked and obtained authority to sink a shaft and drive a gallery under a rebel work, situated about one hundred and fifty yards to the front, on the slopes of a ridge known as Cemetery Hill. This work was carried forward rapidly, and, when finished, a system of mines in close connection with each other, was established, and all the necessary arrangements were made for exploding them simultaneously. The enterprise at first attracted but little attention and nobody had much faith in its practicability or efficiency, but now that the mine was completed Grant conceived the idea that its explosion would afford him opportunity of storming the enemy's works. It has been previously stated that Butler had constructed a pontoon bridge across the James, thus opening close communication with Deep Bottom. General Foster's brigade of troops held this position, and caused Lee to detach a corresponding force with which he kept up communication by a pontoon bridge at Drury's Bluff.

On the 26th of July, Grant silently withdrew Hancock's corps from its place in the investing lines, and directed him to proceed to Deep Bottom where he would be joined by Sheridan with two divisions of cavalry, after which he was instructed to make a strong demonstration in the direction of Chapin's Farm, while Sheridan, strengthened by Kautz, should make a dash towards the Virginia Central Railroad and Richmond. In pursuance of this plan, Hancock turned the left flank of the force confronting Foster, by a skillful maneuver, captured four guns and drove the enemy from his front line to his second beyond Bailey's Creek. Sheridan moving still farther to the right, also drove back the rebels capturing several hundred prisoners. But their new line was very strong, and after a careful examination Hancock concluded that it was impracticable to dislodge them. Lee, as a matter of course, was not long in hearing of these menacing operations on the north side of the James, and therefore hastened to strengthen the troops already there, by large re-enforcements from the defenses of Petersburg. By the next morning five of the eight rebel divisions under Lee were confronting our troops on the north side of the James, and soon after daylight they assumed the offensive, attacking Sheridan on the New Market and Long Ridge roads, in the neighborhood of Darbytown. The dismounted troopers fought stubbornly, but they could not contend with the superior numbers of the rebel infantry and were forced to retire, though under the energetic command of Sheridan they finally succeeded in repulsing their assailants. Hancock remained strictly on the defensive, both on that day and the next; and on the night of the 29th, in compliance with Grant's orders, he returned to his old position in front of Petersburg, followed by Sheridan for the purpose of assisting in the assault already ordered to take place immediately after the explosion of the mine. The mine was sprung between four and five o'clock A. M., July 30th, twenty or thirty minutes later than the time specified, blowing up an entire battery and a part of a regiment. The rebels were much surprised, and not knowing when the next explosion would take place, fled from that part of their line in disorder. But the assaulting column of the Ninth corps through the failure of the engineers to prepare proper debouches from its lines was not able to advance promptly or in proper order, so that twenty or thirty minutes were again lost. In the meantime, the rebels recovered from their surprise, and when the assaulting column reached the crater and the works on its right and left, they were met by a determined

artillery and musketry fire from the enemy who had reformed
on commanding ground somewhat to the rear. The advance
was therefore checked, and although new troops were thrown
forward, many of them into the crater, they did not succeed
in penetrating beyond. It soon became apparent that the
opportunity was lost; and that to save the further effusion of
blood the troops must be withdrawn to their own lines. This
was done, but not till after they had sustained heavy loss.
"Thus," says Grant, "terminated in disaster what promised
to be the most successful assault of the campaign." The
combination of the movements, and the direction of the
forces, had been made with consummate ability. Lee was
completely deceived, and thereby induced to send two-thirds
of his entire army to resist a feint, while Grant had calculated to hurl his entire force upon the weakened lines in
his front, but he was destined to chew the bitter cud of disappointment. His well-laid schemes were entirely thwarted
by the faulty execution of details which he could not possibly
supervise, and yet Grant has been unjustly blamed* for not
having properly regulated these subordinate but essential
matters in person. The simple truth in regard to the affair
of the mine is, that the assault was not made in time; the
troops were not ready for it when the explosion took place,
and no adequate means of debouchment from the works had
been prepared. These were details clearly under the control
of Meade and Burnside, and their engineer officers, for the
regulation of which no specific orders under any circumstances should have been required from the Lieutenant-General. That they were neglected was probably due to a
general lack of confidence that the mine would accomplish
any useful purpose. It was simply another case of failure
to prepare for the contingency of success. The rebels were
considerably elated by what happened, and our own troops
somewhat disheartened, but Grant's confidence, in the ultimate
success of our arms remained unshaken. The disaster may
have taught him not to depend too much upon others, but it

* See Swinton's "Army of the Potomac."

also induced him to hasten his preparations for cutting loose from his base at City Point, and throwing his army boldly into the interior beyond Petersburg with the view of seizing firmly upon Lee's communications, and thus compelling him to come out and give battle. This plan had been conceived immediately after the failure of the first decided attempts to take Petersburg, but it had been deferred or modified from time to time by the adoption of less radical measures which it was hoped might succeed, and was still farther delayed by operations elsewhere on the part of the rebels. But the idea had taken firm hold upon the mind of the Lieutenant-General, and was destined only a few months later to find its embodiment in the final campaign and the closing events of the war.

In the meantime Lee availed himself of the dead lock in operations which followed close upon the mine explosion, and the eccentric retreat of Hunter from Lynchburg, to make a diversion in favor of his own beleaguered forces, by sending a strong detachment towards Washington. He hoped to conduct this demonstration with so much secresy as to capture the national capital, before assistance could be sent to it, or at least that Grant would be compelled to part with so much of the armies about Petersburg, as to throw them completely upon the defensive. Lee looked also to the occupancy of the Shenandoah Valley as a necessary part of his plan, on account of his uncertain tenure over the railroads leading southward by which most of his supplies were obtained. Should they be seized it would become a matter of prime importance that he should keep his troops scattered as much as possible, consistent with safety so as to facilitate their subsistence, and at the same time enable him to draw upon the country occupied by them, for the support of the army retained for the defense of Richmond. The Shenandoah Valley noted for its abundant crops of grain, became towards harvest time, an object of great attraction to the rebels.

In marching northward, Early pursued the beaten track, down the Valley of the Shenandoah, striking the Baltimore and Ohio Railroad, on the 3d of July, just above Harper's Ferry. Sigel, with a small force, holding Martinsburg, was compelled to fall back towards Sharpsburg, and finally after several smart combats, to concentrate his entire command on Maryland Heights.

As soon as Grant discovered this hostile movement towards the frontier of Maryland and Pennsylvania, he ordered Hunter, who had reached the Kanawha River, to move his troops by water to Wheeling, and thence by rail, as rapidly as possible towards Harper's Ferry. But owing to extreme low water, and to the interruption of railway travel, Hunter was delayed much longer than expected. The Government becoming somewhat alarmed for the safety of Washington, called upon Grant to protect it, and for this purpose the Sixth corps was withdrawn from the investment of Petersburg, two divisions of which, under Wright in person, were sent forward by means of steam transports to Washington, and the third under Ricketts to Baltimore. The Nineteenth corps, which Grant had withdrawn from the Gulf Department, immediately after the failure of the Red River expedition, had now begun to arrive at Fortress Monroe, and was also sent forward.

The garrisons at Washington and Baltimore were composed of heavy artillery regiments, veteran reserves, and emergency men called out for a hundred days. Halleck as Chief-of-Staff and the senior General in the Department of Washington, held supreme control, subject only to Grant and the President; Augur commanded the troops in the Department of Washington; Hunter those in West Virginia; Wallace those at Baltimore, and Sigel those near Harper's Ferry; but as these forces were widely scattered and neither of them sufficiently strong to contend successfully with Early, now marching rapidly wherever he chose, the situation was one of imminent danger. On the 6th of July, Early having crossed the Potomac without opposition, entered Hagerstown, but instead of pushing boldly upon Washington, he spent several days in minor expeditions. However, by the 8th, he had concentrated and moved forward to Frederick. By this time, Wallace with his heterogeneous command, including the troops under Sigel, had been re-enforced by the arrival of Ricketts, and had taken up a strong position south of the Monocacy, four miles from Frederick City, where he prepared to dispute the further advance of the rebel troops towards Baltimore. His force was not great enough to contend successfully with Early's well organized army, and after a determined battle of several hours, in which he inflicted a loss of nearly six hundred men upon the enemy, Wallace was compelled to abandon the field and fall back upon Baltimore.

The road was now open, and Early sending his cavalry to destroy the Northern Central, and to burn the viaduct of the Baltimore and Ohio Road, which they succeeded in doing, pushed forward rapidly towards Washington; but his forced delay at the Monocacy, had given time for the arrival of Wright with two divisions of the Sixth and the advance of the Nineteenth corps. Early's advanced troops drew up in front of the fortifications, covering the capital, on the morning of the 11th, and by the middle of the afternoon his entire force was in position for an attack, but did not venture upon it. On the 12th, a reconnoissance was made by a brigade of the Sixth corps, holding the lines about Fort Stevens, during which they fell upon the enemy and drove him nearly a mile losing 260 killed and wounded, but inflicting a heavier loss upon the insurgents. Finding that he was anticipated and foiled by the arrival of the Sixth corps, from the James, Early retired under cover of darkness, and retreated to the west side of the Potomac, crossing at Edward's Ferry, carrying with him "much booty but little glory." Having been advised of this termination to the invasion of Maryland, Grant assigned Wright to the command of all the troops in the neighborhood of Washington, and "directed that he should get outside of the trenches with all the force he could, and push Early to the last moment." The next day Wright began the pursuit, but did not overtake the rebels till they reached Snicker's Ferry in the Shenandoah Valley. Here a sharp skirmish ensued;

but instead of waiting to deliver battle, Early pushed rapidly up the valley. On the 18th, Averill with a division of cavalry fell upon and defeated a rebel detachment at Winchester, capturing four pieces of artillery and several hundred prisoners.

Anticipating that Early would retreat to Lynchburg or Richmond, Grant ordered the Sixth and Nineteenth corps back to Washington with the view of re-enforcing the armies on the James, and using them against Lee before that General's own troops could rejoin him. Hunter, who had reached the valley, was ordered to concentrate his forces, holding a defensive attitude between Washington and any new force which might be sent in that direction. But before this new combination could be carried into effect, it became known that Early was again advancing towards the Potomac with hostile intentions, whereupon Wright's command was ordered back to the vicinity of Harper's Ferry. On the 30th, a small force of rebel cavalry, under McCausland, marching by the way of Williamsport, dashed into Chambersburg, in lower Pennsylvania, and after laying it under tribute, burned the place; they then retreated by the way of Cumberland, near which place they were met and defeated by General Kelly.

From the time of Early's first demonstration in the direction of Washington, General Grant experienced great difficulty on account of the interruption of telegraphic communication in getting his instructions correctly and efficiently carried out. Then, too, under the previous regime, the threatened territory was divided into several departments, and independent commands, and hence the disposition of the troops was more or less faulty, and their movements were incoherent. Grant, on the 2d of August, ordered Sheridan to Washington, and assigned him to the general command. A few days thereafter, the Lieutenant-General went to Washington in person, and thence to the Monocacy where he met Hunter, and after learning the exact situation of affairs, ordered him to concentrate all his available force, without delay, at Harper's Ferry, and after arriving there to go after

Early, no matter where he might be found. If the latter had crossed the Potomac in full force, Hunter was directed to overtake and fight him, and to follow him if he should be driven south of the Potomac as long as it was safe to do so. In case it should be found that only a force of raiders had gone north, he was directed to send a detachment after them, to drive them southward, and to march with the main body of his troops in the same direction, destroying everything that could invite the enemy to return, but taking for the use of his own army, all provisions, stock and forage which were necessary for its support. He was cautioned to bear in mind that his object was to drive the rebels South, and that to do this he should keep them always in sight.

In pursuance of these ringing orders, Hunter, with the alacrity of Blücher in the campaign of 1814, put the troops at once in motion, but on arriving at Halltown he was relieved, with his own consent by Sheridan, who had been stopped at Washington. Grant having already recommended it, the different departments in that theater of operations, were consolidated on the 7th of August, into the Middle Military Division, and Sheridan was assigned temporarily to the chief command, with head-quarters in the field. Washington and Baltimore, with the country adjacent, had up to this time constituted the Department of Washington; Central Pennsylvania and Northern Maryland, the Department of the Susquehanna; North-western Virginia and Western Pennsylvania, the Department of West Virginia; and the Valley of the Shenandoah, eastward to Bull Run Mountains, the Middle Military Department. This arrangement gave rise to petty jealousies between the different commanders, and should have been abolished long before, as it had been fruitful in nothing but indecisive combat and inharmonious combinations.

Grant remained in North Virginia long enough to fix his young lieutenant firmly in the command with which he had been charged, and then returned to the army confronting Petersburg.

17

CHAPTER XXVII.

THE new arrangement of military affairs about Washington, by which Halleck and the various department commanders
were shorn of power, and the control of operations in that
quarter was confided to a thoroughly vital and aggressive
General, was an exceedingly fortunate and judicious measure
on the part of General Grant. The safety of Washington
and the control of the Shenandoah Valley had hitherto caused
him great concern, but he could now give general instructions
and leave his lieutenant to work out the details according to
his own ideas. The latter guided by the orders that had been
given to Hunter, had no doubt as to the policy that he
was expected to pursue. As a preliminary precaution, he
was permitted to gather his troops together to look to their
equipment, and by a thorough reorganization to prepare
them for an active campaign. When Sheridan assumed com-

mand of the Middle Military Division, he found there the Sixth corps, two small divisions under Crook, one division of the Nineteenth corps, and a small division of cavalry under Averill. He was shortly afterwards joined by Torbert's division of cavalry from the Army of the Potomac and still later by Wilson's division. On the 10th of August he began a forward movement from Halltown towards Berryville, thus throwing himself behind the right flank of the rebel army stationed at Bunker Hill. Having made this march, his cavalry and infantry were then headed towards the Opequan, demonstrating towards Winchester. This caused Early to fall back rapidly beyond Cedar Creek to which place he was pursued by Sheridan. At this juncture the latter received information, from his scouts, which was soon confirmed by a despatch from Grant, that Lee had sent two divisions of infantry, twenty guns and a detachment of cavalry to strengthen Early, and that this force was moving by the way of Culpepper and Front Royal. Fearing that he could not cope successfully with so large a body, and knowing that defeat would lay open to invasion both Maryland and Pennsylvania, Sheridan wisely determined to fall back to Halltown, and wait for a better opportunity to strike a decisive blow.

This policy was sanctioned by the judgment of the Lieutenant-General, and was immediately but deliberately carried into effect. On the 16th, Merritt's division, near Front Royal, was attacked by Kershaw's division of Longstreet's corps, supported by two brigades of cavalry, but after a gallant fight succeeded in repulsing the enemy, capturing 2 standards and 300 prisoners. The next day the retrograde movement began; a part of the infantry retiring by way of Berryville, and the rest followed by Wilson's division which had just arrived from Washington, by Winchester and Summit Point, at both of which places there were sharp skirmishes with the advancing rebels. On the 23d, Sheridan had concentrated his entire command, now also increased by the arrival of Grover's division of the Nineteenth corps, at Halltown, and

from his securely entrenched position began a series of well
arranged reconnoissances for the purpose of satisfying himself
in regard to Early's real force and intention.   On the 25th,
he sent Torbert with Merritt and Wilson to fall upon Fitzhugh
Lee's cavalry supposed to be encamped beyond Kerneyville;
but instead of Lee they encountered the rebel infantry under
Breckinridge, on the march towards Shepherdstown.   A determined attack was made, which resulted in throwing the
rebels into considerable confusion, and before they recovered
from it Torbert returned rapidly to the place from which he
had started.   There is no doubt that Early had begun this
movement with the intention of again crossing the Potomac,
but believing from Sheridan's activity that his object had been
discovered, he returned to his position in front of Halltown.
The next day he fell back beyond the Opequan, and was
again followed by Sheridan.   Shortly afterwards Early was
directed to send a part of his force back to Richmond.   Hearing of this, and being convinced that the time for Sheridan to
strike had now come, but fearing to telegraph the order for
an attack without knowing fully the situation as viewed by
Sheridan, Grant hastened from City Point to Washington,
and thence to the Shenandoah Valley, where he arrived on
the 16th of September.   After conferring fully with Sheridan, who expressed great confidence in his ability to overthrow Early, Grant instructed him, as his official report
expressed it, to " Go in ! "

Sheridan's forces were well in hand, Wilson on the left,
near Berryville, Torbert on the right, near Summit Point, with
the infantry well disposed between the two.   The movement
began at three o'clock on the morning of September 19th.
Wilson, with McIntosh's brigade in front, marching rapidly
to the Opequan along the Berryville Turnpike, drove back
the rebel picket, forced a crossing, and dashed through the
heavily wooded ravine, up which the road winds, striking the
right of Ramseur's division about two miles in front of Winchester, before dawn.   A sharp and decisive combat ensued,
in which the rebels were driven pell-mell from their works;

but they returned to the attack at once, and were again repulsed. The ground thus gained was held till after eight o'clock, at which time Upton's brigade of the Sixth corps arrived. By nine o'clock most of the army was in position ready to move forward. Torbert, who was directed to advance with Merritt's division from Summit Point, for the purpose of forcing the Opequan, opposite that place, and forming a junction with Averill at or near Stevenson's depot, met with considerable opposition, and was delayed some hours in getting to the field. The attack was made by the Sixth and Nineteenth corps in handsome style, while Crook's command was held in reserve to be used as a turning column. Early had made hot haste from the time the first shot was fired before dawn, to concentrate his army which he had spread out considerably for the purpose of watching Sheridan, and was soon occupying a strong position on the ridge east of Winchester. The fighting was bloody and obstinate from the start, and neither army being covered by earthworks, the mortality was great. After a successful advance, while our lines were somewhat disordered, Early in turn attacked and drove Sheridan's center back ; but his success was only momentary, at this critical juncture, Sheridan threw forward Upton's brigade of Russell's division, catching Early's attacking force in the flank and driving it rapidly from the field. The gallant Russell was slain, while Upton was severely wounded. Crook, who was still in reserve, was now thrown to the extreme right (instead of to the left as was intended), with orders to find the left of the enemy's line and crush it. Aided by Torbert, with Merritt's and Averill's horse, this movement became perfectly successful, cavalry and infantry vieing with each other in deeds of gallantry. Early's line was crowded back on both flanks, broken in the center and routed everywhere ; his men had nothing to do but to fly southward under cover of darkness. Night alone saved the rebel army from complete destruction.

The next day Sheridan pushed forward in pursuit, finding the enemy at night drawn up in line and partly entrenched at

Fisher's Hill. He again determined to send Crook to turn the enemy's left and fall upon his rear, but in order to accomplish this, great secresy was necessary; the rebels had signal stations on the top of a neighboring mountain from which all our movements could be observed. Crook was therefore concealed in the heavy timber near Strasburg, north of Cedar Creek, where he remained during the 21st. Before dawn the next day, he marched to the position assigned him, on Little North Mountain to the left and rear of Early's line. The Sixth and Nineteenth corps were massed opposite Early's right center, and Ricketts' division of the Sixth corps with Averill's cavalry was then ordered to make a demonstration along the hostile front, which they did in handsome style, attracting the enemy's attention completely. The firing had become pretty general, when all at once, Crook burst from the woods on the hill-side, striking the astonished rebels in flank and rear, and in a few moments swept away their whole line, taking many prisoners and guns, and throwing them into inextricable confusion.

Unfortunately, Torbert, with the bulk of the cavalry, had been sent, with orders to proceed rapidly up the Luray Valley and to cross the mountains for the purpose of falling upon Early's rear; but the road by which he marched, running for several miles along a narrow defile was easily blockaded, by the small force of rebels which had fallen back before him. Everything practicable was done to get forward, but the progress made was slow. Early, in the meanwhile, continued his retreat through New Market, Harrisonburg, Port Republic, and thence to Brown's Gap in the Blue Ridge, closely pursued by the cavalry. Many skirmishes ensued, and a large number of prisoners were taken, but the enemy could not be again brought to a stand. Having cleared the upper valley entirely of the insurgent force, Sheridan withdrew his victorious troops, slowly to Harrisonburg, destroying the forage, grain mills, and such other property as might be serviceable to the rebel army.

"The question that now presented itself," says Sheridan in

his official report, "was whether or not I should follow the enemy to Brown's Gap, where he still held fast, drive him out, and advance on Charlottesville and Gordonsville. This movement on Gordonsville I was opposed to for many reasons, the most important of which was, that it would necessitate the opening of the Orange and Alexandria Railroad, and to protect this road against the numerous guerrilla bands, would have required a corps of infantry; besides I would have been obliged to leave a small force in the valley to give security to the line of the Potomac. This would probably occupy the whole of Crook's command, leaving me but a small number of fighting men." For these and other cogent reasons, he thought it best to continue his retrograde movement to the lower valley and then to send the Sixth and Nineteenth corps back to Petersburg by the way they had been brought from there. He was followed close by the rebel cavalry under Rosser, who attacked the Third cavalry division now under Custer, Wilson having been ordered West to reorganize and command Sherman's cavalry. Sheridan could not brook such insolence, but halted his army and sent Torbert with Merritt and Custer, to check Rosser's career. The two columns met at Tom's Creek and after a short but decisive engagement, the enemy was routed, leaving eleven guns, about four hundred prisoners and all his vehicles in the hands of the victors, who pursued him as far as Mount Jackson, some twenty-six miles. Recalling his cavalry, Sheridan halted his army at Cedar Creek, and on the 10th of October was called to Washington to confer with the Government in regard to further operations. In the interim the enemy advanced again to Fisher's Hill, though he manifested no other evidence of hostile intention. But Early had been re-enforced, and during the absence of Sheridan, on the night of the 18th, and early on the morning of the 19th, he moved silently through Strasburg, sent a strong turning column across the Shenandoah, and after marching below the left flank of the Union army, re-crossed the river at Boman's Ford, under cover of a heavy fog, striking the left of Crook's line, driving in his outposts, capturing his camps, and completely turning his position. This was followed by a vigorous direct attack upon the Union front, and before the true situation of affairs was fairly realized, the whole army was driven back in confusion nearly to Middletown, with the loss of many prisoners, and nearly all the artillery.

Fortunately, however, the rebels did not realize the extent of their success, or being overjoyed at it, they stopped to count the booty found in the camps which they had captured, thus giving General Wright time to partially reorganize his forces. Sheridan, in the meanwhile, had arrived at Winchester, on his way to rejoin his army, and hearing the sound of artillery in the distance, hastened forward, though still not thinking a battle was in progress. He had not ridden far, however, when he met a sickening cloud of fugitives, who had determined to save themselves if running could do it. Putting spurs to his horse he galloped to the front and soon reached the field upon which the army had been halted. Hastily pushing the rear division to the line held by Getty and Torbert, and sending his staff officers to the rear for the purpose of bringing every available man to the front, he soon had most of the army well in hand. Those first on the ground were set to work entrenching. Merritt's cavalry was formed on the left, Custer's on the right, while Powell's (formerly Averill's) held a position on the Front Royal pike. Everything possible was done to restore confidence, and to prepare the army for assuming the offensive. This was delayed by the report that the rebel infantry had made its appearance in Powell's front and was threatening a movement towards Winchester. Having satisfied himself that this was not the case, Sheridan at four P. M., ordered the army to advance, which it did with its accustomed steadiness and confidence, driving the rebels from behind fences, breastworks and hedges, steadily back upon Cedar Creek. The fighting was very determined, and at one time, Sheridan's lines being overlapped by the rebel left, a portion of the Nineteenth corps was thrown into momentary confusion. At this junction of affairs, Sheridan dashed to the head of McMillan's brigade, and led them vigorously against the re-entrant in his front, penetrating the angle fearlessly and breaking the rebel line.

Custer just then charged with his division, and with a simultaneous and impetuous dash by the entire army, the rebels were routed and driven in confusion beyond Cedar Creek, leaving their artillery, (including the captured guns) caissons, wagons and ambulances, besides many prisoners, to grace the victory of the impetuous Sheridan.

This battle practically put an end to the campaign in the Valley of Virginia, for although Early still continued to lurk about in the neighboring mountains, occasionally descending fearfully into the valley, he was never again entrusted with a command large enough to give serious concern, or to prevent the various detachments of Sheridan's army from marching whithersoever they chose in the country north of Richmond. During the winter, Sheridan disposed of his cavalry so as to drive out the guerrillas and to reduce the territory under his control, to comparative quiet, while the Sixth corps being no longer needed, was returned to the Army of the Potomac, to join in the operations against Petersburg. One division of the Nineteenth corps was sent to the Army of the James, and the other to Savannah to join Sherman.

During his brilliant campaign, Sheridan's force never exceeded 30,000 effective men, and never included any other troops than those mentioned above; while Early's force was probably quite as large, notwithstanding the assertions to the contrary, industriously put forth by that officer and his allies. Sheridan took fully 13,000 prisoners as shown by the records of his Provost Marshal, in the various battles and skirmishes, and during this time suffered the loss of 1,938 killed, 11,893 wounded, and 3,121 missing; a grand total of 16,952. It is fair to assume that Early's killed and wounded must have been fully as heavy, or in round numbers 13,800 men, which, added to the captured, gives nearly 27,000 men, killed, wounded, and taken prisoners. Besides this, Sheridan took from them, 100 pieces of artillery, 5,000 stands of small arms, and much valuable property.

CHAPTER XXVIII.

In accepting the grade of Lieutenant-General, and with it
the immediate direction of the Army of the Potomac, Grant
did not in any way neglect the more important and comprehensive duties of his new office. His first care was to secure
for the command of the various armies, military departments
and divisions, Generals who would work harmoniously and
in support of himself and each other; and his next, to devise

such a general plan of operations as would compel them all to do some specific good towards accomplishing the general result to be obtained. The war had hitherto been conducted upon no well established or proper principle. Each General had been assigned to an extended bailiwick, with an uncertain number of soldiers, and although he had been left with few or no instructions, much had been expected of him. When Grant assumed command of the armies of the United States, the loyal troops occupying the insurgent territory, were divided into twelve distinct department commands, with many minor districts, more or less independent of each other,—the troops in which were acting under no general system pointing to the accomplishment of well-defined military results. The different commanders knew that the rebellion must be put down, and that the Government would reward successful military operations; but notwithstanding the fact that the President upon more than one occasion had issued his orders directing a simultaneous movement upon the enemy by all the armies, the military organization was too cumbrous to admit of effective working. The team was not only balky, but badly hitched, and hence one or two of the best horses were doing all the work. It will be remembered that Grant recommended the consolidation of departments and armies before the beginning of the Vicksburg campaign, and that nine months thereafter, the Military Division of the Mississippi was established. On his accession to the command of all the armies, he designated Sherman to succeed him in the command of that military division, adding to it the Department of Arkansas. It has been seen how he consolidated four departments in the Virginia region into the Middle Military Division, and placed it under Sheridan. As Sherman collected his forces and began to operate south-eastward from Chattanooga, a new consolidation of departments took place on the lower Mississippi and the Gulf coast under the title of the Military Division of West Mississippi, with General Canby in command. By these means widely separated regions and armies were brought into the general plan; great power was committed to the hands of able and judicious commanders, acting under the instructions of a clear-headed and far-seeing generalissimo and decided and concentrated action followed throughout the seat of war, bringing down by the terrible onset of 700,000 patriots, in a few months, the well-founded and closely compacted fabric of the slave-holders' rebellion.

The generalship displayed in this wonderful concentration of effort and in the unerring direction given to the national armed forces towards the vital points of the hostile territory, show strategic skill seldom surpassed, coupled with a depth and breadth of comprehension sustained by a high moral courage capable of the greatest resolutions. In bringing the Government to the adoption of such radical measures, Grant displayed all the tact and sagacity of the profoundest statesmanship, and it is doubtful if in the history of the world so much power was ever entrusted by a civilized state to the hands of a citizen, with less hesitation or doubt, while it is certain that such power was never so virtuously and unselfishly wielded. Grant, standing at the head of nearly a million of armed men, held the unlimited sway of a dictator, and yet he never for an instant forgot that he was as far below the law of the land as the most obscure private in the ranks. If the Government ever entertained a doubt of his fidelity, or a shadow of jealousy at his success it is not known; and this is a circumstance as creditable to the General as it is to the President and his Cabinet.

It is not within the limits of this work to give the details of the correspondence and orders by which Grant carried his plans into effect, nor even of the operations which resulted therefrom, but enough of both will be mentioned to show that the success of the national cause was due to the unlimited control which he exercised in the selection of subordinate commanders, and in directing their movements against the armed forces of the enemy in accordance with the true principles of warfare. As a matter of course, the patriotism, liberality, courage and civic virtue of the people were the underlying and primary cause of our success, but they were powerless until guided and controlled by a leader of and from themselves, who comprehended the magnitude of the task assigned him, and was capable of proceeding to its execution fearlessly and confidently.

As soon as Vicksburg had fallen, and complete control had been re-established over the Mississippi throughout its entire length, Grant expressed the opinion that no offensive military operations should be undertaken to the westward of that stream, but that we should content ourselves with holding the river and adjacent territory already conquered, while the entire force, at the disposal of the Government, should be directed to military operations eastward. He believed that that part of the rebellion, lying on the trans-Mississippi region, would die of its own accord like the tail of a snake, whose head and body had been severed from it, and therefore held that operations into that country were not only useless, but positively injurious to our cause, inasmuch as they carried our forces into distant regions, where they could neither be supported nor rapidly re-enforced, and where even if successful, they could render no valuable assistance against the head and front of the rebellion. For these reasons he opposed the Red River expedition under Banks, and urged the Government to send that officer against Mobile instead, with orders to co-operate with Sherman in his operations towards the interior of Alabama. Not having been called to the command of the armies when the Red River expedition was organized and put on foot, his counsel did not prevail, and although he authorized Sherman to send 10,000 of his best men, under General A. J. Smith, by transports, to take part in it, and directed him to order Steele with the available troops in the Department of Arkansas, to move overland towards Shreveport, the objective point of the campaign, he lost no time after he became Lieutenant-General, in withdrawing these armies to the Mississippi, and in sending all the men from them that could be spared to carry out the plan, suggested after the fall of Vicksburg. It is to be regretted that he was not free to do this sooner, for he would not only have averted the defeat which was incurred at Pleasant Hill and Sabine Cross-roads, but would have hastened by several months the fall of Mobile, and probably that of the Confederacy itself.

When Grant was called to Washington, he telegraphed for Sherman, then at Memphis, to meet him at Nashville, and in order to confer more fully with him in regard to the general plan of operations, requested that officer to accompany him to Cincinnati. During this interview, it was decided that Sherman should concentrate at Chattanooga, the bulk of his widely scattered forces, and move against the rebels under Joseph E. Johnston, then at Dalton, for the purpose of breaking up his army and penetrating to Atlanta, and thence operating towards the sea-coast in whatever direction might be found most advantageous, with the view of again severing the Confederacy, and enabling the national commanders to concentrate in overwhelming numbers against the fragments of the insurgent forces. As we have before stated, the first idea of this campaign, so far as known, was developed at General Grant's head-quarters in Nashville, during the preceding January, at a time when it was supposed he would have command in person of the Military Division of the Mississippi. It was now committed to Sherman, the most trusted of his lieutenants, and hence the details of the plan were left to the arrangement of that officer, in all matters, except the time of starting. The Lieutenant-General fixed this so as to make the movement simultaneous with his own from the Rapidan, with the object of keeping the enemy so busily engaged at every point of attack along his extended frontier, that he could not afford to withdraw re-enforcements from any part, for the purpose of concentrating heavily against either of the advancing armies.

Sherman's command embracing the great central belt of country lying between the Alleghanies and the western borders of Arkansas, and extending southward and eastward as far as he could carry his victorious standards, included nearly the entire theatre of war from Savannah to Vicksburg. A large force had already been concentrated by General Grant at Chattanooga, but a greater concentration yet was to take place. It was wisely judged that the territory bordering on the Mississippi could be stripped almost entirely of the force which had hitherto been engaged in holding it and protecting the navigation of the river, provided an active campaign should be conducted from Chattanooga, and the lower part of the great Tennessee Valley. Sherman therefore directed McPherson, commanding the Army of the Tennessee, to concentrate all the available men of his army for active duty at Huntsville, leaving General Hurlbut with the remainder of the force to operate against Forrest in West Tennessee and Northern Mississippi.

General Grant, displeased with operations in East Tennessee during the winter, had solicited and obtained the assignment of General Schofield, an officer of sound judgment, to the command of the army in that region. Burnside's corps was relieved at the same time, and ordered to Annapolis. Sherman's first duty was to concentrate his army, and his next to provide for supplying it with the means of subsistence. It will be remembered that Grant had devoted much care and attention to perfecting the operation of the railroads in Kentucky and Tennessee, but in view of the greatly increased forces to be supplied, Sherman had much to accomplish in that direction before his army could take the field in the sterile region of Northern Georgia. But bending himself with great activity to the multifarious duties of his position, he soon instilled his own energy into the administration of every department connected with his army. By the 1st of May, he had concentrated a force of 98,787 men, and 254 guns, well supplied, thoroughly equipped, well organized and ably commanded, with which to undertake the task assigned him. Promptly at the time designated by Grant for the general advance, he moved forward, and on the 6th of May his forces were distributed as follows: The Army of the Cumberland, General George H. Thomas commanding, consisting of the Fourth, Fourteenth, and Twentieth corps under Howard, Palmer, and Hooker respectively, held positions near Ringgold on the railroad. The Army of the Tennessee, General McPherson commanding, consisting of the Fifteenth, and parts of the Sixteenth and Seventeenth corps, commanded respectively by Logan, Dodge and Blair, was near Gordon's Mill on Chickamauga Creek; while Schofield, with the Army of the Ohio, consisting of a part of the Twenty-third corps, and a division of cavalry under Stoneman, had moved down from East Tennessee to Red Clay, at or near the Georgia line, just north of Dalton.*

General Johnston, with an army of between 50,000 and 60,000 effectives, divided into three corps under Hardee, Polk and Hood, with a division of Georgia State troops under G. W. Smith, and a corps of cavalry under Wheeler lay at Dalton, holding a strongly fortified position on an outlying spur of the Alleghanies, known as Rocky Face Ridge, with his principal force at Buzzard Roost Gap.

The country lying between Chattanooga and Atlanta is broken up by mountain ridges, alternating with deep ravines and rapid streams, and is more difficult, if possible, than the country between Washington and Richmond. It is generally covered with a heavy growth of timber, broken only at rare intervals by farms and villages. The roads are of the most primitive sort, and during the rainy season become almost entirely impassable. Atlanta, the principal town in Northern Georgia, at that time contained a population of about 20,000, and being situated at the crossing of several railroads, the rebels had made it a point for the manufacture and distribution of military stores of all kinds. Recognizing its strategic importance, they had fortified it strongly in

* General Sherman's forces were divided as follows :

	Army of the Cumberland.	Army of the Tennessee.	Army of the Ohio.
Infantry, ...	54,568	22,437	11,183
Artillery, ...	2,377	1,404	679
Cavalry, ...	3,828	624	1,697
Total, . . .	60,773	24,465	13,559
Guns, ...	130	96	28

Grand aggregate of troops, 98,797 ; guns, 254.

1863, and were now prepared to struggle manfully for its defense.

The position of the enemy at Rocky Face, was found to be too strong to be carried by direct attack; Sherman, therefore directed Thomas to occupy Tunnel Hill, a few miles in advance, which he did with but slight opposition, and then to demonstrate strongly in front of the enemy along Rocky Face and particularly at Buzzard Roost. Schofield was ordered to move down from Red Clay, as closely as possible to Dalton, while McPherson was to turn the enemy's position by moving through Ship's Gap, Villanow, and Snake Creek Gap, to Resaca on the railroad eighteen miles behind Johnston. Thomas carried out his part of the programme in handsome style, on the 9th of May. Newton's division of Howard's corps, made a lodgment on Rocky Face Ridge after a gallant fight, and turning to the right tried to reach the gap, but finding the crest quite narrow as well as strongly defended by the rebels, they were compelled to desist. Geary's division of Hooker's corps advanced at the same time, but failed to reach the summit. McPherson got within striking distance of the railroad in good time, on the 9th, driving a brigade of rebel cavalry from Snake Creek Gap, but fearing that Johnston might fall upon his flank and rear, he was unwilling to hazard an attack against the rebel works at Resaca, and therefore withdrew towards Snake Creek Gap, where he took up a strong position. But this flank march had startled Johnston, and although Sherman was chagrined at the failure of the well-planned movement against Resaca, he hastened to re-enforce it at the earliest hour by sending Thomas with Hooker's and Palmer's corps, followed closely by Schofield, while Howard was left with his own corps and the cavalry to keep up the demonstration against Buzzard Roost; but Johnston now evacuated that place and fell back rapidly towards the new position which he had prepared near Resaca.

On the 12th, the whole army, with the exception of Howard's corps, assembled at Snake Creek Gap, and pushed forward at once, McPherson covered by Kilpatrick's division of

18

cavalry, in advance, on the direct road to Resaca, while
Thomas moved to the left of McPherson, followed again by
Schofield. Kilpatrick drove Wheeler's rebel horse steadily
back to within two miles of Resaca, where he was wounded,
and compelled to leave the field, turning his command over
to Colonel Murray his next in rank. At this junction
McPherson's advance pushed forward, and relieved the cavalry, driving the rebels beyond Camp Creek and into the line
of works covering Resaca and the great bend of the Oostenaula River. Johnston had already got there having marched
rapidly and by the best road in that region, while Sherman's
army was compelled to pursue a devious mountain route,
over roads nearly as bad as roads could be. Sherman lost
no time in enveloping the rebel works. Thomas was thrown
forward into position on the left of McPherson; Schofield
pushed through the entangled forest to Thomas' left, while
Howard marched down the main road from Dalton. Sherman also directed McPherson to throw a bridge across the
Oostenaula at Lay's Ferry, below Resaca, and to send
Sweeney's division of the Sixteenth corps to threaten Calhoun, a point still further in Johnston's rear. To give this
movement greater effect, Garrard's division of cavalry was
ordered to march from Villanow towards Rome, for the purpose of crossing the Oostenaula and swinging into the railroad between Calhoun and Kingston.

While these strategical movements were in the process of
execution, McPherson succeeded in crossing Camp Creek
near its mouth, and driving the rebels under Polk from the
commanding ridge, which they held, back to their inner line
of works. Thomas at the same time pressed close into the
Creek Valley, farther to the left, and threw Hooker's corps
across its head to the Dalton road down which he moved till
he had also closed in on the enemy's lines. By the evening
of the 14th, after a good deal of desultory skirmishing and
some sharp fighting, Sherman's forces were all in position and
on the next day moved to the attack. A heavy battle ensued,
without much advantage to any part of the Union army ex-

cept that under Hooker, who drove the rebels from the hills in his front, capturing four guns and a considerable number of prisoners. Finding that his position was no longer tenable, Johnston evacuated it during the night and fell back rapidly towards Adairsville, where he prepared to make a stand. The next day Thomas followed close upon his heels by the main road through Resaca, skirmishing with Hardee, who had been left to cover the retreat. After crossing the river, Jeff. C. Davis' division was sent to Rome, which place it captured, taking ten large guns, and many stores, besides destroying a number of mills and much valuable property.

Leaving a small force to garrison the place, Davis pushed on to rejoin the army. Schofield struggled through the country to the left of Thomas, making roads, or following such trails as promised to lead him in the right direction. McPherson crossed the Oostenaula at Lay's Ferry, and joined in the pursuit with all the speed that could be made in the difficult region through which he marched. Thomas' advance under Newton, came up with the enemy at Adairsville, where a sharp skirmish ensued, but before dispositions for the attack were completed, Johnston again fell back, covering his rear skillfully, and taking up a strong position about Cassville, whither our army pursued him, marching by the way of Kingston. The indications at this place were strongly in favor of a general battle; but as the Union army concentrated for the attack, Johnston acting under the advice of Hood and Polk, though against that of Hardee, abandoned the ground which he had chosen, and fell behind the Etowah, holding Allatoona pass, to cover his future movements. He afterwards regretted this step, but it was too late to change his mind. Sherman, without an hour's hesitation, determined to cross the Etowah and turn the position at Allatoona; after providing his entire army with twenty days' rations, he cut loose from the railroad, and directed his columns on Dallas, whither he had already ordered Davis to move from Rome. Thomas marched by the direct road through Burnt Hickory to that place; McPherson passed still further to the right through

Van Wert, intending to come in on Thomas' right, while Schofield, taking a somewhat more direct line, was expected to take position on Thomas' left; but Johnston seemed to divine the plan, and interposed his left strongly at New Hope Church. On the 25th of May, General Hooker, leading Thomas' column, encountered Jackson's rebel cavalry on Pumpkin-vine Creek, but brushing them rapidly out of the way, he pushed across the creek, saving the bridges which had been set on fire, and about two miles further on came up with the outlying pickets of Hood's corps. These were attacked by Geary, and driven back to the main rebel line. The rest of Hooker's troops, moving on other roads, did not get up till late in the afternoon, when General Sherman ordered Hooker to attack with his whole corps for the purpose of getting possession of the junction of the roads radiating from New Hope Church. The troops assaulted boldly and vehemently, but the rebel works were too strong and too well manned by Stewart's division to be captured. Hooker's loss was considerable. The next morning McPherson moved through Dallas, and deployed in front of the position at New Hope Church, while Schofield was directed to the left with the expectation of overlapping and turning the hostile right. Garrard's division of cavalry operated on the right flank of the army, and Stoneman on the left.

Owing to the dense forests, and the difficulty of finding or making proper roads, much time was lost in working the army into position, and much skirmishing with some heavy fighting took place, during which Sherman decided to work in towards the railroad, striking it south-east of Ackworth. While he was in the act of moving in that direction, the rebels took advantage of the opportunity to strike at McPherson, then fortified in front of Dallas; they made a determined attack upon his works, but met with a bloody repulse. After this several days of inactivity intervened, when Sherman began again to extend his left by moving Thomas towards the railroad four or five miles, gradually closing Schofield and McPherson in the same direction, thus covering all the roads leading back to Allatoona and Ackworth. This was done on the 1st of June, and was at once followed by a cavalry movement upon Allatoona, front and rear, resulting in its capture. Sherman was now relieved of apprehension for his communications, and enabled to take measures at once for the reconstruction of the railroad bridge across the Etowah, a few miles to the rear, and for the establishment of a secondary base of supplies at Allatoona. He did not suspend his movements however, but continued to work to the left, now menacing the right and rear of the rebel lines, and now threatening to push entirely beyond and throw them from their line of retreat towards Atlanta. Johnston was not slow to conform to Sherman's movement, but anticipated him in most cases with ready address; planting his army in well selected positions, and holding it compact and alert in the roads along which his adversary wished to advance.

On the morning of the 5th, he held a strong position with his left at Lost Mountain and his right near the railroad, covering the roads to Atlanta. On the 7th, he fell back, taking up a position behind Noonday Creek, with his right extended to the Ackworth and Marietta Road. On the 8th of June, Sherman was re-enforced by Blair with two divisions of the Seventeenth corps, and Long's brigade of cavalry, belonging to Garrard's division, thus bringing the army up to its original numbers, notwithstanding the killed and wounded and the detachments left at Rome, Kingston and Allatoona. As the rebels fell back they destroyed the railroad, compelling Sherman to weaken and delay himself by detachments for its repair. Johnston showed himself during this time and in fact throughout the entire campaign to be a ready strategist, and a careful painstaking General, always discovering the intentions of his adversary in time to prevent disaster and covering his own movements with consummate skill. Skirmishing was a matter of hourly occurrence, but neither General seemed willing to bring on an engagement till there was a good opportunity for striking a vital blow. On the 9th of June, having re-established his communications and brought forward an abundance of supplies Sherman moved to Big Shanty; meanwhile the enemy fell back to Pine, Lost, and Kenesaw Mountains, covering Marietta and the railroad as far as the Chattahoochee River.

Hardee's corps held the left of the hostile line, resting on Lost Mountain; Polk, the center, thrown to the front on Pine Mountain, while Hood, resting on Kenesaw covered the roads to Marietta. Sherman pressed forward to break the rebel lines between Pine Mountain and Kenesaw, but before the attack could be made, Johnston drew back his center to the rugged ridge joining Lost Mountain and Kenesaw, where he strongly fortified himself and prepared to make a determined resistance. During this operation, General Polk was killed, and was succeeded in the command of his corps, by Lovell. The weather was rainy and disagreeable, and hence the roads became so bad that the army could scarcely get forward, still it did not falter, but kept pressing close upon the rebel lines. On the 11th, Sherman telegraphed to Washington: "I will proceed with due caution, and try to make no mistake," adding, "one of my chief objects being to give full employment to Joe Johnston, it makes but little difference where he is, so he is not on his way to Virginia." On the 13th, he telegraphed: "As soon as possible, I will study Johnston's position on Kenesaw and Lost Mountains, and adopt some plan to dislodge him, or draw him out of his position. We can not risk the heavy losses of an assault, at this distance from our base. Cars now come to our very front camp. All well."

On the 14th, he informed Mr. Stanton that he had received news of the defeat of Sturgis, sent out specially from Memphis to hold Forrest, and to keep him off the Chattanooga railroad; that he had ordered A. J. Smith to be sent after Forrest, and then prepared to move forward, but owing to the elevated position of the enemy could make no movement, not plainly in his view, except under cover of darkness. McPherson held the left, Thomas the center and Schofield the right on the old Sandtown Road, pressing well around on the rebel flank, to counteract which Hood was withdrawn from McPherson's front and thrown to the left confronting Schofield.   On the 22d, Hooker and Schofield advanced their lines beyond the Kulp House, when the rebels sallied from their work, striking Williams' division and Hascall's brigade, driving them back upon the main line, and involving themselves in a terrible battle, in which they were badly beaten, leaving many killed and wounded in the hands of the Union soldiery.   By this time Sherman had gained a thorough knowledge of the enemy's position, and although it was found to be as strong as it could well be made both by natural and artificial defences, he determined to venture upon an assault in the hope of breaking through the left center, and reaching Marietta soon enough to fall upon and destroy the rebel right. He issued his orders accordingly, but owing to the continued rains and bad roads, it was not until the 27th, that the troops could be got into position to carry them into effect.

On that day the assaults were made at points about a mile apart, by McPherson and Thomas, but failed, notwithstanding the gallantry displayed by both officers and men.   It cost the national troops heavily in killed and wounded, including Generals D. McCook and Harker, both officers of fine promise, and the latter already greatly distinguished for gallantry and good management at Stone River, Chickamauga, and Chattanooga.   The rebel loss did not probably exceed 500 men, while Sherman's was not far from 3,000.   In his official report, Sherman frankly says: "Failure as it was, and for which I assume the entire responsibility, I yet claim it produced good fruits, as it demonstrated to Johnston that I would assault, and that boldly ; and we also gained and held ground so close to the enemy's parapets, that he could not show a head above them."   The justification is hardly admissible, but the assumption of the blame is entirely worthy of commendation.

The armies remained in their relative positions till the 2d of July, at which time McPherson drew out of his works in front of Kenesaw, leaving them to be held by Garrard's dismounted cavalry, and in pursuance of Sherman's instructions, moved by his right flank towards Nickajack Creek and the Chattahoochee by the Turner's Ferry road. In this movement his right was covered by a corresponding movement of Stoneman's cavalry, which struck the river below Turner's. Johnston discovering the movement, and fearing for his left and rear, fell back to Smyrna camp-meeting ground, five miles south-west of Marietta. In this position his flanks were protected by Nickajack and Rottenwood Creeks, and his lines covered the approaches to a strong *tête-de-pont* which he had constructed in anticipation of a possible crossing of the Chattahoochee. On the morning of the 3d, Thomas moved by his left flank to the railroad and then turned the head of his columns southward in pursuit. Logan's corps of the Army of the Tennessee, was sent to take possession of Marietta, while McPherson and Schofield pushed across Nickajack, turning the left of the rebel position, and intending to fall upon them while crossing the river, but Johnston had provided for such a contingency, and withdrawing his army into the *tête-de-pont*, held his ground till forced by other combinations to abandon it. Logan was now directed to leave a small force at Marietta, and to push forward and rejoin McPherson; Thomas, also, marched to the river skirmishing heavily with the rebels, while Sherman pushed to the front in person, and finding that the rebel General held a strongly fortified position covering the railroad and pontoon bridges, he did not think it safe to hazard a direct attack, and therefore decided to make a new turning movement.

Withdrawing Schofield from his position in reserve, he ordered him to march by the Smyrna camp-ground road to the mouth of Soap Creek, and to make a lodgment from that place on the south side of the river. This was done with great skill and precision, while Garrard was sent to secure the ford at Roswell, as well as to destroy the cloth factories established at that place. Thomas then directed Newton's division to the same point, whither it was followed rapidly by Dodge's corps, and soon after by McPherson's entire army.

Howard was sent to Power's Ferry, two miles below Schofield, and by the evening of the 9th, Sherman had secured
three points of passage, had built bridges, and united the
most of his force on the south side of the Chattahoochee.
Johnston had distributed his cavalry under Wheeler and
Jackson, to watch the river for twenty miles above and below,
and was therefore kept informed of all that took place on
either flank. On the night of the 9th, he withdrew his army
to the south side of the river, going into position again behind Peach-tree Creek, with his left resting on the river, and
his right extended well out to cover the approaches to Atlanta
now only five or six miles in his rear. He set his engineers
and a large force of negroes to work on the fortifications, and
prepared as well as circumstances would permit, for the crisis
about to burst upon him.

He had doubtless managed his campaign defensively, with
great skill, but had lost according to his own accounts, 10,000
killed and wounded, and 4,700 prisoners,* besides the crops
of grain in the region north of Atlanta, and the extensive
manufacturing establishments at Etowah, Rome, and Roswell.
The campaign had now reached that point, at which both
leaders seemed to recognize the necessity of proceeding with
great caution and certainty. Sherman gave his army rest,
and passed a week in bringing forward stores, strengthening
his detachments along the railway, and perfecting the repairs of the road, his sole dependence for the support of his
army.

On the 10th of July, in pursuance of Sherman's instructions, Rousseau marched from Decatur on the Tennessee River,
with a cavalry force of something over 2,000 men, for the
purpose of breaking up the railroad to Opelika and Montgomery, thus interrupting Johnston's communications with
the South-west. Moving with great celerity, he crossed the
Coosa at Ten Islands on the 14th, defeating Clanton's brigade,
and marching thence to Talladega. On the 16th, he struck
the railroad at Loachapoka, and marched thence to Chehaw

* "Southern History of the War," vol. ii., p. 348.

Station, where he again defeated the enemy, and proceeded to Opelika, destroying about thirty-two miles of track during his march. He then moved to the north-eastward, reaching Marietta on the 22d, having lost about thirty men, killed, wounded, and missing.

On the 17th, Sherman resumed the offensive, directing Thomas to march by Buckhead, and Schofield by Cross Keys, following McPherson who was to march towards Decatur east of Atlanta, by the way of Stone Mountain. Garrard's cavalry was thrown forward on the left flank of McPherson, while Stoneman and McCook continued to watch the river and roads west of the railway. These movements were intended to operate as a general right wheel of the entire army, throwing the left flank against Atlanta and its eastern communications, while the right wing and centre should confront the rebel army an Peach-tree Creek. In this order the different columns closed in, converging on Atlanta, but in the meantime a change had taken place in the opposing army. Davis, the rebel President, it seems had now lost all confidence in Johnston's generalship and courage, and on the 17th, suspended him from command and assigned to General Hood the duty of fighting and beating Sherman. It can not be doubted that in this, Davis committed a grave mistake, viewed from a purely military stand-point, for although Johnston had not risked a battle with Sherman, he had shown himself to be a wily and able antagonist.

Sherman and many of our best Generals had already learned to regard him as the foremost of the Confederate leaders. He had been recognized, from the time of his campaign against Patterson to his defeat of McClellan on the Peninsula, as the exponent of vigorous offensive measures, the basis of the true policy for the Confederacy. In all situations he had shown great boldness, independence and fortitude, and although he never enjoyed the confidence of Davis and his party, he was undoubtedly an abler man than Davis or any member of his Cabinet, and a better General than Lee. He was a better man before the war, a more honest enemy and a better General during it, and has been a better citizen since. His successor, General Hood, noted for nothing except being a hard fighter and a fair commander of a corps, was selected as the exponent of the fighting policy, by which he was expected to overwhelm Sherman, and redeem the waning fortunes of the Confederacy.

CHAPTER XXIX.

SHERMAN CLOSING IN UPON ATLANTA—THE GAP IN PALMER'S CORPS—
RECKLESS ATTACK OF THE REBELS—REPULSE BY HOOKER'S CORPS
—HOOD RETIRES TO DEFENSES OF ATLANTA—THE STRUGGLE UPON
LEGGETT HILL—THE ATTACK UPON M'PHERSON—DEATH OF M'PHER-
SON—GARRARD JOINS SHERMAN—HIS DESTRUCTION OF THE RAIL-
ROAD—HOWARD IN COMMAND OF THE ARMY OF THE TENNESSEE—
THE ATTACK UPON LOGAN'S CORPS—SLOCUM SUCCEEDS HOOKER—
FAILURE OF THE CAVALRY EXPEDITIONS—STONEMAN'S SURREN-
DER—WHEELER'S RAID—SHERMAN THROWS HIS ARMY ACROSS THE
WEST POINT RAILROAD—THE ATTACK UPON HOWARD—EVACUA-
TION OF ATLANTA—RESULTS OF THE CAMPAIGN—HOOD FALLS UPON
SHERMAN'S COMMUNICATIONS—PREPARES HIS SCHEMES FOR INVAD-
ING TENNESSEE.

On the 20th, Sherman's three armies had closed well in
upon Atlanta, but a gap of considerable extent having been
left between Schofield and Thomas, the latter was directed to
send two divisions of Howard's corps to the left, for the
purpose of establishing close communication with Schofield.
This disposition had been but partially completed, when the
rebel leader perceived an opening between Newton's division,
and Johnson's division of Palmer's corps, and massed a
heavy force, with which to penetrate the gap, hoping thereby
to destroy the right of Thomas' army. The attack was
made at a little past three o'clock in the afternoon, and is
described by a rebel writer as "one of the most reckless,
massive, and headlong charges of the war," * gallantly led
by the divisions of Bate and Walker of Hardee's corps ; and,
although it caught the national troops somewhat unprepared,

* "Pollard's Southern History of the War."

it was repulsed by Hooker's corps fighting uncovered, aided by Newton with fence-rail breastworks, and Johnson who had constructed a line of good entrenchments. The rebels left upon the field 500 dead, and 1,000 severely wounded, besides many prisoners. Their loss could not have been far from 5,000 men in all. Sherman's entire loss was only about 500. Such an offensive did not promise the most flattering results, but Hood was not discouraged and determined to try his fortune still farther.

On the night of the 21st, after considerable skirmishing throughout the day, he abandoned the line of Peach-tree Creek, withdrawing to the immediate defenses of Atlanta, and was closely followed in the same direction by Sherman's entire army; Thomas on the right, Schofield in the center, and McPherson on the left. The latter in advancing from Decatur, followed the road parallel with the Augusta railway, and on the 21st, captured from the enemy a commanding eminence, to the south-eastward of the railroad, from the top of which he could plainly see into the heart of the city, not over two miles distant. Blair's corps (the Seventeenth) was ordered to take possession of this hill and fortify it, and in order to render its tenure entirely certain, Dodge's corps, now in reserve on the right, was ordered to Blair's support. It began the movement by a wood road approaching Atlanta and running diagonally towards Blair's left. These movements were in the process of execution, when at about noon on the 22d, McPherson found his left and rear suddenly attacked with great vigor, by the rebels advancing from the south-east. Hood had detached Hardee the night before, with orders to make a wide detour, and to fall upon McPherson's exposed flank. This march had been silently executed, and brought the enemy into position in a most unexpected quarter. McPherson's left division had fortunately been thrown back in a direction parallel with the railroad line, and was thus enabled to make head for awhile against the overwhelming onslaught of Hardee. As soon as McPherson heard the firing, he galloped in that direction, pushing through the woods to the rear of Blair and Logan, and rode towards the railroad evidently expecting to find Dodge, but had not gone far before he ran into the rebels, who fired upon and killed him. Logan, the next in rank, assumed command of the Army of the Tennessee, and was instructed by Sherman at once to hold the ground already chosen, particularly the Bald Hill which had been captured the evening before by Leggett's division. The head of Dodge's column had reached a point within a half mile of Leggett's Hill, when Hardee began his attack through the intervening space. McPherson's last order was to direct Wangelin's brigade of the Fifteenth corps to fill this gap, but the troops did not reach it in time to stop the rebel advance, though they moved at the double-quick. The rebel plan was well laid, and had it been as well executed, a great defeat might have been inflicted upon our arms. Hood had directed Stewart with Polk's corps to attack McPherson in front, while Hardee advanced upon his flank and rear, but fortunately these attacks were not made simultaneously. The latter column had carried Leggett's Hill, capturing the pioneer company engaged in fortifying it, and was pushing on when it was checked by Giles Smith's division, now thrown back nearly perpendicular to its old line, connecting its right with Leggett. At the same time Dodge's lines were thrown forward and attacked Hardee's right, capturing a number of prisoners and breaking the force of the rebel onset, thus giving time to arrange for further defense. A lull now took place in the battle, but the rebels continued their movement along the Decatur road and railway, and at four o'clock again advanced, falling upon an advanced regiment with a section of guns, and pushing on, broke through the lines which had been somewhat weakened by the withdrawal of a brigade, to re-enforce the extreme left.

This break separated the two wings of the Fifteenth corps entirely, and gave the enemy possession of two batteries. At this crisis, Logan, flaming out with the determination of a Ney or a Massena, threw the broken corps forward with irresistible vigor, for the purpose of regaining the lost ground. The movement was watched by Sherman with breathless anxiety, but he was soon gratified by seeing his lines re-established and all the guns regained, except two which had been withdrawn by the rebels towards Atlanta. This was one of the strangest battles of the war, and nothing but the steady valor of the troops and the good management of Logan and his officers, saved Sherman from a great disaster. Logan, Leggett, Giles Smith and Dodge, did all that could be done, while maintaining their position, to inflict damage upon the enemy. The men of Smith's and Leggett's divisions were frequently compelled to fight from either side of the same entrenchments in rapid succession, first driving back Hardee and then jumping the parapets to receive the attack of Stewart. But so coolly did they act that in no case did they forget to take their prisoners with them. In this hazardous work, Colonel Belknap, of the Fifteenth Iowa volunteers, was particularly conspicuous, and a few days afterwards was rewarded for his gallantry by the President with the commission of Brigadier General. Sherman's losses in killed, wounded and prisoners, were 3,722 men; including among the killed the accomplished and much beloved McPherson, the trusted friend of both Grant and Sherman. The enemy's loss was not far from 8,000, killed, wounded and missing, according to the best information which can be obtained.

On the 23d, Garrard's division joined Sherman, having broken the railway towards Atlanta, and destroyed the large bridges across the Yellow and the Ulcofauhatchee Rivers. This left Hood without any line of railway communication except the Macon Road, running into the rich region of South-western Georgia. Sherman was determined to destroy that road also, and for this purpose he concentrated Stoneman's and Garrard's division of cavalry on the left of the army, numbering in all about 5,000 effective troopers; at the same time he sent Rousseau's cavalry, now under Colonel Harrison, of the Eighth Indiana, to report to General E. M.

McCook on the right, bringing that officer's command up to about 4,000 men. These columns were ordered to march respectively by McDonough and Fayetteville, meeting at Lovejoy's Station on the railroad, on the night of the 28th, while the Army of the Tennessee, now commanded by Howard, was directed to withdraw from its place on the extreme left, and marching by the rear of Schofield and Thomas, to swing in behind Atlanta and take position at East Point, the junction of the two roads leading to the south and westward.

Pursuant to this plan, Howard moved his army during the 26th and 27th, to the extreme right, reaching well around to East Point, but while extending in the same direction the next day, the rebels under Hardee and Lee, sallied from the works about Atlanta, on the Ball's Ferry road, and attacked Logan's corps with great fury. But Logan had covered his front with the usual breastworks and received the attack with coolness, repelling it as often as six times, in each instance with great slaughter. The rebel loss was estimated by Logan at fully 5000, while his own did not exceed 600.

On the 1st of August, Hooker feeling aggrieved at the promotion of Howard, to the command of the Army of the Tennessee, was, at his own request, relieved, and was succeeded in the command of his corps by General Slocum; Palmer was relieved at his own request, by General Jeff. C. Davis, while General D. S. Stanley, succeeded Howard. Logan, the only one of these Generals who had any right whatever, to feel aggrieved, continued bravely at his post. The interval between the 28th of July and the 15th of August, was passed by Sherman in gradually working towards the right. The combined cavalry expedition had proved to be a complete failure; for although McCook reached the road at the time and place specified, he had not succeeded in breaking it seriously when he was compelled to desist and withdraw towards the South-west, for the purpose of extricating his command from the toils now being thrown about it. After much hard marching and fighting he succeeded in crossing to the north of the Chattahoochee and rejoining Sherman, with the loss of 500 men and several valuable officers, including Colonel Harrison, who was taken prisoner. Stoneman moved at the appointed time, though not having been joined by Garrard as he expected, he did not go to Lovejoy's at all, but marching by the way of Covington, Monticello, Hillsboro and Clinton, he struck for Macon, which place he approached on the 30th of July, but hearing that in anticipation of his raid, the prisoners had been removed to North Carolina, he started to rejoin the army. The rebels had, in the meantime, gathered a few scattered militia under Armstrong and Allen, and by making a great show of numbers, so imposed upon Stoneman as to induce him to surrender that part of his command which remained to share such an ignominious fate. The brigades of Colonels Adams and Capron cut their way through and returned to the army in good time, though somewhat jaded and disorganized. The rest might have done likewise had Stoneman made an effort worthy of the name to lead them back, or to break through the attenuated lines which environed him.

About the 10th of August, Hood detached his cavalry under Wheeler, to make a raid upon the Union communications. Marching around Sherman's left, by the east and north, Wheeler struck the railroad at Adairsville, and again at Calhoun, capturing in his way nine hundred beef cattle; he then marched to Dalton, where Colonel Leibold held him in check, till General Steedman arrived from Chattanooga and drove him off in the direction of Athens in East Tennessee, where he remained for a short time. He moved thence soon afterwards to the north side of the Little Tennessee, crossed the Holston near Strawberry Plains, and continued his march towards McMinnville, Murfreesboro, and Franklin in Middle Tennessee. From the latter place he was driven towards Florence by Rousseau, Steedman, and Granger, and finally effected his escape with but little loss, though he succeeded in doing no permanent injury to the railroad lines, and really weakened Hood considerably by his absence. Immediately after he started, Sherman seized this opportunity to send Kilpatrick with five thousand cavalry to break the West Point Railroad near Fairburn, and the Macon Road at Jonesboro. Kilpatrick marched rapidly, and met but little opposition, though he did not succeed in damaging the roads seriously. All the efforts of the cavalry having failed, Sherman now saw that there was nothing left for him but to raise the investment of Atlanta, and to throw his entire army across its southern communications. He therefore sent the Twentieth corps, under General Williams, back to the fortified position on the Chattahoochee, and by a series of well executed movements, swung his army across the West Point Railroad; Howard above Fairburn, Thomas at Red Oak, and Schofield at a point known as "Digs and Mims," still nearer East Point. Having effectively destroyed the railroad for twelve miles and a half, he continued the movement towards the Macon Road; Howard on the extreme right towards Jonesboro, Thomas in the center by Shoal Creek Church, and Schofield on the left towards Rough and Ready. These movements were all progressing favorably on the 31st, when S. D. Lee's and Hardee's corps now assembled at Jonesboro, marched out and attacked Howard, but that officer having encountered some opposition after crossing the head of the Flint River, had covered his front by the usual entrenchments, and was therefore well prepared to receive attack. After two hours of sanguinary fighting the rebels were again repulsed, leaving two thousand five hundred men killed and wounded on the field. Thomas and Schofield having both reached the railroad, were ordered to close in towards Howard, breaking the railroad as they marched northward, for the purpose of aiding in a general attack upon the rebels now isolated at Jonesboro. Garrard's cavalry was disposed so as to interpose between Atlanta and the Union left, while Kilpatrick was sent to the extreme right to threaten the road below Jonesboro. The next day, about five o'clock P. M., Davis assaulted the rebel lines, capturing nearly all of Goran's brigade, and eight guns, but the rest of the army, owing to the difficult roads, was not within supporting distance. The advantages gained could not therefore be pressed, and during the night the enemy evacuated both Jonesboro and Atlanta. Lee and Hardee fell back to a strong position behind Walnut Creek, near Lovejoy's Station, whither they were closely followed the next day by Thomas, Howard, and Schofield. Stuart retreated from Atlanta towards McDonough, while Smith with the militia took the road to Covington.

Having thus manœuvered the enemy out of Atlanta, and feeling that it would be impossible to bring him to a stand, or to overtake him in that country, Sherman determined to give up the pursuit and to concentrate his army about Atlanta, for rest and reorganization. Thomas took post in and around that city, Howard at East Point, and Schofield at Decatur.

Thus, after a campaign of four months, Sherman had reached the goal assigned him, and now occupied a position in the very heart of the rebel dominions, eating out its richest products, intercepting communication, and standing ready to push forward with his mighty host towards Virginia, or to the Atlantic sea-coast. The great advantage of his victory was, however, that it enabled Grant to move Sherman towards himself, thus interposing a powerful army between Lee and the rebel forces in the South-west, while the rebel railroad system should be completely destroyed. With the Army of the Potomac investing Petersburg, and Sherman's hundred thousand veterans at Atlanta, Grant felt that the days of the rebellion were numbered; for although the armed forces of the enemy had not yet been destroyed, they had been out-generaled, and henceforward, although they might struggle bravely to retrieve their fallen fortunes, they were destined to gather nothing but the bitter fruits of disappointment.

Hood concentrated his forces at Palmetto Station, on the West Point Railroad, about twenty-five miles from Atlanta, and after confronting Sherman for awhile, reorganized his army under the direction of Beauregard, and threw it to the north side of the Chattahoochee. After some further delay, he struck well around Sherman's left, fell upon his communications, destroying the railroad rapidly, nearly as far up as Dalton. Being closely pursued by Sherman, he drew off to the westward, and prepared to carry out a mad scheme for the invasion of Tennessee, hoping thereby to compel Sherman to abandon Atlanta, and to follow him northward. But, it will be shown hereafter, that this plan also failed, and materially aided in bringing the rebellion to an inglorious end.

CHAPTER XXX.

DURING Sherman's campaign into Central Georgia, Forrest, a bold and skillful leader, occupied Northern Mississippi with a large force of rebel cavalry, which had been extremely busy in striking at isolated posts along the Mississippi and Ohio, and was evidently waiting for an opportunity to fall upon Sherman's communications in Tennessee and Northern Georgia. To neutralize this danger, Sherman before beginning his campaign, directed General C. C. Washburne to send General Sturgis with the bulk of his forces in West Tennessee to attack the rebels, now known to be gathering near the northern border of Mississippi. The contending forces met on the 10th of June near Guntown, one hundred miles south-east of Memphis. After a sharp fight Sturgis was defeated and driven back in confusion to the Mississippi, losing his guns and a number of prisoners. Forrest pursued with such activity and seemed to be so overjoyed at his success that he forgot all about Sherman's long lines of railway communications, and devoted himself exclusively to plundering and galloping over West Tennessee. Shortly after the disgraceful termination of this expedition, A. J. Smith arrived at Memphis, on his way from the Red River to join the army of the center, but before proceeding to Georgia he was directed by Sherman to take the field against Forrest. In pursuance of this order he moved at once from Memphis with a considerable force of infantry, cavalry and artillery, and on the 14th of July, came up with the enemy at Tupelo, where a battle, continuing throughout most of three days, occurred, in which Forrest was wounded and badly beaten.

The country being destitute of supplies however, Smith shortly afterwards withdrew in the direction of Memphis to join Sherman, instead of pressing his advantages and ridding the country of a terrible scourge. Most of Forrest's troops were now ordered elsewhere by the rebel authorities, and shortly afterwards he withdrew to Okolona, where he established his head-quarters, and for awhile assumed a defensive attitude. During the month of August, he again collected his men and pushed rapidly towards Memphis, flanking the covering force, and capturing that city, which he held for several hours. General Washburne, gathering re-enforcements, soon compelled him to retreat again towards Grenada. From here he struck north-eastward, and on the 20th of September, crossed the Tennessee River near Waterloo, Alabama, marching directly upon Athens, which place he captured on the 24th, with 600 prisoners. Soon after the surrender, re-enforcements consisting of two entire regiments arrived, and after a gallant defense, were also compelled to lay down their arms. Forrest now devoted himself to breaking up the railroad westward from that place. At Sulphur Trestle, he captured another small garrison; and on the 27th, he essayed a movement against Pulaski, Tennessee, but was foiled. He then moved against the Chattanooga and Nashville Railroad, Sherman's principal line of supply, breaking it at Tullahoma and Decherd. On the 30th, Buford, with a division of Forrest's command, appeared before Huntsville, and demanded the surrender of the garrison, but meeting with a denial, after lingering in that neighborhood for several days, he withdrew towards Athens, which had been regarrisoned, and on the afternoon of October 1st, and the morning of the 2d, he attacked the defences of the place, meeting with a bloody repulse. Another part of Forrest's command moved northward to Columbia and Mount Pleasant. By this time the Union commanders in Tennessee had succeeded in collecting a considerable force and with them drove the raiders rapidly beyond the Tennessee.

These desultory, but vigorous operations on the part of Forrest, gave both Grant and Sherman considerable uneasiness, although they were of a character which gave promise of greater damage than was actually inflicted upon the national cause. Had Forrest fully appreciated his power, and the facility with which he might have reached the single line of railway at almost any point south of Chattanooga, he could have crippled Sherman most seriously if he had not suspended his operations entirely. Had the rebel President directed the union of Forrest's cavalry with Wheeler's, and authorized Johnston or Hood to use these forces, it is difficult to see how Sherman with his deficiency in cavalry could have possibly maintained his long lines of communication for a single day, instead of four months. Such a consolidation of commands would have given the rebels a force of not less than 15,000 horse, which in skillful hands could have gone almost anywhere within the theatre of operations. Sherman's cavalry, during this entire campaign, was scattered from Memphis to Knoxville, and from Louisville to Central Georgia, the force with the army rarely ever exceeding 7000 men for duty. Having no distinct organization except such as was given it by the different army commanders, it could not have made head for a single day against the rebels. Grant perceiving this, as well as the danger which Sherman was running, and having learned to appreciate the full value of an efficiently organized and well commanded mounted force, he ordered Sheridan to send General Wilson from Virginia, to report to Sherman with ample powers to collect, reorganize and bring into the field the numerous but widely scattered cavalry regiments, belonging to the three armies of the Military Division of the Mississippi. Wilson reported at Gaylesville, Alabama, early in October, and after conferring fully with General Sherman, was assigned to duty as Chief of Cavalry, and was placed in unlimited command over all the cavalry forces in Tennessee, Kentucky and Georgia, amounting to seventy-two regiments. With the hearty concurrence of Sherman, these regiments and the divisions into which they had been previously formed, were withdrawn from the control of the army commanders under whom they had previously acted, and were organized into a corps consisting of seven divisions and fifteen brigades. The best officers that could be found were assigned to their command, and every effort was made to concentrate, remount, equip and properly arm this formidable force. The success which attended these efforts will be detailed hereafter.

Towards the last of August, General Grant received information that General Price with a force of 10,000 men had reached Jacksonport, Arkansas, on his way to invade Missouri, then under the command of General Rosecrans. The detachment of the Sixteenth corps which had been operating under A. J. Smith in Louisiana and Northern Mississippi, was then en route from Memphis to join Sherman. It was ordered to Missouri; a brigade of cavalry under Colonel (afterwards Brigadier-General) E. F. Winslow, was also ordered to accompany Smith. These forces, it was thought, would give Rosecrans such a preponderance, as would enable him to destroy Price's army, or, at least, to drive it back, while the troops under Steele in Arkansas would attack it in rear and cut off its retreat. On the 26th of September, Price attacked Pilot Knob and compelled the garrison to retreat towards St. Louis. He then turned northward, marching rapidly along the Missouri River towards the Kansas border. General Curtis commanding the Department of Kansas, immediately collected the forces within his reach, and prepared to repel the invasion by which he was threatened, while Rosecrans' cavalry, under Pleasanton, was operating in Price's rear. The enemy made a stand on the Big Blue River, where he was attacked and defeated, with the loss of nearly all his artillery and trains, together with many prisoners, after which he retreated precipitately to Northern Arkansas. General Grant, in his official report of this year's operations, aptly says: "The impunity with which Price was enabled to roam over the State of Missouri for a long time, and the incalculable mischief done by him, show to how little purpose a superior force may be used. There is no reason why General Rosecrans should not have concentrated his forces and beaten and driven Price, before the latter reached Pilot Knob."

As soon as General Grant was informed of the defeat of Banks on the Red River, and the paralysis of Steele's co-operating campaign in South-western Arkansas, he directed General Canby, now in command of the Military Division of the West Mississippi, to send the Nineteenth corps to join the armies operating against Petersburg. It has been shown that these troops reached Hampton Roads just in time to be sent to Washington, with the Sixth corps, and thence to Sheridan in the Valley. Canby was directed " to limit the rest of his command to such operations as might be necessary to hold the positions and lines of communication he then occupied."

While charged with the conduct of operations in Virginia, it must not be forgotten that General Grant was responsible for the general plans, as well as for the unity of military policy throughout the entire country; and although he was ably seconded in his efforts to secure efficiency of organization at all points by the Secretary of War, the unprofessional reader will scarcely be able to realize the extent of the personal influence which he exerted by correspondence and otherwise over his numerous and widely separated subordinates, nor to appreciate the continued anxiety which he was compelled to undergo, throughout the entire period in which he held the supreme command. His correspondence during this period took the widest possible range, embracing all subjects connected with the conduct of the war, the movement, supply, support, equipment and organization of armies; his influence was everywhere felt, and always beneficially. While the people desponded, and gold rose steadily in value, he remained constant in the performance of his duties, and confident of the result. The policy of concentration, coupled with that of vigorous action, which he introduced, as well as the combinations which he made, were characterized by a grandeur of conception, and controlled by public considerations of the highest importance. His aim was to use every resource and every armed man of the country for some effective purpose. The armies were no longer permitted to act independently, but were compelled thenceforth to move in concert over a vast extent of country, without regard to time or seasons. Under the relentless policy of the Lieutenant-General, the plan of going into winter quarters had been practiced for the last time, and ceaseless activity was henceforth to be the rule. It was no longer feared that the rebels could be exasperated to a higher degree of hatred than they had already shown for the flag of their fathers. Blow followed blow in quick succession; their lines of supply and communications were wrested from them; their food-producing regions were occupied; their railroads, store-houses, arsenals, foundries, mills and ship-yards, were destroyed; their substance was consumed, and their armies were met at every vital point with a courage and efficiency hitherto unknown. All the time moving, and all the time drawing his lines closer about the visible force which upheld the rebellion, the General-in-Chief knew that by such means he must ultimately succeed in accomplishing the herculean task which had been imposed upon him. He therefore resolutely held his way onward, feeling that victory would be cheap at any price, and yet exerting himself night and day to gain it at the slightest possible cost in blood and treasure.

CHAPTER XXXI.

DURING the entire operations in the Valley, the armies investing Petersburg, in consequence of the detachment of the Sixth corps and the most of the cavalry, were held strictly on the defensive. The greater part of July and much of August were spent in strengthening the entrench-ments, extending now from the Appomattox east of Petersburg, to the outer flank, resting on the Jerusalem plank-road. Extensive and well-constructed siege batteries, and redoubts were constructed on the commanding points; siege artillery was brought forward, and a railroad running from City Point to the advanced lines, was projected for the purpose of keeping the troops supplied with rations and ammunition; it was finished on the 12th of September.

It has already been stated, that early in August the Lieutenant-General notified Sheridan that Lee had detached three divisions of infantry and one of cavalry from the vicinity of Petersburg, for the purpose of re-enforcing Early in the Shenandoah Valley. Believing this information to be substantially correct, Grant determined to avail himself of the opportunity of striking a blow at the rebel force on the north side of the James, covering Richmond; but knowing that such an intention could not be long concealed, after the troops, who were to carry it into effect, should begin their march, he decided to send Gregg's cavalry and the requisite artillery by the pontoon bridge, quietly across the river, and to embark Hancock's corps on board the transports at City Point, as though he intended to send it to Washington. This was done on the 12th of August, and the fleet steamed up to Deep Bottom, where Foster's brigade still held an entrenched position, and although much difficulty was experienced in landing the troops owing to the shallowness of the water near the shore, the debarkation was made by nine o'clock on the next day. Hancock marched without delay by two roads leading towards Richmond, but encountered no resistance until he reached Bailey's Creek. Advancing Mott's division towards the rebel lines which lay beyond, he sent Barlow to the right with two divisions for the purpose of turning the rebel left.

Barlow, however, instead of keeping his force well in hand, in compact order, undertook to make his movement, by stringing out his troops and keeping up the connection with Mott; the consequence was, that his formation was too attenuated to be effective, and hence the entire day was lost without gaining any substantial advantage. Birney, still further to the right, on the north of Bailey's Creek, succeeded in breaking through the hostile force in front of Barlow. Birney captured six guns and several hundred prisoners, but darkness intervening soon after, he was compelled to suspend his advance. It is quite certain that when this movement began, the rebel force on the north side of the James did not much exceed

8000 men, but during the night of the 13th, Lee perceiving his peril, recalled a part of the force sent to Early, and rapidly re-enforced his left wing. By morning it was certain that all the advantages of the surprise had been lost, and that nothing could be gained except by hard fighting or through some unexpected stroke of good fortune. Hancock, however, made a new disposition of his forces, and sent Birney to find the left of the enemy's line, while Gregg, with the cavalry, was directed to conform to Birney's movement; but the enemy's works had no left flank short of Richmond, and hence nothing was done. The movement was now completely checkmated, so far as any chance of success was concerned. On the 16th, Birney and Terry were directed to make a direct attack upon the enemy's works, which was done in handsome style, and resulted in breaking the rebel line, with the capture of several hundred prisoners. The success was, however, short-lived. The rebels soon rallied, and after a sharp fight regained their lost position. Gregg supported by a brigade of infantry under General Miles, at the same time, made a handsome and spirited advance along the Charles City road, driving the enemy before him for some distance, killing General Chambliss and taking a number of prisoners. But Birney's attack having been suspended, the rebels concentrated against Gregg, and drove him after severe fighting beyond Deep Creek.

During the night of the 16th, a fleet of transports was sent up to Deep Bottom, apparently for the purpose of withdrawing the troops, but really in the hopes that the rebels would believe this to be the case, and sally out from their works, thus giving Hancock another opportunity to get at them. But the ruse did not succeed. The four succeeding days were passed in reconnoisances and skirmishing, but without any hard fighting, except on the evening of the 28th, at which time the rebels made a vigorous attack upon Birney's works, but met with a bloody repulse.

Grant now determined to turn his operations on the north side of the river into good account elsewhere. Seeing that

Lee had weakened his right, covering the railroads south of Petersburg, the Lieutenant-General directed Meade to extend his left flank rapidly, and strike the Weldon Railroad, withdrawing Hancock to his old camps in front of the city. Warren was charged with the new operation, and began it on the morning of the 18th; and marching by the most direct line, he struck the railroad by noon, planting his corps firmly across it. Up to this time he had met with no opposition, but pushing forward in the direction of Petersburg something like a mile, he found the enemy well posted and showing a disposition to resist further progress. Warren had left Griffin's division at the point where he first struck the road, and had formed the divisions of Ayres and Crawford in line of battle to the front. In this order he had prepared to advance to the attack, when his left was suddenly assailed by the rebels, marching by the Vaughan road. The left brigade recoiled in some confusion, but Ayres, a cool and practiced soldier, repressed his line so as to conform to the rebel advance, and delivering rapid discharges of musketry and artillery, checked the rebel onset; but not until we had lost a thousand men in killed, wounded and prisoners. In executing this movement, Warren had necessarily been compelled to separate himself from the rest of the army, and fearing that the rebel leader would discover the gap and thrust a force into it, thus isolating his position, he ordered General Bragg, one of his brigade-commanders, to deploy his brigade as skirmishers on the shortest line connecting the right of the Fifth corps with the left of the army near the Jerusalem plank-road.

This order had not been obeyed, when the rebels taking the offensive, broke through the interval, turning the right of Crawford's division, and sweeping rapidly towards Warren's left, captured 2500 prisoners, including General Hays, and compelled the whole line to fall back. Just at the most critical moment, the divisions of White and Wilcox belonging to the Ninth corps reached the ground and moving forward at once, struck the rebels in flank. Warren, with great spirit, pushed his own men also to the front at the same time. The rebels were driven rapidly back in great confusion to their own entrenchments. Warren now strengthened his fortifications and arranged them for artillery. At this stage of the war, the troops never halted in the neighborhood of the enemy without fortifying their front; and even if brought unexpectedly into action, the slightest cessation of fighting was devoted to the construction of rail or log entrenchments. The men had become such adepts in the art of providing cover for themselves that under the most disadvantageous circumstances they were never at a loss how to proceed. In twenty minutes or a half hour, they could render their position impregnable against a direct attack. The method pursued was, after selecting the most favorable ground for the line along a fence, row, ridge or skirt of wood, to fell trees, pile them into rows, and then cover them rapidly with a few inches of earth. Such breastworks, slight as they may seem, were found to be ample protection against musketry, even at the closest range.

During the night of the 21st, the rebel General massed a force in Warren's front, and at early dawn opened a cross-fire upon his position with thirty guns. This was kept up for an hour or more, and was then followed by a direct attack combined with a turning movement against the left flank of the Fifth corps. But Warren's dispositions were admirable, and although the rebel onset was made with unusual vehemence, it was readily repulsed, costing him a large number in killed and wounded, besides 500 prisoners. Warren's loss from the beginning of his movement amounted to 4,455 killed, wounded and missing, but the advantages gained were important in the highest degree, as they rendered his tenure of the railroad entirely stable.

In the meantime, Hancock had returned from the north side of the James, whereupon Grant ordered him on the 21st, to move to the railroad at Ream's Station, in rear of Warren's position, for the purpose of destroying the railroad southward towards the Notaway River. Gregg's division of cavalry was thrown well out towards Dinnwiddie Court House. Hancock executed his orders promptly and without serious trouble, breaking up the road as far as Rowanty Creek, where Gibbon's division was engaged in continuing the destruction when Gregg reported the rebels approaching in considerable force.

Hancock therefore concentrated his troops within the fortifications which had been constructed at Ream's Station some time before by another corps, and had not long to wait when the enemy, under A. P. Hill, fell upon him with great fury. Two attacks were made in rapid succession, principally upon Miller's division, when a lull took place, during which, Hill put his artillery in position and formed Heth's division, with the view of carrying Hancock's lines, at whatever cost. When his arrangements were completed he opened a converging and severe fire upon the national works, under cover of which, his columns again advanced; this time sweeping everything before them. Hancock had only a small force in reserve, but could not induce it to throw itself into the breach. Gibbon was then ordered to re-establish the line and retake the three batteries which had been lost, but his men responded with neither alacrity nor vigor. Miles, however, succeeded in rallying one of his own regiments and leading it in person gallantly to the charge, retook one battery and recovered the most of the line. By this time, the enemy's dismounted troopers advanced against Gibbon's division, and meeting with but slight resistance drove it easily from the works. Attempting to follow up the success, they were caught in flank by Gregg, and in turn, compelled to fall back. Hancock's troops, upon this occasion, seem to have behaved with nothing like their accustomed spirit, for although their position was an exposed one, they should have held it easily against the assaults made upon them. Hancock had sent for aid, but for some reason not sufficiently explained none reached him. Meade, to whom the details of such matters was entrusted, ordered Mott's division of the Second, and Wilcox's of the Ninth, to march towards Ream's Station, but instead of sending them by the railroad, they were sent by a roundabout road, double the distance that they would have had to march by the most direct route.* The affair at Ream's Station, cost us 5 guns, and 2,500 men, killed, wounded, and missing, and the rebels nearly 2,000. It is noted as being one of the few instances during the campaign, in which either party succeeded in carrying lines of rifle-trench and breastwork by a direct attack. After nightfall, Hancock, who had fortified a new line near the station, abandoned his works and rejoined the army. Warren, in the meantime, had made his position impregnable, and had connected it with the investing lines by a well established system of redoubts. A cessation of active hostilities for nearly a month followed the severe struggle for the railroad, during which, the rebel General sent a cavalry force around the left flank of the national army, and by a rapid concentration on a weak part of Gregg's long line of cavalry pickets, broke through, penetrating to the grazing grounds near Coggin's Point, and succeeded in driving off a herd of two thousand five hundred beef cattle, before Gregg could concentrate a sufficient force to prevent it.

Active operations were renewed on the 28th of September, by a strong demonstration from the Army of the James against the rebel works on the north side of the river. This movement was entrusted to Ord, who had succeeded Smith in command of the Eighteenth corps supported by Birney with the Tenth corps, and Kautz's division of cavalry. The object of this movement was two-fold,—to surprise that part of Lee's lines, and to cause him to weaken his right so that the national left might be again extended. The troops designated withdrew from their regular camps, and on the night of the 28th crossed by the pontoon bridge to Deep Bottom, from which place they pushed promptly forward early the next morning; the Eighteenth corps on the left, the Tenth in the center, and the cavalry covering the right, directing their march on Chapin's Farm covered by Fort Harrison and Fort

* "Swinton's Army of the Potomac," p. 538.

20

Morris. These entrenchments with sixteen guns were carried, but in pushing forward his victorious troops Ord was wounded, and compelled to turn the command over to General Weitzel. Birney captured New Market Heights, and Kautz pushed by the right flank to within three miles of Richmond; but Fort Gillmer, a strong work next to Fort Harrison, was so well defended that every effort to carry it was foiled. This necessarily checked the advance, and darkness suspended it entirely. The next morning the rebels having been re-enforced during the night, determined to retake their lost works; and under the direction of Field, Hoke and Gregg, assaulted Fort Harrison on three sides, but timing their advance poorly they were easily repelled, suffering heavy loss. A few days later they advanced against Kautz on the Charles City road, and after a sharp fight drove him back close to the river, capturing 9 guns and 500 prisoners, but losing General Gregg, of Texas, in the combat. Butler now devoted himself to strengthening his new fortifications, and soon put them into condition to defy capture by assault or *coup de main.* These successes on the north side of the James had greatly inspirited the army, and as they threatened Richmond with much more serious danger than at any time previous, Lee lost no time in throwing re-enforcements in that direction for its protection.

Meanwhile Grant caused Warren to make a strong extension of his left, now resting at a point two miles west of the Weldon Railroad, still farther towards the Southside Railroad. Re-enforced by two divisions of the Ninth corps, now under Parke, Warren moved with four divisions of infantry and Gregg's cavalry, directly towards Poplar Spring Church and Peeble's Farm, while Hancock was to march further to the rear, and under cover of Warren's movement, cross Hatcher's Run, to the Boydton plank-road, from which he was expected to advance and seize the Southside Road. In pursuance of this plan, the movement began, on the morning of the 27th of September, but had not proceeded more than two and a half or three miles before the enemy was found occupying a strongly entrenched line resting on Hatcher's Run. It was found in a short time that this position could not be forced by a direct attack, and as had been previously arranged, Warren prepared to cross Hatcher's Run and force the rebels out by an attack in flank and rear. Hancock marching to the south-west by the Vaughan road, struck the river lower down, crossed it and pushed forward by Dabney's Mill, covered by Gregg's cavalry, to the Boydton road, where he intended to turn northward, following the road towards Petersburg as far as the White Oak Bridge, from which point, if reached, he was to march directly towards the Southside Road only about four miles distant. Shortly after striking the Boydton road, however, he was directed by Meade to halt, on the ground that Parke had not been able to carry the works north of the run. As soon as Parke's assault had failed, Warren threw Crawford's division and Ayres' brigade to the south side of Hatcher's Run and directed them to move up the run, with the right of the advancing line resting on it while the left should be extended well out to connect with Hancock, now between four and five miles away.

Crawford pushed through the pine forest bordering the run, with great difficulty. There being no roads, the troops became much scattered and some of them entirely lost, but after three hours of hard work, they reached a position opposite to the end of the rebel entrenchments, on the south side of the run. Now was the time to press the movement with the greatest vigor, but Warren, finding the country entirely different from what it had been represented as being, assumed the liberty of suspending his own advance, while he reported to Meade for further orders. The rebels, in the meantime, were not idle, but discerning with admirable judgment, the object of Grant's movement, and the probable course that it would take, Lee withdrew a force from his entrenchments towards the Boydton road, for the purpose of falling upon the forces already across Hatcher's Run. The interval which now separated Crawford and Hancock, was reduced to a little more than a mile. The latter having been notified by Meade of Crawford's position, deployed two brigades of Gibbon's division, (temporarily commanded by General Egan,) for the purpose of establishing connection between the two forces, but this was not accomplished. Lee's plan seems to have been to attack Hancock's outer flank, but by a piece of good fortune or good management, he changed his mind, and in throwing Hill's corps across the run, gave it such a direction as to bring it abreast of the unoccupied interval between Hancock's right and Crawford's left, but bearing more directly upon the flank of Mott's division. The rebel leader was ignorant of his great advantage, as he could see only a few rods through the tangled growth of scrub pines. But advancing to the attack about four o'clock P. M., he pushed through the interval, striking Mott's right brigade, which it swept back, capturing a section of artillery.

The next division of Hancock's corps, under Egan, now changed front, facing to the southward, and advanced to attack the rebels in flank, supported on the one hand by McAlister's brigade of Mott's division, and on the other by De Trobriand's and Kerwin's brigades. This unexpected onset was too much for the rebels, who broke at once and fled in the direction from which they had come, leaving their two captured guns, with over a thousand prisoners in our hands. Had Crawford advanced at the same time, as he should have done even without orders, Hill's corps must have been entirely routed. The action had nearly ended on the right, when Gregg, covering the left, was violently assailed by Hampton with five brigades of cavalry. Hancock promptly re-enforced him and thus enabled him to hold his own lines and drive Hampton back, but not till night had rendered pursuit entirely out of the question in that region of gloom and thick darkness. Ammunition having been exhausted, the general movement was suspended and the troops withdrawn to their old camps during the night.

The failure of this day's operations, as usual, has been ascribed to the faults of the plan itself, but the candid reader cannot fail to perceive that the movement was in the full tide of successful execution when Warren stopped Crawford, and Meade stopped Hancock.   It is hardly necessary to say that this cessation of operations could not have been made at a more inopportune time; for had it been continued an hour longer Hancock and Warren must have established connection between their lines, and holding a strong position along the south side of Hatcher's Run, or vigorously assailing the rear of the rebel line, on the north side of it, it is difficult to see how the result could have been less fortunate than it was and easy to perceive how it might have been made a perfect success.   In a majority of cases the leader who stops to deliberate, even in the presence of an unexpected danger, after a movement has been carefully matured and judiciously inaugurated, will bring upon himself misfortune and disaster if not absolute defeat.   The best way under such circumstances, is to press forward with increased ardor and energy, or to relinquish his plan without a moment's delay.   There is no axiom in warfare more truthful than this: "Prudence is the virtue of prosperity; audacity that of great emergencies."

A long period of comparative inactivity now intervened, lasting till the spring of 1865, during which, however, no opportunity was lost, to annoy the enemy, by striking at his weak points, and menacing his exposed lines of communication.   The armies before Petersburg were allowed to build huts and make themselves as comfortable as circumstances would permit, but unusual care was taken to keep them constantly on the alert.   The investing fortifications were strengthened, and by the 7th of February, had been extended to Hatcher's Run, while the Weldon Railroad was destroyed as far south as Hick's Ford on the Meherrin River.   Lee studiously maintained his defensive attitude.   The new extension of our lines was preceded by a renewal of the effort to reach and turn the rebel right, but for several days before it began, a heavy bombardment from all the artillery was kept up, so as to distract the enemy's attention.

On the 5th of February, Warren with the Fifth corps,

supported by Major-General Humphreys who had succeeded Hancock in the command of the Second corps, began the new turning movement. Humphreys was directed to march upon the right of the rebel works resting on Hatcher's Run, while Warren, preceded by Gregg's cavalry division, was ordered to cross the run, and fall on the rebel rear. Humphreys with two divisions marched down the Vaughan road, reached the run without any material difficulty, and finding only a small force of rebels on the opposite side, he pushed De Trobriand's brigade across, dislodging the enemy and driving him back. Smith's division closed upon the rebel works, and late in the afternoon its right wing was vigorously assailed, but succeeded, by the aid of McAlister's brigade, in holding its ground. Gregg and Warren marched out the Halifax road, and crossed Rowanty Creek, the former reaching Dinnwiddie Court House, while the latter went into position himself on the prolongation of Humphreys' lines now well established.

The next day Wright's and Parke's corps were also moved westward, to support the exposed flank. The country in the neighborhood of the streams being miry and everywhere densely covered with undergrowth, the troops could not get forward with rapidity—Gregg, who had returned to the left of the infantry was compelled to build corduroy, while Crawford was sent by the way of Dabney's Mill to occupy the Boydton road. At Dabney's he met Pegram's rebel division advancing from the opposite direction to the same point. A sanguinary combat ensued which resulted in Crawford's success. Pegram was driven back, but being strongly re-enforced returned to the attack. Ayres' division was sent, and then Wheaton's to strengthen Crawford, but before these forces could be united, a rebel turning column moving by the Vaughan road, fell upon Gregg and then upon Ayres while another force attacked Crawford in front. In a short time the national left was completely overthrown, but falling back rapidly to Humphreys' position, it reformed behind his works, while the exultant rebels pushed heedlessly forward expecting to complete their victory. Humphreys had taken the precaution to entrench himself strongly and thereby repelled the vigorous but irregular attack with great ease. The Union loss in these operations was about 2,000 men, and that of the rebels quite as great including General Pegram.

This operation put an end to the effort of reaching the Southside Road by successive extensions of the Union lines. In this respect it was probably a blessing in disguise; for it ultimately forced Grant to adopt the policy of swinging boldly into the interior with a force sufficiently powerful to make head against any probable opposition. This policy he had constantly favored, but was prevented from carrying it into effect by a great variety of circumstances, but principally by the desire not to resort to such a measure till he had concentrated all his available forces and could count upon good roads. The complete destruction of the Weldon Railroad to Hick's Ford by Warren in December, forced Lee to discontinue his line of wagon communication between the northern end of that road and Petersburg, and thereby rendered it still more difficult for him to keep his army properly supplied.

The siege of Petersburg, which was neither a siege nor investment, but a continual menace, was now drawing rapidly to a close; but before proceeding to a description of the events which followed, it is necessary to turn for awhile to military operations elsewhere.

CHAPTER XXXII.

THE MARCH TO THE SEA—ITS ORIGIN—HOOD'S MOVEMENT NORTH OF ATLANTA—GRANT SUSPECTS HIS INTENTIONS—HIS CONFIDENCE IN SHERMAN'S DISPOSITIONS—JEFF. DAVIS' VISIT TO GEORGIA—HIS SPEECH—HOOD MARCHES NORTHWARD—TEARS UP THE RAILROAD AT BIG SHANTY—SHERMAN PUSHES AFTER HOOD—THE ATTACK UPON ALLATOONA—SHERMAN THREATENS THE ENEMY'S REAR—HOOD CAPTURES THE GARRISON AT DALTON—HOWARD ATTACKS HOOD AT SNAKE CREEK—WILSON SENT TO NASHVILLE—DETAILS—SHERMAN CONCENTRATES AT ATLANTA—EXPULSION OF THE INHABITANTS—DESTRUCTION OF THE TOWN—FORWARD TO THE SEA—ORDER OF THE MARCH—FORAGING—GEORGIA MILITIA—KILPATRICK'S DASH ON MACON—SKIRMISH AT GORDON—ENGAGEMENT WITH WHEELER'S CAVALRY—THE ARRIVAL BEFORE SAVANNAH—PREPARATIONS FOR ITS INVESTMENT—CAPTURE OF FORT M'ALLISTER—SHERMAN MEETS ADMIRAL DAHLGREN—EVACUATION OF SAVANNAH—SHERMAN ANNOUNCES HIS SUCCESS TO THE PRESIDENT—THE SIGNIFICANCE OF SHERMAN'S MARCH—THE REBEL MISTAKE—JOHNSTON REINSTATED.

IT has already been stated that, so far as known, the march to the sea had its origin in the idea originally discussed at General Grant's head-quarters at Nashville, in January, 1864, and this view of the case is borne out by the following despatch, sent by the Lieutenant-General to General Sherman, from City Point, September the 10th:

"As soon as your men are properly rested, and preparations can be made, it is desirable that another campaign should be commenced. We want to keep the enemy continually pressed to the end of the war. If we give him no peace while the war lasts, the end can not be far distant. Now that we have all of Mobile Bay that is valuable, I do not know but it will be the best for *Major-General Canby's troops to act upon Savannah whilst you move on Augusta.* I should like to hear from you, however, on this matter."

To this Sherman replied the same day, suggesting a mod-
ification of the general idea, on account of the difficulty in
supplying his command; adding:

> "If I could be sure of finding provisions and ammunition at Augusta
> or Columbus, Ga., I can march to Milledgeville, and compel Hood to
> give up Augusta or Macon, and could then turn on the other. * * If
> you can manage to take the Savannah River as high as Augusta, or
> the Chattahoochee as far up as Columbus, I can sweep the whole State
> of Georgia; otherwise I would risk our whole army by going too far
> from Atlanta."

Shortly afterwards Grant replied by letter, in which he
explained the situation in Virginia, and the proposed movement against Wilmington. He also sent Colonel Porter, a
trusted staff officer, to confer with Sherman more fully
than could be done by correspondence. Sherman answered
by letter as follows:

> "I will therefore give my opinion, that, after you get Wilmington,
> you strike for Savannah and the river; that Canby be instructed to
> hold the Mississippi River, and send a force to get Columbus, Ga., either
> by the way of the Alabama or the Appalachicola, and that I keep
> Hood employed and put my army in final order for a march on
> Augusta, Columbia, and Charleston, to be ready as soon as Wilming-
> ton is sealed as to commerce, and the city of Savannah is in our
> possession."

In the meantime, Hood commenced his movement against
the railroads north of Atlanta, and Grant began to suspect his
real intentions. On the 10th of October, Sherman notified
him that with Hood, Forrest, and Wheeler, all turned loose,
"without home or habitation," it would be impossible to protect his communications, and therefore proposed to break up
the railroad to Chattanooga, and "to strike out with wagons for Milledgeville, Millen, and Savannah." Though he
seemed to think that Hood, instead of going northward,
would simply occupy Talledega, and threaten Kingston,
Bridgeport, and Decatur.

Grant feeling sure that Hood would not be satisfied with
this, but would strike for Nashville, was fully impressed with

the necessity of providing for the defense of the line of the Tennessee, but having full confidence in Sherman's dispositions for the protection of Tennessee, as well as in the capacity of Thomas, just before midnight on the 11th of October, he issued the necessary authority for the march to the sea. "It was the original design," says the Lieutenant-General in his official report, " to hold Atlanta, and by getting through to the coast with a garrison left on the Southern railroads leading east and west through Georgia, to effectually sever the East from the West. In other words, to cut the would-be-Confederacy in two again as it had been cut once by our gaining possession of the Mississippi River." If there was any hesitation manifested either by Grant or Sherman in reference to this movement, it arose from the menacing attitude of Hood, and a pardonable anxiety to provide for all contingencies likely to follow whatever plan of operation that erratic General might adopt.

Immediately after the fall of Atlanta, Jefferson Davis visited Georgia for the purpose of suppressing the movements then supposed to be in progress under the direction of Governor Brown, looking to a disruption of the Confederacy and a suspension of hostilities. After attending to this matter in the style of a dictator, he made a " hopeful and encouraging" speech at Macon, which he repeated in substance to the army under Hood. This speech was remarkable for nothing except the frankness with which it made known the rebel plan of operations. Davis is reported to have said to the Tennesseans of Cheatham's division: "Be of good cheer, for within a short while your faces will be turned homeward and your feet pressing Tennessee soil;" and upon another occasion to an audience at Augusta: "We must march into Tennessee; there we will draw from 20,000 to 30,000 men to our standard, and so strengthened we must push the enemy back to the Ohio."

This remarkable declaration was soon followed by the commencement of operations against Sherman's communications. In the meanwhile, anticipating something of this kind, Sherman sent Wagner's division of the Fourth corps and Morgan's division of the Fourteenth corps back to Chattanooga, and Corse's division of the Fifteenth corps to Rome. On the 1st of October, Hood moved westward from Lovejoy's Station and crossed the Chattahoochee, after which he marched rapidly to the north-eastward, striking the railroad in the vicinity of Big Shanty. Meeting with no opposition, he put a large force to work, tearing up and twisting the rails, and burning the ties, bridges and trestle-work for many miles. Sherman did not suffer this to continue long, but leaving Slocum with the Twentieth corps to hold Atlanta, he pushed hard after the rebels with the Fourth, Fourteenth, Fifteenth, Seventeenth and Twenty-third corps and two divisions of cavalry. Fearing that the enemy would fall upon Allatoona, his secondary base, and a position of great strength he ordered General Corse at Rome with a brigade to re-enforce it without delay. Corse arrived there on the night of the 4th, and being the senior officer present took command. The next morning a detachment of Hood's army under General French made a vehement assault upon the national works, but were severely repulsed. The gallant Corse received a dreadful wound in the face, and many of his bravest troops were killed.

Sherman on reaching Kenesaw from which he could see the enemy's movements, pushed the Twenty-third corps to the westward, threatening Hood's rear. This caused him to withdraw from the neighborhood of Allatoona and making a feint towards Rome, he crossed the Coosa eleven miles below. Sherman reached Rome on the 11th, and sent Garrard's cavalry and the Twenty-third corps, to the north side of the Oostenaula for the purpose of threatening the flank of the hostile army, still marching northward rapidly, destroying the railroad wherever a favorable opportunity presented itself. Hood captured the garrison at Dalton, and then withdrew to Snake Creek, where he was attacked by Howard, while Stanley with the Fourth and Fourteenth corps pushed forward to get in his rear. Perceiving this movement Hood retreated to Ship's Gap, where he was again attacked; but without waiting to give battle he hurried on to Lafayette and finally to Gadsden on the Coosa. On the 19th, Sherman's forces were grouped about Gaylesville, at which place they remained several days watching the enemy. On the 23d of October, Hood moved from his camp on the Coosa River, directing his march over Lookout Mountain towards Gunter's Landing and Decatur on the Tennessee. Near the latter place he formed a junction with a portion of General Taylor's army which had moved from Central Mississippi by the way of Corinth and Tuscumbia. Sherman became fully aware of this on the 25th, and having already sent Thomas back to Nashville to resume command of his old department, he detached the Fourth corps under Stanley and ordered it to Chattanooga, to report thence to Thomas. On the 30th, he sent Schofield with the Twenty-third corps from Resaca, where it had stopped, to the rear with similar instructions. Wilson in the meantime had reached Gaylesville and reported to Sherman for the purpose of reorganizing and commanding the cavalry forces belonging to the Military Division of the Mississippi. After receiving full powers, that officer dismounted the remnant of Garrard's and McCook's divisions and turned over the horses thus obtained to Kilpatrick, who was directed to accompany the army to the coast with his division now amounting to nearly 5000 effective men.

Wilson was then sent back to Nashville, with all the dismounted detachments for the purpose of perfecting the organization of his corps, and assisting Thomas in the operations against Hood. Sherman instructed him to collect the largest possible force, and in case Hood should change his mind in reference to the invasion of Tennessee, and should follow him towards Savannah, Wilson was then to follow also, sweeping well down through Central Alabama and Georgia, doing all the damage he could inflict upon the rebel cause, and ultimately joining Sherman wherever he might be found. If Hood continued his threatened movement northward, Wilson was in that case to join Thomas, and after

assisting in the expulsion of Hood, to carry out the foregoing plan as nearly as circumstances would permit. Having
spent several nights over his camp fire in carefully arranging
these details, Sherman completed his arrangements for the
coming campaign towards the sea-coast. The Army of the
Tennessee marched to the vicinity of Smyrna camp-ground,
while the Fourteenth corps moved to Kingston, where it
remained till the sick and wounded, surplus baggage and
artillery, together with the garrisons north of that place,
were sent back to Chattanooga. The railroads and tele-
graphs radiating from Atlanta, were effectually broken up,
severing all communications with the North, and on the 14th
of November, Sherman concentrated his army at Atlanta,
preparatory to the commencement of his operations eastward. This city had already been converted into a purely
military town, by the expulsion of its inhabitants, and was
soon to be reduced to a mass of blackened walls and isolated chimneys. On the eve of its abandonment, all the
public buildings, such as depots, machine shops, and manufacturing establishments were committed to the flames, and as
there was no able-bodied men except the marching soldiery,
near enough to control the fire, and no suitable fire apparatus,
the entire town, with the exception of the suburbs and an
occasional block, was soon in ruins. Rome suffered nearly
the same fate.

On the 16th of November, Sherman left Atlanta in company with the Fourteenth corps, marching by Sithonia, Covington and Shady Grove, directly towards Milledgeville;
having already despatched the right wing of the army with
Kilpatrick's cavalry by the way of Jonesboro and McDonough, with orders to make a strong feint on Macon, crossing the Ocmulgee about Planter's Mills, and moving thence
towards Gordon on the Macon and Savannah Railroad. The
same day, Slocum, with the left wing, was directed to move
along the Augusta Railroad to Madison, burning the railway
bridge across the Oconee, east of that place and then turning south to Milledgeville. The different columns were

ordered to form a junction at the end of seven days, and during the march to inflict as much injury as they could upon the resources of the region which they were traversing. The troops were provided with selected trains, well supplied with ammunition, and light rations, consisting of coffee, sugar, and hard bread, for forty days, with a double allowance of salt. A herd of beef cattle was also driven along with the trains. The corps commanders were directed to forage whenever and wherever desirable articles could be obtained, but the different staff departments were charged with seeing that this important service should not be allowed to degenerate into promiscuous pillaging. The general order of march was admirably drawn, and although much difficulty was encountered in crossing rivers, and moving along muddy roads, fair progress was made. As has been seen, Hood was far away towards the North-west, and as the Georgia militia, although controlled by a powerful array of Generals, were by no means the most formidable soldiery supporting the rebel cause, the Union columns met with no material opposition. Kilpatrick made a dash at Macon, and succeeded in breaking through the line of works on the north-east side of the river, but was soon driven out, and proceeded to join the army assembling at Gordon. Near this place a sharp skirmish took place on the 22d, between Walcott's brigade and the Georgia militia, but the enemy was soon repulsed and driven back in the direction of Macon. From Gordon, Howard and Slocum moved to Sandersville, where the advanced guard of the column had a short engagement with a part of Wheeler's cavalry. Kilpatrick was thrown forward at the same time by the way of Milledgeville to Waynesborough, thus covering the left flank of the infantry. The rest of the army pursued parallel routes farther to the south. In this order, covering a front varying from ten to forty miles, Sherman pushed evenly and regularly forward, driving the rebels into their works about Savannah, by the 10th of December. Measures were taken at once to invest the city on the south and west sides, while General Hazen, commanding the second division of the Fourteenth corps was sent to the west side of the Ogeechee, and directed to move against Fort McAllister, commanding its entrance into Ossabaw Sound. That place was reached by the 13th of December, and although found to be an enclosed work of great strength, it was carried by assault after a brief but sanguinary struggle; 150 prisoners and 22 guns were captured. Communication was at once opened with the blockading squadron under the command of Rear-Admiral Dahlgren. A meeting took place between the Admiral and General Sherman, when arrangements were made for a co-operative attack upon Savannah.

General Foster, commanding at Port Royal, sent a division of troops up Broad River to break the Savannah and Charleston Railway, and then to move towards Savannah for the purpose of completing the investment. After diligent labor the arrangements for the assault were completed, but on the night of the 21st, Hardee succeeded in evacuating the place by crossing to the north side of the Savannah River. Sherman occupied it at once, finding it supplied with 167 pieces of artillery and much valuable property. He immediately announced his success to the President in the following terms: "I beg to present you, as a Christmas gift the city of Savannah, with 150 heavy guns and plenty of ammunition and also about 25,000 bales of cotton."

The present and in fact the only value of Savannah, was mainly as a resting place and the base of future operations. The real significance of Sherman's march, was that it effectually interposed a compact army of 70,000 men between Lee's army and the rebel power in the South-west, and gave Grant the immense advantage of interior lines against the rebellion; an advantage never before attained, and which, properly improved, could not fail to result in the complete overthrow of the Confederacy. Not till Hood had been defeated and driven from Tennessee did the rebel cabinet see the fatal mistake into which they had been led; spurred on by the popular clamor, they reinstated Johnston, in the command

of their widely scattered and decimated forces; but it was
too late.   That able leader hastened to correct the mistake
which had been made under the inspiration of Davis, by
gathering the wreck of Hood's army and uniting it with
Hardee's, at some point north and east of Sherman, so as
to get nearer to Lee than his antagonist could get to Grant.
The adoption of this plan was the last ray of good generalship displayed by any of the Southern leaders, and had the
means for its execution been as adequate to the requirements
of the case, as the conception itself was brilliant, the "lost
cause" might still have made head with a faint glimmer of
hope that Fortune would not prove entirely inexorable.

CHAPTER XXXIII.

IT was a fortunate determination on the part of General
Grant, to permit Sherman to march to the sea-coast, while
Hood was marching northward for the reconquest of Tennessee, and a wise one on Sherman's part, to leave so
prudent and skillful a General as Thomas to direct affairs
throughout the Military Division of the Mississippi. The
latter was anxious not to be left behind, but he was destined
in this case at least to find the rear the post of honor as well
as of danger.

The rebel President had sent forth his fiat of invasion, and
once more brought the trusted Beauregard to the West to
carry his heroic policy into execution. This experienced officer being familiar with the theater of operations, was entrusted with plenary powers over all the rebel resources, and set
himself busily at work upon the desperate task assigned him.
By the middle of October, he arrived at Corinth, his old
head-quarters of three years before, and by extraordinary

21

exertions soon had the railroads repaired and trains running
from Meridian and Central Mississippi, through Corinth, to
Cherokee Station, and with every car, sent forward supplies
of all kinds for Hood's army. Clothing, shoes, equipments,
forage, food, arms, and ammunition, were gathered and distributed with an unsparing hand. Re-enforcements in considerable numbers were also collected from Georgia, and
from the command of Taylor, in Alabama and Mississippi,
thus, in a few weeks, swelling the ranks which Hood's vigorous offensive about Atlanta had so rapidly decimated, to
nearly 45,000 infantry and 10,000 cavalry. Forrest's cavalry command, largely increased in strength and efficiency,
was reorganized and also directed to co-operate with Hood.
As a matter of course these great preparations could not be
long concealed from Thomas, who arrived at Nashville on
the 3d of October, and immediately began to take measures
for strengthening the detachments doing duty along the
Tennessee. The main object at first was to delay Hood's
forward movement till an army could be concentrated, at
some point south of Nashville, and it must be confessed this
was no easy task to accomplish. Thomas had at his immediate disposal only a small force of cavalry, consisting of
Hatch's division and Croxton's brigade about 4,000 men in
all, which he ordered to the neighborhood of Florence.
A small brigade under Colonel Capron, was sent towards
Waynesborough.

Schofield and Stanley were hurried from Gaylesville and
Chattanooga to Pulaski, where they were concentrated as
rapidly as circumstances would permit; the local garrisons
with the exception of that at Decatur, were also drawn in,
but with all Thomas could do, his effective force with which
to resist Hood's first onset did not exceed 27,000 men.
Grant feeling anxious to render Thomas' position in Tennessee entirely safe, sent General Rawlins, his Chief-of-Staff to
Missouri, with orders to gather Smith's command and such
other unemployed troops as could be found, and forward them
to Nashville as rapidly as the transports could carry them.

Wilson was busily engaged in putting the fragmentary cavalry into shape, and raking the cavalry depots for horses upon which to remount the regiments which had given their horses to Kilpatrick. While these preparations for the creation of an army were in progress, Hood began his long threatened advance. But this was preceded by the operations of Forrest in West Tennessee. Immediately after his expulsion from Middle Tennessee, that hardy rider led his forces by the way of Purdy to Fort Heiman, where he established a battery of twenty-pounder guns, and by a successful stratagem captured one light-clad gun-boat and three transports. He then manned the captured vessels, and made a combined movement against Johnsonville.

This place being at the terminus of the Nashville and Tennessee River Railroad, and at the head of low water navigation on the Tennessee River, had acquired considerable importance as a base of supplies for our army and was now quite useful to Thomas. Forrest reached a point near it on the 2d of November, and immediately planted his batteries on the opposite side of the river isolating three more gun-boats and eight transports. He opened fire on the 4th, and although the gun-boats replied with spirit they were soon disabled and set on fire, to prevent their falling into rebel hands. The transports suffered the same fate, but most of the military stores including boots, shoes, clothing, hard bread and hospital supplies and other public property, collected upon the levee at Johnsonville, valued at a million and a half of dollars, fell into Forrest's possession, and were either carried away or burnt. Forrest's troopers laden with the spoils of their fortunate campaign, now hastened to rejoin Hood. On the night of the 5th, Schofield reached Johnsonville but finding the place in ruins and the enemy gone, Thomas ordered him at once to Pulaski, assigning him to the command of all the troops assembling there, with instructions to watch Hood and retard his advance, but not to risk a general engagement till the entire available strength of the military division should be concentrated.

On the 17th of November, Hood's infantry force, now entirely refreshed, well-clad and well-armed, crossed the Tennessee near Florence, and on the 20th began its northern march, covered by Forrest's cavalry, which had been thrown forward some days previous. Croxton and Hatch, commanding the effective force of Wilson's cavalry, reported the movement at once to Thomas, and handling their squadrons with great skill, did all in their power to retard the rebel movement. Schofield, holding his command well in hand, retired shortly to Columbia, on the Duck River; Hood, meanwhile, demonstrated towards Waynesborough, but continued to press northward as fast as possible. Sharp skirmishing took place at Lewisburg and Campbellville, between the cavalry, but no serious engagement was brought on. Schofield remained in Columbia only a short time, disposing the cavalry, now under Wilson, in person along the north side of the river, so as to watch the crossings both above and below, but mainly those above the town. At noon of the 28th of November, Hood's mounted troops made their appearance at the various fords between Columbia and the crossing of the Lewisburg pike, and by dark had forced a passage at several places.

The infantry, during the night, followed close upon their heels, and early the next day struck across the country toward Spring Hill, twelve miles in the rear of Columbia. Schofield, with everything except his rear guard, had already evacuated the latter place, and receiving timely notification from Wilson, of the rebel movements and probable intentions, sent Stanley with one division rapidly by the turnpike to Spring Hill, but not deeming it safe to withdraw from the vicinity of Columbia during daylight, he restrained the main body of the army till after nightfall. He had plenty of time for the retrograde movement, which if promptly made would prevent Hood from obtaining a lodgment on the Franklin pike, while Wilson,—knowing that if Forrest should get possession of the Lewisburg pike, the only other good road in that region, he would reach Franklin first,—lost no time in concentrating the cavalry on the latter highway. The next morning he retired slowly towards Franklin, the rebel cavalry pressing heavily upon his rear guard under Croxton. At Calvary Church, about four miles east of Spring Hill, a stand was made, and the rebels severely repulsed. Forrest then turned towards the railroad and turnpike along which the infantry were supposed to be marching.

But fortunately Stanley was in position to resist his further progress. A sharp fight ensued, lasting all the afternoon. By four o'clock, Cheatham's corps, accompanied by Hood in person, arrived upon the field. Stanley was now sorely pressed by the entire rebel army, except one division of Lee's corps, which Schofield was engaged in holding at Columbia. Perceiving something of the advantage which this fortunate conjunction of affairs had thrown into his hands, Hood ordered Cheatham to make a vigorous attack upon Stanley's hastily constructed works, and to drive him beyond the pike which he was covering, but this was found to be an exceedingly difficult task, for neither Stanley nor his troops were accustomed to yielding a position without a desperate struggle. Cheatham's attack was well made but failed. Darkness put a cessation to hostilities till midnight, at which hour the head of Schofield's column, marching rapidly towards Franklin, made its appearance. The rebel pickets, within a short distance of the turnpike, gave the alarm, whereupon Hood sent an order to Cheatham's head-quarters, directing him to throw his corps across the turnpike for the purpose of arresting the movement of the Union army. This order was not obeyed, nor was any serious effort made to interfere with either the front or the flank of Schofield's hurrying columns. Indeed it is questionable if the order reached Cheatham till after the Union rear guard had passed.

The next morning Schofield concentrated his forces at Franklin, a considerable town, situated on the south bank of the Harpeth, an affluent of the Cumberland, and eighteen miles south of Nashville by the great road connecting the two places. The river making a horseshoe bend in rear of

the town, Schofield disposed his troops in a semi-circular
line covering the place reaching to the river bank both above
and below it.   Stanley with the Fourth corps held the right,
and General (afterwards Governor) J. D. Cox, with the
Twenty-third corps held the left, while the major part of
Wilson's cavalry was posted along the northern bank, guarding the various fords for some distance above and below.
Croxton's brigade held an advanced position on the Lewisburg Pike.   The Union soldiers knowing that they were outnumbered fell to work busily to entrench their position.   By
noon of the 30th of November, Hood's advance began to
press heavily upon Croxton's cavalry and the infantry pickets,
driving them slowly back; by four o'clock his army was in
position, with Stewart on the right, S. D. Lee in the center,
and Cheatham on the left; Forrest's cavalry was mainly on
the right flank.   The ground separating the two armies was
a broad undulating plain, mostly cleared fields across which
Hood advanced gallantly and confidently to the attack.

Before starting he assured his men that victory was certain;
and it was certain, but destined to bestow its laurels upon
Schofield and his stalwart veterans.   The brunt of the first
attack fell upon Wagner's division of the Fourth corps, which
had been permitted to occupy a salient position about eight
hundred yards in front of the general line.   It had fought
gallantly all day before at Spring Hill, and now showed the
same indomitable pluck, but it was too light to withstand the
shock of Cheatham's heavy masses, overlapping it on both
flanks.   Delivering its fire with precision, and holding on till
in imminent peril, it finally fell back in disorder to the main
line, closely followed by the exultant Tennesseeans, into and
across the new entrenchments.   It was a most critical moment for the Union lines; a wide gap had been made, their
works and eight guns were already lost, when Opdyke's brigade of Wagner's division, hitherto in reserve, supported by
Conrad's brigade, dashed forward with irresistible fury, hurling the astounded rebels headlong from the works, and
re-establishing the broken center.   The gallant Stanley, a

soldier like Ney, "terrible in battle," fully realizing the
danger which menaced us, led the attack, mounting the very
parapet in front of his men to hold them to the desperate
work, and after a few minutes was severely wounded. The
rebels struggled courageously to regain their lost ground,
returning again and again to the attack, but the struggle was
hopeless. Cleburne, Gist, Brown, Manigault, Johnson and
Strahl were killed, at the head of their troops, and before
night closed the scene, Hood had lost 6,252 of his best men
and officers. Simultaneously with the conflict in front of
Franklin, Forrest drove back the cavalry pickets, and forced
a crossing two miles above the town, with the intention of
turning Schofield's left and falling upon his communications
and rear. But Wilson had the bulk of his forces under
Croxton, Hatch and Johnson, well in hand at Matthew's
Farm, a mile and a half from the town, and throwing them
promptly forward, mounted and dismounted, after a fight of
two hours' duration, they drove the rebels into the river.
Had the attack of either Hood or Forrest been successful,
Schofield's army must have been destroyed, for it would have
been impossible to withdraw it from Franklin in the confusion of such a disaster. The Union loss in this sanguinary
engagement was 2,326, including in the number, 1,104
prisoners.

Under cover of darkness, Schofield crossed to the north
side of the river, and the next day, covered by the cavalry,
continued his march to the fortifications surrounding Nashville, where Smith's detachment of the Sixteenth corps,
together with various bodies of irregular troops, had already
been assembled. Steedman, with 6,000 or 8,000 men,
gathered from the garrisons of Decatur, Chattanooga, Stevenson and Murfreesboro, arrived soon after, thus concentrating a force of all arms not far from 65,000 men. But
Thomas was in no hurry to attack; feeling confident of his
position, as well as assured of Hood's foolhardiness, he determined to make sure of success before striking a blow.
The cavalry forces were in a bad condition; many men were

dismounted, and many of the horses were disabled by "grease heel" and overwork. Thomas, therefore, directed Wilson to withdraw his command to the north side of the river, and to devote himself exclusively to its re-establishment. Horses were impressed in all directions, and by the 10th of December, 12,000 men were prepared for the field; but of these, 3,000 were detached under McCook, to go in pursuit of a brigade of Forrest's cavalry, which had crossed the Cumberland River under Lyon, for the purpose of operating upon Thomas' communications; 3,000 more were mounted on broken-down horses from the hospital stables, unable to stand more than two or three days' service. General Grant had watched the progress of this campaign from his headquarters at City Point, with considerable anxiety; knowing the inchoate condition of Thomas' army, and the desperate character of Hood, he could not help entertaining a feeling of uneasiness till the great battle had been fought and won. The entire country shared his apprehensions, while the newspapers expressed the greatest fear that Hood, in pursuance of his programme, would cross the Cumberland and carry the war to the Ohio as he had threatened.

Under these circumstances the Lieutenant-General ordered Thomas to wait no longer for the cavalry but to attack at once. Before this order was received, a violent rain-storm, followed by hail, sleet, snow and intense cold set in, covering the entire face of the country with a glare of ice, and rendering it absolutely impossible for troops of any sort to move, much less cavalry. Thomas called a council of his corps commanders, read them the orders, and asked their advice. With one accord they declared it impossible to attack till the weather should moderate, asserting that an attack at that time would be certain defeat, but that if delayed till the ground should become passable for cavalry, it would result in certain victory. General Grant grew still more impatient and started for Nashville in person to put the troops in motion, but he had scarcely reached Washington when he received the reassuring tidings of victory.

On the 11th, the weather began to moderate, and by the night of the 14th, all the arrangements for the battle had been completed. Thomas' plan of attack was admirably arranged and thoroughly comprehended by his subordinates. It consisted mainly of a feint from the left and center, with a direct attack and a strong turning movement from the right. His troops were posted in the following order : Steedman on the left, Wood with the Fourth corps on the left center, covering the Murfreesboro and Franklin pikes, Schofield the right center, A. J. Smith the right, with Wilson's troopers still farther towards the right. General Donaldson with about five thousand quartermaster's employeés was kept in reserve for the purpose of holding the defenses of the city after the army should become engaged. The morning of the 15th of December broke cloudy, and the landscape to the front was obscured by a dense fog, which delayed the movement for an hour or more after the appointed time, and then another delay supervened on account of a movement across the front of the cavalry by a part of Smith's command. Thomas, with unshaken resolution, had declined up to that time to molest Hood, or to disturb the serenity of his confidence, by experiments against his works, and it is possible that the rebels may have thought him weak and irresolute for his pains, but if such an idea had found place in Hood's quixotic brain, it was rudely dispelled by the shock of resounding arms. As soon as the fog lifted sufficiently, the battle opened by Steedman's feint on the left, followed by an assault upon the rebel salient at Montgomery's Hill by Wood's corps. The cavalry corps, had already begun its movement, Johnson on the extreme right, Croxton next, then Hatch, with Knipe and the brigade of dismounted troopers in reserve. Smith moved simultaneously upon the rebel works on the outlying ridges of the Brentwood hills. In a short time the rebel left, well strung out, was reached, broken through and driven back. The enemy had been deceived in regard to the point of attack, and in fact did not seem to expect an attack at all. The Brentwood hills were covered with a thick growth of timber, and being steep and muddy, could not have been more difficult for the passage of troops, except when covered with snow and sleet. But after breaking through the hostile line of investment at Harding's Creek, Wilson wheeled gradually to the left, in order to envelope and overwhelm the left flank of the main line, and if possible to reach Brentwood Station. By noon he came full upon the rebel works, but without hesitation, the dismounted troopers closely followed by the infantry of Smith's corps, each envious of the rapidity and gallantry of the other, sprang with alacrity upon the astonished rebels. McArthur in solid columns, and Hatch with a heavy line of skirmishers, armed with repeating rifles, swept over the first redoubt, capturing four guns and a number of prisoners.

Without waiting to count the spoils, the cavalry pushed forward against a second redoubt on a still higher hill and carried that also, with 4 more guns and 300 prisoners. Wood's corps now moved to the attack carrying the rebel advanced line, while Schofield was thrown to his right to fill the gap between Smith and Wilson, both of whom continued to advance. The rebels were driven steadily beyond the Hillsboro pike, losing sixteen guns and many prisoners. At night, Wilson's right under Hammond, rested on the Granny White pike, behind the rebel left, his center on the Hillsboro pike, and his left connecting with Schofield. The next morning the action was renewed by an effort on the part of the rebel cavalry to dislodge Hammond from his menacing position; Hatch was sent at once to Hammond's assistance, and in a short time a strong line of dismounted troopers was swung entirely across the Granny White pike, facing Nashville and pressing the rebel left and rear with great earnestness. Croxton was ordered into position to cover this line from attack, while Johnson marched across the country from Bell's Landing. The broken region in which the rebel left was now posted could not have been more unpromising for cavalry operations; indeed the cavalry was cavalry only in name; the horses were left far behind, for they could scarcely have clambered up the hills singly, much less, in the order of battle. The dismounted troopers however continued to work their way forward, gradually driving in the rebel rear; by noon their line extended along Hood's rear for a mile; with incredible labor they finally succeeded in getting two pieces of artillery to the top of a rugged hill taking in reverse the hostile entrenchments. Promptly at six o'clock in the morning Wood moved his corps forward, driving the rebel skirmishers back to their works; pausing to form his columns he advanced to the assault of Overton's Hill, the key point of Hood's line, but after a gallant attack was driven back. Steedman conformed to Wood's movement, on the left, while Smith and Schofield threw forward their lines on the right. Meanwhile the cavalry skirmishers continued to press upon the rebel rear, clambering across the ravines and up the hill-sides, and breaking through the dense growth of underbrush as best they could. Finally at two o'clock a trooper captured a despatch from Hood to Chalmers, commanding the rebel horse in the absence of Forrest, directing the latter in most urgent terms to dislodge the Union cavalry from his flank and rear, adding that unless this could be done no human force could save him from defeat.

This despatch was sent to Thomas while the movement of our cavalry continued. Perceiving the effect produced, and that the time had now come for a final and overwhelming advance along the whole line, Thomas launched the entire army directly against the front of Hood's now concentrated but, shaken divisions. Wood's corps, supported by Steedman, advanced again to the assault of Overton's Hill, but again met with a bloody repulse. Schofield and Smith, farther to the right, advanced at the same time, and although they had to climb steep hills and carry a strong line of works, they never faltered but swept right on, crossing the rebel entrenchments from the front, as the dismounted cavalry-men dashed into their rear. The rebel historians say that Bates' division broke and fled in panic, but they forget to explain that it was not till they saw themselves about to be crushed like grain between the upper and nether millstones. Schofield and Smith pressed forward with irresistible ardor, sweeping everything before them. "Excited by the victorious cheers on the right, and the intermingling crack of rifle and carbine, which told of the joint triumph of infantry and cavalry, the Fourth corps and Steedman's command, which had been already handsomely reformed and were chafing for the signal, burst once more with a vigor which nothing could stay, against the stronghold of Overton's Hill." * Human nature could stand it no longer, and shortly after four o'clock the entire rebel line gave way in rout and confusion, retreating rapidly by the Franklin pike, and the fields on both sides of it.

It was now after four o'clock; darkness was coming on, preceded by a sombre and misty twilight. With two hours more of daylight the Union legions could have completed the destruction of their opponents, now hurrying in consternation from the field. The dismounted cavalry saw beyond their reach the reflux of disordered fugitives, but their horses were far in the rear, and without them they were unable to pursue. Croxton was hastily withdrawn from his outpost, the horses were hurried forward, and the troopers mounting rapidly dashed forward in pursuit, but it was too late. The flying rebels had swept beyond the field, vanishing under the pall of impenetrable darkness, which night had kindly spread for their safety. Hatch, Croxton and Knipe used all possible diligence in leading their excited squadrons in pursuit, but had not gone more than two miles when the leading regiment, Spaulding's Twelfth Tennessee, ran full upon Chalmers' cavalry division strongly posted across the road behind rail breastworks. Dark as it was, without a moment's hesitation Spaulding led his men to the charge, striking full upon the barricade, bursting through it and falling with drawn sabers upon the rebel troops scattering them like chaff. The rest of Hatch's men soon joined in the fight; and now occurred one of the most exciting scenes of the war. All order was

---

* Twelve decisive battles of the War.

soon lost in the pitchy darkness, but each man fought his
own battle. Pistol shot and the din of saber strokes, intermingled with the shouts of officers, and the hurrahs of the
supporting squadrons, and the screams of the wounded told
how fiercely the rebels were struggling. But their valor was
unavailing to stay the onset of the Union horsemen. By ten
o'clock the fight was over. The cavalry-men after two days'
incessant fighting were now completely exhausted, and soon
sank hungry to rest upon the sodden hill-sides they had captured. Early the next morning Wilson pushed forward in
pursuit, the bulk of his forces marching toward Brentwood
closely followed by Wood. Johnson's division was sent to
cross the Harpeth, four miles to the right of Franklin, and
turning thence to the left to strike the retreating rebels in flank.
The rebel rear guard was overtaken at Hollow-tree Gap,
where it attempted to make a stand, but Hammond's brigade
by a handsome movement struck it in flank, capturing 400
prisoners and several more colors. Shortly afterwards Johnson dashed into Franklin, driving the rebels from there. This
made the crossing of the Harpeth easy, and without a pause
the cavalry pushed down the Columbia pike, and by such
country roads as were passable. At length, just at nightfall,
they came upon the rebel rear guard, composed of Stevenson's division and two batteries drawn out in line of battle,
six miles south of Franklin.

Wilson pushed Hatch forward at once on the left, Knipe
and Hammond on the right, and his own escort, the gallant
Fourth United States Cavalry, down the pike in a headlong
charge. The rebel batteries opened with grape and canister, but before they could load again the regulars had
burst upon them, and ridden through them like a whirl-wind.
Simultaneously Hatch and Knipe rushed upon the rebel
flanks, sweeping everything before them. Another exciting
night fight took place, during which a number of prisoners
and a battery were captured by Colonel Beaumont and Captain Andrews of Wilson's staff, aided by General Hatch and
a few orderlies. General Hammond and Lieutenant-Colonel

Gresham on the extreme right, crossed the West Harpeth and fell upon the flank of the retreating rebel column, but after losing most of their little band in a gallant charge, they rejoined the main force. At ten o'clock a halt was called, and the weary troopers permitted to bivouac.

The next day, the 18th of December, the pursuit was resumed before dawn, and by night had reached Rutherford's Creek, three miles north of Columbia. It had been raining all day heavily, and much of the day before; the bridges were all down, the railroad bridge destroyed, and the creek running a perfect torrent. The cavalry had no pontoons, and the train which had been hastily improvised at Nashville, was floundering laboriously forward, upon a road already overcrowded by troops and wagons. The rebels had already crossed Duck River, (now deep enough to float the "Great Eastern,") and taken up their bridge. The pursuers had nothing to do but to stay their advance till bridges could be built. This stream once delayed Buell's entire army for ten days, but Thomas crossed it in less than three, and that in midwinter under the most unfavorable circumstances. Hood had availed himself of the time thus providentially given to him to hurry his army towards the Tennessee, leaving a strong rear guard of eight brigades— 5,000 men, under Forrest to cover his flight.

The pursuit was resumed at the earliest moment and pressed with ceaseless activity, but the rebels could not again be brought to a stand long enough for decisive measures. The country south from Duck River is broken, sterile, and heavily timbered, and at that time of year it was utterly impassable for cavalry except along the turnpike, and main country roads. The weather was as bad as could be, alternating with rain, sleet, snow and frost. Both horses and men suffered greatly; neither forage nor rations could be obtained, but still the pursuit was kept up, till the 29th of December, on which day the advanced guard under Spaulding reached the Tennessee at Bainbridge, just in time to see the rebel pontoons swung to the other side.

Thomas had urged the pursuit unceasingly,* sending Steedman by rail to Decatur so as to cross the river and to cut off Hood's retreat, and Colonel W. J. Palmer with a small brigade of Johnson's division of cavalry, to follow and harass him after he had crossed into Alabama. The latter succeeded in overtaking the rear guard at Russellville, where he destroyed the rebel pontoon train of 200 wagons and 78 boats. Pushing on towards Aberdeen, he overtook and destroyed a supply-train, burning 110 wagons and killing the mules. About the same time a raid from Memphis, under Grierson and Winslow succeeded in striking the railroad leading south from Corinth and in breaking it up effectually. Hood's defeat was accompanied by another rebel disaster in the Western theatre. On the 13th of November, Breckenridge defeated Gillem near Morristown, in East Tennessee, capturing his artillery and several hundred prisoners; whereupon, Thomas acting under Grant's instructions, ordered Stoneman, now temporarily in command of the Department of the Ohio, to gather all the available forces and march against Breckenridge, Vaughan and Duke, (Morgan's successors,) driving them into Virginia if possible, and destroying the extensive salt-works at Saltville. By rapid marching and hard fighting, Stoneman executed the task assigned him. Gillem, commanding a part of his forces, defeated Duke at Kingsport, and Vaughan at Marion. Breckenridge was driven into North Carolina, the salt-works were destroyed and the railroads broken up. Thus ended Davis' reconquest of Tennessee. Instead of reaching the Ohio, his troops had beaten vainly "against Thomas, the Rock of Chickamauga," and bore backward the battle-stained flags of defeat. Instead of receiving " 30,000 brave Tennesseans " into their ranks, they left dead or in hospitals 10,000 men, losing besides, 13,189 prisoners, including 8 Generals, 72 pieces of artillery, and many colors.

* " The wisdom of Thomas in delaying attack in order to mount his cavalry, approved itself, for never before in the war had grand victory been so energetically followed by pursuit." Twelve decisive battles of the war—Nashville.

Moreover, during the campaign, Thomas' Provost Marshal received 2,200 deserters. The original army had vanished, and the entire West was lost forever to the rebellion. The broken and dispirited remnant of Hood's 50,000 were returned to Johnston's command, and reappeared again the next spring in the fitful effort which that officer made to stay the progress of Sherman's northward march through the Carolinas.

Thomas now prepared to give his army rest, but under Grant's supreme control winter quarters were no longer allowed. He ordered Thomas to send Schofield with the Twenty-third corps to the Atlantic sea-board, while the cavalry and the rest of the army were concentrated upon the banks of the Tennessee preparatory to pushing forward into Central Alabama. A few weeks' later Smith's corps and Knipe's division of cavalry were sent to assist Canby in the campaign of Mobile, while Wood was started toward East Tennessee for the purpose of penetrating to Lynchburg.

Wilson gathered the cavalry from all directions, and by the 1st of March had in camp 17,000 men, 12,000 of whom were supplied with Spencer carbines and good horses. With this splendid force, well-drilled, well-organized and admirably commanded he was finally turned loose to finish the work of destruction and conquest.

CHAPTER XXXIV.

THE most important seaport yet remaining to the rebels was Wilmington, near the mouth of Cape Fear River. Into this safe and capacious harbor, with its wide entrance, the Confederate cruisers and blockade runners were accustomed to pass in spite of all the navy could do to keep them out. Arms, ammunition, and clothing were carried in to be exchanged for cotton. The Government had long been anxious to break up this business, and during the winter arranged for a combined land and naval expedition, having that object in view. The Lieutenant-General was called upon to furnish the co-operating land forces, and had made his dispositions for sending them to Fortress Monroe, when the object of the concentration of transports and naval vessels at that place became known to the public press, and caused the expedition to be deferred. Late in November, however, it was determined that it should be reassembled and dispatched at once. General Grant went to Hampton Roads,

22

for the purpose of consulting with Admiral Porter, who had co-operated so effectively with him on the Mississippi, and after a conference, it was decided that 6,500 men should be sent, and that the expedition should sail early in December. On the 30th of November, General Grant learned that Bragg who had been commanding in North Carolina, had taken most of his forces to Georgia for the purpose of joining Hardee and making head against Sherman; thinking that the time had now come to strike the long contemplated blow, he designated General Weitzel to command the land forces, and directed General Butler, commanding the Department, to make all the necessary arrangements for sending them forward without delay. On the 6th of December he wrote: "The first object of the expedition under General Weitzel is to close to the enemy the port of Wilmington. If successful in this, the second will be to capture Wilmington itself."

The instructions were sent through General Butler, and he was expected to arrange the details, furnish all assistance and supplies required, but not to accompany the expedition. Much delay occurred, but finally on the 13th of December, the armada, with Butler himself in command, sailed for the place of rendezvous, where it arrived on the 15th. Rough weather intervening, and the naval fleet not being ready, the attack was delayed several days. On the morning of the 24th, a hulk, laden with gunpowder, was run close in under the guns of Fort Fisher, and exploded with the expectation of shattering the rebel works; "but," says General Grant, "it would seem from the notice taken of it in the Southern newspapers, that the enemy were never enlightened as to the object of the explosion, until they were informed of it by the Northern press." [*]

On the 25th the fleet stood up to the coast and a landing was effected without opposition. A reconnoissance was sent

---

[*] The origination of this novel expedient lies between Admiral Porter and General Butler, who procured from the Navy Department and the War Department the powder requisite for the purpose. The Navy Department, however, furnished the greater part of it.

out under Gen. Curtis, and an examination of the rebel works was made by General Weitzel. Thinking them too strong to be carried by assault or reduced by the navy, General Butler ordered the reëmbarkation of his troops and returned to Fortress Monroe. It seems that he had not been able to agree with Admiral Porter in regard to the plan of operations; at all events they had not acted harmoniously.

Grant's instructions were framed with the express intention of shutting the entrance to Wilmington, and therefore did not contemplate the return of the expedition till that object had been fully accomplished. He was, consequently, much chagrined when he received notice that it had returned to Hampton Roads. A few days afterwards, having been informed by the Secretary of the Navy and Admiral Porter, that the naval squadron was still off Fort Fisher, confident of its ability to take the place with the aid of land forces properly commanded, he determined to make a new attempt, but this time under a different leader. Adding a brigade of 1500 men and a small siege-train to the original force, he assigned General Alfred H. Terry to the command, giving him subsequently the same instructions that he had given to Butler, containing the following judicious counsel:

"It is exceedingly desirable that the most complete understanding should exist between yourself and the Naval commander. I suggest, therefore, that you consult with Admiral Porter freely, and get from him the part to be performed by each branch of the public service, so that there may be unity of action. It would be well to have the whole programme laid down in writing. I have served with Admiral Porter, and know that you can rely on his judgment and his nerve, to undertake what he proposes. I would therefore defer to him as much as is consistent with your own responsibilities. The first object to be attained, is to get a firm position on the spit of land on which Fort Fisher is built, from which you can operate against that fort. You want to look to the practicability of receiving your supplies, and to defending yourself against superior forces, which may be sent against you by any of the avenues left open to the enemy. *If such a position can be obtained*, the siege of Fort Fisher *will not be abandoned until its reduction is accomplished. or another plan of campaign is ordered from these head-quarters.*"

Every precaution was taken to provide this expedition against failure. Other troops were prepared and held at Fort Monroe, in readiness to go forward, should an emergency require it. General Grant also sent his aid-de-camp, Lieutenant-Colonel Comstock, an experienced engineer of the regular army, to accompany General Terry. The expedition sailed on the 6th of January, (1865,) reaching its destination two days thereafter, but owing to a stress of weather, the landing was not effected till the 13th. The next day the rebel fort was closely reconnoitered, while one of its detached works was taken possession of, and made to protect Union soldiers during the succeeding operations. Terry and Porter acting in perfect accord, pushed forward their arrangements with great earnestness. The plan of operations agreed upon, was that the navy should silence the rebel guns by a concentrated fire from the different vessels, and this being done, the land forces, aided by the marines and a brigade of sailors, should assault the entrenchments. In pursuance of this plan the fleet steamed in to the attack in three columns, and at a quarter before seven o'clock, on the 15th, began a terrific cannonade, which was continued without intermission for six hours, after the expiration of which time the enemy's guns were silenced. The sailors and marines, under the command of Fleet-Captain Breese, were landed in the meantime, and at the given signal moved forward in handsome style against the water face of the rebel fort, while the land forces, consisting of the division of General Ames, assaulted from the rear. Paine's division of colored troops, and Abbott's brigade of w' ite, held a line across the spit of land, between the fort and Wilmington, for the purpose of covering the assaulting columns from all interruption likely to be attempted in that quarter.

The fort was held by about 2,500 men, and was admirably arranged with ditch and palisade, parapet and traverse on all sides. The sailors found the water work too strong to be carried, but succeeded in attracting more than a fair share of rebel attention to themselves; this was favorable to the operations of Ames, who gallantly led his column forward to the line of bristling palisades which barred his progress till his hardy men had cut them down. Then nobly seconded by Curtis, Pennypacker and Bell, his brigade commanders, the gallant Ames cheered his veterans through the ditch and soon made a lodgment upon the western end of the principal face of the work. The rebels fought bravely, contesting every foot of ground till after nightfall, but all to no purpose, for though their assailants were led by a General upon whose face the beard had scarcely yet begun to grow, they found him as intrepid as Latour d'Auvergne, and as inexorable as fate.* Victory at last rested upon the national standards, but not till 955 men and officers had been killed and wounded. The next day the enemy abandoned Fort Caswell and Bald Head battery, opposite Fort Fisher, thus giving the Union forces complete control of the entrance to Cape Fear River.

In pursuance of the Lieutenant-General's vigorous policy, Terry began his movement against Wilmington at once, but meeting with more opposition from the rebel commander, Hoke, than he was able to overcome, he was compelled to desist till joined by re-enforcements. On the 15th of February General Schofield arrived from the West, and after receiving instructions from General Grant assumed command. Without hesitation that skillful officer prepared. to resume active operations. On the 16th he transferred Cox's division of the Twenty-third corps to Smithville, on the west bank of Cape Fear River, with orders to move upon the rear of Fort Anderson, while the men-of-war should attack it in front. Cox carried out his orders with admirable precision, and was ready for the assault when the rebels evacuated the fort and retired to Wilmington. He then crossed Brunswick River, to Eagle Island, turning the defenses of the Peninsula, and causing the rebels in Schofield's front to fall rapidly back. On the 22d of February, Schofield took possession of Wilmington, the rebels having been forced to evacuate the

* General Ames, the actual Commander of the assaulting division and the hero of Fort Fisher, was a cadet at West Point when the war broke out.

place the night before, after burning their rosin, cotton, and military stores.

Grant immediately erected North Carolina into a Department, and assigned Schofield to the command, ordering him to report to Sherman for the purpose of co-operating with him, in the northward movements, about to begin. Before the campaign from Wilmington opened he gave General Schofield the following written instructions:

* * * * "Goldsboro will be your objective point, moving either from Wilmington or Newbern, or both, as you deem best. Should you not be able to reach Goldsboro, you will advance on the line or lines of railway connecting that place with the sea-coast, as near to it as you can, building the road behind you. The enterprise under you has two objects: the first is to give Sherman material aid, if needed, in his march North; the second, to open a base of supplies for him on his line of march. As soon, therefore, as you can determine which of the two points,—Wilmington or Newbern,—you can best use for throwing supplies from to the interior, you will commence the accumulation of twenty days' rations, and forage for 60,000 men and 20,000 animals. You will get of these as many as you can house and protect to such points in the interior as you may be able to occupy. I believe General Palmer has received some instructions direct from General Sherman on the subject of securing supplies for his army. You can learn what steps he has taken, and be governed in your requisitions accordingly. A supply of ordnance-stores will also be necessary. * * * * The movements of the enemy may justify you, or even make it your imperative duty, to cut loose from your base, and strike for the interior to aid Sherman. In such case you will act upon your own judgment, without waiting for instructions. You will report, however, what you propose doing. The details for carrying out these instructions are necessarily left to you. I would urge, however, if I did not know that you are already fully alive to the importance of it, prompt action. Sherman may be looked for in the neighborhood of Goldsboro any time from the 22d to the 28th of February. This limits your time very materially."

When Sherman arrived at Savannah, the question naturally arose as to what should be his future destination. His grand march to the sea had simply demonstrated the practicability of whatever movement he might be ordered to make. To co-operate with the army in Virginia was clearly the object of all that had been done or yet remained to do, but whether Sherman should be brought with his troops by sea to City Point, and form a junction with the armies operating about Petersburg, or be directed to march northward through the Carolinas, was not at first so clear. Grant favored the former idea, but on further investigation it was found exceedingly difficult to obtain a sufficient number of sea-worthy transports; and as it would have been dangerous to trust so large an army to the mercy of the Atlantic at that time of the year, even in good vessels, Grant countermanded his first order, and after hearing Sherman's views, instructed him to lead his army into the interior again, where difficult roads, numerous rivers, and flooded marshes were yet to be overcome. The Lieutenant-General was confirmed in his final judgment, by the fear, now becoming prevalent, that Lee would abandon Petersburg and Richmond, and throw himself into the interior for the purpose of uniting with Johnston, and gathering the remnants of the rebel forces into one powerful army, with which to continue the war. It was Grant's principal desire, now, as heretofore, to destroy Lee's army and not to dislodge it,—to overwhelm the armed forces, of the rebellion, not to scatter them into distant regions or drive them to mountain fastnesses, where, by resorting to guerrilla warfare, they might prolong the struggle indefinitely. He therefore determined to close all lines of retreat, and block all routes of communication; concentrating from all quarters upon Richmond and Petersburg. Sherman's orders were implied rather than specifically stated; for Grant well knew that his trusty lieutenant would leave nothing in his track that could benefit the rebel cause. When Grant visited Knoxville, after the battle of Chattanooga, patriotic citizens of that region, while praying for peace, expressed the hope that it might never come till Sherman had marched through South Carolina as he had through East Tennessee.

They wished that State to feel some of the pangs that they had felt, and to realize in its own homes and at its own firesides a taste of the manifold horrors that it had so rashly

called down upon the country. With a severe sense of re-
tributive justice, Sherman's veterans were impatient for the
march, and when they heard "the forward," sprang out with
an alacrity never surpassed in war. It was intended that
the northward march should begin on the 15th of January,
and on that day the Seventeenth corps, General Blair commanding, was sent by water from Savannah to Hilton Head,
and thence to Pocotaligo, for the purpose of menacing
Charleston, while Slocum, with Kilpatrick's cavalry, moved
up the Savannah River towards Sister's Ferry, threatening
Augusta. But heavy rains now set in, and continued for a
fortnight almost without intermission. The rivers became
flooded, the bottoms and swamps overflowed, and the roads
impassable, and hence the movement was delayed. In the
meantime, Grover's division of the Nineteenth corps reached
Savannah and relieved Sherman's troops of their charge.
The rains having abated, the entire army was put in motion
on the 1st of February, pointing nearly due northward.
Slocum, with the left column, moved upon Barnwell, while
the right wing, crossing the Salkehatchie and Combahee,
pushed rapidly for the Edisto. The rebels believed it impossible for Sherman to make his way with such an army
through their swamps even if unopposed, but to make his
task still more difficult, the Governor called all the male
population between the ages of sixteen and sixty, to arms,
and put the negroes to work felling trees and breaking up
bridges.

Wheeler's troopers hovered about the Union columns,
while small detachments of infantry were sent to dispute the
passage of the Edisto and Congaree, but these feeble efforts
were of no avail against the confident battalions from the
fields of Donelson, Chattanooga and Atlanta. Steadily these
men of the West pressed forward, tearing up railroads, burning cotton, seizing bridges, and fighting when necessary. Or-
angeburg was reached, then Columbia by a brilliant maneuver,
thus sealing the fate of Charleston and Fort Sumter, and the
other dependencies of that stubborn city. Columbia was

almost entirely destroyed, not by Sherman's fault, but through the criminal negligence of Hampton and the rebel cavalry, who set fire to the cotton in the streets. Similar destruction took place in Charleston, where there were no national soldiers to bear the blame. The rebels seemed utterly bereft of reason, and with passionate ardor consigned their choicest possessions to the flames, forgetting that they were adding to their own cup of bitterness, and in no way injuring the national cause. Indeed, wherever they manifested the slightest disposition to destroy, Sherman and his entire army lent their willing aid, so that between them both, the Carolinas were swept with a besom of destruction from the Savannah to the Roanoke, and from the Atlantic to the Alleghanies. A wide sweep to the westward, and a hurrying march from the Yadkin to the Cape Fear River brought Sherman to Fayetteville on the 11th of March. His army concentrated there the next day, and receiving news from Schofield of what had happened during the six weeks of their campaigning, were permitted to rest for the brief period of three days. Hardee from Savannah and Charleston, Beauregard from Columbia, Cheatham from Tennessee, Bragg and Hoke from Wilmington, Hampton from Richmond and Wheeler from Atlanta, all under the command of Johnston, had finally been concentrated into one army not less than 50,000 strong by Sherman's unheeding advance, and were now prepared to dispute his further progress. Renewing his northward march Sherman demonstrated with the cavalry and Slocum's command heavily towards Averysborough, while he threw forward the rest of the army, on the direct road to Goldsboro. Slocum and the cavalry encountered Hardee, and after a severe battle, drove him from the field in the direction of Bentonsville. Johnston who was then at Smithfield, perceiving that the Union army was divided, concentrated his forces and threw them rapidly upon Slocum, hoping to crush him before Sherman could reach the field. The advance was suddenly attacked, and after a sharp fight driven back, but in a short time Slocum had posted his entire force in order of battle, and successfully resisted the hostile onset. Sherman, hearing the firing in the direction of Bentonsville, hurried thither, and by the next morning had strengthened Slocum sufficiently to justify a renewal of the offensive. The entire army was now concentrated in Johnston's front, but knowing that Schofield and Terry were moving rapidly towards Goldsboro, thus menacing Johnston's line of retreat, Sherman was anxious not to make a general attack too soon, for fear the enemy might fall back without risking a decisive engagement. He therefore made a noisy demonstration in front and maneuvered to get possession of the rebel line of retreat. But Johnston was too wary to be caught in such a trap, and during the next night fell back rapidly to Smithfield and Raleigh, leaving his pickets, and killed and wounded behind. Sherman's loss here was 1,643 killed, wounded and missing, and Johnston's nearly 2,000, of whom 1,600 were prisoners, many of them severely wounded. Sherman now pushed on rapidly to Goldsboro, reaching that place on the 23d of March, resting and reclothing his army, and forming a junction with Schofield and Terry. On the 27th of March, he himself arrived at City Point whither he had been called for the purpose of conferring with the President and General Grant.

The operations in the Carolinas were but a part of the comprehensive scheme which Grant had formed for the final campaign against the rebellion. It will be remembered that he had directed Thomas, after sending Schofield to the Atlantic sea-board, to concentrate the remainder of his available infantry in East Tennessee, with the view of marching into Virginia by the way of Abingdon and Lynchburg. He also instructed him to send a cavalry column under Stoneman into the Carolinas, to break the railroads at Columbia, Charlotte and Salisbury, destroy the rebel resources, and release our prisoners; but Stoneman was so slow in preparing his command for the field, that Grant, in anticipation of Lee's retreating towards South-western Virginia, finally changed his destination to Lynchburg. Before reaching that place, however, Stoneman, who had already devoted a good deal of time to destroying the East Tennessee and Virginia Railroad, turned towards North Carolina, reaching Boone on the 1st of April. He then pushed across the mountains to Wilkesboro on the Yadkin, where he found an abundance of supplies, but tarrying only a short time, he turned north-ward, and went into South-western Virginia, capturing Wytheville and breaking up the railroad to within four miles of Lynchburg. Concentrating his command, he now turned southward a second time, and penetrated North Carolina by the way of Jacksonville and Taylorsville. After destroying the manufactories at Salem and breaking up the Danville Railroad, he pushed on to Salisbury, which place he captured on the 10th of April, taking 14 guns and 1300 prisoners.

On the 14th of February the Lieutenant-General wrote to General Thomas as follows :

" Gen. Canby is preparing a movement from Mobile Bay against Mo-bile and the interior of Alabama. His force will consist of about 20,000 men, besides A. J. Smith's command. The cavalry you have sent to Canby will be debarked at Vicksburg. It, with the available cavalry already in that section, will move from there eastward in co-operation. Hood's army has been terribly reduced by the severe punishment you gave it in Tennessee, by desertion consequent upon their defeat, and now by the withdrawal of many of them to oppose Sherman. (I take it, a large portion of the infantry has been so withdrawn. It is so asserted in the Richmond papers, and a member of the rebel Congress said, a few days since, in a speech, that over half of it had been brought to South Carolina to oppose Sherman.) This being true, or even if it is not true, Canby's movement will attract all the attention of the enemy, and leave the advance from your stand-point easy. I think it advisable, there-fore, that you prepare as much of a cavalry force as you can spare, and hold it in readiness to go South. The object would be threefold,—first, to attract as much of the enemy's force as possible, to insure success to Canby ; second, to destroy the enemy's line of communication and mili-tary resources; third, to destroy or capture their forces brought into the field. Tuscaloosa and Selma would probably be the points to direct the expeditions against. This, however, would not be so important as the mere fact of penetrating deep into Alabama. Discretion should be left to the officer commanding the expedition to go where, according to the information he may receive, he will best secure the objects named above."

The rest of his instructions related to the time of starting, the least number of men which should compose the expedition, and the manner of organizing the troops. Wilson's command was at the time cantoned along the Tennessee River from Waterloo to Gravelly Springs, and by a vigorous system of drills and instruction had reached an efficient state of organization, and was ready for an active campaign by the time specified; but towards the end of February and during the earlier part of March, a season of rains intervened, causing the Tennessee and all its tributary streams to overflow their banks. As similar causes, however, delayed Canby, Stoneman and Sherman, the unity of the general plan was not destroyed. On the 22d of March, the streams having subsided and the weather become settled, the expedition, consisting of the divisions of E. M. McCook, Long, and Upton, and comprising over 12,000 men well mounted and about 1500 dismounted, accompanied by a light canvass pontoon train, began its march. Northern Alabama being a broken, sterile region, the command was as widely disseminated as possible during the first five or six days, in order that subsistence and forage might be better obtained. The general course pursued was south-east, the columns all converging upon Jasper, crossing the east and west branches of the Black Warrior and passing through Elyton. So skillfully was the march combined that it was several days before the rebel authorities were able to determine whether Columbus, Miss., Tuscaloosa or Selma, Ala., was the objective point. Forrest commanding a cavalry department including all the menaced region, was then at West Point, Miss., but as soon as the movement of the national cavalry became fully developed, he gathered his forces and marched with all possible speed to the eastward, his advance arriving at Montevallo where it encountered Upton's division busily engaged in destroying the collieries, iron works and manufacturing establishments in the neighboring country.

On the 31st of March, Wilson having dropped all impediments between the east and west forks of the Black Warrior, reached Montevallo with the bulk of his force, and pushed Upton at once against the enemy, now confronting him in some force under Crossland and Roddy. A sharp action took place, but the rebels were speedily routed and driven from the field in the direction of Selma. Upton dashed forward in pursuit, followed closely by the rest of the corps, and came up again with the enemy, four or five miles further on, when, making a headlong charge, he again broke their lines, capturing fifty prisoners. Night put an end to the pursuit, fifteen miles south of Montevallo, but at dawn the next morning it was resumed with great vigor. At Randolph, Upton captured a courier with despatches, from which it was learned that Forrest was now in front; that W. H. Jackson, with one of his divisions, had crossed the Black Warrior at Tuscaloosa, and was moving on Centreville; that Chalmers, with another division, was at Marion, east of the Cahawba, moving towards Selma, and that Croxton, who had been detached by Wilson at Elyton to take Tuscaloosa, had encountered Jackson's rear at Trion. Shortly afterwards a note was received from Croxton, informing the corps commander that he should postpone his enterprise against Tuscaloosa and fight Jackson, with the view of preventing a concentration of Forrest's forces in front of Selma. Wilson had already sent a detachment to seize the bridge across the Cahawba at Centreville, and now detached McCook, with LaGrange's brigade, with orders to move rapidly by that place to Scottsboro, and assist Croxton in destroying Jackson. The march was made with great celerity, and Jackson was found, but hearing nothing of Croxton, McCook, after a sharp skirmish, and the destruction of a number of factories, fell back to Centreville, destroyed the bridge, and rejoined Wilson at Selma.

In the meanwhile, Wilson pressed forward with the main column towards the South, skirmishing constantly with Forrest, and finally encountered him strongly posted on Bigler's Creek, north of Plantersville. His force, consisting of Roddy's, Armstrong's, and Crossland's commands, was estimated at 5,000 men. Upton's division, with Alexander's brigade in front, moving by the left hand road, and Long's division, with Miller's brigade in front, by the right hand, came upon the enemy simultaneously, and charging him with irresistible ardor, drove him from the field, taking three guns and several hundred prisoners. Forrest himself narrowly escaped capture, and received several severe saber strokes, at the hands of Captain Taylor, whom he killed with a pistol shot. The pursuit was pressed vigorously beyond Plantersville, but the routed rebels could not be brought to a stand again. By two o'clock the next day, Long's advanced guard came in sight of Selma, and by four P. M., the entire force was in position ready to assault the fortifications by which the city was surrounded. Forrest had gathered behind them, a motley force consisting of about 7,000 men, but many of them were conscripts, and local militia, composed of old men and boys, ministers, doctors, editors, and judges. Armstrong's brigade, 1,500 strong, and Crossland's, 1,000 strong were his main reliance, and as he had the assistance of Generals Roddy, Buford, Adams, and Armstrong, he consented to undertake the defense of the place, though his judgment was against it. Dick Taylor, his superior in rank, who secured his own safety by leaving in a special train after the appearance of the national cavalry, had given him positive orders to hold the town at all hazards. A plan of the rebel works had already been secured, and after a reconnoissance for the purpose of verifying its accuracy, the attack was ordered.

Upton, with 300 picked men, was instructed to penetrate a miry swamp covering the right of the rebel works, and after turning them, a general advance was to be made by the rest of his division together with Long's. This movement was not to begin till after dark; but shortly after the details had been arranged for carrying it out, Chalmers' division attacked Long's rear guard with considerable vehemence. Long, therefore, sent a regiment to re-enforce his rear, and with great promptitude threw forward his dismounted line of battle, consisting of 1,550 men and officers, led by Colonels Minty, Miller, McCormick and Briggs, commanded by Long in person. Armstrong's brigade, of equal strength, supported by sixteen guns held the works in their front; but these gallant veterans sprang forward with alacrity, reserving the fire of their deadly Spencers till within close range and then pouring it with withering effect. They clambered over the palisades, through the ditch and over the rebel parapet, sweeping everything before them. Upton was ordered forward at once, and in a few minutes the outer line was ours; but the broken rebels were rallied within a partially finished interior line, where they remained till charged again by the Fourth United States cavalry, Fourth Ohio and Seventeenth Indiana, supported by Upton's movement further to the left. Before such a terrible onset, resistance was of no avail. Selma, with 32 guns, 2,700 prisoners, 3,000 horses, and large quantities of military stores of every kind was ours. It was dark when the second line of works was carried, and hence Forrest and his Generals, with a large part of his force succeeded in escaping.

The gallant General Long, and Colonels Miller, Briggs and McCormick and 200 men were wounded, while Colonel Dobbs and 39 men were killed. The foundry, arsenal, and various factories were destroyed, and after tarrying a few days for the purpose of bringing forward the trains, and building a bridge across the Alabama River, Wilson crossed to the south side of the river, and turned his columns towards Montgomery. He had learned from Forrest that Croxton had pushed on towards Demopolis, and perceiving that the war was over in Central Alabama, he sent a colored courier down the river with a note, advising Canby to push at once for the interior. On the 12th of April, Wilson's leading division under McCook entered Montgomery without serious resistance, and in a short time had hoisted the national colors over the first rebel Capitol. Pausing only long enough to destroy the steamboats, cotton, and public stores found in the neighborhood, Wilson swept on towards Georgia, sending

La Grange to West Point, while Upton and Minty (now commanding Long's division) were directed upon Columbus. The works covering the bridges leading into the latter place were assaulted under cover of darkness by 300 picked men commanded by Colonel Nobles of the Third Iowa cavalry, on the night of April 16th.

Upton and Winslow led the men in person, and after a sharp fight, during which the rebels threw away large quantities of ammunition by an indiscriminate use of their artillery, the works and bridges were captured, and by ten o'clock the city itself with 1,200 prisoners and 52 guns. Our loss was barely 24 killed and wounded. La Grange was quite as successful at West Point, where he assaulted and took a strong enclosed work, containing several hundred rebels under the command of General Tyler, who was killed. The garrison of 265 men was captured, while the railroad stock from Atlanta and Montgomery, consisting of 19 locomotives and 250 cars was burnt. Having thus secured two crossings of the Chattahoochee, the exultant cavalry-men dashed forward to Macon, which place they captured on the 21st of April, with 1,200 more prisoners, including Generals Cobb, G. W. Smith, Mackall and Robertson. Wilson's headlong career towards Virginia, whither he was hurrying with his powerful body of horse to take part in the final struggle, was stopped at this place by the terms of the armistice agreed upon by Sherman and Johnston, and the first clear intelligence was received of what had taken place in Virginia. Croxton who had doubled upon his track and pursued a more northern route, fighting militia, burning bridges, destroying mills and capturing towns, arrived at Macon on the 30th of April. During this campaign of twenty-eight days, the cavalry corps marched on an average 525 miles, captured 5 fortified cities and 22 stands of colors, 280 pieces of artillery and 682 prisoners, and destroyed 2 gun-boats, 90,000 stands of small arms, 235,000 bales of cotton, and all the mills, collieries, iron works, factories, railroad bridges, rolling stock and military establishments, which were found on the line of march.

Besides this three regiments of colored troops, each over 1,000 strong, were organized, armed, and equipped, during the halt at Selma. There was nothing destructible left behind Wilson that could benefit the rebel cause. His command now held possession of the granary of the South, and barred the only road by which the rebel President and his Cabinet could hope to escape. In order to prevent this and to enforce the terms of the final capitulation, Wilson scattered his command on a line from Dalton, Ga., to St. Marks, Fla., sent scouts into all parts of the country, stationed detachments at all the cross-roads and ferries, and succeeded in capturing Jefferson Davis while endeavoring to escape, disguised as a woman, from his camp near Irwinsville, Ga., on the morning of the 10th of May. The actual capture was made by Lieutenant-Colonel Benjamin D. Pritchard, with a detachment of the Fourth Michigan cavalry, although Lieutenant-Colonel Henry Harnden of the First Wisconsin cavalry, first discovered the trail, and followed it to the place of capture, arriving upon the ground immediately after the seizure had taken place. The first entirely trustworthy information of Davis' movements, after entering Georgia, was obtained by Lieutenant Joseph O. Yeoman, of General Alexander's staff. This enterprising young officer, with twenty scouts disguised in rebel uniforms, joined the Confederate Chief and his escort just after they crossed the Savannah River, and accompanied them to Washington, sending information to General Alexander every night, who transmitted it by telegraph to head-quarters. This information coupled with that obtained from other sources was the immediate cause of the movement which resulted in the arrest of the fugitives.

General Canby, commanding the Military Division of the West Mississippi, with his head-quarters at New Orleans, had remained comparatively inactive during the summer and autumn of 1864. The Thirteenth corps, under General Granger, had participated in the operations by which the navy, after capturing Forts Gaines and Morgan, obtained control of Mobile Bay, but no general operations took place

23

till March, 1865, at which time, in pursuance of the Lieutenant-General's instructions, the final campaign against Mobile
was begun.   Dick Taylor, who had been called from the
trans-Mississippi Department, held the supreme command
in Mississippi and Alabama, and had concentrated a force of
about 15,000 men, under General Maury, at Mobile.   General Canby's forces consisted of the Thirteenth and Sixteenth
corps, one division of colored infantry, and one division of
cavalry, in all about 30,000 effective men.   Grierson, instead
of moving from Vicksburg, as General Grant had intended,
was taken to New Orleans, from which place he crossed
Lake Pontchartrain, and marched thence to Mobile Point.
Canby's plan of operations was exceedingly complicated,
owing to the peculiar character of the theatre in which he
was compelled to operate, but withal, it was executed with
great despatch and regularity.   Steele, with a division of
blacks, marched from Pensacola, towards Blakely, above
Mobile ; Granger marched around Bon Secours' Bay, while
Smith's corps crossed the bay in transports, and landed at
Fish River on the 21st of March.   After waiting two days
for the arrival of Granger, who had taken the wrong road
and had been delayed by rains, the two corps pushed forward, and on the 27th of April invested Spanish Fort ;
Steele arrived shortly afterwards, and the next day the siege
was regularly begun, by the construction of parallels, approaches and batteries.   By the 3d of April the result was
no longer doubtful ; and on the 8th our batteries were opened,
and after a terrific bombardment throughout the day succeeded in silencing the enemy's guns.   The fort was taken
possession of during the night by one of Carr's brigades, acting under the direction of Colonel Geddes and Captain Buford
Wilson, Assistant Adjutant-General, but the garrison, with
the exception of about 65 men, had escaped.   Thirty-five
heavy guns and much ammunition were left to the victors.

The guns were at once turned upon batteries Tracy and
Huger near the mouth of the Tensaw, and after a short time
compelled the rebels to evacuate those positions also.   The

way for gun-boats was now opened to Blakely, a remarkably strong position overlooking the river, which had been invested several days before, on the land side, and although it seemed to be capable of indefinite defence, the victorious Union troops made short work of it. As soon as the gun-boats appeared Steele ordered an assault, which took place at half-past five o'clock on the 9th. Garrard's division, supported by two brigades of Andrews' division and Dennis' brigade of Veatch's division, dashed forward, reached the abattis, and tearing it away under a heavy fire of canister and grape, they leaped into the ditch, clambered up the scarp of the fort, and crossed the parapet while two brigades farther to the right gained an entrance and captured General Thomas with 1,000 prisoners. The gallantry of men and officers in this assault was most conspicuous; the rebels, with the determination to make their defence as desperate as possible, covered the approaches to their work with torpedos, which exploded as the assailants pressed forward, and although many men were killed it did not intimidate their companions.

Under a galling fire of canister and grape, round shot and musketry, they steadily advanced, till the victory was complete. The right of our line was led by the colored troops of General Hawkins' command, who in remembrance of Fort Pillow, showed the determination of revenge, and dashed into the ditch and over the works, driving the Mississippians before their terrible energy. By seven o'clock the national colors floated over Blakely, and 3,000 prisoners, 32 guns, 4,000 small arms, and 16 flags were trophies of the victory. The Union loss was nearly 1,000 men, while the rebels, fighting under cover, lost only 500, but the cost was not too much; Mobile, with all its dependencies, fell with Blakely, and during the night Maury retreated with 9,000 men towards Central Alabama, leaving 1,000 prisoners, 132 guns, and much valuable property. Canby now sent one column at once up the Alabama River, to Selma, another to Montgomery, and the cavalry under Grierson, through the country to Eufaula, thus placing another cordon of armed men in the path of the flying rebel President.

CHAPTER XXXV.

SITUATION IN FRONT OF PETERSBURG—THE ARMY OF THE POTOMAC
TO ACCOMPLISH ITS OWN TASK—MR. LINCOLN'S VIEWS—GRANT'S
INSTRUCTIONS TO SHERIDAN—SHERIDAN MOVES FROM WINCHES-
TER—DEFEAT OF EARLY—SHERIDAN AT THE WHITE HOUSE—HE
JOINS GRANT—GRANT'S APPREHENSIONS FOR SHERMAN—REVIEW
OF OPERATIONS—THE FINALE APPROACHING—THE ORDERS FOR
THE GENERAL MOVEMENT—PLANS OF OPERATIONS—LEE'S SORTIE
AGAINST GRANT'S RIGHT—LEE'S PLAN FOILED—PRELIMINARIES—
BATTLE OF FIVE FORKS—SHERIDAN'S SUCCESS—REJOICINGS IN
THE ARMY—LEE DECIDES TO ABANDON RICHMOND AND PETERS-
BURG—JEFF. DAVIS PREPARES FOR FLIGHT—THE OVERWHELMING
ASSAULT—A FIERCE STRUGGLE—LEE ABANDONS PETERSBURG—
GRANT'S ARMY IN PURSUIT—LEE ATTEMPTS TO REACH THE MOUN-
TAINS—SHERIDAN WATCHFUL—HE CAPTURES THE REBEL TRAIN—
LEE'S PROGRESS CHECKED—CORRESPONDENCE BETWEEN GRANT
AND LEE—THE SURRENDER OF LEE'S ARMY—ITS RESULT—JOHN-
STON'S SURRENDER—SHERIDAN'S MOVEMENT TOWARDS THE MEX-
ICAN FRONTIER—GRANT'S OPINIONS IN REGARD TO MEXICO—DIS-
BANDING OF THE VOLUNTEERS—GRANT PROMOTED TO THE FULL
GRADE OF GENERAL.

DURING the course of events which resulted from his magnificent combinations in the West and South, Grant himself
was not idle, but all through the winter maintained such a
menacing attitude in front of Petersburg as to compel Lee to
stand constantly on the defensive. At no time would it have
been safe for that General to detach a brigade from his beleaguered forces for the assistance of Hood and Hardee.
Before the spring campaign commenced, the President urged
Grant to bring Sherman's army from Savannah to City Point,
and to join it with the armies near Petersburg for a final and

crushing blow, but the far-seeing Lieutenant-General steadfastly adhered to his plan of keeping Sherman in the interior,
marching and destroying as well as barring all lines of retreat.
He had other reasons not purely military, but rather belonging to the domain of statesmanship which influenced him in
requiring the Army of the Potomac to accomplish the task
which it had undertaken. If the gallant fighters of the West
should be allowed to join their strength with that of their less
fortunate, but not less courageous, compatriots from the East
before the final blow was struck, it would give rise to never-
ending jealousy, and never-satisfied claims for the honor of
having conquered the last stronghold of the rebellion.

Patriotism is a controlling characteristic of American soldiers, in all matters concerning the public enemy. but amongst
themselves, they are slow to sink their individuality in defer-
ence to the claims of others, and therefore Grant's apprehension that the arrival of the Western army would not be
productive of harmony, was probably well founded. At all
events, Mr. Lincoln, with his usual candor, frankly admitted
that he had not considered the question in that light, and
after reflection agreed with Grant, that if the Armies of the
Potomac and James could, without assistance, crush Lee's
army, they had better be permitted to do it. Grant really
entertained more fear of failure for Sherman's movement, than
he did for his own; and instead of drawing support from
him, except of that moral kind which would come with a
victorious march northward, he exerted himself to the utmost
to send troops to Sherman. Schofield and Terry, with a
column of 25,000 men, went out from Wilmington, menacing
the rear of the rebel army gathering under Johnston. Stoneman was ordered to cross the mountains from East Tennessee,
and after breaking the railroads, was expected to form a
junction with the marching columns, and in order to make
all the operations outside of his own immediate presence,
secure beyond the chance of failure, Grant directed Sheridan,
now the undisputed master of North Virginia, to cut off all
hostile communication from Richmond with that region, and

then to move by the way of Lynchburg, to the westward of
Danville and join Sherman.

On the 27th of February, Sheridan, with 10,000 cavalry
under Merritt and Custer, moved from Winchester, and on
the 1st of March secured the bridge across the north fork of
the Shenandoah at Mount Crawford, in spite of the efforts
of the rebels to destroy it.   He reached Staunton the next
day, driving the rebels before him in the direction of Waynesborough.   Without pausing he pushed forward in the same
direction ; found the enemy under Early occupying a strongly
entrenched position, and with audacious confidence, spurning
the preliminary of even a reconnoissance, he dashed headlong
upon their works, sweeping over them with the violence and
ease of a tornado, capturing 1,600 prisoners, 11 guns with
horses and caissons complete, 200 wagons and 17 battle-flags.
Early, with one orderly, fled to the mountains and disappeared
from the war.   Sheridan, sending his prisoners back to Winchester, pushed forward to Charlotteville, breaking up the
railroad and burning the bridges as he went.   At Charlotteville he stayed his rapid swoop till his trains could overtake
him.   The roads being exceedingly bad, several days elapsed
before he could resume his march ; and owing to the delays
already experienced, he relinquished the idea of going to
Petersburg.   On the morning of the 6th of March, dividing
his force into two columns, he sent one to Scottville under
Merritt, with directions to destroy the James River Canal as
far up as New Market, while Custer moved toward Lynchburg destroying the railroads as far as Amherst Court House,
and there forming a junction with Merritt at New Market.
The James being very high, Sheridan could not cross it with
the small number of pontoons that he had brought with him,
and the enemy having destroyed the permanent bridges span-
ning that stream at Hardwicksville and elsewhere, it was impossible to reach the Southside Road as he desired.   Under
these circumstances, having done all the damage he could on
the north side of the river, there was nothing left for him but
to return to Winchester or to march to the White House and

thence to the James River below Richmond for the purpose of forming a junction with the armies about Petersburg.

"Fortunately," says General Grant, "he chose the latter course," and set out at once by the canal towards Richmond, destroying the locks and cutting the embankment as far down as Goochland. Thence he moved to Columbia, communicating from that place with Grant, and halting a day for the purpose of closing up his columns. On the 19th of March he reached the White House. After refitting and resting his command, he moved across to the James and rejoined Grant, from whom he had been absent nearly nine months.

Still apprehensive for Sherman, and fearful that Lee, as the toils were drawn closer and closer about him, might undertake to withdraw his army to the mountains, the Lieutenant-General, on the 7th of March, ordered Thomas to repair the railroad in East Tennessee, and to throw a good force forward to fortify Bull's Gap, where he could hold himself in readiness for a campaign towards Lynchburg, or into North Carolina. Having taken this final precaution, and fully matured his plans, the time was at hand for the forces under his immediate command to strike the final blow. He had made his preparations with consummate skill, infusing into the armies, from the Potomac to the Mississippi, an unconquerable spirit, and directing them with a skill and unity never before realized in modern warfare. Under his chosen leaders they had ceased to be "a balky team," and were now pressing forward with a zeal and harmony that made light of labor, and darkened the closing days of the rebellion with a series of overwhelming defeats.

"Thus," says General Grant, "it will be seen that in March, 1865, General Canby was moving an adequate force against Mobile and the army defending it, under Dick Taylor; Thomas was pushing out two large and well-appointed cavalry expeditions,—one from Middle Tennessee, under Brevet Major-General Wilson, against the enemy's vital points in Alabama; the other from East Tennessee, under Major-General Stoneman, towards Lynchburg; and assembling the remainder of his available forces preparatory to offensive operations from East Tennessee. General Sheridan's cavalry was at the White House; the

Armies of the Potomac and James were confronting the enemy under Lee in his defences of Richmond and Petersburg; General Sherman, with his armies reinforced by that of General Schofield, was at Goldsboro; General Pope was making preparations for a campaign against the enemy, Kirby Smith and Price, west of the Mississippi; and General Hancock was concentrating a force in the vicinity of Winchester, Va., to guard against invasion, or to operate offensively, as might prove necessary."

The orders for a general movement of the armies operating against Richmond were issued to General Meade on the 24th of March, and as one object of this work is to show the methods resorted to by the Lieutenant-General, in the conduct of military operations, they are inserted entire, as follows:

"On the 29th instant, the armies operating against Richmond will be moved by our left for the double purpose of turning the enemy out of his present position around Petersburg, and to insure the success of the cavalry under General Sheridan, which will start at the same time, in its efforts to reach and destroy the Southside and Danville Railroads. Two corps of the Army of the Potomac will be moved at first in two columns, taking the two roads crossing Hatcher's Run nearest where the present line held by us strikes that stream, both moving towards Dinwiddie Court House.

"The cavalry under General Sheridan, joined by the division now under General Davies, will move at the same time by the Weldon Road and the Jerusalem plank-road, turning west from the latter before crossing the Nottoway, and west with the whole column before reaching Stony Creek. General Sheridan will then move independently under other instructions which will be given him. All dismounted cavalry belonging to the Army of the Potomac, and the dismounted cavalry from the Middle Military Division, not required for guarding property belonging to their arm of service, will report to Brigadier-General Benham, to be added to the defences of City Point. Major-General Parke will be left in command of all the army left for holding the lines about Petersburg and City Point, subject, of course, to orders from the Commander of the Army of the Potomac. The Ninth Army Corps will be left intact to hold the present line of works so long as the whole line now occupied by us is held. If, however, the troops to the left of the Ninth corps are withdrawn, then the left of the corps may be thrown back so as to occupy the position held by the army prior to the capture of the Weldon Road. All troops to the left of the Ninth corps will be held in readiness to move at the shortest notice by such routes as may be designated when the order is given.

" General Ord will detach three divisions, two white and one colored, or so much of them as he can, and hold his present lines, and march for the present, left of the Army of the Potomac. In the absence of further orders, or until further orders are given, the white divisions will follow the left column of the Army of the Potomac, and the colored divisions the right column. During the movement, Major-General Weitzel will be left in command of all the forces remaining behind from the Army of the James.

" The movement of troops from the Army of the James will commence on the night of the 27th instant. General Ord will leave behind the minimum number of cavalry necessary for picket duty, in the absence of the main army. A cavalry expedition from General Ord's command will also be started from Suffolk, to leave there on Saturday, the 1st of April, under Colonel Sumner, for the purpose of cutting the railroad about Hick's Ford. This, if accomplished, will have to be a surprise, and therefore from three to five hundred men will be sufficient. They should, however, be supported by all the infantry that can be spared from Norfolk and Portsmouth, as far out as to where the cavalry crosses the Blackwater. The crossing should probably be at Vinton. Should Colonel Sumner succeed in reaching the Weldon Road, he will be instructed to do all the damage possible to the triangle of roads between Hick's Ford, Weldon, and Gaston. The railroad bridge at Weldon being fitted up for the passage of carriages, it might be practicable to destroy any accumulation of supplies the enemy may have collected south of the Roanoke. All the troops will move with four days' rations in haversacks, and eight days' in wagons. To avoid as much hauling as possible, and to give the Army of the James the same number of days' supply with the Army of the Potomac, General Ord will direct his commissary and quartermaster to have sufficient supplies delivered at the terminus of the road to fill up in passing. Sixty rounds of ammunition per man will be taken in wagons, and as much grain as the transportation on hand will carry, after taking the specified amount of other supplies. The densely wooded country in which the army has to operate, making the use of much artillery impracticable, the amount taken with the army will be reduced to six or eight guns to each division, at the option of the army commanders.

" All necessary preparations for carrying these directions into operation may be commenced at once. The reserves of the Ninth corps should be massed as much as possible. Whilst I would not now order an unconditional attack on the enemy's line by them, they should be ready, and should make the attack if the enemy weakens his line in their front, without waiting for orders. In case they carry the line, then the whole of the Ninth corps should follow up, so as to join or co-operate with the balance of the army. To prepare for this, the

Ninth corps will have rations issued to them, the same as the balance of the army. General Weitzel will keep vigilant watch upon his front, and if found at all practicable to break through at any point, he will do so. A success north of the James should be followed up with great promptness. An attack will not be feasible unless it is found that the enemy has detached largely. In that case it may be regarded as evident that the enemy are relying upon their local reserves principally for the defence of Richmond. Preparations may be made for abandoning all the line north of the James, except enclosed works—only to be abandoned, however, after a break is made in the lines of the enemy.

" By these instructions a large part of the armies operating against Richmond is left behind. The enemy, knowing this, may, as an only chance, strip their lines to the merest skeleton, in the hope of advantage not being taken of it, whilst they hurl everything against the moving column, and return. It can not be impressed too strongly upon commanders of troops left in the trenches, not to allow this to occur without taking advantage of it. The very fact of the enemy coming out to attack, if he does so, might be regarded as almost conclusive evidence of such a weakening of his lines. I would have it particularly enjoined upon corps commanders that, in case of an attack from the enemy, those not attacked are not to wait for orders from the commanding officer of the army to which they belong, but that they will move promptly, and notify the commander of their action. I would, also, enjoin the same action on the part of division commanders when other parts of their corps are engaged. In like manner, I would urge the importance of following up a repulse of the enemy."

But Lee, who had long contemplated the evacuation of Petersburg, had also formed a plan of operations, based upon a vigorous offensive. Early on the morning of the 25th of March he threw forward Gordon's division against the right of Grant's line held by the Ninth corps, at Hare's Hill or Fort Steedman. The concentration of troops for this attack was made with secrecy, and as the sortie began before daylight, it fell quite unexpectedly upon the advanced works of the Union line. A brief struggle ensued resulting in the loss of the works and many guns, but the troops behind forming promptly, advanced to regain the lost ground. Meade threw forward the Second and Sixth corps at the same time, and after a sharp contest not only dislodged Gordon, but captured 1,900 prisoners. Lee's object was doubtless to break through Grant's right and seize his railroad to City Point, thus com-

pelling a contraction of the Union left and securing for the
rebels an opportunity to abandon Petersburg and throw
themselves into the open country for the purpose of uniting
with Johnston. This well conceived plan was admirably
foiled; Grant was not changed in his resolution in any way
by it. It neither accelerated nor retarded his movements;
but he delayed to consult with Sherman, whose army was
now at Goldsboro, while he was in person hastening to City
Point, with assurances of his ability to move forward to any
designated point for the purpose of co-operating in the final
movement. Grant directed him to demonstrate upon Raleigh
and then turning north-eastward to cross the Roanoke at
Gaston and move forward to Burkesville, or join the armies
operating against Richmond as he might think best. He
explained fully the plan of his own movement, and informed
his Lieutenant that in case of failure or only partial success,
Sheridan would be detached to move down the Danville Railroad and form a junction with the army from the West.

"I had spent days of anxiety," says General Grant, "lest each morning should bring the report that the enemy had retreated the night
before. I was firmly convinced that Sherman's crossing the Roanoke
would be the signal for Lee to leave. With Johnston and Lee combined, a long, tedious, and expensive campaign, consuming most of the
summer, might become necessary. By moving out, I would put the
army in better condition for pursuit, and would at least, by the destruction of the Danville Road, retard the concentration of the two
armies of Lee and Johnston, and cause the enemy to abandon much
material that he might otherwise save. I therefore determined not to
delay the movement ordered."

On the 28th of March, he informed Sheridan that the
Fifth corps and Second corps would move at an early hour
next morning, and directed him to march in the same direction with his cavalry, but without confining himself to any
particular road or roads. The object of his march was to
find and fall upon the enemy's right flank and rear, with the
intention of compelling him to abandon his entrenched position in front, and seek the open field for battle. Sheridan
was allowed ample latitude in carrying his orders into effect,

but was urged to fight as hotly as circumstances would permit, should he find a favorable opportunity, receiving the
assurance that the infantry would attack with vigor, or follow in close pursuit.   Should it be found impracticable to
force the enemy from his works, he was in that case to cut
loose and push for the Danville Railroad, and after doing all
the damage he could upon rebel communications he was
authorized to return to Grant or to proceed to join Sherman
in North Carolina.

The next day, at the appointed hour, the different corps
moved forward as directed.   Warren marched by the Quaker Road, with Griffin in advance skirmishing heavily with
Bushrod Johnson ; Humphreys crossed Hatcher's Run and
pushed through the dense woods to Warren's right ; while
Sheridan trotted briskly by the usual route to Dinwiddie
Court House, some six miles to the left and rear of the Fifth
corps.   Ord had already crossed from Deep Bottom, and
taken his place on Wright's left, while Parke still held his
old position, thus extending the Union line, without a break,
" from the Appomattox to Dinwiddie."   The various movements of the day were made with such regularity and precision, and the prospect at night was so favorable, that Grant,
in order to make sure of Sheridan's powerful co-operation,
wrote :

" *I now feel like ending the matter if it is possible to do so before going
back*.   I do not want you, therefore, to cut loose and go after the enemy's roads at present.   In the morning, push around the enemy if you
can and get on to his right and rear.   The movements of the enemy's
cavalry may, of course, modify your action.   We will act altogether as
one army here till it is seen what can be done with the enemy."

Early the next morning, notwithstanding a heavy rain-
storm during the night, and throughout the day, Sheridan
pushed forward to Five Forks, where he found the enemy
strongly entrenched.   Warren's corps advanced, crossing the
Boydton plank-road, and after heavy skirmishing took up a
position in front of the rebel works along the White Oak
road.   Humphreys drove straight forward with his right on

Hatcher's Run, while Ord, Wright and Parke made demonstrations along their respective fronts, with the view of ascertaining the feasibility of an assault. Lee, in extending towards Five Forks, seems to have weakened his left considerably, discovering which, both Wright and Parke expressed the opinion that they could assault successfully. Grant, therefore, decided to extend the left no further, but to re-enforce Sheridan with a corps of infantry, which would enable that officer to "cut loose" and fall upon the rebel rear, while the other corps should assault in front. Preparations were made to carry this determination into effect, but the sodden condition of the roads caused a considerable delay. On the morning of the 31st, Warren having expressed a belief that he could take the White Oak road, was directed to do so, though previous instructions had been issued from Meade's head-quarters suspending all movements for the day. The operations of Warren, however, were not fully begun when Lee, who had massed a heavy force on his right, assumed the offensive, falling upon the advanced brigade under Winthrop, sweeping it back upon the rest of the division, throwing the whole into confusion, and compelling it to recoil upon Crawford's division. Warren, in the meantime, threw forward Griffin's division, and after a gallant struggle checked the rebels till the arrival of Miles' division of the Second corps ultimately enabled him to drive them back to and beyond their works on the White Oak road.

Sheridan, who had advanced to Five Forks and made a lodgment at that place, now caught the brunt of the rebel attack. Rapidly massing infantry and cavalry in his front, they fell upon him with great fury, driving him, after a continuous and bloody battle lasting till nightfall, nearly to Dinwiddie Court House. During the entire afternoon, Sheridan managed his force with great skill; dismounting all his available men, and sending the horses to the rear, he formed an extended line of skirmishers, whose operations were favored by the heavy forest through which he was compelled to retire. The rebels, after pressing him back some distance,

swung off towards his right as if to march towards the
Boydton road for the purpose of attacking Warren in flank
and rear. Divining their intention and perceiving a fine
opening, he threw forward his left, under Gibbs and Gregg,
striking the enemy in rear and flank, and compelling them to
change front at once. After this, they continued to press
heavily upon him, but by hard fighting he succeeded in
retarding their advance long enough to permit Merritt to
throw up a rail breastwork in front of Dinwiddie, behind
which, a final and successful stand was made. During the
afternoon he notified the Lieutenant-General of his perilous situation, and Grant sent him MacKenzie's, (formerly
Kautz's) division of cavalry, and Ayres' division from Warren's corps. During the night, Meade, by a confidential
order, directed Warren and Humphreys to contract their
lines and retire to the east side of the Boydton plank-road,
apparently looking to an abandonment of the advantages
already gained, if not of the entire movement. But Grant,
with immovable resolution, shortly afterwards directed Warren, with the rest of his corps, to hasten to Dinwiddie, notwithstanding the intense darkness of the night, while Humphreys was instructed to maintain his position on the Boydton
road. This idea seems to have occurred to Warren at the
same time, but unfortunately the bridges across Gravelly Run
were down, and hence the movement was much delayed.
In the meantime, the rebels fearing that Ayers would fall
upon their rear, about midnight abandoned their position in
Sheridan's front, and fell back to Five Forks. This was the
turning point in the campaign, for at an early hour the irrepressible and "belligerent Sheridan," clothed now by the
Lieutenant-General with ample authority over all the troops
within his reach, moved once more confidently towards Five
Forks, (so-called because of its being the point of radiation
for five roads or paths.) But the infantry having been delayed by the darkness of the night and the long distance to
be marched, the day wore on well into the afternoon before
the general attack could be made. Sheridan had with him

about 9,000 cavalry, commanded by Merritt and MacKenzie, and about 12,500 infantry of the Fifth corps. His plan of operations was exceedingly brilliant. After reaching the immediate vicinity of Five Forks, he threw forward most of the cavalry, menacing a direct attack, while Warren's corps was moved to the right by the Gravelly Run Church, for the purpose of striking and breaking through the enemy's left. MacKenzie was ordered to reach the White Oak road and cover the right flank and rear of the infantry. The first part of the plan was executed with great skill, by Merritt, who pushed Davies and Custer vigorously against the rebel skirmishers, by two o'clock driving them into their entrenchments in front of Five Forks, and then demonstrated heavily upon the extreme right of the rebel line. MacKenzie's movement to the White Oak road was also fortunate and opportune, for shortly after he struck the road he encountered a rebel force moving towards Five Forks, and attacking them boldly, drove them back towards Petersburg. At length Warren reached the position assigned him, and advanced straight upon the White Oak road, Crawford on the right, Ayers on the left, and Griffin in support. Immediately after striking the road, the corps wheeled to the left till it was faced westward, at right angles with its original direction. MacKenzie was then thrown forward, to the right of Crawford. In this order the assault was made ; but Ayers, swinging on a fixed pivot and advancing, at once found himself hotly engaged and thrown into considerable confusion before the rest of the corps had completed the wheeling movement. Griffin was thrown forward to his assistance, and the two veteran divisions now sprang out with alacrity, breaking through abattis and sweeping over the enemy's works with an irresistible impulse. The heavy firing on this front was the signal for Merritt to sound the charge for the cavalry, and, eager for the fray, the gallant horsemen dashed straight at the works in their front, sweeping over them like a tornado. The rebels finding themselves assailed in front, flank and rear, gave way and fled in hopeless confusion, hotly pursued by the victorious cavalry-men. They left behind them 6,000 prisoners, 4 guns and many colors, while the Union loss did not exceed 1,000, all told. Merritt and Mac-Kenzie chased the fugitives westward till far into the night. The victory was complete, and put a fitting climax to the fame which Sheridan had won at Stone River, Chickamauga, Chattanooga, and in the Valley of Virginia.

The news was instantly borne to Grant and communicated to the army, where it was received with deafeni..g cheers by the gallant troops who gathered confidence for the morrow, feeling that their reward was near at hand, and that the dawn would usher in their last struggle against the rebellion. Fearing during the night lest the rebel chieftain should gather in his detached forces, desert the entrenchments he had held so faithfully, and fall with his entire army upon Sheridan, the Lieutenant-General sent Miles' division from Humphreys' corps to re-enforce him, and caused the guns and mortars all along the investing lines to open fire upon the hostile position and continue the bombardment till four o'clock in the morning, at which time a general assault was ordered. Lee in the meanwhile had also heard the news from Five Forks, and decided at once that Petersburg and Richmond must be abandoned ; but he was too good a soldier to go in disorder or confusion and therefore maintained his position till the proper arrangements could be made for the retreat. He made known to Davis, however, the necessity which had been precipitated by the disastrous defeat of his right wing. The rebel President received the news while at church, and left instantly to prepare for flight from the capital he had declared it would be cowardice to abandon. Precisely at four o'clock on Sunday morning, April 2d, the impatient soldiers of the Union leaped forth in one overwhelming assault, extending from the Appomattox to Hatcher's Run. Wright's Sixth corps, which had returned from the Shenandoah filled with confidence, swept forward from the center with the impulse of an avalanche, carrying everything before it ; glacis and ditch, parapet and rifle-trench alike failed to check their progress. Parke, with the Ninth corps on the right, and Ord, with the Army of the James on the left, joined nobly in this crushing and annihilating assault. Parke was checked after carrying the outer line of works, but Wright and Ord pushing their destructive march through all obstacles, capturing cannons and prisoners, reached the Boydton road and turned towards Petersburg. Humphreys hearing the sounds of a triumphant advance from the right, threw forward his line and swept over the Confederate works. Sending a part of his corps towards Sutherland Station, with the rest he pushed on towards Petersburg in support of Wright and Ord. Before eight o'clock the entire chain of exterior defences had been captured by the Union troops, but without halting to count the spoils, they pressed forward against the strong interior line which had been drawn close about the city. The highest enthusiasm prevailed, officers and men felt an elasticity and prowess that nothing but victory can give, corps vieing with corps, division with division, man with man. But the works against which they were now hurling themselves were as strong as those of a feudal citadel, and their defenders though rudely shaken from their fancied security, and depressed by the fate whose baleful shadows were but too plainly visible, stood to their guns, and clasped their muskets with the courage of brave men.

As the surging lines and serried columns of the assailants dashed bravely forward, they were received with a deadly fire, and after a brief struggle were hurled back, broken and bleeding, to reform and dash forward again and again. By noon the strife had ceased, and Lee had gained a brief but delusive respite from the troubles now gathering so rapidly about his intrepid but fated army. During the night he quietly abandoned the works about Petersburg, and withdrew to the north side of the Appomattox, turning the heads of his columns westward along the northern bank of that stream. By daylight he was sixteen miles away, having collected the bulk of his army not far from Chesterfield. At

24

early dawn the flight was discovered, and Grant, without a moment's delay, put his army in motion. Sheridan, followed by the Fifth corps, marched by the most northern route directly towards Burkesville; Ord, along the Southside Railroad, followed closely by the Second and Sixth corps towards Jettersville. The Union forces had gained the shorter line, but Lee hurried forward with the energy of despair, hoping to pass beyond Burkesville and reach North Carolina where he could join Johnston, and make still another struggle. On the morning of the 4th, he reached Amelia Court House, where he expected to find rations for the army, but the cars which brought them had gone to Richmond to remove the rebel archives, and by a strange fatality carried with them the rations upon which the rebel army depended for its lease of life. His troops were weak and hungry, and were therefore allowed to break up into small parties for the sake of foraging. Two days were thus lost, whilst Grant drew his cordon closer about them. Sheridan had reached the Danville Road, seven miles in advance of Lee, and planted the Fifth corps firmly across it, while the cavalry watchfully guarded every road by which a forward movement could be made. Grant directing everything in person, reached Wilson Station on the Southside Railroad, on the 5th. Ord arrived at Burkesville the same day, and by night the entire army stood ready to bar Lee's further progress southward. Forgetting nothing that could possibly render the national triumph more complete, the Lieutenant-General wrote to Sherman:

" All indications now are that Lee will attempt to reach Danville with the remnant of his force. Sheridan, who was up with him last night, reports all that is left, ' horse, foot, and dragoons,' at 20,000, much demoralized. We hope to reduce the number one-half. I shall push on to Burkesville, and if a stand is made at Danville, I will, in a very few days, go there. If you possibly can do so, push on from where you are, and let us see if we cannot finish the job with Lee's and Johnston's armies. Whether it will be better for you to strike for Greensboro or nearer to Danville, you will be better able to judge when you receive this. *Rebel armies now are the only strategic points to strike at.*"

But Lee had already discovered the hopelessness of trying to force his way through the Union lines towards the South, and during the night of the 5th resumed his march towards High Bridge and Lynchburg for the purpose of reaching the mountains of South-western Virginia; Sheridan, however, with sleepless vigilance discovered the march almost as soon as begun, and hurrying forward with the cavalry, leaving all the infantry to Meade who had overtaken him at Jettersville, he hung upon the flank of the rebel column. Near Sailor's Creek, six miles east of High Bridge, he dashed in upon Lee, severing his marching column and seizing 400 wagons, 16 guns, and many prisoners. By repeatedly charging the rebel train guard with terrible earnestness, he succeeded in holding it till Wright with the Sixth corps, now hastening forward, arrived upon the field. After a vigorous combat, during which the Sixth corps attacked in front and the cavalry in rear, Sheridan compelled the enemy to surrender at discretion. It was found that three divisions of the rebel army under Ewell had laid down their arms. While this action was in progress, Humphreys, pushing farther to the north, struck another column of rebels and captured 200 wagons, many guns, prisoners and flags. At the same time Grant threw Ord forward in the direction of Farmville. His leading brigade under General Read, by marching rapidly succeeded in throwing itself in front of Lee's advance guard, near that place, and by heroic resolution checked the rebels till Ord with the rest of his army arrived. During the night Lee fled again, recrossing the Appomattox, and pushing towards the west, but with the faintest streak of light the pursuing army hurried forward with unflagging energy.

Lee's force was now reduced to less than half its original number. The divisions of Mahone and Field about 10,000 strong were all of that once splendid organization now in a fit condition for marching or fighting; but they had been sorely tried in covering the rear and forcing the disordered stragglers forward in their weary flight. Early on the 7th, Barlow's division, leading Humphreys' corps, pressed forward to High Bridge in time to capture eighteen guns and to save the bridge from destruction. Humphreys continued the pursuit by two roads, sending Miles upon one and Barlow upon the other. The former soon came up with Mahone, strongly entrenched five miles north of Farmville, and attacked him with great vigor but was severely repulsed, losing nearly six hundred men. But this was only a temporary gleam of victory for the rebels. Meade hurrying the Army of the Potomac onward in pursuit allowed the rebel host no place of rest. On the 8th, Sheridan spurred his jaded horses forward by the road through Prospect to Appomattox Station, capturing many prisoners, four trains containing supplies for the rebel army, and twenty-five pieces of artillery, and driving Lee's advanced guard back towards Appomattox Court House. On the morning of the 9th he planted his forces squarely across Lee's road, and having already seized the supplies intended for his staggering and disheartened enemy, prepared to hurl his irresistible horsemen once more headlong into battle.

But Lee, failing to realize the desperate strait into which he had fallen, ordered Gordon to attack the yet dismounted horsemen and drive them from the road. The advance was made with the vigor of despair, and resulted in driving the cavalry; but it was too late, for Ord and Griffin, with 20,000 infantry, stood at their backs. Perceiving that to struggle longer could result in nothing but the slaughter of his half-famished soldiers, Lee decided to surrender. His army was reduced to less than 10,000 effective men; his artillery had been captured, his trains destroyed, his ammunition exhausted, his depots and supplies were burnt, and worse than all, 80,000 victorious troops were bearing down upon him, under the supreme command of his relentless adversary. Withal, that adversary had offered him, two days before, the most generous terms of capitulation, and under the present circumstances there was no alternative left him but to accept such as could now be obtained. Mounting his horse, he rode to the rear for the purpose of conferring with General Grant, leaving Longstreet in charge of the little band now confronting Sheridan. During the hurry of the pursuit, Grant became convinced that the condition of the rebel was entirely hopeless, and accordingly, on arriving at Farmville, on the 7th of April, he had written, and sent by flag of truce to General Lee, the following humane and characteristic note :

" GENERAL,—The result of the last week must convince you of the hopelessness of further resistance on the part of the Army of Northern Virginia in this struggle. I feel that it is so, and regard it as my duty to shift from myself the responsibility of any further effusion of blood, by asking of you the surrender of that portion of the Confederate States army known as the Army of Northern Virginia."

To which Lee replied at once, but with his accustomed caution :

" GENERAL,—I have received your note of this date. Though not entertaining the opinion you express on the hopelessness of further resistance on the part of the Army of Northern Virginia, I reciprocate your desire to avoid useless effusion of blood, and therefore, before considering your proposition, ask the terms you will offer on condition of its surrender."

This letter did not reach the Lieutenant-General till the morning of the 8th, just as he was setting out from Farmville to hurry forward the pursuit, but he answered immediately :

" GENERAL,—Your note of last evening, in reply to mine of same date, asking the conditions on which I will accept the surrender of the Army of Northern Virginia, is just received. In reply I would say, that *Peace* being my great desire, there is but one condition I would insist upon, namely : that the men and officers surrendered shall be disqualified for taking up arms again against the Government of the United States until properly exchanged. I will meet you, or will designate officers to meet any officers you may name for the same purpose, at any point agreeable to you, for the purpose of arranging definitely the terms upon which the surrender of the Army of Northern Virginia will be received."

This communication reached Lee late in the afternoon, while hurrying his army forward in its weary flight to save it from entire destruction ; and although sorely pressed, he replied the same evening in the following disingenuous and diplomatic terms:

"GENERAL,—I received, at a late hour, your note of to-day. In mine of yesterday I did not intend to propose the surrender of the Army of Northern Virginia, but to ask the terms of your proposition. To be frank, I do not think the emergency arisen to call for the surrender of this army; but as the restoration of peace should be the sole object of all, I desired to know whether your proposal would lead to that end. I cannot, therefore, meet you with a view to surrender the Army of Northern Virginia, but as far as your proposals may affect the Confederate States forces under my command and tend to the restoration of peace, I should be pleased to meet you at ten o'clock A. M. to-morrow, on the old stage-road to Richmond, between the picket-lines of the two armies."

General Grant was not for a moment deceived by the confident tone of this letter nor misled by the anxiety of its writer to treat for peace. The letter reached him at midnight, but knowing that he could lose nothing by letting the negotiation take its natural course, he did not reply till the next morning after the army had been put in motion towards Appomattox Court House. His answer, dated April 9th, was as follows:

"GENERAL,—Your note of yesterday is received. I have no authority to treat on the subject of peace; the meeting proposed for ten o'clock A. M. to-day could lead to no good. I will state, however, General, that I am equally anxious for peace with yourself, and the whole North entertains the same feeling. The terms upon which peace can be had are well understood. By the South laying down their arms they will hasten that most desirable event, save thousands of human lives and hundreds of millions of property not yet destroyed. Seriously hoping that all our difficulties may be settled without the loss of another life, I subscribe myself," &c.

Lee had by this time discovered that an emergency * had

---

* There can be no doubt in history that General Lee, in taking his army away from Richmond and Petersburg, had decided, in his own mind, upon the hopelessness of the war, and had predetermined its surrender. The most striking proof of this is, that in his retreat there was no order published against straggling—a thing unprecedented in all deliberate and strategic retreats—and nothing whatever done to maintain discipline. The men were

arisen to call for the surrender of his army, and receiving General Grant's letter at the outposts, he replied at once:

"GENERAL,—I received your note of this morning, on the picket-line, whither I had come to meet you and ascertain definitely what terms were embraced in your proposal of yesterday with reference to the surrender of this army. I now ask an interview in accordance with the offer contained in your letter of yesterday for that purpose."

General Grant was in the meantime pushing on towards the head of the army, when this clear and unequivocal demand for a meeting, overtook him; staying his horse for a few minutes, he wrote as follows:

"GENERAL,—Your note of this date is but this moment (11.50) received. In consequence of my having passed from the Richmond and Lynchburg to the Farmville and Lynchburg Road, I am, at this writing, about four miles west of Walter's Church, and will push forward to the front for the purpose of meeting you. Notice sent to me on this road, where you wish the interview to take place, will meet me."

Hurrying on to Appomattox Court House he stayed the threatened onset of Sheridan and Ord, and sent word to Meade to restrain his army during the negotiations. The

not animated by the style of general orders usual on such occasions. They straggled and deserted almost at will. An idea ran through the Virginia troops that with the abandonment of Richmond the war was hopeless, and that they would be justified in refusing to fight outside the limits of their State. Nothing was done to check the well-known circulation of this notion in the army. The Virginia troops dropped off to their homes at almost every mile of the route. We have seen that Pickett was left with only a handful of men. Some of the brigade commanders had not hesitated to advise their soldiers that the war was virtually over, and that they had better go home and "make crops."

But there are other proofs, besides the omission of the measures against straggling usual on retreats, that General Lee had foreseen a surrender of his army. He carried off from Petersburg and Richmond all the transportation of his army, sufficient, perhaps, for one hundred thousand men, certainly largely in excess of the actual needs of the retreat. The excessive number of Virginia troops who were permitted to drop out of the ranks and return to their homes, shows very well that there was no firm purpose to carry the war out of the limits of the State. Prisoners taken on the retreat invariably reported that the army was soon to be halted for a surrender; and General Custis Lee, when captured, is alleged to have made the same revelation of his father's designs.—"Southern History of the War," pp. 507-8.

meeting between General Grant and General Lee took place
at the house of Mr. Wilmer McLean, in the village of Appomattox Court House. The Chieftains were attended by the
members of their staffs, and proceeded, after polite greet-
ings, at once to the business which had brought them together,
and by half-past three o'clock the agreement for surrender was
perfected. The deportment of the Lieutenant-General is described by Pollard, the rebel historian, in the following words :

" It is to be fairly and cheerfully admitted that General Grant's conduct, with respect to all the circumstances of the surrender, exhibited
some extraordinary traits of magnanimity. He had not dramatized
the affair. He had conducted it with as much simplicity as possible,
avoided ' sensation,' and spared everything that might wound the feelings or imply the humiliation of a vanquished foe. Such conduct was
noble. Before the surrender, General Grant had expressed to his own
officers his intention not to require the same formalities as are required
in a surrender between the forces of two foreign nations or belligerent
powers, and to exact no conditions for the mere purpose of humiliation."

The conduct of the entire army was governed by the same
high sense of honor and propriety. No rebel soldier or officer was harshly addressed or unkindly treated, but everything was done that generous men could do to alleviate their
sufferings and supply their wants. When the surrender was
definitely announced the different divisions and brigades
throughout the victorious host rent the air with deafening
cheers ; men and officers went wild with delight. The war
was now ended ! The citizen soldiery, whose constancy and
courage had so long maintained the integrity of the Republic
were finally blessed with a triumph such as few armies have
ever gained. That night they dreamed of home and friends,
or around their camp fires, with hearts too full for sleep, talked
of the bright future which now seemed assured for their
country and themselves.

The terms of surrender as fixed by General Grant are set
forth in the following letter, dated April 9th, and addressed
to General Lee :

" GENERAL,—In accordance with the substance of my letter to you
of the 8th instant, I propose to receive the surrender of the Army of

Northern Virginia on the following terms, to wit: Rolls of all officers and men to be made in duplicate, one copy to be given to an officer to be designated by me, the other to be retained by such officer or officers as you may designate. The officers to give their individual paroles not to take up arms against the Government of the United States until properly exchanged, and each company or regimental commander to sign a like parole for the men of their commands. The arms, artillery, and public property to be parked and stacked, and turned over to the officers appointed by me to receive them. This will not embrace the side-arms of the officers, nor the private horses, or baggage. This done, each officer and man will be allowed to return to his home, not to be disturbed by United States authority so long as they observe their paroles and the laws in force where they may reside."

General Lee at once accepted these terms, and General Grant appointed Generals Griffin and MacKenzie to remain with their commands at Appomattox Court House for the purpose of carrying them into effect, while the rest of the army returned to Burkesville Junction, where they could receive supplies by rail.

General Grant did not yet regard his labor as finished, though Lee's surrender was the signal for the surrender of all the other armed forces of the rebellion, and as soon as the news could be spread, put an end to hostilities throughout the land.

Johnston surrendered to Sherman on the 25th of April, on the same terms that had been accorded to Lee; Cobb surrendered to Wilson at Macon on the 20th of April; Dick Taylor, at Citronville, Ala., surrendered to Canby on the 4th of May; but Kirby Smith, commanding the trans-Mississippi Department, seemed defiant till he heard of Davis' capture, and the movement of a heavy army to his Department under Sheridan, when he left his army to disband itself; Buckner, with the small force which retained its organization, surrendered on the 26th of May.

The movement of Sheridan with a large and well-appointed army to the Mexican frontier, had a deeper significance, however, than could be attached to any movement against the remnant of rebel power which might show itself in Texas. General Grant had long looked upon the French invasion of

Mexico, and the forced establishment of the Mexican Empire under Maximilian, as acts of open hostility against the United States, by the avowed allies of the slave-holders' rebellion, and therefore regarded the French army, then occupying that unfortunate country, as the next objective against which the Government should direct its forces. It is due to the Lieutenant-General to add that the avowal of this well known opinion on his part, did more to bring about a peaceable solution of the Mexican question than all the arguments of the Secretary of State, supported by the entire strength of the Mexican people.

As soon as the insurgent forces had been paroled and sent to their houses, Grant collected the different armies at convenient places, and, under the instructions of the Secretary of War, disbanded them with all possible despatch—and that mighty host of citizen soldiery, which, under his leadership, had been taught every secret of the military art, now returned to the pursuits of peace, becoming at once the most quiet, orderly, law-abiding, and respectable members of society. When European nations can thus disband their huge standing armies, and depend for the safety of Government upon the virtue, patriotism, and intelligence, of their people, a happy epoch will have dawned upon the world.

As a more substantial reward for his extraordinary services than collegiate degrees and popular ovations, which were bestowed upon him in profusion, Grant was promoted to the full grade of General on the 25th of July, 1866.

CHAPTER XXXVI.

ON the 12th of August, 1867, General Grant was appointed
Secretary of War *ad interim*. This being the first civil office
he ever held, it is interesting to inquire into the manner in
which he discharged its duties.

Throughout the fifteen months that had intervened since
the surrender of the Confederate forces, he had been desirous
of seeing a reconstruction of the Union on a just, liberal and
safe basis. He had not been required to devise or propose a
plan of reconstruction, that task being confided to the Legislative and Executive Departments. As head of the army,
he had stood ready to co-operate in carrying out any plan
which they might agree upon.

When Congress presented to the States, for their ratification, the Constitutional Amendment, commonly known as
Article XIV., he saw that it opened a way through which
the South might, at an early day, emerge from its anomalous
and irksome position, and resume the exclusive control of its

affairs. Acting upon the promptings of unwise counsels, the Southern States repudiated this magnanimous plan by rejecting the amendment; and thereupon, Congress, after mature consideration, passed the reconstruction acts of March, 1867.

These acts imposed upon Grant as Commander-in-Chief many weighty and delicate duties. The five military commanders of the several districts provided for by these acts, were selected by the joint advice of the President, the Secretary of War and the General-in-Chief. The selection was deemed eminently wise, and the assignment to the respective districts highly judicious. In his original instructions to the district commanders, and in his subsequent correspondence with them, Grant, while impressing them with the idea that the letter and spirit of the law were to be the guide of their conduct, counseled moderation and forbearance towards the people of the South. From the time of the surrender down through the entire period under consideration, his official intercourse with the Southern population of all classes was that of an urbane magistrate rather than a soldier clothed with supreme powers; and no man below the Potomac and the Ohio can justly say that he has ever felt the undue pressure of his mailed hand.

General Grant had not sought the office of Secretary of War *ad interim*, and he took the post with great reluctance. He did not recognize the necessity of a change in the Department at that juncture, having, to use his own language in his letter to Mr. Stanton, full confidence in "the zeal, patriotism, firmness and ability" wherewith that gentleman had discharged its duties. He had privately remonstrated with the President against the change, and he finally lodged with him an earnest written protest against it.

He feared that the suspension of Mr. Stanton, at that critical stage in the reconstruction measures, would operate injuriously in the South, encouraging opposition to a plan of restoration, which, in its essential features, he deemed inevitable, inspiring hopes that it could be broken down, inflaming the smouldering embers of rebellion, and disheartening those

Southern citizens who were laboring in good faith to carry it into effect. He regarded the suspension as inopportune so soon after the adjournment of the Senate, when no new reasons to justify it had since arisen. "It is," said Grant in his protest, "but a short time since the Senate was in session, and why not then have asked for his removal if it was desired?" He deprecated it because it would widen the existing breach between the President and Congress, at a period when it was especially important that all branches of the Government should harmoniously co-operate in the delicate work of restoring the Union.

General Grant was averse to taking the position himself because it would throw upon him the burdens of two important offices, when he was already heavily laden with the cares of one of them; and he felt that every thing he could do in aid of the work of reconstruction, he could as well perform in his sole capacity of General-in-Chief. But the President thrust the office upon him, and Grant has since avowed, that inasmuch as the suspension of Stanton was a foregone conclusion, he took the place rather than that it should fall into the hands of some supple or unpatriotic person. If Grant's motives in accepting it did not comport with the President's intentions in conferring it, this is not discreditable to Grant, however it may affect the President. If, as the sequel proves, Mr. Johnson had sinister ends in view in these proceedings, and hoped ultimately to mould Grant to his purposes, or in some way use him in attaining those ends, his failure only reflects the more honor upon Grant, while it leaves Johnson in the unenviable predicament of a baffled seducer, who had the will but lacked the honor to accomplish his evil designs.

Grant held the post of War Secretary five months, performing at the same time the duties of General-in-Chief. He took the office at a period of great embarrassment. The difficulties that beset his administration from the opening to the close, were constant and harassing. Sharp collisions between the President and Congress, which had been increasing

in asperity for more than a twelve-month, had kindled a spirit
of inflamed hostility to the Federal Government in the five
military districts, which, in many localities, had risen almost
to the height of insurrection, in some had broken out in
actual violence, while in New Orleans there had been a pro-
fuse shedding of blood. Hostility on the part of the President towards three of the district commanders, serious when
Grant took the office, increased in intensity till Johnson
finally dismissed them from their posts.

Five days after Grant entered the Department, General
Sheridan, who had managed his turbulent district with marvelous skill, was, against Grant's protest, removed from
command, throwing the district into confusion, and heaping
unexpected troubles upon the shoulders of the General-in-
Chief. As this protest exhibits a warmth of sentiment not
usually attributable to its author, we for that reason, as well
as because of the important character of the document, copy
its main paragraphs. It is addressed to the President, and
bears date August 1, 1867. After objecting to the suspension of Mr. Stanton, General Grant goes on to say :

" On the subject of the removal of the very able commander of the
fifth military district, let me ask you to consider the effect it would
have upon the public. He is universally and deservedly beloved by
the people who sustained this Government through its trials, and
feared by those who would still be enemies of the Government. It
fell to the lot of but few men to do as much against an armed enemy
as General Sheridan did during the rebellion, and it is within the scope
of the ability of but few in this or other country to do what he has.
His civil administration has given equal satisfaction. He has had difficulties to contend with which no other district commander has encountered. Almost if not quite from the day he was appointed district
commander to the present time, the press has given out that he was to
be removed; that the administration was dissatisfied with him, etc.
This has emboldened the opponents to the laws of Congress within his
command to oppose him in every way in their power, and has rendered
necessary measures which otherwise might never have been necessary.
In conclusion, allow me to say, as a friend desiring peace and quiet, the
welfare of the whole country, North and South, that it is in my opinion
more than the loyal people of this country (I mean those who supported

the Government during the great rebellion) will quietly sumbit to, to see the very man of all others whom they have expressed confidence in removed."

Regardless of these protestations, Johnson issued the order for the removal of Sheridan on the 17th of August. On the same day, before the order was past recall, Grant, in his double capacity of General and Secretary, addressed an eloquent letter to the President, hoping to stay his hand, assuring him that there were "military reasons, pecuniary reasons, and above all, patriotic reasons, why this should not be insisted upon;" and reminding him, that "General Sheridan had performed his civil duties faithfully and intelligently;" and warning him that "his removal will only be regarded as an effort to defeat the laws of Congress. It will be interpreted by the unreconstructed element in the South, those who did all they could to break up this Government by arms, and now wish to be the only element consulted as to the method of restoring order, as a triumph. It will embolden them to renewed opposition to the will of the loyal masses, believing that they have the Executive with them." But all was in vain. The hero of Winchester was sacrificed. Ten days afterwards, General Sickles, who had so wisely conducted affairs in the Second District, composed of the Carolinas, as to win the confidence of the great majority of all classes of their population, was also removed against the earnest wishes of Grant, thus increasing his anxieties and cares, and causing unusual disquietude in that important district. Ultimately General Pope, who had shown rare judgment in managing the great department of which Georgia was a leading member, was removed, disarranging his well matured plans for hastening forward reconstruction in that State and in Alabama.

For the removal of these three distinguished commanders, scarcely a specious pretext was offered by the President. Certainly no solid reason was ever given for dealing such wanton blows over the head of Grant at his trustworthy subordinates. Under the circumstances in which he was then placed, the South trembling on the verge of anarchy, it was hardly less embarrassing to deprive him of the sagacious judgment and ripe experience of these three officers than it would have been to have taken Sherman and McPherson from him at Vicksburg, and Meade, Sedgwick and Hancock at the Wilderness, and Sheridan at Five Forks. But he bore these more than insults with his proverbial equanimity, and zealously co-operated with the successors of his tried Generals in prosecuting the work of restoring the Union.

When General Grant entered the War Office, the reconstruction acts as they had been modified at the session of Congress in July, were just going into active operation in all the districts. The registration of votes, the calling of State conventions to frame constitutions and other preliminary steps towards restoring the South to its former relation to the Union, were being initiated. This daily demanded from him as Secretary of War and General-in-Chief, expositions and applications of unprecedented and not always lucid statutes, necessitating the solution of complicated problems which involved conflicts of jurisdiction between the military and the magistracy, collisions between antagonistic and rival classes of the people, the removal from office of governors, judges, and custodians of public money, and the appointment of incumbents to supply the vacancies, and, indeed, all conceivable questions of right and of policy that could arise in ten inchoate States, smarting under humiliation, whelmed in poverty, two-thirds of whose populace were inflamed with passion and prone to disorder, while the other third, though peacefully disposed, was steeped in ignorance and could exert but little influence upon public affairs. To evoke order, contentment and prosperity out of this civil, social and financial chaos, and to construct a solid political edifice out of the *debris* of the shattered Confederacy was the task committed to Grant and his subordinate commanders.

The execution of this task would have been to the last degree difficult, even if Grant had been sustained by the harmonious co-operation of the great branches of the Government, and encouraged by the united loyal sentiment of the country. But instead of this, Congress and the President were at open war, and each was jealously watching him. A large part of the Republican press was sharply criticising him for having accepted the War Department, while the Democratic journals were either insidiously flattering him in the hope of drawing him into the quarrel between the Executive and Congress, or coldly waiting to see whether he would prove to be a "radical" or a "copperhead," and not seeming to care which he might turn out to be. Mr. Johnson, too, aided by wily members of his Cabinet, was on the alert to entangle him in the toils so that he might, through him, carry out the sinister purposes which had inspired the suspension of Stanton and his appointment.

Thus sorely tried, it would have been natural to expect that his administration would, at the least, have been marred by numerous and serious blunders; nor would it have been surprising if he had made utter shipwreck of his department and of his own fame. But the dispassionate pen of history will record that in the face of these severe provocations, and in spite of these harassing difficulties, he bore himself with exemplary caution, patience and urbanity, and performed his high duties with extraordinary ability, vigor and success. Suffice it to say, that during these five eventful months, he *filled* both his offices up to the measure of the expectations of his most sanguine friends.

The correspondence and documents emanating from the War Department while under General Grant's charge, many of them of great importance and marked ability, would alone fill volumes. It was one of the busiest periods of the last seven years of his life. In tracing his course while in the War Office, we must necessarily refrain from going into details, and be content with viewing the subject in its general aspects. Nor need we do otherwise; for his words and deeds while officiating in this capacity are familiar to his countrymen. Turning our attention from the higher duties we have been contemplating, and scanning the minor measures

25

that distinguished his administration, we find him instituting searching and salutary reforms in all branches of the Department.

In his annual report as Secretary *ad interim*, he says: " Retrenchment was the first subject to attract my attention." To the solid value of his services in this particular, as well as to the useful reforms he introduced during his brief term of office, the President, no partial witness, bears ample testimony. Mr. Johnson, in his message to the Senate, giving reasons for the suspension of Mr. Stanton, says, speaking of Grant: " Salutary reforms have been introduced by the Secretary *ad interim*, and great reductions of expenses have been affected under his administration of the War Department, to the saving of millions to the Treasury."

By his direction while Secretary of War *ad interim*, the duties of the Bureaus of Rebel Archives and of exchange of prisoners, were transferred to the Adjutant-General's Office, thus dispensing with the services of a great number of officers and clerks. He reduced the number of agents and subordinates in the Freedmen's Bureau and largely curtailed its expenses; closed useless hospitals and dispensaries; discontinued a long list of superfluous mustering and disbursing offices, discharging their numerous incumbents and attendants, and thus stopping the needless expenditure of considerable sums. He sold surplus animals, ambulances, wagons, etc., to the amount of $33,535; and superfluous and useless stores and war material of various kinds, amounting to $268,000; and one thousand temporary buildings used by quartermasters, for the sum of $112,000. He ordered the chief quartermasters throughout the country to make every practicable reduction in the number of employes on duty under their direction.

The result was, that in a short time the monthly expenses of that Department, arising from the hire of civilians, had been reduced by $407,065, making an annual saving in this item alone of nearly $5,000,000. Besides the class of employes just mentioned, the numbers of mechanics, laborers, and others, in various branches of the service, were so reduced that the monthly expenditures in this particular were curtailed full $100,000, making an annual saving of more than $1,200,000. He caused many unnecessary commissaries of volunteers to be mustered out, reduced the number of paymasters, and greatly curtailed the cost of transport for men and munitions of war in the Western States and territories where Indian hostilities were then prevailing. He recommended the sale of four small arsenals and two or three armories, they, in his opinion, not being needed for the service. He stopped the manufacture of large guns, then going on at great expense, until their efficiency could be more thoroughly tested. He warmly seconded all the suggestions of the heads of Bureaus which aimed to reduce the expenditures of their several branches of the service, and secure greater efficiency and a more rigid accountability among their subordinates and agents. In a word, he instituted or recommended economy and retrenchment, the reformation of abuses, and measures tending to produce greater vigor, closer scrutiny, and a keener sense of responsibility in the Adjutant General's office, the Freedmen's Bureau, the Inspector General's office, the Quartermaster's, Commissary, Pay, Engineer and Ordnance Bureaus, and in the Military Academy at West Point.

. In his annual report he bestows commendation upon his associates and subordinates with the same liberal and generous hand that characterized his reports of army operations during the continuance of hostilities. Speaking of the commanders in the Southern States, he says : "I am pleased to say, that the commanders of the five military districts have executed their difficult trusts faithfully, and without bias from any judgment of their own as to the merit or demerit of the law they were executing." Like everything from his pen, this report is plain and concise, wisely selecting and appropriately arranging its materials, and exhibiting much valuable information in a style at once compact and luminous.

CHAPTER XXXVII.

AFTER the assembling of Congress, the President, on the 12th of December, 1867, sent to the Senate a message containing his reasons for the suspension of Mr. Stanton. This was an admission that the suspension was effected under the Tenure of Office Act. Otherwise, why submit this message to the Senate? It afterwards transpired that on the 14th of August the President addressed an official communication to the Secretary of the Treasury, informing him that he had, by virtue of this act, suspended Mr. Stanton and appointed General Grant in his place. Mr. Johnson further recognized its binding force by making removals and appointments in accordance with its provisions; and his Cabinet acted under it by so changing the forms of commissions of officers as to meet its requirements.

In this act, therefore, Johnson stood committed when he entered upon his controversy with Grant in January; and in any inquiry into the merits of that controversy, he cannot be allowed to change his ground. In regard to this act, Grant's position has always been, that like all other laws imposing duties upon him, he must obey it till some competent tribunal declares it invalid and releases him from his obligations. *

The Senate, on the 14th of January, after considering the reasons of the President for the suspension of Stanton, refused to concur therein, and thereupon immediately notified Johnson, Stanton and Grant of their decision. By the terms of the law, Grant's duties as Secretary *ad interim* then instantly ceased, and the functions of the office devolved upon Stanton; and any person thereafter attempting to prevent his exercise of them incurred the penalties of fine and imprisonment imposed by the law.

Subsequent events have proved that Johnson, in the suspension of Stanton, intended to keep him out of the War Office permanently, in spite of the law and of the Senate, and to obtain the control of the Department for ulterior objects. His purpose was fixed. His mode of accomplishing it was sinister. He sought his ends by hypocrisy and double-dealing. Pretending to yield to the requirements of the act, he practically disregarded it. Professing to respect the authority of the Senate, he meant to defy it.

Though one of the agencies through which he hoped to attain his ends was the temporary installment of Grant in Stanton's place, he never dreamed, confident and presuming as he is, that he could secure his aid in an illegal seizure of the Department. He only aimed to keep him there till his plans were matured for thrusting some pliant tool into the office. So long as Grant remained, one point was gained— Stanton was out. If, under some plausible pretext, he could induce him to stay after the Senate had acted adversely, he could gain the next point by carrying on his contest with the Senate under the shadow of his popular and powerful name.

Up to this stage of the proceedings, Grant, wholly absorbed in his multifarious duties, had not detected his devious designs. Grant probably believed the Senate would regard

the Tenure Act as valid. Whether they would refuse to concur in the reasons for Stanton's suspension was not so certain.
On Thursday, the 9th of January, Grant had an interview
on this general subject with Johnson. He had not then
critically examined this act; for, being constantly engaged
in studying laws with whose execution he was specially
charged, he had no leisure to examine those with whose execution he had nothing to do. So in this interview he did not
combat but rather assented to the President's interpretation,
to the effect that he might legally retain the War Office,
even if the Senate should fail to concur in the reasons for
Stanton's suspension, and thus send him to the courts for
redress; but he told the President he would examine the law
and inform him if he changed his views.

On Saturday, the 11th of January, having in the meantime carefully read the law, he again met Johnson, and then
distinctly informed him that, according to its provisions, if
the Senate refused to concur in the suspension, Stanton's right
to resume the office was fixed, and his own powers ceased;
and in the event of the Senate's so deciding, he should
retire. What did Johnson do? Grant had fulfilled his
promise by notifying him of his views and intentions. Johnson then had the matter in his own hands. If he wished for
a conspirator in the War Department, who would defy the
Senate, resist the law, and drive Stanton to the courts, he
could have removed Grant and installed a servitor in his
place. But, as is the wont of a man offensively self-confident
and prone to contention, instead of accepting the circumstances, he undertook to combat Grant's construction of the
law, even generously offering, in case he was mistaken, to go
to jail in Grant's stead if he would only set the law at defi-
ance! After much argument by the President in favor of
his interpretation of the act, they separated with some vague
idea of meeting again on Monday.

Mr. Johnson subsequently asserted, that on this occasion,
Grant promised that he would either resign the War Office
or remain and resist the reinstatement of Stanton. This

statement Grant explicitly, and under his own hand, denied. In his letter to Johnson, of January 28th, he says: "I made no such promise." And here the question of veracity between them arises.

On such an issue the unprejudiced public will take, and have taken, but one side. According to the experience of hundreds of his fellow-citizens, Johnson is a frequent violator of his plighted word. He calls these verbal infelicities "misunderstandings." Using plainer language, the people call them falsehoods. The probabilities of the case are all in favor of Grant and against Johnson. Grant has ever been scrupulously obedient to law. He is the soul of honor, and never forfeits his word. He had protested earnestly against the suspension of Stanton, and had shown extreme reluctance to take the War Department. Is it to be credited for a moment that he would deliberately violate the Tenure Act, incur its penalties, defy the Senate, become the subject of a wrangle in the courts, and cover himself with disgrace, solely to keep Stanton out of an office which belonged to him, and retain possession of a place which he was reluctant to hold?

To the point in controversy the President cited witnesses; not however be it noted, as to what was said at the interview between him and Grant on Saturday, when, as Johnson had asserted, this promise was made; but, as to certain alleged conversations at a Cabinet meeting on the following Tuesday, in regard to what had been said by Grant on Saturday—a very important distinction in respect to the subject-matter inquired into; while the testimony (it may be remarked in passing,) is of a species which courts of Justice and the general experience of mankind, have always viewed with great distrust and suspicion, so liable are such conversations to be misunderstood or misrecollected, or misinterpreted, or misrepresented.

The place where these conversations of Tuesday occurred, was in a Cabinet council at the Executive Mansion. Why was Grant invited thither? He was not a member of the Cabinet as the President well knew, for he had informed him that, in consequence of the proceedings of the Senate on Monday, he had withdrawn from the War Department. Was he invited into the presence of Johnson and his counsellors and allies, that they might "entangle him in his talk?" And these counsellors and allies — we will not call them co-conspirators—are the witnesses whom he summoned to sustain his version of what was said by Grant at this pre-arranged Cabinet council.

When these witnesses were called to testify, the President's case was involved in this dilemma. Without consultation with the more moderate members of the Cabinet, Johnson had ostentatiously proclaimed to the country, through certain journals, not only this alleged promise of Grant, but also his version of the conversations in the Cabinet meeting, insisting that the members of the Cabinet concurred with him in regard to what had taken place in their presence; and these statements were made in language very bitter and offensive towards Grant. When Grant, by his denial, raised the issue of veracity, Johnson imperiously demanded the support of his Cabinet, whom he had already committed to his side of the controversy. Their position was embarrassing; but hesitation was ruin. For his counsellors to have gone back on him then, would have provoked his ire and ruptured his Cabinet; and the House of Representatives which they had with much difficulty kept at bay for many months, would have entered the breach with articles of impeachment against the President. Therefore, to save their Chief, upon whom their official existence depended, and who would have sacrificed them on the instant had they faltered, it behoved them to sustain him with the best endorsement which their slender materials afforded.

And what does their testimony, given under these circumstances, amount to? Messrs. Welles, Randall and McCulloch merely echo the President's statements, to which he had previously committed himself and them before the country. By refraining from all details of the conversations of Tuesday, and by merely giving the President "an endorsement in blank," they consign themselves to that class which the courts call " willing witnesses," whose testimony is contemptuously dismissed as not entitled to the weight of a feather.

Mr. Browning, while evidently anxious to support the President, goes into detail; and he effectually disposes of the case on the only material issue involved. General Grant, in his letter to the President of January 28th, had denied giving a promise to resign if he concluded not to resist the reinstatement of Mr. Stanton. Mr. Browning, in reciting what Grant said at the Cabinet meeting on Tuesday, says, Grant on that occasion stated, that on examining the Tenure Act " he had come to the conclusion that if the Senate should refuse to concur in the suspension, Mr. Stanton would thereby be reinstated, and that he, Grant, could not continue thereafter to act as Secretary of War *ad interim* without subjecting himself to fine and imprisonment, and that he came over on Saturday to inform the President of this change in his views, and *did so inform him*." This contradicts the President's assertions, verifies the statements of Grant, and settles the question of veracity in his favor.

Mr. Seward does not essentially alter this view of the matter, though he, as also Mr. Browning, leaves it barely possible that Mr. Johnson may have inferred that the discussion of Saturday was postponed to a contemplated interview on Monday. But General Grant did not so understand it. He had done his errand; he had redeemed his pledge; he had notified the President of his change of views, and of his fixed intentions, and he retired from the interview, leaving the President to pursue his own course. If the latter cherished the hope that by a subsequent interview, he could bend his inflexible opponent to his wishes, and induce him to change his determination or postpone its execution, the unexpectedly prompt action of the Senate afforded him no opportunity to ply his arts in that direction. He was caught in the snare he had spread for another, and he emerged from the controversy a baffled conspirator.

Mr. Johnson has contended that his sole object in these

strange proceedings, was to test the constitutionality of the Tenure of Office Act. This is an afterthought, suggested by the exigencies of his impeachment. The inference from all the facts then existing and those which have subsequently transpired, is irresistible, that his purpose was to get and keep possession of the War Department. Assume, however, that his object was as he alleges. Has the President, any more than the humblest citizen, the right to violate a law in order thereby to test its constitutionality? While this would be reprehensible in a private individual, and subject him to pains and penalties, such conduct in the President would be a far higher crime, tending by its evil example upon inferior officials to whelm the country in anarchy. Like all his fellow-citizens, Mr. Johnson was bound to obey the laws, while as President he rested under far weightier obligations. He was the Chief Executive Magistrate of the Republic, whose sworn Constitutional duty it was to "take care that the laws be faithfully executed;" and upon no pretext, and for no ulterior objects, and in pursuance of no advice, and under no preconceived motives as to their validity, could he refuse to execute and obey any laws which imposed duties upon him.

But, concede that his object was to test the constitutionality of the Tenure Act. Why did he fix his eye exclusively and persistently upon the War Department for the purpose of trying this issue? With swarms of minor officers and retainers all over the land, ready to do his bidding, a score of cases involving this question could have been made up and the issue sent to the courts for a decision within a week after his wishes were made known. Why then aim at the War Office? His subsequent appointment of General Thomas to this post, and the events that attended and followed it, afford an answer to the question.

Mr. Johnson, for ulterior purposes, desired to get the absolute control of this Department. Through it perhaps he imagined he could suspend or supersede Grant as General-in-Chief, manage the army, defy the Senate, overawe the House, prostrate the Congressional plan of reconstruction, control the elections in the five military districts, bring to the Capital from the Southern States, Senators and Representatives who would, through his aid, either force their way into Congress, or by uniting with the minority of the two Houses, create a legislative body with which he could co-operate; and thus, by a startling display of power, he would make a bold stroke for his own election as President.

The ungenerous and unfair treatment which General Grant received from the President and his coadjutors during this controversy, would have aroused, in a mind less patriotic and more liable to be swayed by passion and revenge than his, intense bitterness towards his foes, which would have awaited its opportunity for inflicting upon them summary retribution. Such an opportunity soon occurred when the House of Representatives adopted articles of impeachment against Johnson, and the Senate entered upon his trial. But throughout these proceedings, Grant pursued the same wise course that had marked his conduct during the entire period of the collision between the President and Congress.

Prudently resolving to leave those upon whom the Constitution had devolved the responsibility of initiating and determining this complicated case, to discharge their several duties, he attended to the performance of the manifold trusts committed to his keeping as General-in-Chief. Continuing to enforce retrenchment and reform in all branches of the service, he devoted himself with untiring energy to the completion of the plan of reconstruction. The fruits of his labors in this field were early seen in the adoption of Constitutions, and the election of State Officers and members of both Houses of Congress, in a large majority of the ten Southern States, leaving it no longer doubtful that, under the vigorous and conciliatory policy and measures of Grant and his faithful coadjutors, all the lately rebellious States may be prepared to crown the work of restoration by participating, in common with the rest of the Union, in the next Presidential election.

On the 19th of May, 1868, a National Convention of soldiers and sailors met at Chicago, and nominated General Grant for the Presidency. It was composed of officers and men who had borne a part in the great contest for the preservation of the Republic. Numerous representatives were in attendance from all parts of the country, who greeted the name of Grant with intense enthusiasm. Two days afterwards, the National Convention, of the Republican party, also sitting in Chicago, presented him as a candidate for the Presidency. As in the previous Convention, so in this, he was nominated by acclamation, and amid the most hearty applause.

The presentation of Grant as the nominee of the soldiers and sailors, was natural and appropriate. In installing him as their Chief in the pending political campaign, his com-·panions in arms only renewed and revived a leadership which they had followed through the perils of the war, and which had conducted them to victory and the country to peace. His nomination by the Republican Convention, was only the recognition and ratification of an existing fact. He had previously been placed before the nation, as a candidate by numerous organizations, in various sections of the Union, composed of men of all parties. Though doubtless concurring in sentiment with the leading principles of the Republican party, he had never been a member of it, nor voted its ticket, and, so far as he was a politician at all, he was known as a War Democrat. Large numbers of the Soldiers' and Sailors' Convention were prominent Democrats, while many of the most conspicuous members of the Republican Convention had been distinguished as leaders in the Democratic party. They united with the Republicans in presenting the name of Grant to the country, not because they had ceased to be Democrats, but because they believed him to be the best and safest man with whom to entrust its destiny in the pending emergency, and to secure this end they naturally coalesced with the largest body of his supporters to carry out their common object.

His nomination at Chicago, by these two Conventions,

under these circumstances and surrounded and supported by
such adjuncts, did not require that he should vacate the position of political independence which he had always occupied;
and though Republicans will support him with fidelity and
enthusiasm, he will still be regarded as the candidate of
other organizations as well as theirs, and will be sustained
by a large and influential body of those who are distinct-
ively known as War Democrats, while the great mass of the
people, should he be elevated to Chief Magistracy in November next, will not entertain the slightest fear that the Union
and the Constitution will suffer detriment at his hands.

CHAPTER XXXVIII.

POPULAR MISCONCEPTION OF GRANT'S CHARACTER AND ABILITIES—
HIS PECULIARITIES AND VIRTUES—HIS PHYSICAL AND MENTAL
ENDURANCE—PERSONAL HABITS AND APPEARANCE—HIS LIBER-
ALITY—HIS STRICT REGARD FOR TRUTH—GRANT AS A SOLDIER—
HIS COURAGE AND RESOLUTION—AS AN ORGANIZER—COMPARISON
BETWEEN THE ORGANIZATION OF THE ARMIES OF THE WEST AND
EAST—CONFIDENCE IN THE PATRIOTISM AND INTELLIGENCE OF HIS
SOLDIERS AND IN THE ULTIMATE SUCCESS OF THE WAR—HIS
ESTIMATION OF CHARACTER IN THE SELECTION OF HIS SUBORDI-
NATES—HIS CHARACTER FOR GENERALSHIP AS JUDGED BY NAPO-
LEON'S AND MARSHALL MARMONT'S RULES.

IN following General Grant through the incidents of his eventful life, it has been impossible to dwell upon his personal peculiarities, or to delineate his qualities as a leader in that bold relief which may be necessary to illustrate the man as he is. Notwithstanding the long array of admirable performances that have marked his career, there is scarcely any character in history in reference to whose real merit so much doubt has existed. The reasons for this are somewhat complex, but are sufficiently indicated by a reference to the remarkable reticence of the man and his utter abhorrence of the arts of the demagogue in whatever shape. He has studiously avoided sounding the trumpet of his own fame, either in public or in private, and has been so persistently generous in awarding praise to others, that the world has really heard more of his subordinates than of himself. Then, too, in the very outset of his career as a soldier during the war of the rebellion, he was denounced before the country as being

intemperate as well as incompetent.* His brilliant and
entirely successful movement against Belmont, was studiously reported, even by those who knew better, as a disastrous failure; his splendid campaign of Fort Donelson in
mid-winter, resulting in the capture of an entire army and in
the infliction of the first staggering blow upon the rebellion,
was so marvelous and incomprehensible to the people at
large, but so persistently misrepresented, that many excellent
persons came to believe that Grant had retarded that victory

---

* The following letter, from Mr. F. L. Olmsted, will serve to show
the origin of such reports:

THE GENESIS OF A RUMOR.—*To the Editor of the Nation:* One day in
the spring of 1863, Mr. Frederick Knapp and myself were guests of
General Grant, at his head-quarters, on a steamboat lying at Milliken's
Bend, a few miles above Vicksburg. A curtain had been hung in such
a way as to give a certain degree of seclusion to the after-part of the
main cabin, and when we rose from dinner we were asked to sit with
the General behind the screen, where there was a writing table with a
pitcher and glasses. The General then told us that he had a few hours
before received unfavorable intelligence from General Sherman's expedition up the Sunflower. Inviting our enquiries, and replying to all
we thought it proper to make, with an unexpectedly generous freedom
and painstaking thoroughness of explanation, he was gradually led into
a comprehensive review of the existing conditions of his campaign,
which it was easy to see were of the very gravest character. We were
impressed as much by the remarkably methodical clearness of the narration as by the simple candor and ingenuousness with which it was
given to us who, the day before, had been strangers to him. He took
up several hypotheses and suggestions, and analyzed them in such a
way as to make prominent the uncertainties and uncontrollable elements which were involved in them, and I could not but think, so
musing and quietly reflective was his manner, and yet so exact and
well-arranged his expressions, that he was simply repeating a process
of "thinking it out," in order to assure himself that he fully comprehended and gave just weight to all the important elements of some
grand military problem, the solution of which he was about to undertake.

(The last attempt to attack Vicksburg on the north ended that day,
and a few hours after our interview the first step was taken looking
toward the approach from the south; but of this no hint was given us,
and we only heard of it the next morning.)

instead of having organized and achieved it by his own incisive judgment and indomitable courage. His arrest and
confinement at Fort Henry was looked upon as a legitimate
punishment for misbehavior. The bloody battle of Shiloh,
followed by Halleck's disgraceful siege at Corinth, convinced
the public that Grant must be entirely incompetent; and it
was not till after Vicksburg that the real truth began to be
suspected. First it was McClernand who had "furnished
him with brains;" then it was C. F. Smith who had led his
army to victory; then it was Halleck; and finally Sherman
and McPherson to whom all praise was due. It was not till

All at once he stopped short, and, with an expression of surprise if
not of distress, put his cigar away, rose, and moved his chair aside. A
moment before we could not have imagined that there was a woman
within many miles of us; but, turning my eyes, I saw one who had just
parted the screen, comely, well-dressed, and with the air and manner
of a gentlewoman. She had just arrived by a steamboat from Memphis, and came to present General Grant with a memorial or petition.
In a few words she made known her purpose, and offered to give in
detail certain facts, of which she stated that she was cognizant, bearing
upon her object. The General stood listening to her in an attitude of
the most deferential attention, his hand still upon his chair, which was
half in front of him as he had turned to face her, and slightly nodding
his head as an expression of assent at almost every sentence she
uttered. When she had completed her statement, he said, speaking
very low, and with an appearance of reluctance: "I shall be compelled to
consult my medical director, and to obtain a report from him before I can
meet your wishes. If agreeable to you, I will ask him to call upon you
to-morrow; shall I say at eleven o'clock?" The lady bowed and withdrew; the General took a long breath, resumed his cigar and his seat,
said that he was inclined to think her proposition a reasonable and
humane one, and then went on with the interrupted review.

A week or two after this, having gone up the river, Mr. Knapp met
this lady at a hotel, when, in the course of a conversation, she referred
with much sadness to the deplorable habits of General Grant, and the
hopelessness of success while our army was commanded by a man so
unfit to be charged with any grave responsibility. Mr. Knapp replied
that he had the best reason for stating that the reports to which she
referred were without foundation, and proceeded to give her certain
exact information of which he happened to be possessed, which, as far as
possible, refuted them. "Unfortunately," said the lady, "I have cer-

Vicksburg was followed by Chattanooga that the world came to look upon Grant as possessing any merits of his own. It is a safe rule to judge men by the results of a life-time, but an unsafe one, particularly in reference to military men, to judge from past reputation or isolated actions. In this day of skepticism there are but few people who believe entirely in ability, honor, vigor and manly virtue as the sure means of making life successful. And fewer still who are able to separate from their estimate of successful characters the idea that chance or fate may not have had as much to do with achievements of high distinction as real worth and ability. A very large number of intelligent persons will

tain knowledge that they are but too true." She then described her recent interview with General Grant, and it appeared that, from her point of view, the General was engaged in a carouse with one or two boon companions when she came unexpectedly upon him; that he rose to his feet with difficulty, could not stand without staggering, and was obliged to support himself with a chair; that he was evidently conscious that he was in an unfit condition to attend to business, and wanted to put her off till the next day; that his voice was thick, he spoke incoherently, and she was so much shocked that she was obliged to withdraw almost immediately. The next day, being ashamed to see her himself, he sent his doctor to find out what she wanted.

Mr. Knapp then told her that, having been one of the boon companions whom she had observed with the General on that occasion, and that having dined with him and been face to face with him for fully three hours, he not only knew that he was under the influence of no drink stronger than the unqualified mud of the Mississippi, but he could assure her that he had never seen a man who appeared to him more thoroughly sober and clear-headed than General Grant at the moment of her entrance.

Notwithstanding his assurances, the lady repeated that she could not doubt the evidence of her own senses, and I suppose that to this day Mr. Knapp and myself rank, equally with General Grant, in her mind as confirmed drunkards.

This experience is by no means a unique one, and the zealous devotion with which I have often heard both men and women undermining the character of others for temperance on equally slight grounds, has often led me to question if there are not vices in our society more destructive to sound judgment and honest courses than that of habitual overdrinking. Yours respectfully,   FRED. LAW OLMSTED.

26

doubtless be found to claim that no man is or can be exclusively the architect of his own fortunes, and that without the favoring circumstances of life, in the shape of that mysterious and indefinable agency compounded of time, place and opportunity, no amount of talents or energy or good management will secure true renown.

It is not our intention to discuss the doctrine of chances, nor to say which of the foregoing propositions affords the best rule by which to measure the deserts of public characters. There is doubtless some middle ground which is nearer the truth in most instances, but in war, if in no other human pursuit, success must be made the sole criterion of merit. To assume a different principle or to base opinions upon the idea that we may have formed of the mental parts or culture of a General, is to enter upon fallacious and uncertain ground.

" If we sometimes deceive ourselves," (says Marshall Marmont, in the " Spirit of Military Institutions,") "in judging by facts, we should deceive ourselves much more in directing ourselves solely by personal knowledge of individuals. Fortune may once or twice overwhelm with her favors, a man who is not worthy of them ; she may betray the finest combinations of genius, and humble a noble character ; but when the struggle is prolonged, when events are multiplied, the man of true talents infallibly conquers her favors; and if continual reverses occur, we may boldly conclude, that in spite of a superior mind and qualities, which have dazzled us, a lack of harmony and adaptation in these faculties, destroys their power." Before making an application of these principles to Grant's character as a General, let us consider him as a man.

His special peculiarities as a boy, his modesty, honor, and steady self-confidence, have been set forth at considerable length, and some estimate has been given of his characteristics as a soldier, at various epochs of his life ; but no full and ample description of the man and his habits has yet been ventured upon.

He is somewhat under the medium size, though his body is closely and powerfully built. His feet and hands are small and neatly shaped; his dress is plain, and exceedingly unostentatious; his eyes are large, deep, leonine and very strong, equally capable of blazing with a resolution that nothing can withstand, and of shining with the steady light of benevolence and amiability. His fibre is like that of steel wire, elastic, close-grained, and enduring; his temperament is admirably compounded of the sanguine, nervous and lymphatic, but the last is in such proportion as to tone down and hold in equilibrium the other two, perfecting both mental and physical organization. His capacity for labor surpasses comprehension; neither mental nor physical exertion seems to produce the least wear and tear in his case. He rides at a dashing speed hour after hour and day after day with the same ease with which he plans a battle or issues the instructions for a campaign. There is no noise or clash or clangor in the man; his voice is as quiet and orderly as a woman's, and his language judiciously and tastefully chosen. He was never heard to give utterance to a rude word or a vulgar jest; no oath or fierce fiery imprecation has ever escaped his lips. No thundering order, no unfeeling or undignified speech, and no thoughtless or ill-natured criticism ever fell from him. When angry, which is rarely the case, or at least, he rarely shows his anger, he speaks with well-ordered but subdued vehemence, displaying his passion by compressed lips and an earnest flash of the eye. But it must be said of him, that of all men he is the slowest to anger. He has been heard to say that even under the severest insult he never became indignant till a week after the offense has been given, and then only at himself for not having sooner discovered that he had been insulted or misused. This arises rather from an unconscious self-abnegation than from any incapacity for choler. It is precisely this quality which has made him so successful in the personal questions which have arisen between him and his subordinates. They have usually mistaken his slowness for dullness or a lack of spirit, and have discovered their mistake only after becoming rash and committing a fatal error. Grant is as unsuspicious and pure-hearted as a child, and as free from harmful intention; but he is stirred to the very depths of his nature by an act of inhumanity or brutality of any sort; while meanness or ingratitude or uncharitableness excites him to the display of the liveliest indignation. He is not slow in the exhibition of contempt or disgust for whatever is unmanly or unbecoming.

In issuing orders to his subordinates or in asking a service at the hands of a staff-officer, he is always scrupulously polite and respectful in manner; and orders or requests rather as he would ask a friend to oblige him personally, than as a military commander whose word is law. His consideration for those about him is admirably shown by the following incident: On the night after the battle of Mission Ridge, while returning from the front to his head-quarters at Chattanooga, he desired to know what had become of Sheridan's division, which had been reported at noon as engaged in building a bridge across the Chickamauga at Mission Mills, and although it was then after midnight, he requested one of his staff to obtain the desired information. The officer, after a long and tiresome ride, reported at head-quarters just at sunrise, and found the General not yet asleep. It seems that in returning to Chattanooga at about one o'clock, he found a full explanation of the day's operations, and instead of going to sleep he spent the rest of the night in thinking of the long and tedious ride he had required from his officer, all for no purpose, as he expressed it. Such solicitude for the comfort of others, it is needless to say, was rare even among the most humane of our Generals. Many of them would not have hesitated to save themselves even the slightest trouble at the expense of others; and not a few would have given themselves scarcely a moment's thought had an aid-de-camp been killed, much less if he had only gone on a long and difficult ride upon a wintry night.

Grant's personal habits and tastes are exceedingly simple; he despises the pomp and show of empty parade, and in his severe simplicity and manly pride he scorns all adventitious aids to popularity. He lives plainly himself and cannot tolerate ostentation or extravagance in those about him. His mess was never luxuriously, though always bountifully, furnished with army rations, and such supplies as could be transported readily and easily in the limited number of wagons that he permitted to follow his head-quarters. His appetites are all under perfect control. He is very abstemious, and during his entire Western campaign the officers of his staff were forbidden to bring wines or liquors into camp. He has been represented as one of the most taciturn of men, and in one respect he is such. He never divulges his thoughts till they are matured, and never aspires to speech-making; and even in private conversation he falls into silence if he suspects that he is likely to be reported. He is the most modest of men, and nothing annoys him more than a loud parade of personal opinion, or personal vanity; but with his intimate friends, either at home or around the camp-fire, he talks upon all subjects, not only fluently and copiously, but in the most charming and good-natured manner. His life has been too busy to read history or technical works, but he has always been a close and careful reader of the newspapers. He has a retentive memory, and is deeply interested in all matters which concern the interests of humanity, and particularly his own country. Upon all such subjects, in fact, upon all the vital questions of the day, he thinks carefully and profoundly, and expresses himself with great ease and good sense. His understanding is of that incisive character that soon probes a question to the bottom, no matter how much the politicians or newspapers may labor to confuse it; while his judgment is so deliberate, honest and truthful in its operations that it may be implicitly relied upon to arrive at a fair and unbiased conclusion. His memory is stored with personal incidents illustrative of men and manners in all parts of the country, showing that he has evidently been a profound student of human nature throughout life; his appreciation of men and character has never been sur-

passed. This was well shown in the reorganization of the
army after he became Lieutenant-General. It is well known
that he did not fail in a single instance where a change was
made, in putting the right man in the right place. This was
due neither to chance nor snap judgment, but to his habit of
careful observation. He warms towards a bold outspoken and
loyal nature; full of ardor and zeal himself, he naturally
admires these qualities in others. He has no patience with a
weak, complaining and selfish disposition, and cannot endure
double-dealing or indirectness of any sort. Straightforward
and frank in all things himself, he respects these qualities
wherever they are found. Indeed the most striking peculiarity of his nature, both as a man and a General, is a profound and undeviating truthfulness in all things. Those who
have known him best will bear a willing testimony to the
statement that he never told a falsehood, or made a voluntary misrepresentation of fact; and will believe us that it
would be almost as impossible for him to do so as for the
needle to forget its fidelity to the pole.

He is a true friend and a magnanimous enemy. His liberality is boundless, and his charity as broad as humanity
itself. He has neither vanity nor selfish ambition; no promotion has ever been sought by him, and none has ever
turned his head or changed his character in the slightest
degree. Naturally a strong believer in the goodness of
Providence, as exerted in the affairs of mankind, he yet
possesses none of that blind fatalism, which has at times,
characterized military chieftains. So confident was he in
the moral strength and rectitude of our cause, and the superior intelligence and endurance of the Northern people, that
he never, even in the darkest hour, despaired of a united and
prosperous country. In this respect he is a perfect embodiment of the great American characteristic, faith in the
manifest destiny of the republic.

" We rarely find," said Napoleon, " combined in the same
person all the qualities necessary to constitute a great General. The most desirable is that a man's judgment should be

in equilibrium with his courage; that raises him at once above the common level. If courage be a General's predominating quality, he will rashly embark in enterprises above his conception; and on the other hand he will not venture to carry his ideas into effect if his character or courage be inferior to his judgment." By way of illustrating this principle Napoleon went on to assert that it was impossible for Murat and Ney not to be brave, but added that "no men ever possessed less judgment." Speaking of moral courage, he said: " I have very rarely met the two-o'clock-in-the-morning courage ; I mean unprepared courage ; that which is necessary on an unexpected occasion. Kleber was endowed with the highest talents, but was merely the man of the moment, and pursued glory as the only road to enjoyment, while Desaix possessed, in a very superior degree, the important equilibrium just described." After fully considering this subject, and discussing the merits of his own subordinates, he did not scruple to say that he was himself the only General of his time who fully possessed the courage ready for every emergency.

While we are forced to admit that this opinion of himself, was not unusually partial or singular at that time, it is but just to add, that it is now well established in history, that both his judgment and courage were at fault upon more than one occasion. Without enlarging here upon the events of his remarkable career, it is only necessary to call attention to the attempted conquest of Spain and Russia, the war of 1812–13 in Germany, the campaign of 1814 in France, and finally the campaign of Waterloo, in order to establish sufficiently the fact that the necessary equilibrium did not always exist in Napoleon between the conception and execution of his plans.

Marshall Marmont classifies Generals into four categories, counting, first " those who have never lost a battle, whose courage and judgment were equal to every emergency," such as Alexander and Cæsar in ancient times, and Gustavus Adolphus, Turenne, Condé, Luxembourg, and

Napoleon until 1812, in modern times. In the second class he places "those who, if they have often gained victories, have sometimes lost them" in spite of desperate fighting and good Generalship. Among these are the Archduke Charles, Suwarow and Wellington. The third category contains "those Generals who have been habitually unfortunate in war, but have never allowed their armies to be destroyed, nor been personally discouraged, always offering a menacing front and impressing the enemy with fear." Such in ancient times, were Sertorius and Mithridates, and in modern times Wallenstein and William III. of England. Finally, the fourth category contains "that numerous class, common to every country and every epoch, who have lost their armies without serious fighting, or without making the enemy pay dearly for his victory." In describing the qualities of a great leader, Marmont speaks of a union of intelligence and courage, but prefers, if either be in excess, that it should be courage, for reasons which are obvious. Another writer declares that the distinctive characteristic of genius, is the apparent ease and simplicity with which it accomplishes the most difficult things. Now let Grant be tried by these rules, and what rank must be assigned to him in history? Where must he be placed? Clearly in the highest category of great soldiers; but in order that this may be still further beyond the pale of dispute, let us consider the grounds for this conclusion somewhat more in detail.

Grant having been educated as a soldier, at West Point, the first military school of America, if not of the world, and having served under both Taylor and Scott, had at the outbreak of the rebellion, received all the training, both theoretical and practical, that was requisite to a thorough understanding of the military art, as applicable to warfare in America. In the very outset of his more recent career, he showed plainly that he had not been an idle or unobservant student of his profession. He was, from conviction, always opposed to that spirit of martinetism which Frederick the Great succeeded in making the basis of military discipline in nearly all modern armies; and believed in developing the individuality of the soldier, as much as possible, trusting to his intelligence and patriotism for a full performance of duty, instead of relying exclusively upon the capacity of officers to control brute masses. He had the sagacity to perceive that the system of Frederick, while it might do well enough for feudal Europe, before the days of the revolution, could not be made to apply to citizen soldiery, and he therefore wasted no time in trying to enforce the strict rules of fixed military establishments. He did not make the usual mistake of supposing that the common soldier was ignorant and thoughtless, and therefore to be considered as a mere machine to be provided with a musket or sabre, and then to be harassed into a reluctant performance of duty, but was profoundly impressed with the idea that the volunteers were intelligent citizens of the republic, whose business had been to become acquainted with public affairs. Withal, he was not unmindful of the necessity of drill and organization, for the purpose of ensuring coherence and uniformity of effort, though he acted upon the reasonable supposition, that volunteers would obtain more of the practical knowledge of warfare, in a week's campaigning, than a year's drilling in camps of instruction. He has been often heard to say, that the officer who could not tell that his movements were in the way of successful execution, by reading the faces of his men, was already defeated; he believes that American soldiers "are as smart as town folks," and what they do not know, or cannot find out, is scarcely worth the knowing. Looking at the army in this light, he wisely devoted more time to the selection of good officers, and the weeding out of bad ones, than in working from .the men upwards.

He held from the first that the Government in conducting the war should have acted upon the hereditary policy of the nation, and disbanded the regular army entirely, distributing its officers, non-commissioned officers and privates among the raw and untrained volunteers, thus, by a wide dissemination of the trained and disciplined element, thoroughly impregnating every branch of the volunteer army with experienced and accomplished soldiers. By this means, one or two commissioned officers and ten or twelve non-commissioned officers and privates of the old army could have been put into each new regiment. The rebels having no standing army to maintain, pursued exactly this course with their officers educated for the military service, and although they had very few, comparatively, their army for the first two years of the war was under much better general discipline than ours. To be sure, the Southern people had been preparing for this outbreak for several years before it actually took place, but the only satisfactory explanation of the efficacy with which they conducted operations at first is to be found in the fact that they wisely used their trained officers in the organization and command of new troops, while the National Government studiously pursued just the opposite policy. So rigidly was this system adhered to that not till after Grant became Lieutenant-General did he have the assistance of trained military men even upon his staff.

McClellan has been much praised for the organization of the Army of the Potomac, and while it is not our intention to detract from his deserts on that account, it must not be forgotten that in his greatest performance he was aided by those who became his successors, or that he had the help of nine-tenths of the trained soldiers in the Regular Army at the outbreak of the war. He absorbed the best of everything,—officers, troops, arms, ammunition and supplies of every sort. His infantry was commanded by Sumner, Franklin, W. F. Smith, Hooker, Kearney, Heintzleman, Casey, McCall, Stone, Ord, Meade, Humphreys, McDowell, Keyes, Fitz John Porter, French and Richardson ; his cavalry, by Stoneman, Cooke, Buford, Emory, Pleasonton, Bayard and Averill; his artillery, by Barry, Hunt, Ayers, Gibbon, Griffin and a galaxy of younger officers. The various departments of the staff were presided over by regular officers, many of whom were already distinguished for conspicuous services, including among their number, Barnard, Duane, Michler, Mendall and McComb of the Engineers; Ingalls, of the Quartermaster's Department; Clarke, of the Subsistence Department; Letterman, in the Medical Department; and Seth Williams and Marcy, in the Adjutant-General's Department. In fact, every corps, division and brigade, besides many a regiment and battery, was led by an experienced commander. The result is well known: the Army of the Potomac, "that splendid army of citizen soldiery," had its origin in this organization, and for four long years steadfastly struggled under every sort of commander till it finally found its hero in the Lieutenant-General, and gained a signal triumph.

But fortunately for the cause of free Government, there were other armies in the field whose history is not less glorious than that of the Army 'of the Potomac. Buell organized the Army of the Cumberland, whose distinctive feature was rigid discipline and methodical performance of duty; and although its commander was a military favorite and one of the prodigies of the earlier days of the war, he was permitted to have but limited assistance from the regular army. His staff officers alone, with a few division and brigade commanders like Thomas, Wood, Stanley, McCook, Hazen, Terrell, and Harker, with two batteries of artillery and four new regiments of infantry, were drawn from the regular army. The case with Grant was incomparably worse. Sherman and McPherson were the only graduates of the military academy who were permanently identified with the Army of the Tennessee. C. F. Smith made the campaign of Fort Donelson with it; Rosecrans that of Corinth and Iuka; Sheridan commanded a cavalry regiment in it for a while, and was then transferred to the Army of the Cumberland. Wilson belonged to the staff, and Ord, Sooy Smith, and Comstock, and several inferior officers joined it during the siege of Vicksburg; but with the exception of a small battalion of the Thirteenth (new) infantry, and a few hundred of the First infantry during the Vicksburg campaign, not a regiment of regular soldiers ever formed any part of its columns. It was made up, Generals and all, of raw

Western volunteers, with no knowledge of warfare except that derived from family tradition or based upon their mother wit ; and no military training except in the use of the rifle. Having served with all these armies and had ample opportunities of observing their habitual deportment in camp, on the march and in battle, at various epochs of their career, we may be permitted to speak unhesitatingly.

In the routine and detail of duty, and in the minor matters of discipline and organization, the Army of the Potomac was undoubtedly superior to either of the others. But in the subordination of its Generals, in the promptitude, zeal, and energy of its lower officers; in the self-reliance, earnestness and physical characteristics of its rank and file, in short in every moral military quality, the Army of the Tennessee has never been excelled. No General ever more successfully impressed his own character upon an army than Grant did his upon the one which grew up so silently under his care. No army was ever more loyal to its Chief or more clearly embodied the spirit of the people from which it sprung. It is a curious fact, too, not otherwise sufficiently accounted for, that it is the only army organized with the war, and continuing in existence till the establishment of peace, which, as a whole, never suffered a defeat. Its endurance and courage were unconquerable, so much so that before the war had terminated, it came to be a boast in its ranks that it was sure to win any battle that lasted over one day, no matter what the odds or who the enemy. Officers and men seemed to be endowed with the gift of persistency to a degree never surpassed except by their commander. As an organizer Grant's reputation must continue to increase the more his performances in this direction become known.

The attention of the reader has already been called to his recommendation of a united command in the Mississippi Valley, and to the tardy action of the Government in carrying this recommendation into effect. It is hardly necessary now to say that this combination was the foundation of all our substantial victories, not only in the West, but throughout the entire theatre of war. Fort Donelson was won by celerity, audacity and heroic resolution. Shiloh, by stubborn fighting and unconquerable heroism. Vicksburg, by the most brilliant and original strategy, by rapid marching, judicious combination and self-reliance, which remind one of the invasion of Russia by Charles XII., or of the vigor displayed in Bonaparte's campaign of 1796; but it must not be forgotten that Charles lost his army at Pultowa, and that Bonaparte did not cut loose from his base and plunge headlong into the interior of the hostile country; but by a judicious and well-formed plan of operations he broke through the enemy's lines at such a point as to retain his communications with France constantly uninterrupted, while by rapid combinations and severe battles he drove these lines before him. But Grant, in the Vicksburg campaign, boldly threw himself into the midst of hostile forces, leaving an army entirely behind him, until he had seized the most important point in the theatre of operations, and then turned upon and defeated that army, and drove it into the fortifications from which it was destined never to emerge except at the will of its conqueror. The closing victories of the war were won by a rare combination of military agencies. The consolidation of four vast territorial departments into one grand military division, enabled Grant to concentrate at Chattanooga a splendid army, heavily out-numbering the enemy, and it should be remembered that Providence favors strong battalions. By a series of strategic and grand tactical combinations, these superior numbers were so directed upon the field of battle as to take the enemy at disadvantage, striking him in flank, and actually getting closer to his base of supplies than his base was to his own head-quarters.

The Atlanta campaign and the march to the sea; the selection of Sheridan and the formation of the middle military division; the consolidation of the Western cavalry; the establishment of the military division of the West Mississippi, under Canby, followed by the campaign of Mobile; Sherman's grand holiday excursion and picnic party through the

Carolinas, again severing the Southern territory, isolating and scattering its armies, breaking its communications and eating out the vitals of the Confederacy; and, lastly, but not least, the magnificent campaign of the Army of the Potomac, from the Rapidan to the James, and from Petersburg to Appomattox Court House, bear ample testimony not only to the grandeur of Grant's conceptions, but to the heroic and unshakable resolution with which he carried them into effect. There was no defeat in all this, no hesitation, no doubting, but the clearest comprehension of the ends to be aimed at, the most careful preparation of materials, and the most perfect confidence in the men and means by which they were to be attained. No modern General except Bonaparte ever wielded such vast and prolonged power; and not even that great conqueror displayed such remarkable sagacity in his organizations and selections of subordinates. Massena and Soult were driven from Spain; McDonald was overwhelmed at Katzbach; Marmont was defeated at Montmartre; and Napoleon himself was driven from Russia, beaten at Leipsic, and finally, after a series of unaccountable blunders, was hurled from his throne, recovering it again only to repeat his blunders and meet an ignominious fate.

But Grant knew that no genius, however remarkable, could sufficiently command the national armies in a war of such magnitude without the assistance of lieutenants who could be trusted "to make their own orders" for the emergencies that were sure to arise. He therefore gave more thought to the proper organization and direction of armies upon the vital points of the enemy's territory and lines, and to the selection of men competent to command them, than to issuing the detailed orders of battle. Neither Sherman, nor Sheridan, nor Thomas, nor Canby ever failed him, and had circumstances enabled him to devote himself exclusively to the command of the Army of the Potomac, he would doubtless have displayed as much skill in the tactics of battle as he did in the strategy of campaigns.

The quick judgment by which he discovered the enemy's

plan to evacuate Fort Donelson, and the sudden resolution which he based thereupon, to attack at once, are evidences of something more than aggressive temper or mere brute courage. The tactics of Lookout Mountain, Chattanooga Valley and Mission Ridge have never been surpassed. The tactics, or more properly, the grand tactics displayed during the overland campaign, are worthy of the highest commendation, and had the execution of details been as faultless as the conception of the movements, there would have been nothing to regret. But it was precisely in the details with which Grant studiously avoided interfering that the greatest, and in fact the only failures took place. Grant's conduct at Belmont, Fort Donelson, Shiloh, Vicksburg, and in the Wilderness, was all that could have been wished, and shows, beyond chance of dispute, that he possesses, in the highest degree, that "two-o'clock-in-the-morning courage" which Napoleon declared to be the rarest thing among Generals; while his conception and execution of the Vicksburg campaign, are complete proof that his judgment is in exact equilibrium with his courage. His unvaried course of success through four years of warfare, shows that he is entitled to be ranked in the category of Generals who never lost a campaign or a battle, and the easy simplicity with which he did the most extraordinary things points strongly to the possession of a remarkable genius for war.

THE number of persons is small indeed who will not concede that General Grant possesses military genius of the
highest order. Steadily winning his way upward from a Col-
onelcy to the command of a district, and thence to the control of a department, and ultimately to the head of the entire
forces of the nation, he directed the movements of more than
a million of men, divided into many armies, and spread over
an area larger than Western and Central Europe. In all
branches of the service his companions in arms have, with
one accord, conceded to him the highest place.

After the capture of Corinth he was consulted by the
War Department and the President in regard to all army
movements in the Western States, and his plans were adopted
with scarcely an exception. After the fall of Vicksburg his
advice in respect to military operations throughout the country was constantly sought at Washington, and his advice was
influential till the close of the war. When the rebellion suc-

cumbed, he alone prescribed the terms under which all the Confederate forces laid down their arms—terms, whose generosity surprised the insurgents, and whose wisdom is vindicated by the fact that in the three years that have since intervened, and which have been characterized by great civil commotions in the unreconstructed States, not a rebel officer has lifted his sword, nor a rebel soldier resumed his musket.

While so much will be freely admitted respecting his military genius and services, it is contended in some quarters that General Grant has given no evidence that he possesses statesman-like abilities. In reply to this it might be insisted that to accomplish the great objects we have enumerated, required something in addition to mere soldierly qualities, and that the tasks were of such a complex character that their successful performance demanded the talents of a statesman not less than those of a warrior.

The advocates of the contrary theory will, in proof of their assertion, cite the fact that Grant has never held civil offices of trust and influence; that he has never been a member of a legislative body, nor the Governor of a State, nor represented his country at foreign courts, nor conducted diplomatic correspondence, nor been accustomed to address popular assemblies on public questions, nor even mingled in politics. All this must be admitted. Grant has never been an office-holder, nor an office-seeker, nor a partisan politician. He has issued orders for the government of millions of men through years of peculiar peril, but he has never delivered a speech in Congress, nor shone as a stump-orator. He has planned campaigns, proclaimed truces, received the capitulation of cities, and negotiated the terms of surrender of an armed Confederacy, but he has never waited in the presence chamber of Kings, nor wearied the patience of Ambassadors with vapid diplomatic dispatches. His genius has been invoked to save a Republic of forty millions of people in war, and his wisdom to reconstruct a shattered Union of thirty-seven States in peace, but he has never sent an annual message to a Legislature nor to the Common Council of a city.

27

Those who would measure the extent of one's abilities as a statesman by the number of offices he has held, should remember that Washington, Franklin, Knox, Hamilton, Jackson, Taylor and Lincoln had never had much official training or experience of any sort in civil affairs, and especially in legislation, till they were called to discharge the highest civic trusts. Knox and Hamilton went almost directly from the camp into the Cabinet of Washington ; Lincoln had only served a single term in the lower branch of Congress when he was summoned to the Executive Mansion ; and Taylor cast his first vote at the polls at the election when he himself was a successful candidate for the Presidency. Though enthusiastic parties rallied around Washington, Jay, Madison, Monroe, Wirt, Tompkins, Jackson, Calhoun and Taylor, and bore them into office, they were never, in the popular acceptation of the term, politicians ; they never breathed the fetid air of the caucus ; they never addressed political meetings ; but their countrymen, testing their character and achievements by no such narrow standard, have ranked them among the great statesmen of their times.

Now, we are not claiming that Grant is the equal of all these eminent civilians, but only citing their lives to show that it does not necessarily follow, that men do not possess statesman-like qualities, merely because they are not partisan politicians or have not been trained in a particular routine of civil employments. It would be thought flattery to assert that Grant is the peer of many of the distinguished characters just named ; but he is certainly entitled to a place in that class of public men of whom Franklin, Knox, Jackson, Taylor and Lincoln, were illustrious types.

It hardly admits of a question that his education was better adapted to fit him for statesmanship, than that afforded by most of the higher grade of colleges in this country. The academy at West Point, not only thoroughly tests and trains the intellectual faculties, but its routine of studies embraces law in its application to the ruling of States, the history of nations, political economy, the Federal Constitution and the general science of civil government. He passed the severe ordeal of the academy with great credit. Moreover, he possesses in large measure those native qualities and cultivated habits, which enable one to supply deficiencies, resulting from want of experience in the conduct of civil affairs. He has quickness of apprehension, breadth of comprehension, patient industry, persistency of purpose, self-reliance, and common sense; and, better even than these, he has had a seven years' discipline in one of the greatest schools of modern times, wherein he has been constantly engaged in dealing with some of the most important and intricate concerns, political and military, ever entrusted to the care of a civilian or a soldier.

Grant entered this incomparable school on the firing of the signal-gun at Sumter. Through the earlier portion of these seven years, he was one of its most assiduous and apt scholars. For the remainder of the period, he was one of its ablest and most successful masters. He who regards him as a mere soldier in an era so crowded with civil, social, financial, and military events of the first magnitude, takes a narrow and one-sided view of the part he performed in this grand 'chapter of the world's history.

It is the misfortune of distinguished military chieftains, that their achievements in the field so attract and dazzle the eye, that observers are wont to overlook their less brilliant but ofttimes equally valuable services in dealing with political subjects and matters of a *quasi* civil nature. Viewed in this aspect, Grant's position is not unlike that of Wellington, whom, it may be remarked, he somewhat resembles in the salient points of his character. The political aid rendered by Wellington to the cause of the allies during the five years he commanded in the Spanish Peninsula, was as important as his military campaigns. Though the British Cabinet knew that throughout these five years, much of his time and patience were spent in healing the strife of political factions, regulating the administration of justice, counseling with the feeble and impracticable Ministers of Portugal, and dictating a policy to the proud and implacable grandees of Spain, it was not till long afterwards that these facts became known to even his well informed fellow subjects, who had only recognized him on that theater of his exploits, as the hero of Vimeira, Talavera and Vittoria, just as the masses of our citizens, not aware of Grant's civil services during the past five years, only know him as the conqueror at Donelson, Vicksburg, Chattanooga and the Appomattox.

The like statement may be made respecting General Scott. His military record is all aglow with brilliant deeds. But his civil labors were hardly less important than these, though for years they were unknown to the great majority of his countrymen. Throughout his life he was a skillful negotiator, and apt at dealing with embarrassing public questions, more than once by his informal intervention averting the calamities of war. But Scott lived so long that his fellow-citizens became familiar with his good deeds as a pacificator, and they now revere his memory not less for these than for his more dazzling exploits in the field.

In suggesting this comparison between Grant and the two distinguished soldiers just mentioned, it need hardly be added that the parallel does not run on all-fours; for it would be absurd to imagine that in all particulars he was the counterpart of two men who but slightly resembled each other; and as we have seen, as a soldier he is greatly superior to either. But there were points in the character of Wellington and Scott beside those already named, which bear a striking likeness to traits in the character of Grant.

Like Wellington, Grant is reserved in manner and speech; apt to give dry, curt answers to those who would pry into his thoughts; accustomed to state the conclusions at which he has arrived without detailing the mental processes through which he reached them; thoroughly digesting plans in his own mind ere he announces them to others; accurate in his estimate of character, so that in selecting his subordinates and coadjutors he intuitively puts "the right man in the right place;" with a cool and impassive exterior, through which, however, there occasionally bursts a glowing phrase, hot from the heart, that becomes a talisman, like, " I shall fight it out on this line if it takes all summer,"—an echo of the slogan at Waterloo, " Up guards, and at them !"

Though Scott was one of the most vain and loquacious of men, and Grant is one of the most retiring and taciturn, Grant, like him, has rare tact in conducting difficult negotiations to a successful termination. It is universally conceded that Scott excelled in this respect. A striking illustration of Grant's skill therein was shown in the happy manner in which he disentangled the meshes wherein General Sherman had become involved in the terms of surrender he proposed to General Johnston in April, 1864. Destitute of accurate information, because of his isolation in the heart of the enemy's country, the terms he had tendered did not comport with the wishes of the Government. These terms were promptly disavowed and countermanded, by the civil authorities at Washington. Deeming himself rudely treated, his pride was wounded, his warm blood was inflamed, and the hero of the " the grand march to the sea," was in a state of extreme irritation. In this unpleasant condition, Grant was despatched to North Carolina to settle the matter. After mutual explanations and a thorough survey of the field of controversy, the high-spirited victor promptly and heartily yielded to the views of his calm and modest commander. The friendship of Grant and Sherman, so dissimilar in every prominent trait of their characters—a friendship tested by rare vicissitudes of fortune, and growing stronger with every trial—is one of the most interesting facts of its kind which the war, so fruitful in striking incidents, has brought forth.

Resuming the thread of our narrative, we shall find that during the last two years of the war, and more especially in the winter of 1863–64, no important civil measure bearing on the rebellion, was initiated by the Government without Grant's judgment thereon being invoked by the Cabinet; and the opinions of no one man, not actually in high political office, were more carefully considered or generally adopted,

than his.   In the winter of 1864–5, when it became apparent
that the rebellion was about to yield, and it was of vast importance that all our civil as well as military measures should
be so shaped as to contribute to that result, his proximity to
the seat of Government, made him a frequent participant in
the Counsels of the Cabinet and in conferences with leading members of Congress; and his unimpassioned and sagacious advice essentially aided in moulding a policy wherein
energy and conciliation were wisely combined.

In the three years that have transpired since the war terminated, Grant, as Commander-in-Chief, and for five months as
Secretary of War, has been required to deal constantly with
civil matters, of the most rare, complex, and delicate character, deeply affecting not the South only, but the entire
country.   In the discharge of his high duties, he has never
forgotten that he was a citizen as well as a soldier, and has
wielded his vast powers rather as a civil magistrate, than as
a military commander.   The nature of these services is understood.   Their extent and value can hardly be overestimated.
The unimpeachable and enduring record of his acts bears
testimony to the zeal, urbanity, patience and ability with
which he has executed his responsible trusts.

In the face of these facts, can it be affirmed that General
Grant has no statesman-like qualities?   Rather do they prove
that he possesses a capacity for civil affairs which needs but
the pressure of duty and the occurrence of opportunity to
exhibit rare administrative abilities.

It has been an axiom in American history, that to the
training which Washington, Knox, and Hamilton, for example, received in the Revolutionary War, and in the intervening period down to the adoption of the Federal Constitution, were mainly due those qualities that so admirably
fitted them to discharge the duties which devolved upon
them after the new Government went into full operation.
And is it not safe to infer, nay, fair to insist, that long and
thorough discipline in the events of our late war, and varied
experience in handling those still pending and unsettled ques-

tions which have resulted therefrom, are quite as necessary
to prepare a ruler for the wise administration of national
affairs for a few years to come, as it was necessary in the
analogous case of the revolutionary era, to train Washington
and his compeers for the discharge of the political responsibilities ultimately imposed upon them?

Rather may we insist that such a training and discipline
are more necessary for the public men of our times than they
were for the Fathers of the Republic in their day. The contest of 1776 was a war, practically, between foreign nations,
divided by the ocean. Ours was a civil conflict, between the
citizens of one country. When the Revolutionary War
closed, the defeated party retired to its home beyond the
seas, leaving the whole body of our people to rejoice as victors, homogeneous in feeling and united in opinion. But the
beaten party in our late strife are Americans, dwelling side
by side with their conquerors, the humiliation that followed
their defeat being aggravated by the impoverishment and
ruin that have resulted from their wild crusade. Through
the term of the next National Administration the subjects that
will press upon the public attention and demand solution and
adjustment, spring directly out of, and in truth are part and
parcel of the same subjects which, during the administrations
of Lincoln and Johnson, have agitated the councils and
shaped the destinies of the American people, whether dwelling in the North or in the South.

During both of these administrations, the clear mind and
strong hand of Grant have been employed in devising and
executing the plans and measures that carried the nation
through its perils in war, and have secured to it so much of
peace and prosperity as it now enjoys. In view, then, of the
present condition of the country, and of the peculiar character of the calamities that afflict it, and the dangers that beset it,
and of the complexity and delicacy of the political and military problems that will demand solution in the immediate
future, it cannot be doubted that the employments and experiences of Grant, through the seven years wherein these

grand events were passing across the stage of history, have more thoroughly prepared him for wisely and safely guiding the nation, than could twenty years spent in the ordinary routine of civil offices of even the highest grades.

Standing at the close of the eventful epoch we have been surveying, we need not hesitate to affirm, that to play the part in this great drama which Grant has performed, has required talents of a very different kind, if not of a higher grade, than those which produce the mere soldier, however illustrious. His enlightened counsels, the actual services he rendered in regard to civil, social, legal and financial matters of unprecedented character and transcendent importance, affecting the interests of large populations and the destinies of powerful States, prove that he possesses abilities and attainments that entitle him to a place among the wise and prudent statesmen of the country.

Marshall's Line Engraved

PORTRAIT OF GEN. GRANT.

MESSRS. TICKNOR AND FIELDS take pleasure in placing before the American people this superb Engraving, which must be regarded as the only authentic and satisfactory portrait yet produced of General Grant. It is from the same hand that executed those portraits of WASHINGTON and LINCOLN which have taken rank among the masterpieces of lineal art; and it is confidently believed that this likeness is destined to become the historic portrait of GENERAL GRANT.

The engraving has been made from Mr. Marshall's own painting. In the execution of this portrait, the artist had unusual facilities for becoming acquainted with his illustrious subject, and obtained numerous sittings. As a portrait of General Grant, it differs widely from all others; but the publishers believe that it is at once the best and the truest portrait of him; and, as corroborating this opinion, they invite attention to the following testimonials from persons well qualified by acquaintance, taste and culture, to pronounce upon the merits of this engraving as a portrait, and as a work of art:

[From Mrs. Grant.]

WASHINGTON, Feb. 25, 1868.
MR. W. E. MARSHALL—*Dear Sir:* I am delighted with your splendid engraving of my husband. I cannot say too much in its praise. As a likeness I do not think it could be better, and I shall always prize your elegant gift. Yours truly, JULIA D. GRANT.

[From Hon. E. B. Washburne, of Ill., the intimate friend of General Grant.]

WASHINGTON, D. C., Feb. 3, 1868.
MESSRS. TICKNOR & FIELDS—*Gentlemen:* It has afforded me great pleasure to see and examine an artist-proof of Marshall's *Line Engraving* of General U. S. GRANT. In the execution of the work, art seems to have achieved its highest triumph. The likeness is most perfect, and the wonderful skill displayed by the artist must excite the warmest admiration of all lovers of art. Very truly, yours &c., E. B. WASHBURNE.

[From Senator Sumner.]

SENATE CHAMBER, Feb. 18, 1868.
GENTLEMEN—Lincoln and Grant were associated in a great crisis of history. They are again associated in the immortality of art. The same talent which so successfully engraved the portrait of the former, now gives us a companion portrait of the other. I have always admired Marshall's engraving of our late President, and now have, among my most valued possessions, the first proof of the plate. The engraving of the Commander of our armies is not less admirable. It is a rare and finished work, excellent as a likeness, and altogether worthy of a place in any collection, or on the walls of any house. Faithfully yours,
MESSRS. TICKNOR & FIELDS. CHARLES SUMNER.

[From Mr. Curtis.]

NORTH SHORE, STATEN ISLAND, N. Y., April 3, 1868.
MY DEAR SIR:—I thank you most heartily for the noble and satisfactory portrait of General Grant. The same force and fidelity, the same exquisite skill and delicacy which you have made us all admire in your Washington and Lincoln, are renewed in this masterly work. It shows all that simplicity, tenacity, sagacity, modesty and moderation, which explain Grant's career, and commend him so closely to the regard and respect of his countrymen. We are all your debtors again, and I am most truly, Your obliged friend and servant,
MR. MARSHALL. GEORGE WILLIAM CURTIS.

[From Mr. Bryant.]

NEW YORK, March 26, 1868.
MESSRS. TICKNOR & FIELDS—*Dear Sirs:*—I am entirely satisfied with the portrait of General Grant, engraved by W. E. Marshall, from a portrait painted by himself. It is really a noble specimen of the art engraving. It is admirable as a likeness, and appears to me to give the character of the original, more perfectly than any engraving which I have seen.
I am, Sirs, very truly yours, W. C. BRYANT.

☞ This Engraving will be sold by subscription only. Agents are wanted to canvass every town of the United States. For terms and territory immediate application should be made.
Address, for the New England States, TICKNOR & FIELDS, Boston.
For the Middle and Southern States, Ohio and Michigan, TICKNOR & FIELDS, No. 63 Bleecker Street, New York.
For the Western States, except Ohio and Michigan, JOHN H. AMMON Western News Company, Chicago.

JUST PUBLISHED:

Life of Ulysses S. Grant,

THE CONQUEROR OF THE REBELLION AND GENERAL OF THE UNITED STATES ARMY,

COMPRISING A COMPLETE AND ACCURATE

History of his Eventful and Interesting Career

WITH

ANECDOTES OF HIS BOYHOOD, HIS EDUCATION AT WEST POINT,

His Gallant Conduct as a Young Officer in Connection with the War with Mexico, his Resignation from the Army, Life as a Farmer near St. Louis, and as a Leather Dealer at Galena, Illinois,

UNTIL THE

Breaking Out of the Great Rebellion,

WITH AN AUTHENTIC NARRATIVE OF

HIS INVALUABLE MILITARY SERVICES,

INCLUDING THE

Organization of Armies, Battles, Sieges, Plans of Campaigns and Achievements,

Adding also an impartial estimate of his character as

A MAN, A SOLDIER, and A STATESMAN.

Containing Splendid Portrait of Grant, and numerous Maps and Diagrams.

By CHARLES A. DANA,

Late Assistant Secretary of War, and

J. H. WILSON,

Brevet Major-General United States Army.

HOLLAND'S

Life of Abraham Lincoln,

LATE PRESIDENT OF THE UNITED STATES,

COMPRISING A FULL AND COMPLETE

HISTORY OF HIS EVENTFUL LIFE,

WITH

Incidents of his Early History, his Career as a Lawyer and Politician, his Advancement to the Presidency of the United States and Commander-in-Chief of the Army and Navy Through the Most Trying Period of its History,

TOGETHER WITH AN ACCOUNT OF THE

TRAGICAL AND MOURNFUL SCENES

Connected with the Close of his Noble and Eventful Life.

By Dr. J. G. HOLLAND,

The widely known and favorite author of the "Timothy Titcomb" Letters, "Bitter Sweet," "Gold Foil," &c., &c.

The author's aim will be to describe as graphically as may be the private and public life of the humble citizen, the successful lawyer, the pure politician, the far-sighted Christian statesman, the efficient philanthropist, and the honored Chief Magistrate. The people desire a biography which shall narrate to them with a measurable degree of symmetry and completeness, the story of a life which has been intimately associated with their own and changed the course of American history through all coming time. Such a narrative as this it will be the author's aim to give—one that shall be sufficiently full in detail without being prolix, and circumstantial without being dull.

The work will be published in a handsome Octavo volume of about five hundred and fifty pages, on fine paper, printed from electrotype plates, and will be embellished by an elegant Portrait of Mr. Lincoln, with a finely engraved view of his residence in Springfield, Illinois, and other Steel Engravings.

The work will also be issued in the German Language at the same price of the English edition.

JUST PUBLISHED:

Sacred Biography and History of the Bible;

OR,

ILLUSTRATIONS OF THE HOLY SCRIPTURES;

CONTAINING

Descriptions of Palestine—Ancient and Modern; Lives of the Patriarchs, Kings and Prophets, and of

CHRIST AND THE APOSTLES,

TO WHICH ARE ADDED

Notices of the Most Eminent Reformers, Luther, Melancthon, Calvin, etc., with Interesting Sketches of the Ruins of Celebrated Ancient Cities—Palmyra, Nineveh, etc.,— mentioned in the Sacred Writings.

EDITED BY OSMOND TIFFANY,

Author of "The American in China," "Brandon, or a Hundred Years Ago," etc.

ILLUSTRATED WITH NUMEROUS AND BEAUTIFUL STEEL ENGRAVINGS.

In One Volume of over 600 Pages.

THE HISTORY
OF THE
CIVIL WAR IN AMERICA,
COMPRISING A FULL AND IMPARTIAL ACCOUNT OF THE
ORIGIN AND PROGRESS OF THE REBELLION,
OF THE VARIOUS
NAVAL AND MILITARY ENGAGEMENTS,
OF THE
Heroic Deeds performed by Armies and Individuals,
AND OF
TOUCHING SCENES IN THE FIELD, THE CAMP, THE HOSPITAL, AND THE CABIN.

By J. S. C. ABBOTT,

Author of the "Life of Napoleon," "History of the French Revolution," "Monarchs of
Continental Europe," &c.

**ILLUSTRATED WITH DIAGRAMS AND NUMEROUS STEEL ENGRAVINGS, OF BATTLE SCENES
AND PORTRAITS OF DISTINGUISHED MEN, BY THE BEST ARTISTS.**

IN TWO VOLUMES.

And containing over 1,100 large Royal Octavo pages. The author of this work is well
known as one of the most talented and popular historical writers; and his History of
the Great Rebellion will not be surpassed in merit and attractiveness by any other that
may be offered to the public.

The Illustrations are all from original designs, Engraved on Steel, by the best Artists,
expressly for the work, and comprise portraits of distinguished commanders and civilians, with the prominent battle scenes by sea and land.

This work will be published in the German language as well as in the English.

THE ILLUSTRATED
LIFE OF WASHINGTON,
WITH

VIVID PEN-PAINTINGS OF BATTLES AND INCIDENTS, TRIALS
AND TRIUMPHS OF THE HEROES AND SOLDIERS OF
708
REVOLUTIONARY TIMES.

By HON. J. T. HEADLEY,

Author of "Washington and his Generals," "Napoleon and his Marshals," "Sacred
Mountains," &c.

TOGETHER WITH AN INTERESTING ACCOUNT OF

~~708~~ MOUNT VERNON AS IT IS,
By BENSON J. LOSSING.

The whole embellished with numerous Steel and Wood Engravings, and a
splendid Colored Lithographic View of Mount Vernon
and Washington's Tomb.

This beautiful Royal Octavo volume of over 500 pages embraces a brilliant narration
of the facts and incidents in the life of that remarkable man, and Father of his Country—George Washington; together with his connection with the Revolutionary War, &c.
Comprising much new and important information, derived from the papers of General
Putnam, and the researches of Mr. Lossing.—information embraced in no other book.

When every heart throbs with enthusiastic gratitude, and public feeling is thoroughly
aroused towards the memory of Washington, a biography from the pen of Mr. Headley,
of that great and good man, is of peculiar interest, and would necessarily be in great
demand. Already thousands of copies have been sold, and the demand is every day
increasing, as the success of our agents abundantly prove.